Even Thoughts Hurt

by

Patricia Grigg

Grigg Publishing, LLC ~ Arizona ~ USA

Grigg Publishing, LLC
P.O. Box 6154
Peoria, AZ 85381

ISBN-13: 978-1-62555-010-1

This story is a work of fiction. Names, characters, places, and incidents are either a product of the author's imagination, or used fictitiously. Any resemblance to actual persons, living or dead, events, or places is entirely coincidental.

Printed in the United States of America

First Edition, 2025

www.griggpublishing.com

Books written by

Patricia Grigg
***

The Nothing Girl

Children of the Nothing Girl Series:

Windy With Hell

Nobody's Hero

Even Thoughts Hurt (This Book)

Soon to come:

When Darkness Falls and Night Has Yet to
Come

To my dear friend Susan Young
For the people in my life who traveled the long
journey to this point in time, who have seen the
underbelly of life and reached out to pick a friend up
off the ground.
To the protectors. Those who give up hours at home
to see to another's safety.
For those in my family. Who came when the need
was dire. And the dear ones who were left to worry.
This book is for you.

Acknowledgements

As I have worked on The Nothing Girl series of books over the years, many people have entered my life. I feel blessed to have these dear friends.

Ray Bilcliff has generously supplied the photos used on the book covers. Butterflies are only a small part of Ray's talented photographs. To appreciate his talent, visit Ray's website at https://www.raybilcliff.uk/

My family and the many friends in Lake Charles, Louisiana, kept me afloat when I doubted myself.

Then there are the people willing to be test readers. I hope they will hang on to the next and, I think, final book in this series.

Thank you one and all for being in my life.

To all of you many thanks.

Chapter One

THE NEW SS

The new Secret Service guy was counting again. Susan was annoyed and relieved, hating the constant counting yet not wanting to know what the SS guy was trying to keep hidden from her. The numbers continued, "4533, 4534, 4535, 4537… Car… Alert!" The SS turned to Susan, standing just inside the door. She nodded immediately, going to the secure bunker under the house. It was a safe room with monitors so she could see what was going on above ground. Cameras were positioned to reveal where an intruder might go in or around the house. Susan watched a black car slowly drive up the long dirt road to the house. That road was the only way in or out of Susan's home, designed to make it difficult for anyone to approach her. The safe room was carved into the rock that formed the mountain under the house. A lot of consideration went into protecting her. Because, as her grandfather was prone to say, she is a weapon without equal.

She watched as people piled out of the black car parked in front of the house. A door was held open, and a Four-Star General stepped out. Susan watched her Secret Service guy keep his weapon leveled at the General. This SS agent took his job seriously, and for that, Susan was thankful. She turned on the sound to hear what they were saying to each other. "I received no notification of your visit here. Until I do, I don't care if you are the King of France. You don't get by me. Sir." The sir seemed an afterthought as if the SS did not feel any respect for the Four Stars yet knew better than to disregard someone of that rank.

The General held his hands out, palms open. "Please, calm down, son. I've no idea why you were not brought up to date on these arrangements. I am certain that information is soon to come."

As if on cue, the SS guy's phone rang. "Talk," SS said to the air. Irritation filled the SS guy's voice. "You realize you nearly got your General and his men killed. End call." With a grimace on his face, the SS guy holstered his gun. "Stand down," He said. Susan knew the snipers on the mountain had been told everything was okay. They didn't take chances with Susan's life. The SS guy looked at the nearest camera and nodded at it.

Upon exiting the safe room, Susan immediately knew why General Richards was there. Susan had an assignment in the Capital. Dread filled her, so she only wanted to crawl back into that safe room. And shut the door. She didn't. The price she paid for this isolation was going when the need was great. They considered the need to be great. She glanced at her SS guy. This trip would be the first time the new SS man went on an assignment with Susan. It was the first call to duty since the new guy had arrived. He might irritate her, yet she found him more competent than those stationed with her previously. She gave him a slight nod of approval, then turned to face the General.

"Miss Whiting, we have made arrangements for you. Believe me. We will try to minimize any contact. We have arranged a concrete bunker for your off-time during the assignment. Clothing, as usual, has been provided to fit the occasion and is on the plane. Plus, you will be allowed to dress and care for yourself. Everything possible we could think of that you might need during your stay to make this less painful for you has been provided," he hesitated before continuing. "Two dinner parties. We won't ask more than that of you. We will bring you home if you haven't found anything by then. Are these arrangements to your satisfaction, Ma'am?" The General looked at Susan as if he feared she would object to the terms.

"Hold it right there! You are not taking her to any place that is harmful to her. It is my job to protect her, and I will not allow her to come to harm, General." The SS guy was fuming. He had heard that this would hurt his charge and jumped to her defense. He glared at General Richards and his men, so he missed the look Susan gave him.

He was new to handling her and hadn't even offered her his name yet. Susan knew the departing SS had warned him to guard his thoughts. Thus, the counting. Yet here he was, facing down these men on her behalf. She reached out and gently touched his arm. He looked down at her hand on his arm, furrowed his brow as if puzzled, and exhaled. She caught his name with that brief contact. Susan hadn't meant to invade his mind. "It is okay, Tex. I've been through this before, and it is painful, but this is my job. It is something only I can do. You serve your country by protecting me. I know this assignment has been painful, even scary, but you are doing it. Do you expect less of me?"

He looked at Susan, doubt in his eyes and mind. He had stopped counting. "You want to do this even if it hurts you?"

Susan nodded. "They don't even realize their thoughts are so painful, Tex. You, them, and everyone else can't hear all the snide comments, the rantings of rage and hate, the fear, or the pain of heartbroken lovers. A child's skinned knee is just a woeful child crying; I feel their pain. I experience it all, the slimy, greasy sickness of men who plan to rape women. The people who are planning to hurt another person simply because they don't feel the person belongs or should even live. Hate, fear, pain, rage, and even joy hit me with such force that all I want to do is crawl away and die, but I can't. So I hide away up here and enter the trenches when duty calls.

The furrows deepen on Tex's forehead. And Susan could feel sympathy from him. "Count." She told him, turning away and entering the house to get her go-bag.

"One, two..."

"You heard her, all of you assholes count and don't stop," Tex growled. "… three, four, five."

Tex was worried now. He hadn't thought of what it must be like for his subject, hearing all the thoughts around her. Hell, there were so many times he knew his thoughts were vicious. She had been right. He had been scared that she would be able to hear his thoughts. A girl like her hears all the nasty things people keep inside. It was…. It had to be horrible. His job had taken an unexpected turn, and he took his work seriously. So he would shield her in every way he could. If it meant telling some strutting General to count, he damn well would make him count. Eyes narrowing, Tex took Susan's bag and placed it with his go-bag in the car's trunk assigned to him for this job. He wasn't about to have her ride with those other men. Isolate, protect, and keep her from as much mental pain as possible. He was ready to take on this twist to his job.

The entire area around Air Force One had been cleared of all but the essential people. Susan cringed inside at the thoughts pouring into her mind. Thoughts. She hadn't found a way to block them. They were thoughts that were not of her mind but belonged to other people. The man pulling the blocks broadcast hate that privileged people got rides on such special planes. The guy directing the airplane towards them was worried his kid sister might be on drugs. Ever thought beat at her, making her head throb. She placed the 'I don't care' look upon her face and bore up to the constant assault on her mind. Nobody looking at her would notice the slight tremble of her fingers and the beads of sweat on her brow. She hid it all well.

It was with new eyes that Tex watched over his subject. This assignment scared him when he learned his subject could hear his thoughts. Who wants all their thoughts heard? He'd never be able to look at a pretty girl and have lustful thoughts about her. Or consider punching some idiot out because he had been disrespectful to a little old lady in the grocery line. He had to reconsider every thought, every emotion. It wore him out.

His thoughts paled to what his subject must go through. Hearing all those things had to be a million times worse. He did what a good tracker does. He let himself become attuned to his subject. He noted the slight tremble of her fingers and the stiffness of her facial muscles as if determined not to give away her distress. His eyes swept the area again and again. He noted how the area had been cleared and watched for the flash of a weapon. Ready, ever ready, for a threat to his subject. He was the first to look inside before they entered Air Force One. And the last one to enter as he swept once more for any threat to his subject. Then he glared at each of the men aboard, mouthing "Count" at them. "500023, 500024."

Susan sat as far away from the men as possible, taking the President's refuge when flying as her hiding spot. Leaning back in the very comfortable chair behind the desk of this flying office, Susan tried to let the constant counting work for her instead of causing her pain. She concentrated on the numbers in Tex's head while wondering how he came by the name Tex, as it didn't seem like a real first name. Maybe it was a nickname. These thoughts were running through her mind, along with the constant numbers, until Susan fell asleep.

As quiet as a shadow, Robin Shadow, nicknamed Tex, peeked into the room where Susan had taken shelter. She was sleeping curled up in the President's chair, looking tiny and helpless. Careful not to disturb his subject, Tex got one of the heated blankets for the President to tuck around her. This flight wasn't his first ride on one of the transports, Air Force One when the President was on board. Feeling something like satisfaction, Tex went back to guarding his subject. "501990, 501991." The corner of his mouth lifted. He was getting the hang of this, keeping the doggies in line and keeping his subject safe.

It was too soon, Susan thought. If only she had a little more time to prepare for this trip. The people, the constant thinking people. She felt too enclosed with these men in the long car making its way through the crowds outside the White House. The thoughts of chattering outside were so angry. Susan held up her hand as a person's thoughts hit her hard. "Stop the car," the General ordered, turning all his attention to Susan. "Who and where, Miss Whiting?"

Slowly, Susan's head turned left and then right. She went back, left halfway, and pointed. "The man in the green baseball cap with a blue shirt. He has a gun and plans to shoot my Grandfather."

Tex gazed along Susan's finger and got a bead

on the man. The Capital was his territory. The
Secret Service was in charge here.

"We have a threat to the Old Man. I'm
sending a video. The guy is in a green baseball cap
and blue shirt. Take care not to let him dump the
gun."

The car continued, taking Susan out of harm's
way. It wasn't long before Tex confirmed the SS had
the man, gun, and all. For the first time, he had seen
Susan in action. Now he understood why Susan
was well guarded. You'd think the Old Man would
keep her at his side to see threats. What torture
that would be for Susan. Tex thought kindly of the
President for keeping Susan at her mountain retreat.
"505221, 505222."

So many, there were so many of them,
Susan thought, looking out the car window at the
people. Some were standing in line to have a tour
of the White House. Others in groups protested,
wanting something to be handed over to them for
whatever grievance they had, whether related to the
government or not. The anger radiating from them
was like a sickness eating at them, enhancing their
angry thoughts and making them even more upset.
Why didn't they step back and look for a solution
rather than blame someone else? Hate, unreasonable
hate, radiated from them like pus oozing from an
infected wound, which was ugly and smelling of rot.

Susan looked at the dress picked by her
grandmother. The woman always tried to dress
Susan and her family in her image. Thankfully,
Susan didn't have to wear jeans to be herself.

Clothing meant nothing to her; it was just something to wear. So she dressed in the floor-length evening gown, placed the jewelry sent with the dress on her body, and steeled herself for an evening of torture. While on this assignment, her escort was waiting outside the concrete bunker they set up as her living quarters. Susan exited the bunker to face the first trial of the evening. A tall man in a tux was waiting beside the General and Tex. Susan knew this was the man who was her escort to the first party she had to attend. Just as was her immediate rejection of the leering, I will do her monster inside the man.

The General straightened even more than his usual stance when Susan came over to the three of them waiting on her. "This is Raymond Holbrook. He will be your escort for the evening. Mr. Holbrook is well-known and often brings a lovely woman with him to these events. So we will not need to explain who you are to anyone."

"No," Susan stated, her voice flat and uncompromising.

Tex's eyes went to Holbrook. The danger in that look would have brought any man to his knees had Holbrook noticed Tex, but Holbrook only had eyes for Susan.

"My Lady, I assure you you will have a marvelous time with me. I know all the people. There will not be a moment when you will be bored with me as your escort."

Susan held up her hand in a stopping motion. Tex was between her and the fancy pants Holbrook before the other man could blink his eyes. "You heard her. Leave."

"Go on, Holbrook. I apologize for bringing you into this," The General told Holbrook. He looked back at Susan with contrite. "Without an escort, you can not attend the party. The event is a dinner party. The man we are seeking to ally with, his culture, does not allow women to go about on their own. We must set up another reason you are at the social and another escort. I'd take you myself. Only everyone knows I never bring women to these events. You have placed us in a difficult situation, Miss Whiting. Tell me who you will accept as an escort to tonight's and tomorrow's event."

Without hesitation, Susan answered. "Eric."

The General seemed unhappy to hear the name. Still, he nodded and pulled out his phone, walking a distance away to avoid being overheard. "I need a tux on Eric Whiting and transport to my location. Tell him his sister needs him. How long until he arrives?"

Tex didn't like this at all. Some strange guy, someone he had not vetted, was going to be his gal's date. If the guy so much as touched Susan, Tex would make him pay in the most painful manner possible. The Holbrook guy was already on his list. He was thinking of barbed wire for the guy. And look at that creepy General. The guy was smiling as he walked back to them. Wire and ants for him. "One, two, three, four." Tex counted like crazy, not wanting his subject to hear his thoughts about these loser men.

"Eric is being prepped and will meet us at the limo. Excellent that he was already in the area," The General said as he rang for the elevator to take them topside.

The man waiting by the limo had to be five years older than Susan. The man's face lit up the moment he saw Susan. He hurried to her and wrapped his arms around Susan, hugging her so tight that Tex was ready to make him let go before he broke Susan's ribs. The only thing that kept Tex from stepping in was that his subject was hugging the man. Was this a lover? A weird feeling hit Tex in the gut. He almost rubbed his tummy to lessen the queasiness in his stomach. Instead, he scanned the area repeatedly, trying not to watch the happy look on the faces of the two people embracing each other. He was a bodyguard, nothing more. As he scanned the area, he saw another SS agent watching the happy couple. The man looked like someone Tex should know, but he didn't know many agents as he wasn't social with others on the job.

Bobby Jay saw the new guy taking in the surroundings, and Bobby had already checked a hundred times or more while waiting for Susan to come up from the safety bunker. He walked over to the man to introduce himself. "Looks like we are teamed tonight. I have Eric's back. You have Susan. Let's make it quick if we must get them out of there. Agreed?"

Susan noticed Bobby Jay and spun around to hug the man quickly. "Bobby Jay, you are still with Eric. How nice. You know he has abandonment issues, right?" Behind her, Eric blushed.

"Yes, Ma'am, Miss Susan. He puts up with me as much as I put up with him. We'd be fine if he could get his cat to stop licking my hair."

"Bruce has a girlfriend," Susan laughed, hearing that tidbit in Eric's thoughts. It was the first time Tex had heard her laugh or seen her smile. It was like the heavens had opened up and rained bliss upon them. Then she sobered. "Eric will know when I've reached my limit. The same goes for Eric. If he needs to leave, we go and go fast. I don't care what the snobs all think about us leaving. Grandfather will have to make up an excuse. Let's get this over." Her voice held determination; her body gave her away; the slight tremble of her fingers and the flush on her face all spoke of stress.

It was a dinner party, with the food, seating, music, and Susan all part of the arrangements. She was to sit next to Eric and be the humble woman he was presently sleeping with, humble to the point that she had to raise her hand to ask to speak to him. This signal was acceptable, as her hand raised signaled that she had something.

Tex and Bobby stood against the wall behind where Eric and Susan were seated, playing the dutiful bodyguards of a rich man. Unable to get his mind off the new name Susan threw out without explanation, Tex gave in and asked Bobby about it. "Who is this Bruce guy? Will he be showing up next?"

Bobby had trouble not chuckling, as a mean bodyguard wouldn't be laughing while on duty. "Bruce is Eric's cat, and he does have a girlfriend. We are a bit worried about that at the moment. Convincing Bruce that romance isn't safe for him… needs handling carefully. He is pining away in Eric's rooms at the moment…." All talk stopped. Susan's hand was up.

Trying to show anger at Susan's whisper when he allowed her to speak to him, Eric shoved his chair back and took her by the arm. It appeared he was hustling her out of the room in a rage. His bodyguards are hot on his heels. Nobody spoke until they were on the elevator headed down to the garage level.

"Send out a silent alarm. The king was not at the dinner yet, which was planned by his brother. The brother plans to kill the king and blame the United States. You have to send men now to rescue the king. Do it now!" The words were barely out of Susan's mouth before Tex and Bobby used their cells.

The tension was high as they rushed Susan and Eric to the waiting car. Once Susan hit pay dirt, it was up to the Secret Service to take over. They removed Susan before anyone suspected her of being the intelligence source. The threat, the reason, was handled. They all settled into the limo, and the driver took off as if the hounds of hell were on his tail until Bobby suggested he slow down to the speed limit- well, more like growled it. They were heading to the safe bunker along a street with a small amount of traffic when Susan's hand went up.

Susan had heard the pain before she knew what it was. Then, the mind behind that agony began to clear. Someone had thrown a puppy out of a car onto the street. "Look for a bag. She is scared. We need to find her before a car hits her."

Sure enough, in the middle of the road was a plastic bag that wiggled. The limo stopped, blocking any cars from hitting the plastic bag, as Eric and

Susan sprang out of the vehicle and ran to the bag. Susan picked up the bag and ran back to the limo, practically shoving Eric into the car before she scrambled in and opened the bag. A small golden-colored ball of fur lay very still inside that bag. The only part that moved was the puppy's tail, which weakly wagged as if saying thank you. Eric scooped the puppy to his lap and touched it with a finger. "She won't last long without a heal."

Bobby Jay straightened and took over. "Drive to the nearest place that has a medical service. We also need high-protein food items. You are to drive until you get us what we need. Texas, be ready to catch Susan." Bobby looked at Eric. "Neither of you has eaten. Don't take it too far, kid."

Eric took over. "Susan, you are my battery but don't you dare to give me all of you, or Dad will kill me. I'm going to do enough to save her life. I promise Susan I'll save her. Don't you cry."

Tex went on full alert even though he was confused about what was happening. Bobby Jay was the senior Secret Service agent who took over the operation. Whatever they were talking about seemed to be serious. The limo leaped ahead and sped up, passing the other traffic like a high-speed chase. The General looked green-faced as if he was about to puke. The General's aide had pulled away from Eric and Susan, who huddled over the puppy. As if making as much room as possible for the two to work. Eric placed his hand on top of the puppy and closed his eyes. Susan put her hands on Eric's shoulders. Her face was so profound that signs of tears were forming in her eyes. The limo was quiet. It was as if everyone held their breath, afraid to move.

Eric fixed the worst of the bleeding first, infusing the puppy's body with the need to make more blood. He caused the crushed ribs, probably from a kick, to go back to where they should be instead of lodged in the wee one's lung and to mend. The kidney took time to repair. Eric could feel the weakness taking over his body and fought to keep going. Just before he blacked out, he felt his sister, Susan, slump and knew she had passed out. Dad would kill me was his last thought as darkness wrapped his mind.

The shock when Susan went limp, sliding off of Eric, hit Tex hard. He caught her before her head hit the drink console. Not knowing what was happening, he held Susan to his chest and looked to Bobby Jay for instructions. Bobby had Eric under the arms, his mouth set in a straight line of either anger or worry. "General, take the puppy. You hurt it, and I'll ensure you hurt ten times worse." Bobby turned his head to speak to the driver. "What is the ETA?"

"Here, Sir." The driver responded, whipping the limo into a sports medical clinic.

Bobby glanced at the Medical Clinic and began to bark orders. "You run in and tell them to set up two drips with glucose and electrolytes, warming blankets too. Don't let them give you any shit." As the driver ran towards the clinic, Bobby continued. "Tex, you carry Susan. I have Eric. General Richard, you carry the puppy, and be sure it has a warming blanket. We are in the second phase, recovery. Time is critical for our subjects. Move!"

Ignoring the stares from the medical staff, Bobby carried Eric at a dead run into the clinic. He headed for the black-suited limo driver standing over a person scrambling to set up the two drips, his hands shaking. The gun in the driver's hand may have had something to do with the guy's trembling hands. Bobby lay Eric gently on a med-bed. Bobby nodded his approval to the limo driver. "Go take over care of the puppy from the General. I don't trust him to do what is best for the pup."

The limo driver smiled. "Yes, sir. My pleasure." The limo driver was having the time of his life, and ordering the General around was the icing on the cake.

Tucking the warming blankets around Susan, Tex had never felt so helpless as he did then. This emergence was something that was outside of his experience. What the hell had happened? He had taken his cues from Bobby Jay, uncertain what caused his subject to faint. The real worry was that the guy Eric had fainted, too. Both Subjects went down, and at the same time, they had the stink of a plot. Some unseen enemies. Who? What? He needed something to fight, something he could smash into submission, something he could do. He remembered Bobby saying high protein foods and pulled out his cell—finally, something he could do. The chef for the White House was snippy, telling Tex they were not a delivery service. "I don't care who you are. You will deliver several high-protein meals to this medical clinic ASP. If I don't see them here in 30 minutes, I will inform the President." He hung up and let the creep chew on that.

Susan moaned, and Tex was instantly at her side. The medic was causing her arm to bleed. Didn't he know how to insert a catheter? "Move the hell out of the way. You are hurting her." Tex grabbed a new catheter. He had put in many a field catheter. Tex rubbed his finger over the area in the bend of the elbow. It was there, the pulse slow and weak. Worry tripped his heartbeat as he inserted the catheter and hooked up the drip. Tex glanced at the guy lying so still in the other med bed. Bobby Jay and Eric had worked as a team. As if they had done this many times in the past. Was that why Bobby Jay knew what action to take? It ate at Tex that he had been unprepared for this crisis. Tex had to know if there was an enemy to be on the lookout for. Or was this some medical problem these two people had in common? So he watched and waited until first Susan woke and then Eric, each of them going to the table set up with food kept steaming hot by the President's chef.

Going up to Bobby Jay, his eyes promising dire deeds if he didn't get straight answers, Tex started his interrogation. "Someone has kept me out of the loop, Bobby. Start explaining."

Motioning for Tex to follow him, Bobby stepped far enough from the others to keep from being overheard. He spoke in the low non-whisper the SS were trained to use so as not to be heard by the enemy. "They never clue Miss Susan's men in because they get spooked and leave. Everything I'm about to tell you is so classified; just telling you may be the end of you and me. This all started with the mother. Fredrick Whiting's wife is a healer. She can touch a person and heal whatever is wrong with them. The catch is that it takes a terrible toll on her. She can die just from healing a person, and she has several times. If you ever meet her, don't touch her. Mr. Whiting will rip your heart out if you do. Fredrick Whiting learned to support his wife like a battery, giving energy to a flashlight. Then Eric learned this same ability... plus developed talents of his own. Susan, you know, hears and feels everything from the people around her. It is a horrible life for her to endure. She is so brave to come here to help her country. Eric is another story. He can heal a little like he healed the puppy with Susan's help. But his real talent is seeing future crimes. He sees them, and we find a way to stop the crime or capture the stupid bastards doing the crime. Middy, well, Middy is a force to be reckoned with. I know she has wind power, plus I suspect she has more elements. Maybe she just hasn't owned them yet. The healing power is the most draining of the powers, that and being a battery. So you and I have to protect them from others and themselves. They... well, they give too much of themselves to those they are healing. Too damn much." Bobby cleared his throat. "Now, I need to warn you that should you betray the trust just placed in you, I will find and kill you. You understand?"

Tex's brows had knitted a crease in his forehead as he listened to Bobby Jay. It all sounded much like a bunch of bull. If not for him seeing Susan at work, he'd have punched Bobby in the face and walked away. He looked over to the blanket where the golden puppy was snuggled fast asleep.

Had Eric healed the pup? Tex wondered what was happening when Eric swore to Susan he'd heal the puppy. And the way the pair of them had suddenly passed out wasn't fake. He looked Bobby in the eyes. "Understood." He grunted.

Chapter Two

NO SUGAR COAT

It was clear Eric was reluctant to leave Susan when they reached her bunker. The fact that he was pale and barely able to stand was also apparent. Bobby Jay finally put his foot down and ended the long goodbye. "You won't recover in time to catch our plane home if we don't leave now and get you hooked up to Dr. Andy's magic brew." Bobby looked over at Tex. "I'll send a bag over for Susan. It is intravenous, okay?" Tex nodded, his eyes hooded as if keeping his thoughts to himself. Bobby didn't think keeping one's thoughts hidden was possible with Susan. But he nodded farewell to the new agent, practically lifting Eric back into the limo. As the limo door closed, Tex heard Eric asking if they could pick a steak up for Bruce to calm him down when they got to the hotel. Steak for a cat. Damn, rich people. "One, two, three, four…"

His focus was on his subject. Susan was weak. Her muscles kept jerking in minor spasms. Tex's instincts told him to take her to a hospital. Then there was this whole critical secret crap over what she and Eric could do. National Security. National Treasures. They could stuff that crap right where the sun doesn't shine. His subject was his only priority. He watched her cradle the golden puppy to her chest, leaning heavily against a wall. First, he needed to get her inside the bunker and secure the area. "Ma'am, let me get you inside where you can rest." Tex took her arm and let her lean against him as she slowly shuffled to the elevator that would take them down into the concrete bunker set up just for her visit. The puppy rolled her head over and licked Tex's hand. "Good dog. 500, 501, 502…."

Susan let the constant numbers wash over her, hoping to block the worry of the King's brother getting caught. So many things could go wrong. People might be killed if she said so; this was one of the nightmares she lived with, the knowledge that others might suffer harm or death because of what she revealed. Yet, what was the alternative? Did they let the assassination happen, and did the country become embroiled in a war with a government that could have become a friendly nation? Would young men and women have been killed during that war because she had kept quiet? She shook as the possibilities spun in her mind. "519, 520, 521…." The constant counting anchored her, giving her a comfort she didn't deserve as the elevator traveled swiftly down and down, and the voices in her mind faded. Once they left the elevator and entered the bunker, there was just the counting left in her mind. She sank gratefully into a lounge chair. "When…"

She paused to gather enough strength to speak. "When Andy's magic brew arrives, you must insert another catheter. You might as well set up for that now, as the bag should be here soon," Susan told Tex.

Tex nodded, understanding the situation, leaving to fetch a blanket to wrap around her first. He hadn't checked all the drawers and equipment in the bunker. His initial check was for danger. Now, he noticed a whole section for tending to someone very ill. They knew. The bastards knew that she was going to be sick at some point. "Barbwire, anthills, cactus beds. 532, 533, 534." He heard his subject sigh as he gathered cotton wipes, tape, and the catheter. She was out when he got to her side. Worry for his subject ate at him. So did the anger at those who had put her in harm's way. They hadn't told him the truth about what care his subject needed. They only warned him to hide his thoughts. They said nothing about what she needed. Anger curled inside him until he had to calm himself or take action. He was a Texan and would behave like a Texan. He might even warn the bastards, maybe.

Action on the monitor drew Tex's attention. A skinny youth surrounded by armed men stood in front of a camera and waved a paper bag at the camera, clutching a bag of puppy chow to his chest. "Stand down. Let the boy put the bags into the elevator when it arrives. Then give him $100.00 as a tip." Tex watched as the guards and the boy waited for the elevator. He could see the discomfort on the faces of the guards. The boy was the most relaxed of the bunch. Tex's lip lifted in a slight smirking smile as the elevator arrived, and the boy put the bags on the floor. The boy stepped back quickly as if he knew the doors would slam shut and the elevator would speed away. The sweat dripping down the face of the closest guard gave Tex some satisfaction. They all deserved to suffer. He would not easily forgive what they had done to Susan.

Tex ensured no explosives were in the plain paper bag or puppy chow using the elevator's scanners. Three of the intravenous setups were inside the bag. Bobby Jay's offer for Susan. If what Bobby Jay had told him was true. And Tex had no reason to doubt his fellow SS man. There may be a need for the other two bags in the future. It angered Tex that he had been kept out of a vital part of the loop regarding his subject. What the hell had the previous SS done? Run like hell the moment she revealed she could hear their thoughts? Susan's SS didn't stay long enough to be given the vital information that was needed to save her life. His opinion of his fellow SS dropped to zero. With angry thoughts rumbling, Tex set up the life-saving bag, inserting the catheter and regulating the drip. Taking the golden puppy from Susan's arms, Tex fed the pup. He rubbed the golden head, and his face seemed to relax for a fraction of a moment.

Mind still in a storm over his briefing on the subject being so lacking in the information needed, Tex sat beside Susan's sleeping form to monitor her. He studied her face, thinking of how mistreated she had been. The rage boiled inside him. She gave a slight moan, her face developing a frown. Were his thoughts upsetting her sleep? "You are right. They are not worthy of anger. They are all pansies dressed in pink, dancing around a fountain of piss. They look ridiculous and smell bad. I feel sorry for them now." The side of his lip twitched at the vision, and his subject relaxed. Tex took a small satisfaction at seeing her relax, wondering if he had managed that bit of ease for her. If outrageous thoughts gave her some slight relief from all the bad she heard, Tex would give her that. He would learn how to take care of her, protect her, and give her some tiny happiness. He knew he would not be leaving like the others. Tex had committed, and neither hell nor high water could change his mind now.

As she awoke, the tadpoles crawling out of the water on their new legs filled Susan's mind. They were so cute, crawling about and taking their first clumsy hops. Sunlight filtered down through the trees along the little creek, moss growing on rocks half in the water and the edges of the creek bank. Susan smiled and opened her eyes. She was in the bunker. Her IV bag was almost empty. Goldie must have been very close to death for Eric and her to have been so drained. A butterfly flew over the new little frogs on the creek bank, and Susan realized she had not been dreaming. Tex. They were thoughts from Tex. She knew the moment he realized she was awake by how the counting started again in his mind.

"Ma'am, do you want me to go now that you are recovering?" he asked. "Bobby Jay sent some food for the puppy. Her little tummy is full. She will need to go out soon for a walk. Will you be okay if I take her out?"

"No, unhook me, and we will both walk her. Goldie needs to know she isn't being dumped again.

There is a lingering fear in her mind." Susan sat up straighter to see where the puppy had gone.

The SS man's mouth tightened as if biting back an objection. "Yes, Ma'am. I'll take the bag and some paper towels for the puppy's offering." Gently, he removed the catheter and placed some tape and a cotton ball over the injection site. "Did you wish to change into walk clothing?"

Susan nodded and gathered some casual jeans and a blouse before disappearing into the bathroom area to change. This was the strangest experience she had ever had with any of her SS guys.

Susan found a long soft belt to tie around the neck of the puppy for walking. Tex had alerted the outside guards to the fact they were coming up to go for a walk. The dread of being among people hit Susan as soon as they stepped out of the elevator. The guards were all wary and taking sidelong glances in her direction. Their minds were fearful, fighting not to think anything. And this made their thoughts go to everything they wanted to hide. She took a deep breath, bracing herself, seeking the counting in Tex's mind to center her concentration. "Frogs," she said to Tex. "Tell me about frogs."

For a moment, Susan thought she had made a mistake when she told Tex about the frogs. It always spooked the SS guys when she said something they had thought. Then he began to talk.

"When I was a kid growing up in Texas, there was this creek that I thought held all the world's wonders. It was so clear you could see the fish swimming and the critters hiding in the rocks on the bottom. The frogs would sing in the spring, trying to get a mate. My dad told me it was a love song. I would listen to those croaking notes and wonder at frogs being in love. I was a romantic little boy who grew out of that later. Every day, I ran down to the creek and looked for frog eggs because Daddy said I would know if the frogs found love when there were eggs in the water. One day, I saw all these tiny, round, clear-looking specks in the water and knew some frog had found love. I watched over those eggs. I saw the eyes form on the babies and watched them develop and grow. I was all set to see tiny little frogs emerge from those eggs. When the eggs began to hatch, I was so disappointed. Instead of frogs, they looked like some baby fish, odd-looking, but not frogs. I went home and told my dad the frog did not find love. The eggs had just been the fish eggs.

"Daddy just looked at me and smiled. He proceeded to tell me that frogs were magical critters. They did not look like frogs because they had to trick the world into letting them live long enough to become frogs. He told me how my fish were tadpoles and that these magical critters would grow legs. And one day, when they were ready to be frogs, they would leave the water. I was doubtful, but I knew my dad had never lied to me, so I continued to watch the fishy beings. Sure enough, the little ones began to grow front legs. I became excited about them, running home to tell Daddy the magic was starting. He told me to be patient because magic took a while to come true. So I watched those little tadpoles grow front legs, then back legs, and before I knew it, the long swimming tails disappeared. The day the first little one crawled up on land and took a wobbly hop, you could hear my whoop of joy all across Texas. That day, I believed in magic. It has been a memory I hold onto."

Susan's eyes glistened. "We have them on the farm. One time, I helped Eric heal a leg on a big frog. I slept for two days. My father talked with Eric and told him that, being the oldest, he had to be the one to stop me from helping. Mother did not let either of us do chores for two days. I think that hurt us more than when Father was talking to Eric. We knew she was disappointed in us when she did not assign us chores. Although Mother told us we had done a good thing by healing the frog, I used to think I saw that frog whenever I went down to the pond. I imagine he would smile at me. Silly, huh?"

Tex could see a little black girl smiling down at a frog in his mind. "At least you did not kiss him and try to turn him into a prince," he said, then wanted to kick himself.

"Like in the fairy tales?" Susan shook her head, giving a sad little laugh. They walked in silence after that. Goldie found a small grass patch to her liking, ending the reason for the walk. By the time they had returned to the safety of the bunker, Tex had a lot on his mind, none of it good.

Tex's phone buzzed just as they were about to enter the elevator. He answered it with a growl, "Report."

"You okay, SS?" General Richards inquired. He cleared his throat before continuing, following the silence from the agent. "We were able to stop the assassination. The brother confessed and was escorted home under not-so-friendly guards—the alliance discussion we will have in the future. Let us say the King is very, very grateful to have his brother's plans spoiled. This assassination attempt worked well for our side. Miss Whiting may return to her home."

"That's it? You don't even have the guts to tell her Thank You? This behavior is going to change. You will personally thank Miss Whiting and apologize to her for her suffering for you. Understood." Tex's low voice and chilling unspoken threat convinced the General.

"Please put Miss Whiting on the phone." The General listened as Tex approached Susan.

"Ma'am, there is an important call for you."

"Hello," Susan said, fearing they were sending her on another assignment before she had time to clear her head.

"Miss Whiting, we wanted you to know how grateful we are for your bravery. You have my eternal thanks for the service you gave your country. I can not express how honored I am to know you. I thank you, and your Nation thanks you. Have a safe trip home, Miss Whiting." The General tried to speak with cheer and appreciation, unaware he had failed.

Susan didn't speak, merely disconnected the phone. This call was a first. Once an assignment was over, everyone went as far away from her as possible. Susan picked Goldie up and hugged the warm, happy puppy to her chest. Then, she slowly looked to where her SS was standing. His face was passive, showing little expression. He was counting like crazy. Inside her, a small drop of wonder dripped into the black pool of despair that was her constant companion. She didn't ask if he was responsible for the General's call. She didn't need to ask.

"SS, I am going for a walk. Please let the guys know," Susan announced to Tex as she walked outside her home. Almost the only pleasure left her in life was walking the mountain pathways. Today, she would have the company of little Goldie. She wanted to introduce Goldie to her mountain's deer and creatures. Goldie leaped forward when she realized they were going outside. The pup seemed to have grown overnight. It was a delight to watch as she romped around, tripping over her feet and falling flat on her face, only to get up again and take off running again. It was a beautiful day, sunny with a light breeze and perfect walking weather. Taking a deep breath of the mountain air, Susan started to walk on one of her favorite pathways. She was always aware of the SS guy following her and of the snipers in their cubbyholes higher on the mountain. The snipers were talking bull crap to each other. They tried to relieve the boredom of watching for someone out to harm Susan, but nothing happened. She felt sorry that the snipers were up there because of her. Susan carefully monitored them for signs of stress from their jobs. Susan often sent one or two snipers off to have fun for a week or two to relieve their boredom and worry for their families. Today, she planned on just enjoying Goldie and the patches of woodland on the sides of the mountain.

Wanting to enjoy her walk did not mean Susan was allowed that small privilege. Thoughts from the snipers bombarded her mind. They shadowed the area around her through their scopes, looking for any threat to her. Joe was worried about his daughter, who her ex-boyfriend had threatened. Before leaving for this assignment, he thought about how he should have taught her more self-defense. And what he needed to do to prepare his family for any situation life dealt with. Mick was worried about his father. His father needed to take it easy as his heart was in bad shape. On and on went the thoughts behind the banter of bull they talked. Ironically, the people Susan needed to protect were those protecting her— them and Goldie. Goldie must learn how to survive. She would start learning today.

Tex walked with a weapon behind Susan. He watched everything: the trees, the shadows, the faint glint off of a rock, but often, he watched Susan. She looked to love the outdoors. The life this young woman lived bothered him. Tex found himself trying to figure out how to make life happier for her and failed. He needed to be so careful of his thoughts that he caused her pain or stress.

As he watched the surroundings and Susan, the puppy began to act strangely. The pup would suddenly scurry under a bush to disappear, only to dash out of hiding a moment later to attack a stick. That persistent frown line popped up between Tex's brows as he saw the pup slink to her belly and crawl into a pile of leaves. Goldie wiggled until only the tip of her nose could be seen. He closed up behind Susan as she went to uncover the pup. He heard her softly talking to the puppy. "Good girl, Goldie. You've learned how to hide quickly. Tomorrow we'll practice in the house. Remember, don't come out once told to hide until Tex or I tell you it is safe. If you need to run away, go fast and far. You are such a bright girl."

Tex realized Susan was training the puppy to hide if she was in danger. How messed up was life when the first thing a young woman thought to teach her puppy was to hide from bad guys? Tex took a chance, bending down to pet Goldie. "If Miss Susan is in trouble, Goldie, you come to get me fast. Understood?"

Susan was startled when Tex spoke. She had been so involved in teaching Goldie safety measures that she had forgotten he was there. "I don't want her risking herself. Our family dog was wounded protecting my mother and father. If not for Mom healing him, he'd be dead." She took a deep breath. "I can't heal." She had said the words as if it was a failing on her part.

"But you helped Eric heal Goldie. You saved her life. Don't discount what you can do." Tex argued.

"My brother needed more than my poor battery. Dad will be mad at him for letting me give him that much. If Bobby Jay hadn't been there, I'm not certain we would have survived," Susan said. "Eric seldom gives that much at one time. He did it for Bruce, and we think that changed Bruce; he made it so he could shift. It is the most reasonable answer. Bruce's heart barely beat when Eric healed him, like Goldie's. He quite literally brought them both back from the brink of death. Only mom has been able to do that with people. She dies sometimes, you know, healing someone? Dad won't trust anyone to care for her other than himself. It wrecks him each time he sees the life go out of her." After saying this, Susan stood and continued her walk, not going far before heading back to the safety of the house and bunker. What had been a pleasant day had turned dismal for Susan. She spent her life worrying about others, hiding from would-be threats, and unable to do much for others except to spy on the thoughts of bad guys—a national treasure locked away in a vault.

On the walk back, Goldie was a happy puppy. She fetched sticks, sniffed at all the many scents, and returned to Susan for pets and love. For a brief moment, the heavy mantle Susan carried lightened, and Susan felt happy. Here in the forest was the closest she came to being free. A fox ran onto the trail, and Susan smiled. "Hello, my friend. You are looking beautiful today. Has your mate had her babies?" Susan asked the fox. The fox stared at Goldie and Tex, undecided whether he should run or remain. "This is Goldie. She is a friend like you and will not hurt you or yours." Susan half-turns to Tex. "This is Tex. He has sworn to protect. He will protect you and all your kind. You must let us know if anyone presents harm." The fox bowed.

Tex watched this exchange between Susan and the fox, wondering if she was crazy. That is until the fox bowed to him. Then his 'this is nuts' meter went off the scale. She was communicating with a wild animal. He didn't know what to do, so he nodded to the fox. The nod seemed to satisfy the fox as he turned to look slightly off the trail. A doe stood, shock-still, watching them. More craziness, it seemed, was about to happen.

Noticing the doe, Susan smiled at it. "You heard they are friends and a protector. You need not fear them when we do our walks," Susan told the doe. The doe walked carefully over to Susan, always watching Tex with his gun. "Yes," Susan said, "I've brought you your treat." She dug into her pocket and produced a handful of corn for the doe. And a bit of what looked like dried liver for the fox. They both came up and took their offering. They each took a whiff of Goldie and Tex, committing the scents to memory.

Susan had another two months of a peaceful routine at her home. Goldie was growing at a fantastic rate, only a few months old, and she looked like a grown dog. They met the fox and doe in the forest several times—the three of them. Goldie, the fox, and the doe often played a game of chase through the trees. What game it was, Tex didn't know. Seeing the three of them running and playing like little kids was quite a sight. He knew his job had expanded to include the creatures of the forest. For some reason, that thought didn't distress him. He felt the dark shroud around his mind starting to lift. Still, he was ever-vigilant. There was no way he would neglect his duty to his subjects. Then the call came.

The first problem with the call was that it went directly to Susan's inside line instead of being directed through Tex. Both Tex and Susan turned to stare at the phone. They were about to go out the door for their walk. A chill went down Susan's back. A call on that phone was seldom anything pleasant.

As much as she dreaded what the phone call was about, even stronger was her sense of duty to keep the world safe.

Tex held his hand out to stop Susan as she approached the ringing phone. Calls were his domain. He would not have her have to talk to some self-centered creep. He let the phone ring a third time before picking it up, allowing them to wait. Finally, he picked up the receiver. "State your business," he growled into the mouthpiece.

There was silence for a moment before a hesitant voice began to speak. "I'm calling for Susan Whiting on a matter of some urgency. Did I dial the wrong number?"

"This number has not been released. The fact you have this number means men in black suits will visit you. State your business or be taken out of life as a free man," Tex was bluntly truthful. Nobody but Susan's immediate family and the President of the United States should have Susan's number. As Tex spoke to the man, he also sent a text on his cell, requesting the call be traced to the source. And men were sent to apprehend the caller. The SS would have the man incarcerated within minutes.

"You don't understand; listen. We have 24 missing children here, and the count keeps going up. Someone is snatching the most treasured gift the world has given us. God only knows what those children are going through. Please, will Miss Whiting help the children if not …." There was a scuffling sound, and the phone dropped from the caller's hand. A few grunts sounded as if the caller was wrestled down. An SS agent came on the line.

"We have him. From his identification, he is a State Trooper. He has a murder board filled with pictures of children. He isn't going to hurt anyone where he is going."

"Hand me the phone," Susan said/ordered Tex. Tex didn't question why she wanted the phone; he just handed it over. "This is Miss Whiting. You will take this man to a secure location in his state. Bring all his gathered evidence. We will meet you there. You may give my SS the particulars." Susan handed the phone back to Tex. So much for our walk, Tex thought, as he gathered details of where to meet up with the prisoner. He watched Susan as she packed her go-bag. Noting the extra go-bag she packed for Goldie. It seemed the whole family was going to meet some strange caller. Well, Susan and Goldie were. Tex called his night relief to tell him to pack a go-bag. His go-bag was always ready. He could never take the chance of a subject trying to lose him by running away.

"May I ask why you decided to go, ma'am?" Tex asked, convinced she could not hear the other end of the conversation.

Susan looked at him as if judging his reaction to the words she was about to say. "You thought about children. Your thought was distressed, as though it hurt you to have the man arrested. No matter what, we help the children."

Tex almost smiled in relief. He had been worried that he was having the wrong guy arrested. Missing children was always a priority for him. Still, he had done his job, protected his subject, and set his feelings aside. He wasn't even upset that she had read that information from his mind.

He watched as Susan fitted a vest on Goldie, which allowed her to go anywhere they went. Tex had not heard of this type of vest before. He had seen vests on dogs for the handicapped, bomb dogs, and so on, but never one that allowed a pet to go anywhere in the world.

As if still reading his mind, he heard Susan explaining to Goldie why she had to wear the vest. "These vests were originally made for Dog. So he could travel with my mother. They made one for you and registered you the same as Dog, Goldie. Eric wanted one for Bruce. But they refused to do one for a cat, which is silly. Bruce guards Eric as much as you, and Dog guards us. They will change their minds on a vest for Bruce the first time Bruce saves Grandfather. Eric has seen that outcome."

An attack cat! The idea just wouldn't set in Tex's mind. He realized he was as closed-minded as the vest maker or the government branch that regulated the vest. Something Susan had once said flashed through his mind, something about we think that is why Bruce can change. Change? Change to what? He couldn't let his mind go there, to the impossible; right now, there were children to save, 24 and counting. He had started counting as his thoughts were turning dark. "One, two, three…."

Chapter Three

MONSTERS

The safe house was just that, a house in a
neighborhood of working-class people. Tex and
his partner looked at each other. The night guard,
Simon, nodded, letting Tex know he agreed. This
place would never do for their subject. She needed
somewhere insulated against the thoughts around
her. They glanced at Susan, noting the tension
knotting her into a stiff, straight statue. "We will try
to find an old bomb shelter or somewhere for you to
rest up, Ma'am," Tex said softly, as if afraid to add to
the burden of thoughts bombarding her mind. Her
lips were white, and Susan nodded.

Worry, grief, and anger were in the safe house.
It all hit Susan hard before they were parked. One
of the missing children belonged to the trooper's
sister. That made this very personal for him, and he
desperately needed action. Both could be dangerous
areas for Susan's mind. She held up her hand before
they left the car. The two SS were alerted, guns out,

ready to protect her. "Go, tell the trooper to count like crazy. I can't go inside there until you do."

Tex stayed at Susan's side while Simon took off at a run to the house. His gun was still out, and a look of determination was on his face. He might be new to this assignment, but he already knew to count in his head when around Susan.

Surprise and anger burst from the house in a wave, nearly knocking Susan off her feet. She reached out blindly and grasped Tex's arm. "One, two, three, four, five." Susan sagged, managing to stay on her feet. "It is okay; now we can go inside," she told Tex, releasing his arm.

He watched her closely as she walked ahead of him. Simon came out and fell in step with Tex. "She nearly passed out for a moment. Did he give you trouble?

"I think he was more surprised than anything. Took a gun to the head to get him to listen," Simon said. Tex nodded. He would have reacted the same way if someone burst in on him with a gun. Only the guy would be dead.

Tex looked the trooper up and down, sizing him to what sort of man he might be. "This is Miss Whiting. You may call Simon and me by our names. I'm Tex. There are certain rules you must follow while Miss Whiting is here. Always count. Not counting will cause Miss Whiting stress, making it hard for her to work. Don't touch her. We also need a place where she can relax away from everyone in a bunker or bomb shelter. Even a concrete basement that is isolated as much as possible from all people will do. She has no privacy from the thoughts around her. They torment and hurt her. Meaning you have no private thoughts from her. For the moment, counting will cover the worst of what you think. Simon and I have learned to count and think at the same time. You bring the counting to the fore, the active area of your mind, and think deep inside, as silently as you can. At all costs, you will protect Miss Whiting…" Susan raised her hand, and Tex and Simon immediately went on alert.

"There is a robbery taking place across the street. I don't have an address. The man has a gun," she said.

Simon called the locals, vaguely explaining how he knew this was happening. He nodded to Tex to let him know the locals were on it.

"This is another thing to watch for, Miss Whiting's raised hand. This signal is how she indicates we are to stop and listen to her, for she has picked up thoughts of trouble. Or something we need to be aware of around us. Do you understand all I have said?" Tex asked.

The trooper glanced nervously at Susan and nodded. Had the poor guy had any idea what he was doing calling her? Somehow, Tex doubted it. For the first time, the man spoke. "I'm Jess Kurt with the state troopers. I happened upon this whole thing when they kidnapped my nephew Robby. All the abductions have occurred in separate places. The different locals have not connected their cases with any others. I think this is because the abductor is taking children from places around the state. That makes them strung out in areas covering a large distance. I have a friend in the border patrol who mentioned hearing about an abduction similar to Robby's in a little town called Roanoke. A few inquiries revealed that there seemed to be a pattern shaping up. By child number twelve, I had no doubts. The problem is the Feds won't listen. They consider these to be isolated incidents. After a lot- I mean a lot of arguing, begging, and desperation. A Federal agent took pity on me and sent me your way. Can you, will you, help?" He turned hopeful eyes on Susan.

Tex and Simon both moved as if prepared to catch Susan. "You are leaking, man, count," Tex barked. Almost instantly, Susan's mind filled with numbers. They shouted at her. "ONE, TWO, THREE!" Susan put a hand to her forehead and whispered, barely loud enough for three men to hear her, "Please, not so loud." The noise toned to a bearable level, and she nodded her thanks.

Sweat popped out on the trooper's forehead. He felt as if he was jumping through hoops while juggling knives. Still, he persisted in trying to gain the help of this weird woman who was so sensitive to his thoughts it seemed to hurt her. Opening a large yellow envelope, he poured out photos, reports, and sealed baggies with physical evidence of his nephew's abduction. "Some of this has not been to the lab yet. Once I realized what was happening, I returned and collected any scrap. I hoped your lab could do a more in-depth analysis than the state lab. Take it all. I've documented each sample and the location. And in those boxes are samples from the kidnapped other children," he told them, stumbling over his words as if counting and talking were difficult for him. "There were never any real witnesses, although some places had noticed strangers passing through their little towns. Remember, these are all small communities where people trust each other. And don't expect real bad things to happen near their homes. Most families initially thought their child was spending the night at a friend's house. So the people taking the children got a head start on everyone."

Susan picked up each item, not so much looking at them but more looking inside them. She discarded some of them, placing others one by one out. "These are the only ones related to the case," she told the trooper. He looked doubtful but nodded. "I must rest now. In the afternoon, we will begin the search." Susan turned and headed for the door, her two shadows falling behind her.

"Wait! Let me give you a number to reach me," Jerry Kurt said.

Susan rattled off the number in his head. If he had doubts before, they were gone now. He nodded and said no more.

The search for shelter for Susan was a challenge. The state was a wetland and had few, if any, underground buildings. They finally settled on an old concrete structure, once an ice house. The building had long been abandoned, having several holes in the walls from vandals or teens. The SS support team swooped down to the place, cleaned it, and put it in beds. One faucet had rusty colored water, making it only usable for cleaning. Bottled water and a portable bathtub for bathing were the first order of business. The tub and a port-a-potty were set up behind a screen for privacy. They would be eating take-out food while there. Tex's scowl darkened when he looked at the setup. He would have threatened if Susan had not appeared pleased with the arrangements. In the meantime, Simon went to pick up their lunch.

A sigh of contentment escaped Susan as she finished the last bite of food on the paper plate. Rising, she walked over to the bed set up for her, laid down, and was almost instantly asleep. The nightmare began once Susan was in a deep sleep. Susan was locked up in a room filled with children. Most of the children were crying silently. Some just stared vacantly into space. She cuddled as many children as possible. The others sat or lay packed against each other. The horror from the children's minds had Susan in tears. She could barely function, yet she had to be there for the children. So she toughened her resolve and tried to think of what her mother would do. Her mother would have suffered even death for those kids. She could do no less. She relaxed her mind, gathered her strength, and sent a thought out to Tex. "Help." It was the first time she had attempted to send her thoughts to a human. As a child, she often called Dog when she felt overwhelmed by the thoughts people continually broadcast. It was time to explore other uses for her mind. With that thought, Susan awoke.

She woke frustrated and angry with herself. She should have explored other possible uses for her mind long ago. Only she had never faced danger or had another need her help. All she had ever needed to do was point out the bad guy. Her SS or the locals took care of the problem. Susan knew her parents and siblings had fought for their lives when she was just a baby and was unaware of the danger. Urgency filled Susan. Children were suffering, and she needed to find them fast. Determination became a driving force. She would explore the limits of her mind, and she WOULD find the children.

Once Susan decided to do something, she displayed her family's stubbornness. Scooting off the bed, she attempted to send Tex a message. "May we go now?"

"Yes, ma'am," Tex replied from across the room, his brow furrowed as if trying to figure out what had just happened. Simon was snoring in the bed set up for him. It wasn't an ideal arrangement with the men in the same building she was to sleep in, but she could stand just the two men she trusted being here. It was time to find the missing children.

This first plan was simple: they would drive from warehouse to warehouse district with Susan scanning for any sign of the children. Except it wasn't around the warehouses where Susan first felt the utter despair of frightened children. They were driving to the next small town with warehouses. They based the whole theory around the small towns. The outlying areas were where the kidnappers struck. It was logical to think the monsters taking the children would be somewhere near the small towns. There were miles and miles of fields for growing crops and little else between each dwelling. It was in the middle of such a stretch of fields when Susan raised her hand. "Stop the car," Tex barked to the trooper, who drove them around the state.

Susan's face had taken on a chalky look. Her dark skin had almost a look of being smeared with ashes. Susan heard Tex speaking to her from what seemed a long, long way off. "Should I set up an IV? Do you need the hospital?" There was a pause. "Whatever she is sensing must be very bad. Go back to the trunk and bring me the medicine bag. Get on the other side of her and hold her steady while I get a rig setup. Bring the blankets I put back there. It is important to keep her warm."

Everything was quiet. The only sounds were the opening and closing of the car door and the snap of the trunk being popped open. Susan barely registered the sounds. Her mind was overwhelmed with the fear of two dozen children. She knew she had to control her emotions. And overcome the way it was paralyzing her so she could help them. Fighting her way free was like trying to swim up a waterfall. Suddenly, the fear moved away from her, giving her enough control to break free. They were moving the children! She pushed past a body that blocked her from the road. Once out, Susan extended her arm and slowly turned in a circle. She had a direction. "That way. They are moving the children. Hurry." Climbing back in the car, she extended her arm to Tex.

As he struggled to insert the needle in Susan's arm, Tex barked orders to the trooper. "Start moving in the direction she pointed. Take my phone and push number 2. Then hand it back to me. Call your guys and have them look for a large truck on any road in this area." With barely a pause in the action, Tex wrapped tape to secure the needle in Susan's arm.

Hooking the bag of life-giving liquid to the clothing hook above the car door, he snatched his phone out of the trooper's hand. "Simon, zero in on my phone. Do a grid search for five, no ten, miles around it. We are looking for a moving truck with the body heat of many children. Also, have them look for a building where they could hold the children. Call up a satellite if needed." Damn it, Susan, don't you die on me, Tex thought.

Tex watched Susan with a critical eye. If she blinked slowly, he would take her to the hospital. It was one thing when a doctor cared for her, but he was not used to the role. Had he done right with the IV? Should he call Doctor Andy? He was so uncertain of what he should do that it was eating him up inside.

Susan, all of a sudden, went almost limp. She raised her head and looked at Tex. "They are out of my range," she said sadly.

Pulling her head over to his shoulder, Tex soothed her. "Don't worry. The troops are out. If at all possible, we will catch them."

The radio blasted them, "Two trucks just passed going north on I-10. I am crossing over to pursue." The voice on the radio proceeded to give details on the mile marker. And a description of the trucks. He stopped talking when a second trooper called in a report of a large truck on a back road. Each team went to one of the locations. The two trucks spotted on the interstate were stopped first. Both were cleared and let go. That left the back road truck.

The patrol car tailing this suspected truck stayed back to prevent the driver's panic. Hanging back became a problem. The road began to twist and turn around sharp bends. Around one such bend, the truck disappeared. It was with great reluctance that the patrol officer reported the loss. "This intersection has only two cutoffs just past the turn. That I see. I will take the right-hand one heading east. Anyone who gets here, go down the west one."

A patrol car rounded the turn just ahead of the one carrying Susan. The trooper driving slowed, looking for traces of a truck driving down either side of the road. It was then that Susan's hand went up. She was barely able to sit up. But, Tex thought, she had felt the children. Only she rolled her window down to watch, of all things, a butterfly dancing beside the car. "Susan," he warned.

Susan ignored Tex, watching as the butterfly flew back the way they came to disappear in a clump of trees. "Turn around. There must be a road in that bunch of trees."

"Do you feel the children?" Tex and the trooper ask together.

"No, but the blue butterfly is my mother's mentor. Sometimes, it will come to help us during a dark moment, and there is none darker to me than losing the children."

"You expect us to believe that?" The trooper asked.

Susan turned to Tex. "Do you trust me?" She asked him.

"Completely. Turn around. If we don't find a road, we will have only lost a few minutes," Tex said.

Jess's face was red in anger, which he did not try to hide from Susan. He blamed her for this delay. Jess spun the car violently around. He was sure they would have seen any road. They were halfway past the clump of trees when Susan pointed. That damn butterfly was dancing in the middle of an overgrown track that had recently had the vegetation disturbed. "I'll be damn," he muttered.

Jess went on the radio immediately, calling it in. Finally, they had a break. Tex hopped out and planted his white handkerchief on a stick to guide the others to the track. They went barreling down the barely-there track, bouncing up and down in teeth-jarring ruts. After Susan's head hit the roof of the car, Tex strapped her in. She was still recovering from the earlier instance, and Tex's main objective was to protect her.

They drove across overgrown fields, rough patches of trees, and areas neglected for years. Who would have guessed all this was just off a country road? Suddenly, Susan picked up on the terror the children felt. Most of them believed they took them to this remote location to die. These were country children for the most part. They were trying to find a way to escape. Susan fought the overwhelming emotions of the children. She tried to send thoughts of encouragement, telling the children repeatedly that help was coming. "They are so scared," she said.

Tex raised his hand with a bark. "Stop here. This spot is where we set up and decide how to go in. Susan, can you tell how many men are guarding the children?" he asked.

"Three. I sense a fourth," Susan said, stepping

out of the car and doing her circle turn. "In that direction, watching. He is bad. Very bad, and will kill the children should he feel threatened."

"Perhaps we can circle and take him out," Tex said without so much as blinking an eye at the idea. He counted like crazy, not wishing Susan to hear his thoughts. "Let me know if he moves."

Although she was shocked at Tex's matter-of-fact manner, Susan kept a blank face. The man, hidden in the trees, could be listed under monsters. She would not weep for him even though killing went against all she believed. The fact that this monster was watching them was unsettling.

It felt like hours, but it could only have been minutes when the first trooper's car arrived. Moments later, a swat team dropped from the sky and landed in one of the fields Susan's bunch had passed. They fast marched to the field command center, each with a heavy pack of equipment on his back. Their leader approached Tex as he updated the others on what they knew. "One of our primary concerns is the man acting, we assume, as the lookout. We have information this man is capable of killing the children. Use every caution when approaching this man.

"Our objective is to save the children and take their guards alive if possible. We need to find out how large this group of perverted human flesh has become. Questions?"

As Tex asked for questions, Susan felt the intent of the watcher. "Down," she said in her most commanding voice, dropping and rolling to cover

herself. She had been drilled as a child on what to
do when monsters threatened her. Around her, the
SWAT team did the same. They were well-trained.
Tex threw his body on top of Susan. Glass shattered
in the car window behind the place where Susan had
stood. The state troopers were a tad slower to follow
orders, only hitting the ground after the shot fired.

Immediately, the SWAT leader began the
role call. All his men answered. One trooper did
not. Later, it was determined the unresponsive state
trooper had been behind Susan. Fortunately for him,
Susan was shorter than all the men around her. The
bullet, meant as a kill shot for her, hit the trooper
in his vest. All it did was bruise and knock him out
for a long moment. The shattered window was from
the impact of the trooper's head. Still, this changed
things. Now, the watcher was going down.

"He is moving. Rapidly. You must hurry if
you are to catch him." Susan advised.

Swat took the car with the busted window.
Three team members drove all out in the direction
Susan had pointed them in. Bouncing over the field,
sometimes the whole car was airborne. Yet they were
too late. The guy had his escape plan down to the
last second. On that side was a well-paved road with
a car parked and ready for a quick exit.

While part of the SWAT team went after
the shooter, the others went for the children. Tex
was super protective. He had Susan put on swat
protection and robbed the wounded man to deck
her out. He didn't want her near the action, but she
insisted the children needed a woman to comfort

them. Finally, he agreed to let her stay in the back, just outside the building, until they cleared it. The look she gave him at all his orders had Tex worried. She could have him removed from protecting her and doing her own thing instead of listening. Either was a bad outcome, so he stuck to her like super glue.

Susan asked the children to pinpoint where the kidnappers were so she could tell the men. She also told them to move away from the kidnappers and lie down. "The bad guys are one by each door and one watching for movement out a little window. The children are lying down," she told Tex. Tex whispered orders to the teams through the communication setups. He listened for the confirmation that each take-down group was in position. The guy by the window would be the most difficult. The window was too small to enter. The plan was to come in behind the door closest to the window and take him down.

He sent the signal to the teams to go in. Operation Rescue went into action. The doors were rammed open. The men behind those doors wrestled to the floor. That left the window man who hadn't been idle. Quickly, he reached down on the floor and pulled a little boy in front of him. He crouched down to use the boy as a shield. The boy was Jess Kurt's nephew. Tears began to run down Robby's cheeks until Jess stepped in front of the SWAT team with their guns pointed at the kidnapper's head. A calmness seemed to settle on both the boy and the trooper. As if seeing each other meant that everything was going to be okay. Looking at Robby, Jess spoke, "You remember what I told you?" Barely nodding, a determined look upon his face, Robby relaxed, his body slumping forward. Suddenly, he reared back with all his might, slamming his head into the kidnapper's face. The kidnapper let go of Robby, grabbing at his face. That was all Robby needed to be off, like a shot straight into Jess's waiting arms. "It worked, Uncle Jess," Robby crowed as he held tight to his uncle. The SWAT team soon had the man who had held Robby on the floor. They were not gentle.

Susan came in behind the troopers. She had eyes only for the children. Kneeling, she opened her arms to let them know she was there. It was like a stampede as little bodies ran to her, all but one which lay motionless upon the floor. "Children, give this trooper your names so we can contact your parents," Susan told them after ensuring each child had been hugged and kissed. She rose as the flood of children went to the trooper with the clipboard. Approaching the little boy lying still on the floor, Susan felt Tex's presence beside her. Together, they knelt to examine the little boy. His skin was cold to the touch, but a slow rise of his chest proved he still lived. "Emergency medical team here first," Tex barked, "blankets now!" he was in full protector mode, and this child had entered among his priorities.

"I can't heal," Susan mumbled to herself as if it was a failing on her part.

"You found him. We would have never known to look here if not for you. So you have saved him," Tex told her, not about to let her blame herself for anything.

"Who is he? We need to contact his parents so

they will be there for him," Susan inquired.

Again, Tex took over. Rising, he went to the trooper with the clipboard of names. "We need to contact the parents of the sick boy. What is his name?"

"Sir? We've already checked off all the kids on the list. They are all accounted for," he said.

"Then, who is he? Let's get his picture and fingerprints. We'll go over the list of missing children. Someone must be missing this boy," Tex ordered. "Miss Whiting and I will go to the hospital with him. Send Simon and me both a copy of the picture and fingerprints." Tex knew there would be no way Susan would leave the boy's side since he wouldn't have his parents with him.

Outside, the transport choppers and the medical team arrived. Tex wasted no time getting one of the doctors to the boy. Surprisingly, the first thing the doctor did was smell the boy's breath. "I suspect it is diabetes," he said. He pricked the child's finger to draw a drop of blood. He touched a blood machine with a test strip attached to the blood. Within seconds, he had a reading. "Glucose," he bellowed to the medical team.

One medic came at a run with an IV bag. "What do you have, Doc?"

"Worse sugar low I've ever seen. We need to keep the child warm. And check his blood every half hour since we put glucose directly into his veins," the doctor said. He turned to Susan and Tex. "Have his parents come directly to the hospital. They have to be worried sick over him."

"At the moment, he is a John Doe. Susan and

I will stand in for them until we find out who he is," Tex said.

"He will need a legal guardian—or social services to sign hospital forms so they can treat him. I'll call social services," the doctor said.

"No," Susan said, with the air of the issue being settled. "I will be his legal guardian before we reach the hospital." She turned away, her phone already in her hand.

"She does know that is impossible?" The doctor asked Tex.

"No, it is quite possible for her," Tex said. He could hear Susan talking on the phone.

"Grandfather, I need to become this little boy's guardian until we locate his parents. I will have Tex send you the information. Grandfather, it needs to become legal in the next 20 minutes," Susan said before hanging up.

Tex was already sending the known facts. He sent the boy's picture and fingerprints to the President and the place to send the legal documents. He knew the forms would be at the hospital by the time they arrived.

Late into the night, Susan watched the sleeping boy. He had not woken yet from the coma he was in from low-sugar blood. Susan saw so much of her brother, Eric, in this sleeping child. It was the stories her sister, Middy, had told her of when Eric first came into their lives that often haunted Susan. It was hard for her to imagine being so frightened as to have any noise send her running to hide. Her poor brother had suffered so much already. Now, he suffered horrible visions. Susan hoped to spare all the horrors of the world for this boy. It was why she championed the boy. And would protect him from the world.

The night nurse came into the room. They had run out of fingers to prick and were using his arms now. She smiled at Susan, "It is staying steady. If this keeps up, perhaps he will wake up after all."

Those words sent a chill down Susan's back. "You mean you all do not think he will wake up?" she questioned.

The nurse looked uncomfortable. "I need to finish my rounds. The doctor will be here in the morning. He will answer any questions you may have then."

Standing, Susan stood beside the boy as he slept. She ran her fingers through his limp hair, then tucked the covers around him to be sure he stayed warm. Reaching over, she took one of his limp hands. "Do not worry. I will call my mother after talking to the doctor in the morning. We are going to get you well." She turned as the door opened. Tex slipped into the room. The hospital would only allow Susan to stay inside the room with the boy after visiting hours.

"We will get him a specialist. Do not let her worry you," he said.

"I have decided to call my mother after we talk to the doctor in the morning. If he has lied to us, she will know," she told him with conviction.

The worry line in the center of Tex's forehead deepened. Was it better not to know the worst was true? Or understand the worst was happening and begin to face up to it? All he knew was that anyone who had lied to him was dead in his eyes. He suspected Susan would be equally hard on someone who lied to her. Only she could cause such a fool endless trouble. Being that powerful and not taking advantage of it showed great honor. The boy was the only time he knew her to call upon that power. The truth was he would have done the same if able. He pulled up a chair on the other side of the boy's bed and sat. There would be no more banishing him from the room. The nurse had stressed Susan, and that would not happen again. "Rest. I will watch over him for a while," he told Susan. She nodded and rested her head on the edge of the bed. He would have a bed set up in the room for her.

Simon popped his head in the door. "You know I have nights. Get some rest," he gave a wicked grin. "And that's an order." Quickly, he closed the door. Simon chuckled to himself. It wasn't often he got to tell Tex what to do.

In the morning, bright sunlight glared into the hospital room. Susan woke up feeling she needed to brush her teeth. A shower would have been nice, but having a fresh mouth was at the top of her list. She glanced to where Tex sat dosing, looking for once more like a boy than a hardened man. That boy side of him was something she had only glimpsed before, and it made her wonder what sort of childhood he had. Her own was filled with love, not always the loving/hugging type, yet there was no doubt in her mind that her family loved her.

At last, she let her eyes settle on the boy in

the hospital bed. His eyes fluttered open, and he huddled back as if cringing from any threat that might be present. "You are safe," Susan said, clearing her throat as her voice sounded scratchy. "Will you tell me your name?"

The boy stopped the cringing. He seemed to think a moment before answering, "Useless."

"What?" Susan asked, not sure she heard him correctly.

"Useless. My mother said my name is Useless because I am," the boy said, his voice a little stronger.

Susan bit into her lip rather than say anything about his mother. She smiled at him, "Well, I'm not calling you that because you are not useless to me. What name do you like?"

"Me?" the boy asked. Susan nodded. The idea of picking a name seemed to be so strange. He couldn't speak for a moment. "I may pick any name, any at all?"

Susan nodded. She could hear names flooding his thoughts. They flicked through so fast none had time to settle. They were all strong names of warriors or heroes. "York," he said. "He was a man of honor and morals. He didn't believe in killing, yet he went over to do his duty for his home and country, where he earned the Congressional Medal of Honor." As the boy, who would be called York, talked, he became animated for the first time, having a glow to his face that reflected his pleasure. Quickly, the animation disappeared from his face. He cringed back against the sheets, his face reflecting fear now. "Don't hit me. I didn't mean to talk. I know I'm useless," was pouring from his mind.

Susan clenched the sides of her seat to keep from passing out. "Nobody will ever hit you as long as you are with us," she told him. "I meant to tell you that because we have been unable to locate your father or mother, I have become your legal guardian. We will continue to try to locate your family. Do you know where they live?"

His thoughts were a jumble of fear and hope. It was a long moment before he said anything. "My mother dumped me on the side of the road and told me to go die. I don't have a father."

Tex opened his eyes a crack at the boy's words. He had been listening to the conversation all this time. Quickly, he closed his eyes again.

"Then I will look into adopting you. I'm adopted, and the people in my family are all loving. They will love you too," Susan told him. "That is if you decide you want to live with me. I'd like you to meet Tex. He is my protector. Now, he will protect you as well. Tex, wake up, please." She smiled as Tex made a show of waking up. "Tex, meet York. For now, he will be living with us."

"York? Like the Congressional Medal of Honor York?" he asked. "I believe I know of a museum where he is honored. I'm pleased to meet you, York."

York's eyes seemed to sparkle at the mention of the museum. He was careful not to say anything. He did put his hand in the hand Tex offered. It was a start.

Chapter Four

ADJUSTMENTS

It was a question of getting York released from the hospital. Doctor Fryer was in charge and wanted to run a test on York. To determine any brain damage caused by low sugar levels, what he wanted to do was to experiment on him. Doctor Fryer thought of masking his intent with the excuse of tests. The man had no idea who the person was that he was trying to fool. "It is simply, we need to determine how much brain damage happened," he told Susan and Tex.

"Doctor Fryer, you saved his life, and I am grateful for that. I will not have you experiment upon York. You will sign the release forms now," Susan said, her voice firm and commanding.

"But you don't even know how to care for him," he said.

"My whole family is very experienced in sugar lows. We have a knowledgeable doctor with practical experience in the subject. There is no need to worry about that score," she told him, her voice growing cold, harder than Tex had ever heard it. He knew then the doctor was now on his list, on the dark side.

Tex stepped forward. He flashed his SS badge. "This child is under the Secret Service's protection. We have to approve any matters concerning him. I say your services are no longer needed. We will be leaving here now," he stated, turning on his heel, Susan following in his wake.

It seems the hospital had destroyed York's clothing. Tex and Susan began preparing York to leave while Simon ran to buy clothing. "We are getting you out of here and going home," Susan explained to York. Tex went to have York released. They worked as a team, each doing their task quickly. Shortly, they regroup, with York looking at his new clothes in wonder. Susan saw the hesitation in the boy's mind when putting on the clothing. "They are yours," she reassured him.

"For real?" he asked.

"For real," she said, being very positive with him. "We will buy a couple more sets for you after we get out of here."

"From the Salvation Army?" York asked, still uncertain of it all.

"No, new clothes. Those, too, will be yours to keep," Susan told him. "And shoes."

York was quiet after that. He was afraid that if he spoke, they would take the clothes away. And they would leave him on the side of the road again. Susan wept inside for York. A child should know love and not be tossed away like so much trash. Tex and Simon were both tight-lipped. They counted like crazy to be careful not to stress Susan. Inside, there was anger for the parent who had so abused this boy.

The shopping affair was a start and stop. York would become overwhelmed with all the nice things in a store and need a quiet place to adjust enough to continue. When Susan would feel York becoming too stressed, she would take him to a quiet area and only continue when she felt his mind settle. Simon would buy them a Coke or ice cream during these breaks. This way, York would be distracted from all his fears. She would also explain to York why he had been in the hospital. And how to avoid becoming so low again. They gave him a couple of the bars her family used when they supported her mother's healing.

"Eat a bar when you start to feel weakness or feel you will pass out. You will find yourself gradually gaining strength. The rise in your sugar won't happen all at once. It takes time for the bar to digest. And the benefits enter your bloodstream. Just rest and let it happen. My mother and the kids in our family all become very low when our systems are stressed. Dr. Andy invented the bars for our family. So you are not the only one with this condition. Will you remember to take care of yourself?" she asked.

York nodded, then sat for a long moment in thought. Susan could hear him wondering if his mother had taken him to see a doctor, would they have known what was causing his blackout spells? He didn't ask Susan. He decided he didn't want to know if his earlier childhood could have been so much better. It was what it was, which was a very mature way for such a little boy to look at things. Susan felt pride bloom in her chest for York. She decided it was best to stop shopping now that he had a few clothing changes. The whole shopping bit was so strange to York that he was starting to have culture shock.

The airport fascinated York. He craned his head this way and that, watching everything. He tried to take in every plane that landed or took off. The escalators gave him a thrill. He wanted to ride them again but was afraid to say anything. Susan told Tex to take him up and down them again, then watched as her oh-so-serious SS protector played with York. For once, Tex's face looked relaxed. York was going to be good for him to have around.

It was almost a letdown when they stopped to continue to the private plane. York came to a complete stop when he saw they were approaching an airplane to ride. His eyes grew huge in his face. After standing to stare at the plane for a very long moment, he turned to Susan, unable to ask if they would ride in it. Susan squatted down to York's level, looking into his eyes. "We are going to where I… we live. It is far away from this place, so we must ride on this plane or drive for days to get there. If you are afraid to ride on an airplane, we will take a car and drive. The decision is yours. Whichever way you pick, I will see to it we do it. Okay?" she asked him.

Still unable to speak, York pointed at the plane. She saw in his mind that he wanted to experience a plane ride. He was just scared of something so new happening. Most of all, York didn't want to let Susan down. York squared his thin shoulders and took a step forward, then another and another. His bravery touched all three of his escorts deeply. They watched him go up the steps into the plane. He was still moving very slowly, taking each step forward. When he reached the top, the flight's steward greeted him with, "Welcome, Young Sir. Please enjoy your flight." York's mouth dropped open. Yet, he managed to nod. The steward smiled at Susan as York entered the plane. The smile brought a frown from Tex.

The flight home filled York with wonder. He saw the tops of clouds and buildings so tiny below the plane that they looked like toys. Susan monitored York the whole time to ensure he wasn't too overwhelmed. When they finally landed, York turned to Susan. "Can we do it again?" he asked.

On the long drive home, York fell asleep, not waking until they turned off to Susan's mountain. As the house came into view, Susan pointed up at it. "This is where you will be living for now. Tomorrow, I will introduce you to some animal friends of ours, but tonight, we eat and get some sleep. Simon will have the night watch. Tex is on days. So we are well protected here."

Susan hadn't thought about where York would sleep. She realized that being a mother may be more involved than she thought. Fortunately, Tex and Simon took care of making sleeping arrangements for Susan. Already, a room had been added on and furnished for York. However, Susan would not let York be the one sleeping outside of the bunker. So they were all busy for a while as they moved furniture from one room to the other. The SS was not happy. Their subject was putting herself in danger by not sleeping in the safety of the bunker. Immediately, plans were sent out for a second safe room to be built. It would be alongside and joining where York slept. They would have a connecting door between the two rooms. For now, the two SS would be extra vigilant.

The code for opening the door was something York had to learn. He asked them, "Why?" They reminded him that recently, he was kidnapped. The bunker was to keep him and Susan safe. They told him that he and Susan would do whatever they wanted during the day if whoever was on duty was with them. But they had to enter and secure the safe room if an alert went up. They showed him how to use the monitors to see what was happening during an alert. York was big-eyed in wonder by the end of his briefing. And he was a bit nervous.

Susan thought he needed some happy time now. Over breakfast, she smiled at York. "Are you ready to meet some special friends?" York nodded. "We will need to be quiet and not move too fast, or they will be scared," Susan told him.

Once they were done eating and cleaning up the dishes, Susan and York dressed for a walk. Goldie danced along the path, so happy to be home. Tex followed the three as they walked through the woods with a rifle in his hands. He watched everything around them. Tex listened to Susan explaining the trees and flowers along the path. She slowed her steps and became soft on the woodland path. Tex cracked a half-smile as York copied Susan. She stopped standing still, waiting.

Almost as silently as Susan, a doe approached Susan and York. She offered her head to Susan to pet, then Goldie to lick. Speaking softly, Susan introduced York to the doe. "My friend, this is York. He is staying with us. Please do not fear York."

The doe stepped over to York and offered her head. Eyes opening wide, York reached out to rub the doe's head. "Thank you," he stammered with a big smile. The wonders were not over. A slight rustle of the leaves was the only warning before a red fox came on the path. The fox was wary of being petted, but he did come over and lick York's hand. The fox scurried off when a noisy raccoon waddled out of the woods. Even Goldie backed away from the coon. Tex hadn't seen the coon before. The coon was a bossy animal seeming sure of itself. Both the coon and the doe moved away when a piercing cry from the sky sounded. The eagle swooped down from the sky at an alarming speed. Quickly, Susan pulled a leather wrap out of her pocket to wrap around her arm. Sharp talons pierced the leather as the eagle landed on Susan's arm. It fussed, ruffling its feathers. Susan laughed, "I take it that you missed me."

For the rest of their walk, Susan's animal friends followed them. They were not tame pets. Susan made that clear to York as they walked on, softly talking. Only the doe was willing to accept petting. The eagle showed affection for Susan. The rest of the forest animals wanted the company. Mostly Susan's company. She talked in soft tones to the animals and York. York was beginning to feel affection for Susan. For most of the walk, the animals entranced York. It was the perfect distraction after being frightened by the idea of harm coming to them.

On the way back, Susan showed York the skills Goldie learned in hiding. After mouthing practice to Tex, Susan whispered one word. "Alert." Goldie reacted immediately. She ran forward and disappeared.

"Now, we must find her. She hides well but often forgets not to wag her tail when she hears us approach." "Keep your eyes open, or you will miss seeing her," said Susan.

They walked on a little bit before Susan spotted the tell-tale flick of Goldie's tail. She waited to see if York saw her. His face was scrunched up in concentration. The closer they got, the more the end of Goldie's tail flicked. Finally, York saw her. "I found her. I found her. She is under those branches," York said, jumping up in glee. "May I try, please?" This reaction was just what Susan hoped for: a chance to begin defensive training with York.

"Okay, I'll find you both. Alert," she said. Immediately, the pair were off. Susan gave them a moment before walking down the faint path. It was Goldie that Susan spotted first. "Goldie, you forgot to hold your tail still," she said. Goldie came dancing out of the thick bush she had used for cover, happy despite the slight scowling. Susan looked around, expecting to see York. Only she didn't. She looked under bushes, behind trees, even in loose leaves, but no York.

Tex had spotted the boy right off. The child had climbed a tree and was lying very still along the top of one of the larger branches. He had Susan bested. Finally, she announced that York was the winner. He shimmed down the tree with the biggest smile on his face. "People never look up," he said. "That was in a movie."

Tex hated to break York's bubble of happiness, but he needed to know that some people would look upward. "York, I saw you right off. I'm a train Marine, a sniper, and a Texas Ranger. We never miss anything up or down. Sometimes, the bad men are trained too and will know to look upward. When in the trees, secure yourself so nothing shows. That was a smart move, climbing the tree. Just remember, some bad guys know to look up. I am proud you thought of doing that. Good job."

"It won't work again, Susan knows now," York said, but his smile returned.

Life for York was completely different from before he lived with Susan. York hadn't had a fainting spell, and he had enough energy to do her assigned chores. Gradually, York was gaining weight and developing muscle. He and Goldie would romp and play hide for hours.

The boy was inventive of places to hide. Susan told York that if they were inside when an alert sounded, he must first enter the safe room, locking it. From there, he should watch the monitors. He was to come out when Tex or Simon told him to. Should both of them be out, York was to push the rescue button near the monitors and wait for SS to arrive. Never leave the safe room until the all-clear. First, insist that the person saying it was alright show his identification. It was a lot to put on a little boy. York accepted the rules. He had experienced what bad guys could do up close in person. For the first time in his life, York felt safe. That feeling was of great comfort to him. He owed Susan his life for so many reasons.

The days passed quickly. Before they knew it, the weather had turned cold. York and Susan stayed inside more and more. It was on a cold, windy day. Tex gave an alert. Two cars came up the road without advance notice. Susan and York entered the safe room. Where they could watch the cars come up the road. York was nervous. He looked up at Susan and asked, "What about Tex?"

It was a question Susan had asked herself many times. There was no answer to satisfy Susan. Tex had said it was his job to be out there when she asked him. It just wasn't right. "We have to trust Tex to be careful. I've tried to get him to wait in here with me. He won't do it. He says his job is to be out there to protect me. It helps to know there are snipers up the mountain watching over him. Not much, but some," she said truthfully.

"There are snipers on the mountain? Are they there all the time?" York asked.

"Yes, a different team takes over at night to watch over Simon," Susan told him.

By then, the two cars were pulling up in front. Susan sighed when the General stepped out of one of the black cars. "The man never learns," Susan said, turning the sound up.

"Oh, come on. You know me, put the gun away," the General blustered, his face turning a terrible shade of red.

"You have no appointment. For all I know, you are here to harm Miss Susan. There is no way I will accept your word alone," Tex barked at the General.

"Oh, for God's sake, do we have to go through this every time?" asked the General.

"Yes, any time you show up without prior notice, you will be turned away," Tex said with steel.

"Okay, look, I'm making a call to the President. Are you happy?" mocked the General.

"Not until you leave. This second is your last warning." So saying, the mirror on the car next to the General shattered. He jumped back and dove into the car, slamming the door. For five more minutes, the standoff continued. The General stayed secure in his bulletproof car, and Tex stood at the ready. It took that long for the President to call Tex. Tex then proceeded to rip the President a new one.

"This is the second time this has happened. You are supposed to care about your granddaughter. Is this how you show you care? This causes her to become stressed, with the belief that an assassin has arrived to harm her. You will not let it happen again, understand?" Tex said. "You get your shit together!" Tex snapped the phone off in the middle of the President's blustering. He had had it with pompous jackasses.

"You may exit the car and state your business," he said, still angry.

The car door slowly opened, and the General, pale of skin yet red in the face, asked, "May I please speak to Miss Whiting?" he asked, his hat in hand.

"You must first tell me. If I approve, Susan will

hear you out," Tex stated.

Clearing his throat, the General began, "We have reason to believe one of the most trusted members near the President is a traitor. We need Miss Whiting to find them. It is impossible to investigate any of these people without tipping them off. Only Miss Whiting can do this," said the General.

"Stand down," Tex said. The General visibly relaxed now that Tex had told the snipers to back off. Tex was unaware he had been calling Susan by her first name. Tex turned to the house. "It is okay to come out, Miss Whiting," he told Susan.

The General started to repeat himself, but Susan held up her hand, and he stopped. "I know," she said.

"Of course you do. We do not have a bunker for you this time." When he saw Tex was going to object, the General rushed on. "But we have outfitted a basement with extra shielding. Will that be okay with you?" Sweat began trickling down his face as he waited for an answer.

Before committing to the deal, Susan asked, "Will it also be outfitted for York, Tex, and Simon?"

"Ma'am, who is York?" asked a puzzled General.

"York, come out, please," Susan called. York stepped out, his shoulders square and his back straight. He glared at the General and stood between Susan and Tex. "York will be living with me from now on. So any arrangements must accommodate him too. Be certain of it. Else we will not come," Susan said. With her, there was never any doubt she meant what she said. Such was her power over these men. They ran the country, but they needed her. She did not need them.

"Yes, ma'am. Everything will be ready when you go to your rooms." What else could the General say? Susan turned on her heel, motioning for York to follow. Tex called Simon to gather their go-bags and join them. Simon didn't ask why. The fact that the go-bags were needed said it all. He brought their car, for he felt Tex was in no mood to travel in a car with anyone else.

Susan had a go-bag, as did Goldie, but York didn't. Susan pulled out a bag that matched hers except for color. "This will be your go-bag. We all have them. What they are is a bag already packed. And ready for us to leave at a moment's notice, such as today. We are going to Washington, DC, where I will try to determine if any person close to the President is a traitor to this country. This job is the work I do," Susan told York. York nodded as they packed his clothing and essentials, along with protein bars for York's sugar blood. "We will repack our bags each time we come home, so they are always ready to go," she added.

York was delighted he got to ride another plane. However, the greeting and rush to a limo with dark windows once they landed slightly put him off the trip.

The secrecy of the whole thing had the SS escorting Susan tight-lipped and tense. She and the others were taken to a secluded place and told to wait. Tex and Simon had that stubborn look in their eyes that meant somebody would pay for treating them in this manner. York looked nervous. The whole thing gave him flashbacks to being kidnapped. He stuck to Tex as if his life depended upon it.

"This stops now," Tex proclaimed. He pulled his phone out, ready to push the connection to the President, when the door opened, and the man stood there.

The President rushed over to Susan and hugged her. He looked around until he saw York. "He is the one soon to be my great-grandchild?" he asked Susan.

"Just as soon as we can wade through all the paperwork. York is brave," Susan told him. "York, come here, please."

York approached, looking wary and suspicious of this fat man. "You better not hurt her," he told the President.

"York, this man will be your great-grandfather once you are adopted," Susan explained.

"I don't trust him. He locked us in this place," York said, not bothering to lower his voice. He had watched Tex face down the General and was trying to copy him in his actions.

The President laughed. "I like him. Like you, Susan, he is not afraid to speak his mind. We will get along just fine," he said, smiling at York. "Now, to get down to business. We have a traitor. Of that, I am certain. We don't know who. Until we do, there is nobody I can trust. This situation is very grave, Susan. Discover the traitor as soon as possible. What I thought might be the best approach is to hold a security meeting. I will pretend to discuss something important related to that recent African development. We will have you in a room next to the meeting where you can feel everyone. When you know who our traitor is, the meeting will suddenly close due to urgent business. We will then arrest the traitor. Sound okay to you, dear?" he asked Susan.

Tex stepped up. "How many will be in the meeting?" he demanded.

President Whiting took a half step back. Tex was the one man who scared him. He was like a bulldog when it came to Susan's protection. It was why he would never remove him from taking care of her. The President trusted him to have her interest in mind. He wished he had been there this last time the General went up unannounced. To have been able to see Old Bluster Nose's face. It would have made up for all the times the man disobeyed orders. "About 100. These will be the first batch to be tested. If there is nobody in the first bunch, then there will be a series of small meetings arranged. Most of which I will not be present. We don't want to overwhelm Susan's system."

The arrangement seemed to agree with Tex as he stepped out of the President's immediate space. Tex nodded. "We need to get Susan to her room. Give me directions now."

It was more of an order than a request. President Whiting didn't even blink. Instead, he gave the address for the basement. One last hug for Susan, a handshake with York, and the President was gone.

Simon came over to York. "You realize you just shook hands with the President of the United States of America, York?"

York's eyes grew wide. "He is going to be my grandfather?"

"Yes, if all goes well and the adoption happens. It is a matter of waiting now. Believe me. The best lawyers worldwide are working hard to see you and Miss Susan become family," Simon said.

York became quiet after that as they picked up food and headed to the basement.

They were two blocks from the basement when Susan's hand went up. Simon pulled over. "What is it, Miss Susan?" he asked.

She didn't answer, just stared off in one direction. At last, she spoke, "The sniper, a whisper of him, but it went so fast he must have been at the edge of my reach." A shiver ran through her body before she sat back.

"What would he be doing in DC?" Simon mumbled to himself.

"Reporting, it was the fraction I caught before he was gone," Susan said. It gave them all something to think about besides a traitor among the country's leaders.

It was a great relief to be inside the basement. The shielding was good enough to block most thoughts. And for the first time since landing, Susan had no thoughts except for her companions. She had grown used to having their thoughts constantly in her mind. Worn down with all the responsibility placed on her shoulders, Susan ate, kissed York's cheek good night, and collapsed on the nearest bed, falling asleep.

York looked over at Susan, worry etched on his face. "What is wrong? Is she sick?" York asked

Tex as he prepared to bunk down.

"No, well, in a way, she is sick. All these people in this city hurt her mind. It makes her very tired. You notice we are down in a basement instead of a plush hotel. Being underground with concrete around her keeps the many thoughts from flooding her mind from the city's people. It gives her the relief she needs to sleep. She is so brave to put herself through all this pain to help our country," Tex told him, settling down in bed.

A troubled look came over York's face. "Do my thoughts hurt her?" he asked, clearly distraught.

"If it worries you, do what we do, count. Count and do your thinking deep inside. Soon, it becomes easy to do overtime," Tex yawned. "You best get some sleep. Simon has the night watch. He will sleep when I wake up."

The yawn seemed to be catching, and soon, York was curled up asleep.

The morning brought dread to Susan for what lay ahead today. They expected her to listen to 100 people's thoughts. National secrets would be mixed with despair, greed, lust, and downright evil. These people looked up to by so much of the nation were human. They worked not so much for the good of the people but for their own interests. The few who cared about people were the rare birds in a flock of vultures. And Susan was expected to wade into that pool of minds, working each to best the other. She sighed while eating breakfast. Rising, Susan cleared her area. It was the way she ran her house. York was not far behind her with his plate. He had been quiet all morning. She first noticed that York was counting like Tex and Simon in his mind. She had wondered what brought this on and was about to ask him when he looked up at Susan with tears in his eyes. "Whatever is the matter, York?" she asked, kneeling before him.

"My thoughts hurt you. I'm sorry." Tears were rolling down his cheeks now in huge, hot drops.

"Oh, honey, your thoughts don't hurt me. Of all the thoughts I hear, you, Tex, and Simon have thoughts that are the only ones besides my family's thoughts that don't hurt me. You are not thinking about hurting someone or planning on making money on some family's misfortune. Thoughts like that are the ones that cause me pain. I walk into a room of people, and so many are out to cause someone harm that it makes me feel sick inside. You don't do that. I don't think you would ever do those things to others, honey," Susan said.

York fell into her arms, hugging her tight. His mind burst out one thought, "I love you."

"I love you too, sweetie," Susan told him. He smiled, realizing she had heard his thought, and stopped counting. "Do you know what you just did for me?" York shook his head. "You made a day of having people invading my mind worth bearing."

Tex and Simon had been shamelessly listening to Susan and York. There was a sense of pride and relief that they didn't cause her pain. Listening to her talk of the thoughts that did hurt her made them wince, for their own lives had held a few moments when anger swept reason away, and they wished harm on another. Right then, they knew they could never let that happen again. It was their job to bring down those who hurt others but to wish it on someone in their life was different. They both counted like crazy to avoid letting these thoughts leak out.

Simon settled to sleep while everyone else headed off for Susan's ordeal. The President was waiting when Susan arrived. He made a great show of greeting her. "Susan, my dear. How nice it is for you to come to visit. I am sorry, dear, but you must wait a bit. You know how it is, constant meetings of one sort or another. This young intern will show you to a room where you may wait. Handel, please show my granddaughter to the rose-colored room. And have some snacks and drinks brought to them." He kissed her on the cheek, then rushed off.

Handel felt scandalized that Susan was a black person. He held his bland expression well, but inside, his mind was going, "Oh my God!". Susan waited until he brought the refreshments to relieve his mind. "You do know I'm adopted?" she asked.

The young man betrayed the relief on his face, causing a look of irritation to flash on Tex's face. "Ma'am, you need not explain it to me. I'm here to serve. Is there anything else I might get you?" he quickly said.

"No," Susan said. Once alone, Susan explained to York that she would be sorting through many thoughts and might require one or two of his power bars. Susan didn't have to say what it was that she was sorting. They had gone over that earlier. First, she sat down and ate a large portion of the food Handel had brought.

Settling in one of the plush seats provided, she closed her eyes and began searching the many minds in the meeting room. Secrets, lies, plots, and bits of information about the country's business that she should never know flashed through her mind. She wanted to retreat into a happy memory. And never see another person's thoughts again. Only life was cruel, and it never let her escape the constant invasion of thoughts. She was only a third of the way through the 100 when her hands began to shake in her lap.

Tex and York had been watching over her. York's face scrunched up in worry, while Tex's had pure determination set on his. Tex asked York for a power bar and knelt beside Susan. Gently, he shook her shoulder, "Honey, eat a bar."

Weakly, she nodded, taking the offered bar. Her hands shook so much she couldn't open the wrapper on the bar. Little York was there in a flash, tearing the wrapper open. "Thank you," Susan whispered, biting into the bar and devouring it as if she were starving. Which her body was telling her she was.

Tex brought a plate of the leftover food to her. "Eat," he ordered. Susan nodded again and ate the food. Finally, she resumed her sorting. They had moved around some in the room. She had to flip through them to find those she hadn't done. The search began again.

With the power bar in her system and a second one added before she needed it, Susan managed to get through to the rest of the people. She shook her head no to Tex when he raised his eyebrows in question. "None of them," she said aloud for York's benefit.

"Does that mean you have to do the sorting again?" York asked, clearly stressed out for her going through this again.

"Not so many next time, sweetie," Susan assured him. "A quick talk with my grandfather, and we will go to a fun museum." That, at least, perked York up.

It was another twenty minutes before the President could break free and join Susan. Susan made a show of leaving once her phone beeped to let her know her grandfather was on his way. She met him as he rushed down the hallway to the room she had stayed in. "Oh, Grandfather, I'm so sorry. My schedule requires us to move along, I'm afraid. I will have to come back, maybe tomorrow?" Susan inquired. Giving him their signal that the search had been fruitless, so he would have to arrange another meeting.

"My dear, it seems our schedules are always at odds. I have a staff dinner tomorrow night. Perhaps you could join me, share a meal, and give me a chance to win this young man over to my side?" he said. And so the plans were made for the next ordeal.

Susan refused to let York down. So, while they toured the promised museum, tailors worked frantically to finish a tux for him. Tex and Simon always brought a tux when traveling with Susan. They knew it was very likely something like this dinner would come up. Susan had no worries about clothing when in DC. Her grandmother always thought she had no idea how to dress and kept clothing at hand for her to wear.

The fun part of the day came when Tex and Simon dressed York in his tux. Some of the laughter from the boys' dressing hit the belly-holding-pain-in-the-side stage. The men were every bit as silly as York during the whole thing.

It was time to face the ordeal. Susan sobered and put on her in-charge face, causing all three guys to stand straighter. An aide hustled them to the President's side. He took Susan's arm, and a path cleared as if by magic before them to the head table. York was seated between Susan and the President.

Susan relaxed as much as she could in a crowd. She knew who the person was leaking important information. She gave her hand signal to Tex, nodding; she knew. He slipped up to her side and pretended to whisper in her ear. She acted annoyed, asking for a slip of paper and a pen. "Tell him this is my answer." Around them, staff members nodded to each other as if they had a bet going on how long it would be before somebody tried to get a date with the lovely Miss Whiting. What she wrote was the name of the traitor.

So it was over. The girl who took the President's notes at meetings was arrested as the dinner broke up, and she exited the building. No one would ever know Susan had uncovered the truth about the girl. Susan was relieved they would tour the Smithsonian with York before going home—a good outcome.

Chapter Five

LEARN TO RELAX

The museums, the water slides, and the plane rides had all been tremendous fun for York, but the sight of home brought a peaceful smile to his face. This mountain was the home he never had, the first place he felt at peace.

Home. No pressing humanity to throw thoughts out to crush her. It was the closest Susan came to being happy. She heard relieved thoughts from the snipers up on the mountainside. It was strange how she had missed hearing them. Their thoughts let her know she was home.

They went out to visit the animals as soon as they had finished eating. York was as eager as Susan felt to check on their friends. They didn't have far to go before the doe appeared. She allowed York to pet her and even nuzzled Goldie. It was clear she had missed them. Just when they were about to go on. There was a screech from above. Falling like a stone came the great eagle who had befriended the humans. At the last moment, the eagle backed the wind and settled on a branch low enough that York could approach him. Susan laughed softly, "I missed you too, Great One." The bird preened at the praise. He swung his head to stare into the shadows where the red fox crouched. The busybody raccoon pushed past the fox and chattered as if scowling at everyone for being gone even though they had not been gone as long as on other trips they had taken. Susan smiled knowingly the coon fussed the most at those he cherished. To Susan, they were a family, close in ways most did not understand. Tex was even graced by the coon and the fox. And was that a hint of a smile on his oh-so-serious face?

Tex watched everything. Each shadow could be a threat. He was glad to be back on the mountain with more security. Under his breath, he asked the snipers if there had been activity while they were gone. He got a negative on that. Somewhat relieved, at least the man who shot at Susan hadn't found her yet. Tex felt, in his gut, that this man was dangerous. If only they had killed him right off. The delay in explaining things to Swat and the troopers had allowed the guy to plan his escape. He kicked himself mentally for not going immediately after the guy. Only that would have left his subject unprotected, something he could not do to satisfy his agenda.

He watched Susan and York as they enjoyed the animals, the mountain, and the forest. When Tex was with Susan, he noticed she had grasped such moments with happiness. She had blossomed with the addition of York to her oddly mixed group of friends, and he had accepted that these animals were indeed her friends. He was grateful that Susan had some joy in her life. Too much of which she spent inside the dark minds of criminals. Tex could not imagine what it would be like to have your mind invaded by even the people walking casually down the street. He would become a hermit in the deepest forest if it were him, but not Susan. She used her curse to help others, to save the world from unspeakable evil often, just like she had saved York.

His thoughts turn to the man who had tried to kill Susan. Why had he targeted her? Susan was in grave danger until he knew the answer to that question. His eyes swept the peaceful surroundings, searching for a killer lurking in the shadows.

Susan became aware of Tex's concerns as he let a tiny thread of thought slip. She didn't want gloom and worry to overshadow their first day home. It was with that thought that she decided to practice sending messages. "Goldie, Tex needs some love and cheering up." It was short and to the point, not sent as a shouted thought but more as a whisper. The results amazed Susan as she watched Goldie go to Tex. The Golden Retriever began to bounce around Tex, inviting him to play. She brought sticks for him to throw and made a big show of retrieving them to present each one to his hand. Briefly, a smile twitched at his mouth, trying to escape. Still, he remained ever alert, not letting a shadow go without a glance to see if death waited there. Susan could see he was worried about the sniper. She decided to give him his space and avoid getting into dangerous situations again. There was something Susan wanted to try with Goldie and York. She thought it might be just the thing to lighten the mood.

After breakfast the next day, Susan announced they would only have a short walk today. "I have something for all of us to learn. It should be fun and give us a little exercise. Let's walk and see our friends. Then, when we get back, I will explain what I have in mind."

York's eyes filled with excitement, wondering what Susan had in store for them. He greeted their friends with warmth and energy. Bounding over logs with the doe, letting the coon chase him around a tree. Then they practiced disappearing in the woods, which York was getting very good at, blending into the trees. Even Tex missed seeing him once.

They returned to the house to enjoy lunch before Susan revealed her plan. She put a DVD in the player and sat down with York to watch it. Music begins to play as the action starts to play across the screen. Soon, York was sitting on the edge of his seat, his eyes glued to the screen. At times, his body swayed as if trying to follow the action on the television screen. Once, he bounced in his seat in excitement, his eyes glowing.

"Do you think we can do that?" York asked, turning to Susan with hope in his eyes.

"I think we can do anything we put our minds to doing. What do you say, want to do it?" Susan said, her own eyes holding a spark of excitement. York gave an eager nod and leaped to his feet in a hurry to begin.

Outside, Tex could hear music playing inside the house. He was surprised at the fast tempo of the music. It was different from the music Tex thought Susan usually enjoyed listening to. He heard sounds like furniture knocked around, with near-hysterical giggles and laughter. Tex's eyebrows shot up. It sounded like a wild party was going on inside the house. She is having fun, Tex thought, his heart beating quickly. He smiled, thinking of Susan having a good time for a change. He was curious about what had put the laughter in her belly and the giggles on her lips.

"Okay, okay," Susan said, barely able to talk for laughing so much. York and Susan discovered that watching a video and trying to do it wasn't all that easy. "What we need to do is to synchronize our moves. Let's map it out and plan what we are going to do. One of us will call it side jump, side jump, back and forward, Goldie weave. Sound good?" Out of breath, York nodded. He was having so much fun that he would agree to anything if Susan didn't change her mind about them doing this.

"Let's begin," Susan thought to York and Goldie. "Step forward, back, spin, sidestep, sidestep. Legs wide, Goldie weave, spin legs together, hop back, hop sideways, spin, spin, spin."

A sense of achievement settled on York as he stepped, spun, hopped, and let Goldie weave through his and Susan's legs. They were doing it!

Susan continued mentally calling out commands as she bowed to York and Goldie so they could do a round without her. The boy and dog were so intrigued by the dancing that time flew by. Before anyone knew it, the night was approaching. Susan called a halt, and with York's help, they placed the furniture back where it had been. Dinner was going to be a little late.

York and Susan were both pleased with their attempt at dancing with Goldie. At the same time, they weren't telling the others about what they were doing. York kept giving Tex glances as if wanting to talk but was determined not to give away the wonderful secret he and Susan had.

Tex heard the music and laughter each day after lunch for a week and a half. It gladdened his heart to know Susan and York were having such a good time. Yet, curiosity ate at him. Part of him wanted to be in there with them, laughing also. That part he held in tight check. His world seldom allowed for laughter to happen. He might have a tiny smile creep in, but laughter never.

Simon showed up early. He was looking worried. Tex studied him a moment before doing his thing and cutting any bullshit before it began. "Just spit it out." He growled.

Frowning, Simon nodded. "Got a call to relieve you early. Sounds fishy to me," Simon said.

"Sounds like a visit from a blow-hard on the horizon to me. Sucks for him that I'm not tired yet," Tex stated.

Simon nodded as he listened to the music inside. "They sound like they are having a good time. That kid has been good for Miss Susan," he said, no longer frowning. "She doesn't seem so lonely now."

"Yep," was Tex's simple reply. He was looking

down the road where a plumb of dust had appeared. Silently, he cursed that he was right about the visit. He thumbed the direct Mic for Susan's house. "We have a car approaching. Lock-down."

Lock-down. Susan and York heard the words and went down into the bunker after Susan shut off the stove's burners. She secured the door and sat beside York in front of the monitors, turning on the sound. "You did great! We are going to surprise Tex and Simon," Susan told York. By then, a black staff car pulled up outside. For a long moment, the occupants stayed in the car as if considering the wisdom of stepping out with two armed men pointing guns at them.

"Step out of the car with your hands up," Tex barked. When the doors closed, Tex spoke softly into his Mic, "Prepare to shoot out the tires if they don't comply after the next warning." Readying himself for a gunfight, Tex motioned to Simon to take cover. "This is your final warning. Exit the car with your hands over your head. Now."

Slowly, a door cracked open. "Don't shoot! I'm trying to contact the General." A frantic voice called out. Two shots rang out in the distance, and the staff car leaned to one side. A little man scrambled out of the staff car. His hands are raised as if he is trying to touch the sky. "I'm just an intern doing a favor for the General. He has the flu and could not come himself. He told me it was safe to come here. And he would take care of things. I'm just the messenger. Please don't kill me."

Behind Tex, the door to the bunker opened. He started counting in his mind, almost shouting the numbers at himself. Susan shouldn't hear his thoughts about that low-life General. Hell, his Mom would have taken a switch to him if she had ever heard him say those thoughts. "Ma'am, please return to the bunker."

"No, I have this now," Susan told him, stepping up beside Tex. She looked at the scared little guy. "Tell the General I am not a paid escort. He must find someone else to take the Minister to the White House party. And if he ever sends some unsuspecting intern to contact me again, I will allow Tex to shoot him when we lay eyes on the General next. Now, leave."

"But the tires are flat," the little guy protested.

Susan shrugged her shoulders. "The price of not exiting the car. Some lessons are hard. Don't listen to fools. There is a station a few miles to the west."

The shaking man got into the car and started it. The tires thumped, and the car wobbled as it slowly turned around and went down the road.

Her SS agents were so wound up after the late-evening visitor that Susan asked York if he would like to show them what they could do after dinner. York was excited about the idea but nervous.

When she served up dessert, Susan informed the two SS agents that they were to push the furniture back, and she washed up the dishes. Simon gave Tex an inquiring look. Tex shook his head.

After finishing the cleanup and moving the furniture, Susan told her SS agents to sit down. Both shook their heads no. "One of us needs to be outside," Simon said.

Susan placed her hands on her hips, her face stern. "You will sit down for a few more minutes. Now sit," she said, pointing at two chairs. They sat, and that was the end of any argument.

Tex assumed they were about to receive a lecture of some sort. It may have had to do with their handling of the intruder. But he kept his mouth shut, waiting for the sword to fall. Music began to play. He looked over at Simon. Only Simon didn't seem to know what was going on either.

Susan, York, and Goldie walked to stand in the middle of the room. "For your entertainment, we present The Dance of Joy," Susan announced. She, York, and Goldie spun in place, starting an intricate dance pattern they had assembled. They stepped, hopped, and did what looked like impossible moves in perfect harmony with each other. They took up fifteen minutes of the agent's time. They filled that time with fast-paced action. By the time they ended up back in the center of the room, all three spinning around once more to end in a bow, they were breathless.

Tex and Simon stood up, clapping and whistling like mad. Both men had huge grins on their faces. York's eyes were sparkling as he ran over to them. "Did you see my backflip?" he asked, an eager look upon his young face.

"We sure did," Tex said. "It was amazing. Everything you all did made my mind go, wow."

"I gave it a ten," Simon said, patting York on the head. "The whole dance was incredible. I must return to work, but you have made my day wonderful, York. Thank you," Simon said, then looked up at Susan and smiled, mouthing a 'thank you' to her. She nodded, looking happy.

Once Simon left, Tex walked over to Susan. "So this is what the three of you have been doing. I've been scratching my head, wondering what was happening here. You were amazing. All of you were. I'm going to dream of this tonight, I hope," Tex said.

Susan suddenly felt shy, but she didn't show it. "I'm glad you guys liked it. York and Goldie worked so hard on it. Most of the ideas were York's. He is very talented. I best give him an extra dessert and some milk," Susan said, worried York would have a low sugar level.

Tex felt disappointed as he felt she was dismissing him. He started for the door. A hand touched his arm. Looking over, he saw Susan and wondered what was going on.

"Won't you join us?" she said.

"Sure, I have a moment," Tex admitted, feeling a strange shift inside him. It almost felt like he cared. "You want us to fix the furniture first?" he asked. Susan nodded. "Come on, York. Let's fix the room back like it was," he told the boy.

Once they finished the furniture, York and Tex joined Susan at the table. Milk and peach pie with a scoop of ice cream on top of the pie waited for them. The boy and man looked so much alike as they dug into their treat that Susan smiled. She remembered her family and how it had been before she developed her super-spy power. Susan had trusted everyone back then. Now that she had seen in so many minds the underside of people. Susan could only trust her family. Friends were something she didn't have. People just wanted to use her or hated her because Susan was a black girl living in a white family. Susan mentally pushed the negative thoughts away to enjoy this moment with York.

Between bites of pie and ice cream, York went on about everything he wanted them to try in their dancing. There were leaps, spins, and wiggles of the hips, and he got up and demonstrated the wiggling hips. Susan was shaking her head. Tex's mind was conjuring up images of her wiggling her hips until he realized what he was doing and clamped a lid on it, counting like mad.

At last, Tex said his good-nights to York and Susan, stepping outside to stand with Simon. "The boy is over the moon happy over dancing," Tex told Simon. "He is in there planning some wild moves which were making Miss Susan blush." Tex looked at Simon, "They were good, weren't they?"

"Pretty much made my day. It took the sour taste out of my mouth that pompous ass put in there. What are we going to do about him?" Simon asked.

"Shoot him?" Tex joked. And they both laughed. Like it or not, the man was in their lives because of their subject. That didn't mean they had to bend over for him. Most certainly, they would not allow him to use Miss Susan.

Tex drove to the SS house, set up for those who watched over his subject. As he arrived, he remembered the man he had replaced standing outside the house with his bag in his hand. He had been brief and curt, telling Tex to guard his thoughts by constant counting. "This one will get in and read every secret you are protecting. We guard secrets vital to our country, so don't let your guard down momentarily. Keep alert. Don't let her steal secrets from you. Now I'm getting the hell out of here. Good luck, you will need it." After giving that briefing, he had left in a cloud of dust, leaving Tex to wonder what he had been assigned to guard.

It was one of those rare days when Susan went shopping. York needed new clothing. They could have ordered clothes for him over the Internet, but Susan wanted to let him pick out what he wanted and try it on. Roger, the new Secret Service agent assigned to guard York, came with Tex.

Goldie was wearing her allowed everywhere vest. She behaved like a highly trained dog, walking in perfect sync with Susan. York had just picked out some shirts he liked when Goldie alerted. She put herself before York and would not let him move forward.

Tex stopped counting. "Down," he told Susan, stepping in front of her. He reached out and grabbed York, pulling him back by Susan, then glared at Roger, the new guy. "Keep yourself alert. You missed seeing Goldie move to protect York," he growled.

Roger paled. He had missed it. His subject may have faced danger as Roger worked up a fit of anger because of needing to count in his head. He glanced around, trying to see what the dog had sensed: nothing, people shopping. The dog whined and looked back in the direction she had been alerting on.

"Someone is hurt," Susan said. "You need to call for medics. It is a woman just ahead of us. She became conscious for just a moment. Long enough that I heard her."

"Roger, stay here and protect them while I check it out. Call for an ambulance and the locals," Tex ordered. He slipped from sight as he searched the area ahead—every shadow he suspected of being more. There were too many places a shooter could hide in here. He shouldn't have allowed York and Susan in here. Who was he kidding? Susan went where she wanted. Tex stopped moving. Two. Two people lay in a growing pool of blood: a man and a woman. The woman gasped as if drawing air into her lungs was hard. Both had been stabbed—a silent killer then, up close and personal.

"Move, she will die without help," Susan said behind Tex. He gave her a stern look. He was shouting mentally at her for moving from where he had left her. "Count," she told him, squatting down by the woman. "I know you thought I should have stayed put. But Goldie didn't growl. She whinnied. In dog talk, that was a concern, not a danger. Mom's dog taught us all how to tell the difference."

Tex nodded, never stopping his search for that danger around them. There movement. He sighed as York and Roger appeared. Did he have no control here? "What is she doing?" Roger asked.

Tex shifted his eyes to Susan. She was starting to pale before him. "Stop," he barked at her. She looked up at him. Her own eyes held a haunted look in them.

"She will die if I do," Susan whispered. A

paramedic knelt beside her, and Susan relinquished the woman to him.

Tight-lipped, Tex helped Susan to a chair. He dared not stop counting, so she couldn't pick up his thoughts. Most of them held more than a few curse words. "York, Roger, get over here." He said in that barking, angry tone. "If you have to. Tie her to the chair. She nearly spent all her energy pumping it into the victim. I need to see what info I can gather from them and the scene. York, make her eat two of your bars." He got in Susan's face, "Behave. I have to find who did this."

"They are gone. If anyone guilty of this is still around, I could detect thoughts from them," Susan said, looking as if she could barely speak.

Of course, she would have, Tex thought. Look how far away the children had been when she heard them. His adrenaline was pumping heavily into his body, screaming at him to take action. So he went and examined a dead man, hunting for anything that might point him at someone to shoot or beat the hell out of to calm himself down.

York was scared. Susan looked so weak. He unwrapped the energy bars for her and watched to ensure she ate them both. She couldn't die on him, not when he had come to trust and love her. She was going to adopt him. What was going to happen if he lost her? "Please don't die," he thought over and over until she spoke to him.

"I'm not dying, Sweetie. You know how a low sugar level makes you weak?" she asked. York nodded. "That is what happened to me. That woman was dying. The only way I could keep her alive was to give of myself. I'm not a healer like my mother is. But, I am one of the people who can give her my energy, letting her continue to heal. So, I took a chance that giving my energy to that poor woman would keep her alive long enough for the medics to arrive and save her. Understand, Sweetie?"

York stood a little straighter. "Teach me how to do that so I can help you when you work for Grandfather," he told her.

"I can try, but not many people can be a battery. Don't be disappointed if it doesn't work, okay?" Susan said, already starting to feel her strength returning.

"I will do it," York said as if he had decided to do this battery thing.

Roger listened to this crazy conversation, keeping alert for any danger that might pop out of the clothing racks around them. He stood where he'd be blocking his young subject's sight of the dead man, sure that the child should never see something so gruesome. Roger counted slow, deliberate counting to mask the turbulence in his mind. An unselfish act by this woman, he feared, had flipped his preconception upside down. He had made a mistake that didn't sit right with him.

Susan suddenly stood, surprising Roger. She began to turn in a circle. Tex saw her and drew his weapon, which caused Roger to go on alert, shoving York down. Tex turned with Susan, scanning as they did the crowd around the medics and coroner. "There," Susan said. "The man in the dark suit and blue shirt. It was him."

Roger's eyes went wide. He hadn't known she could do this sort of thing. It shed new light on why they protected her. Then it dawns on him that Tex hadn't been following her hand. He had been hiding her from prying eyes. He felt that had been his second mistake. Always, you protect the subject first and foremost. He had pushed York down only when he'd seen Tex draw his weapon.

After Tex informed the locals and forwarded them a picture of the killer, Susan turned towards Roger. "You need to relax. Stop thinking of yourself and start thinking of York. He is yours to protect," she told him.

"Yes, ma'am," Roger said, and there was a difference in his tone, indicating a shift in his attitude. He immediately gave York all his attention. The killer moved to the back of the crowd of onlookers and slipped away.

"He is leaving. He won't think of his name. People seldom do. He is considering options. Going home, a white house, or visiting his sister, Sophie. He thinks she will forget how long he has been there," Susan said. "He is in a red car now and going out of range."

"He probably went up on the freeway to get away fast. We know that when he left, he was in a red car and headed to the freeway. There had to be a security camera that caught him on film. Mall Security office," Tex said, his face grim.

They had a plate number for the suspect's car fifteen minutes later. Police cars were sent to his and his sister's homes, but they did not find him. Susan was left feeling she had failed the murdered man and the woman in critical condition in the hospital. It was a feeling she didn't like, not one tiny bit. She had always been right when she gave out information she found pushed upon her from someone's mind. It seemed Susan still had work to do.

"He is on the run," Tex said when he saw the way Susan tensed upon hearing the news about the killer. He lowered his voice for Susan to hear and added, "We should go eat. I don't want to expose York to any more of this."

Inside, Susan cringed. What sort of mother was she? Here, she was prolonging York's exposure to this horror. "How would you like to go to Down Home to eat? They have some of the best food and serve tea in Mason jars." Susan asked York.

"What is a Mason jar?" he asked.

"When people preserve their food, like fruits and vegetables they grow, they use jars. Long ago, everyone did their canning to preserve food to last over the winter until the weather became warm enough to grow food again. Because the jars are glass, you can see what is in them. People would go down to the cellar and choose what vegetable or fruit they would cook that night. Those are Mason jars," Susan said with a smile.

"Cool! I'd like to see those," York said, jumping up in excitement. "I didn't know you could… can… is that right?… at home. Could we try that?"

"We can, can," Susan laughed at her joke. "I need to warn you it is a hot job. We did some canning when I was little. The whole house would smell like whatever we were canning. Usually, it was peaches. We could have peach pie all year round. It was easier to freeze the blackberries, but we would make a field trip out of picking the blackberries. Mother used to tell us anything that good was worth a few stickers. She was right."

They talked about the different canning methods to where they were to eat. Susan kept trying to pick up thoughts from the killer the whole trip there. She felt she had let down the dead man and the woman stabbed. How could she be so wrong?

Tex and Roger took the table next to their subjects. They were all in one corner of the homey dining room, seated where they could see York, Susan, and the entire room, including the exits. "She will eat a huge meal to replenish what she gave to the woman," Tex told Roger. "You need to make certain York always stays well fed. Here," Tex handed Roger some of the protein bars. "Always carry some of these. There is a carton at our house and a couple of cartons at Susan's place. You see York starting to look the slightest bit weak. Hand him one. He knows to eat it." Tex did not want Roger to come in blind as he had been. He was still super pissed that nobody had clued him in on caring for Susan.

They gave their orders and were almost finished with the meal when Susan raised her hand. Tex had dropped his fork, and he stood up, causing Roger to alert. Walking over to Susan, Tex bent down as if to whisper something in her ear. "He is two buildings away, I think. Happy," Susan whispered.

Tex nodded. "I'll go. You stay here. You can't

be around again. Roger will watch over both of you. Don't move. Order dessert for us all," Tex told her, then updated Roger. He walked back to his table and sat down. "She has the killer again. You keep watch over our subjects. I'm going after this creep. She said he was happy. We'll fix that," Tex vowed, leaving.

Checking the picture he had taken of the killer, Tex went outside. Finally, he could release the anger he had built up inside him. Give me a fight, please, he thought. Two buildings over, left or right? She hadn't pointed. So, it must be in the direction she had been facing. Which was? He returned to the door he had just exited, picturing them entering and going to the tables.

To the left was a parking lot, beyond which stood two buildings. Tex made short work of reaching his first goal by walking fast. A bank? That sucked. He'd have to identify himself to the security before they went wild over his gun. The door opened as he flipped through contacts. He felt that rush of adrenaline surge through his body. Luck was favoring him for a change. With a smile, Tex walked up, his right hand extended as if to shake the killer's hand. The guy laughed and shook his head as if he was too good to shake Tex's hand. As he made a shooing wave at Tex, Tex's left hand clocked him one. The guy went down like a limp noodle. Tex pulled out his phone and dialed the locals. "Saw that picture of a man you are searching for on that stabbing. The idiot tried to hit me. Send a car to…."

Returning to his seat at the table with Roger was a relaxed Tex. "Got him," he thought to Susan, then dug into his dessert with gusto.

Chapter Six

SIMPLE

The excellent mood lasted four days for Tex. A call came for Susan from Bobby Jay. Once Tex confirmed this was from Eric, he handed the phone to Susan and stood listening to her side of the conversation. "I am on my way," she said before hanging up. Then, she turned to Tex. "Book an emergency flight to my sister. I need to talk to York," she said, dismissing him.

He did not like this. An emergency flight meant trouble. Tex stuck with Susan even when she looked annoyed. They booked the flight. Simon was up and on the way with a car and their go-bags by the time Susan had York sitting down talking to him.

"Honey, I need to leave for a few days. My sister, Middy, needs help. It is the sort of help where I cannot spend time doing anything else. Will you stay here with Roger so you can look after our friends? I do not know if I can call you as we will be inside a hospital. You know I love you. It will be hard not being able to be here with you. Can you be strong and keep me in your thoughts? I think that will help me more than anything else in the whole world, just knowing you are thinking of me," Susan told him.

Tears were threatening in York's eyes, but he didn't let them fall. "I will think real hard. Hard enough, you can hear me," York told her.

"Hope I can, but I will be very far away. I'll think just as hard about you, Honey. When I'm on the way home, we will see how close I have to get for you to hear me," she told him, hugging him to her.

Tex sought out Roger and updated him. "You have to keep York safe until we return. That means his mental health as well. Do you know his birth mother told him to die? We do not need him to feel deserted. You up for this?" Tex challenged. Roger nodded, his face looking grim. There was no time for anything but rushing to Susan's sister.

"Love you bunches, love you bunches," Susan sent over and over to York, all the way to the hospital where Middy's SS agent, Ritter, lay crushed and dying.

It was the worst thing Susan had ever seen. A man crushed. Only his head was unmarred. Susan immediately knew Middy loved this man, and he loved her. It was all there, so clearly in his thoughts. He wanted to spare her from seeing him die. It was the only thought in his head. The pain didn't matter. The only thing he wanted was to keep her from having more pain. Middy was determined to heal this man. She would not admit she still loved him. He had rejected her.

It was time to be a battery. Susan's mother, Felith, touched Ritter's forehead and began healing him. Susan, her two siblings, and her father placed their hands upon her mother. Immediately, Susan felt the drain on her system. This healing was one of those times when her mother would have to heal and rest, as would they all. It was very draining to be a battery. They ran out of energy like a car battery or a flashlight's batteries. Unfortunately, humans needed to rest and eat. They took time to recover. On a heal like this, there was very little time left.

To Susan, it seemed they were touching their mother for hours. However, only a few minutes had passed before they made her stop. Everything inside her was screaming out in pain. She needed food. And to sleep. More than those physical needs was the desire to help her mother. She couldn't let her mother die, and her mother would, without them to boost her up. So, she rested, stuffing protein bars into her mouth and drinking the brown energy drinks that would boost her up somewhat. Her brother was curled up asleep in a lounge chair. Only Middy and her father still supported her mother.

Fred started talking their mother down, telling her what she needed to remember to get her out of the healing mode. Always, he reminded her of how much he loved her. And how it would hurt the kids to see her die. Finally, she slumped back into his arms so he could take care of her. Susan wanted love as they had. One who was there for her and didn't care that she could hear his every thought. She wanted the impossible.

They exiled Tex to the hallway. He fumed and worried about Susan. They were to keep anyone from entering the room. Tex took that to heart, daring the busybody doctor who kept trying to get past them to try again. Bobby Jay placed a hand on his shoulder. "Settle down. You can only help her now by ensuring they get whatever they need in there and are not interrupted. She will need you big time when she reaches the end of her strength. You have a place to take her, set up?" Bobby asked, trying to direct Tex in some helpful direction.

"Simon is on that. No cellars in this place." He grumbled. He glanced at all the SS who had shown up because Susan's mother was there. "You better all be counting," he said with a glare. One man started as if he was lacking. Tex walked up to him and stared him down.

"I'm counting. I just forgot for a moment," the agent admitted.

The phone in Tex's pocket was muted. He had refused to turn it off even though the higher-ups had declared a freeze on phone use while here to prevent any news of this healing from leaking out. He felt it vibrate and nodded to the agent in front of him. "I'm going to be certain that the doctor isn't sneaking around again. All of you count!" he abolished as he rounded a corner of the hallway. Checking to be sure the hallway was clear, he took a peek at his phone. Simon had a place to secure Susan. Relief flooded Tex's system. Now, he just had to get her out of there.

The hours dragged by slower than time should pass. If only Tex could be in the room with her, Tex wouldn't feel so stressed. He didn't know how long he'd kept his vigil outside that hospital room. Simon had shown up twice to try and take over for Tex, but he refused.

He saw Simon coming down the hallway again, and Tex was already shaking his head no when he heard his name called inside the room. He was inside the room so fast he might as well have ported. Susan was curled up in a lounge chair, barely breathing. His heart nearly stopped beating when he saw her.

"Take her to the hotel," Fred, Susan's father, told him.

Gently, Tex picked Susan up, clutching her to his chest. He rushed her out of that room as if the hounds of hell were on his tail. He gave Simon a knowing look. Simon drove, while Tex held an unconscious Susan tightly as if afraid she would disappear on him, to the concrete bunker Simon had found. Neither man spoke. Taking care of Susan was theirs to do. Both men knew what they had to do and did it.

The journey home gave Susan enough time to recover to near feeling human. The whole flight back, she worked on connecting with York. The first time she heard a reply from him, she was able to, finally, relax. Being a mother made her feel emotional. She put on the face her mother always presented to the world, feeling she now understood how hard it had been for her mother to maintain that indifference.

A cloud of dust drifted up behind the car, taking Susan home. Roger knew Tex and his subject were due back, but it would be irresponsible to take a chance with York. "You need to go into the safe room, York. Stay until I give the all-clear," he said.

"It is Miss Susan," York countered.

"Go in the safe room. I need to do my job to ensure you are protected." Roger gave York a stern look. "Do you want them to replace me? They will. All it takes is one more mistake. Already, I'm on thin ice, not picking up on Goldie alerting. Believe me. Tex will not allow another mistake."

York made a face, but he went into the bunker and shut the door. Roger was okay. Suppose he got a real grump next time? He knew Susan was a person with power. But could she force the Secret Service to leave Roger with him? Sitting before a monitor, he turned on the sound, waiting to see what Susan would say to Roger.

The agent was upset. He was blasting Susan with thoughts of regret for having insisted that York go into the safe room. And guilt over what he considered his mistakes in this assignment. The fact that he was upset over not letting York greet her boded well for him. Turning towards the camera, Susan waved at York. She smiled her approval as she mentally told him how proud she was of him listening to Roger.

Feeling a glow inside at Susan's praise, York looked to where Roger stood. He waited until Roger nodded to the camera before unlocking the bunker door. It could only be opened from the inside once locked down. He grinned and ran to Susan, throwing his arms around her. Never again

did he want her to leave him like that. He'd learn
to be a battery, so she'd have to take him next time.
Knowing he owed Roger an apology, he let go of
Susan to face the SS man. "Thank you for being so
good at your job. I hope you will stay as my SS man,"
he told Roger.

What had just happened? Roger wondered
if he had entered an alternate Universe. Everyone
knew kids and teens could be the worst to protect.
They didn't listen and often rebelled by running off.
He cleared his throat to relieve the tightness there
from the kid's words. "You are worth it," he said,
hoping that didn't sound too corny. Roger risked a
glance at Tex. Tex nodded at him—high praise from
a man rumored to have ice in his veins. A deep sigh
of relief escaped from Roger.

The phone rang as they stepped into the
house. Simon, who had been about to leave and get
some rest before his shift started, froze in place. A
call was seldom a pleasant thing. The three SS agents
shared a look. Simon and Tex had run on fumes
since leaving for Middy's place. Both had been
relieved to reach home finally. Tex answered the
ringing sound of dread.

"Speak," he barked.

"This is Homeland Security. We need to speak
to Miss Whiting," a bored voice said in his ear.

"Regarding what?" Tex growled. He was tired
and in no mood to listen to fools.

"That is for her ears only," was the annoyed
reply.

"Sorry, she is unavailable," Tex clicked the
phone off. His expression said it all. He was pissed

off. He glanced at Susan, checking her reaction as he hung up on a call to her. She didn't look upset, but he knew she hid her feelings deep. Great, he may have just messed up again. There was no sense in second-guessing himself. Reluctantly, Tex went outside to take up his post and guard his subject. Only a part of him didn't want to leave her.

"We have time for a walk," Susan told York. "How have our friends been?"

York bounced up and down to the door. "Chatterbox has fussed and fussed. Sly came up to me twice. I think Dewy has been sad you have been gone. She came up to me and laid her head on my shoulder like she needed a hug. They are going to be so happy to see you," he gushed as if a dam had broken open inside him. He nodded his head in Roger's direction, lowering his voice. "He carries corn for Dewy now, but he tries to sneak it to her. He wouldn't let me play the hiding game."

"That is because he was worried that something would happen to you if you were out of his sight. We need to consider the strain he is under to keep you safe. Do you know their job is to die instead of us? I'm so proud of you for listening to Roger when you knew I was coming up the road. You showed great intelligence. You know why I went to my sister to help?" Susan asked. York shook his head. "Her SS agent was dying. He saved her, knowing he would die. My mother didn't let him die. It took my whole family to support her so she could heal him. Don't ever disrespect your SS agent, okay?"

Nodding, York became very quiet. A screech overhead made him look up and smile. "Look, it is

Eagle Eye. He didn't come till now."

"I think he was here watching over you all along," Susan said, holding her arm for the eagle to land. Once the eagle had landed, the forest around them rustled with activity. Their woodland friends came eager to visit with Susan and York. The raccoon Chatterbox went at a run, scattering the others in his rush to scowl Susan for being gone. Even Goldie scrambled away from the fussing raccoon. Susan smiled at them as they came up for the little treats she handed to each. She relaxed, knowing she was home.

Two cars came up the drive to the house the following day, and dust clouds sprayed plumes into the air behind and over them. Tex gave the alert a grim look on his face. He had little doubt as to who was coming. Homeland Security. They had not accepted his blunt answer that no one talked to Susan. "Be alert. These creeps didn't like being told no," he whispered. He could almost hear the snipers readying to fire. They would listen to every word said.

The two cars approached much faster than they should have, skidding to a halt in front of Tex, throwing dust and dirt over him. Tex saw one driver smirk. Strike two. One more strike, he thought, and you are out of here. "Turn around and leave. You are not authorized to be here," Tex warned, taking a stance with his gun drawn and steady upon the passenger in the first car. The guy smiled at Tex. Tex didn't blink. "This is your final warning. Leave now before we take action." Slowly, Tex counted to ten.

At ten, he whispered, "Side mirrors."

The smiling creep of a passenger jumped when the side mirrors of both cars shattered. He gave a frantic signal to get them out of there. If anything, the two black cars traveled faster, exiting than entering Susan's domain.

Tex gave a thumbs-up as he said, "Good job." He smiled; it was something he rarely did, and it felt strange on his face. Now, to wait for the next call. Life was never simple. "I'm going to see about getting you each a peach pie hot from the oven," he whispered to the men who spent long hours lying on a mountain. He nodded at the camera, knowing Roger stood guard over Susan and York.

Roger was the first to exit, sweeping the area with his weapon drawn before motioning for the others to come out. Now he knew why they said Tex had ice in his veins. Roger had a great deal to learn from Tex. Roger didn't know if he could ever do a face-down like he had just witnessed, but he was determined to try.

Many thoughts were running through Susan's mind. Dread was among them. Glancing at Tex, she knew they needed to talk only out of hearing of York. Before they hustled her off to the bunker, Susan had picked up thoughts from the men in the cars. Trouble was at her door. What she didn't know was why. Someone was after the reason that Susan stayed secluded on this remote mountain. A person who thought they were powerful enough to have whatever they wanted. She would not put York in danger.

"Roger, stay with York. Tex, follow me," Susan ordered. Years ago, she decided that if she was needed so desperately by her country. She would be the one in charge. Susan took Tex into the bunker and locked the door behind them. He was frowning with his brows when he turned to question Susan, but she was the one who spoke. "Those men were under orders. They were to bring me to be questioned by a man I don't know. The feeling is that this man is rising to power and feels he can do whatever he wants. They were not Homeland Security." Susan took a breath and sat down.

"Do you think they intended to take you by force?" Tex asked, his eyes narrowing and his stance broad as if the threat was just outside.

"No, they did not expect to be turned away either. There was a confidence that you, being just one man, would be easy to overcome. I have no doubt you would be threatened with a fake charge and expected to allow them access to me," Susan told him.

"Moving you to a different location will take some time, but I believe we should consider it," Tex mused. "The question is, how did they find where you live and get your phone number?"

"There are always ways to betray a secret," Susan said. "Loose lips on the General's team. Don't forget that someone in the FBI gave out my number. I can't believe my grandfather would take a chance and tell anyone. But people are always spying on him. It makes sense that I'd be the one they would go after, even though Middy is more powerful. They can't take a chance that I'll reveal whatever they are plotting."

"Your sister is more powerful?" Tex asked,

puzzled.

Susan smirked, "The General never bothers her. He is afraid of her. Once, he had made her mad, a mistake he would never repeat. She blew him on top of a silo and kept him there until our father had her let him down. She was my hero that day." A smile was on her face as Susan thought about how the General had been bullying her. Middy found out, taking matters into her own hands literally. "He has attempted to be civil to me since then. When we were little, the General thought he owned us and tried to order us around. Middy made him understand he was wrong. At least while she was around."

"Barbed wire hanging from a tree is what he deserves," Tex thought. "If we find the leak, we can track and deal with the threat. Only, how do we find the person responsible?" Tex wondered out loud.

"We visit the suspects. I'll know," Susan said flatly, with a determined look.

"No!" was Tex's instant reaction.

"Yes, I will not stand by when it is possible for something as simple as a visit to find a traitor. My country uses me to spy on the enemy. It is time for me to find a traitor, even if the government may be unaware of among them," Susan stated.

"What about York?" Tex reasoned.

"True, he must be protected. We will have Roger and two alternates take him to museums," Susan said. "You and I will visit old friends. The General was sick, remember? I'll bring him a get-well gift and ask that he show me around. I think he might end up touring the FBI. Two birds with one gift." A simple plan.

Tex kept his mouth shut. Nothing was simple.

It was a simple plan. The team only had to carry it out. Simon would fly ahead of them to set up a bunker for the stay. The visit was unscheduled as they didn't want to give the traitor a chance to run far enough to hide from Susan's mind.

York could sense the tension but was still excited about visiting the museums. There was a reason they had not told him why they were going to a place Susan hated to dwell in. He kept his mouth shut, sure that he would eventually learn why.

Holding a box of home-baked cookies, Susan went to the General's office. She didn't knock before entering, as he never gave a warning when invading her home. The General was lounging behind a large desk. His feet were up on the desk, and he had a drink in a coffee cup in his hand. When Susan and Tex walked into the office, his feet hit the floor with a thump. "Miss Whiting, what a pleasure. What brings you to my office?"

Susan didn't answer as she scanned everyone in the nearby offices. "Your intern mentioned you were ill. I've brought you some cookies to brighten your day."

"Thank you. I didn't want you to be that man's escort. That is why I sent the intern. For me, backing down was not right. But my intern could leave and not have his reputation ruined. Do you understand?" he asked, giving Tex a nervous glance.

"If not you, then who wanted to do that to me? I can't believe it was Grandfather," Susan said.

"Someone must have gotten to a person in his office. The call didn't come from him. Which I thought was odd. It seemed valid at the time, but now I wonder. They put pressure on me when I delayed, saying they would reassign me if I didn't try to make you come. I was counting on him," the General said, pointing at Tex with his chin, "… to kill the deal." He shook his head. "I had to pay for new tires. But it was worth it."

Walking over to the man who had aggravated her from childhood, Susan placed her hand on his shoulder. "Thank you," she said. Turning away, she hastened to the exit.

Walking swiftly, Tex cleared the way for Susan. His mind was racing. Someone near the President was a traitor. Was this person involved in the Homeland Security scam? And, more importantly, why?

"Count," Susan whispered to Tex.

"One, two. Three…" Tex counted, upset with himself that he had let his guard down and exposed her to his thoughts. For once, the General had shown some backbone in working the system to protect Susan. For that, Tex would not shoot at him the next time he showed up for her. He pulled out his phone and speed-dialed Roger. "Something that smells of rot is going on. Keep your eyes open and protect York at all costs," he said, then hung up. He didn't ask Susan where they were going next, as Tex had a good idea.

As their driver approached the next destination, Susan raised her hand. The car slowed to a crawl while Susan did her directional search.

She stopped immediately and pointed to a man dressed in a business suit. "That man is wondering where the best spot would be to leave his briefcase. It contains a small bomb. At least he thinks of it as small," Susan told them.

Tex relayed the information, waiting until he saw security close in on the suspect before giving the order to drive on. There was no way he would allow Susan near a bomb. "We do this tomorrow," he told Susan. "For now, we join York and go to lunch. You can't be associated with a bomb found." His tone was reasonable, so Susan didn't protest as the driver circled away from the area.

Everything felt like it was going sideways to Susan. She had seen the thoughts of so many self-centered and thoughtless people that little if anything, surprised her. This plot, however, was pointed at her. What had she done that had drawn the finger to point in her direction? She was always gone before her grandfather acted on the information she gave him. Where had she slipped up? Had she endangered York? Someone knew where she lived; that thought sent chills down her back. She felt violated in her home.

York looked at the display about one of the first capsules to be sent into space and recovered. York envisioned all the discoveries in outer space. This one event opened the door to so many extraordinary things. Science, he thought, investigates all these things in real life. He looked back to see if Roger was as awed as he felt. Science went clear out of his mind when he saw Susan and Tex. York started to run to them, then checked himself, walking over as if they had been there the whole time. "We saw so many planes and old bones, clubs, arrows made by hand, a part of the moon, a real moon rock and… and," he had to take a breath, "a chimp, as Tarzan had, that went up in space. It was so smart."

"How amazing. Tell me all about everything while we eat lunch. A real moon rock?" Susan smiled as York continued telling her about the wonders he had seen that day. She had to find out who was after her to protect York. He needed to have the childhood that had been robbed from him by a heartless birth mother. That did not mean there wouldn't be chores and duties, for they, too, were part of being a child. It was how you learned to survive as an adult, but he needed these wonders, which he had experienced today, and joy in his life, not constant fear.

Lunch was seafood, ice cream, and a touch from a traitor's mind. While laughing at York's description of a pigeon, he saw having a standoff with a rat. "The grandpa tossed the treat on the sidewalk. The rat wanted that treat, but so did the bird. They stared at each other, and then the rat dashed for the prize. That pigeon just grabbed it up and swallowed it. The rat couldn't believe a bird outsmarted him," York laughed.

Susan chuckled at the image of the bewildered rat's face in York's mind. The whisper of a thought touched Susan's mind. Slowly, she turned her head to the right, then back to the left. Tex saw the movement, alerted, and poked Roger in the ribs to get his attention. "Watch over them once Susan tells me where to go," he whispered. Roger nodded his ice cream, feeling like a cold lump in his belly because he had missed Susan doing her thing.

"Where?" Tex asked in a soft micro whisper behind Susan's chair. "It was to my left but at a distance. Gone now." Came the thought in his mind. What the hell? Had she just talked in his mind? He didn't have time to worry over that there was a traitor to catch. He knew it was the person they were after; Tex didn't even consider it. He just knew. The problem was, how could he identify a thought without its face? He couldn't. For once, he was at a total loss on what to do unless…. Pulling out his phone, he dialed a base team. "I need all the video footage within a five-mile radius heading north from my location," he said softly into his phone.

That night, Simon and Tex looked through all the traffic and security feeds for Susan's period of hearing a traitor's mind. They were hoping to find anyone who had learned of her gift. Near midnight, Tex went to bed. He had to be alert the next day when they visited the President. He checked on Susan and York before willing himself to sleep. An agent had to catch sleep when he could. Even in his sleep, Tex's mind reviewed what he should have done differently. Nothing.

The following day, they treated York to a visit to a pancake house for breakfast. They sent York and Roger to one of the few locations left where the history of the United States of America was still displayed. Susan and Tex reluctantly left the cheerful pair to play the spy on the people around the President.

Because this was not a time when Susan had an appointment with the President, they shuffled from one waiting area to the next. You don't just drop in on the highest man in the country. But that was the plan. Each level of clearance allowed her to scan the minds around her. She felt like she needed a wire brush to scrub her brain. Too many people were voted into office to serve those who didn't. They were plotting on how to take advantage of them instead. All they wanted was to continue to make money. Where was the interest in bettering the country and the lives of the people? Her skin crawled with repulsion. Susan tucked her hands into her jacket pockets to hide the slight tremble that was starting.

Something was not right. Tex could see the tension building in Susan. He stood where he was, close enough to cover her if shots were fired or if a scumbag approached her. He suspected everyone but kept his distance like a good guard dog. He also counted like mad so as not to stress Susan with his dark thoughts.

"How could they have failed? He had given them all the information needed. Now he'd have to be the one reporting failure." The thoughts slammed into Susan's mind. They were angry thoughts of a man desperate and filled with fear. Susan lifted her hand slightly, not enough to draw attention to herself, but so that Tex saw it. He came immediately to her. The man was moving away from them. Shivering, Susan stood, turned to get a directional reading, and swiftly returned to where they had entered.

Lips pressed tight together, Tex followed. He didn't like this one tiny bit. Susan was tracking the traitor, and he was sure of that. Something inside his chest twisted into a knot of fear. She was his to protect, but how did you protect a subject from finding a traitor only she could locate?

Down one hall after another, Susan followed the thoughts. She constantly flinched as those thoughts turned to things she didn't want in her mind. Susan saw him striding along ahead of them. "There, in front of us," she thought to Tex. He nodded and slipped in front of her. There was a problem that Susan hadn't anticipated: the man was only a servant of a larger organization. They needed him to talk. She was about to tell Tex to capture the suspect when the team he had summoned to take the guy down arrived. Everything went to hell.

Tex saw when the man he kept in sight realized he was in trouble. The guy glanced at the two SS agents closing in on him, looked behind him, and saw Tex. He pulled a gun. Tex immediately turned and pushed Susan to the ground, covering her body with his own. He heard shots fired. With his gun in his hand, he flipped so his body blocked Susan's body, ready to kill if he must protect her. It was over. The SS team was standing over the body of the traitor, calling it in—time for cleanup. Quickly, Tex helped Susan to her feet, rushing her away from the area. They would join York and Roger as if nothing had happened and return home. Her visit with her grandfather would not happen this time around.

Chapter Seven

UNSOLVED LOOSE ENDS

They spent a wonderful day with York after leaving the White House and a dead traitor behind. Susan told Tex the little she had learned from the mind of the man before he had died. He thought being killed for his cause was a great deed. The most disturbing thought was that he had managed to infiltrate the government. How many others were there that they didn't know?

The search through this man's past went under investigation. Other than a Muslin connection, they could find no hint of involvement with organizations or governments that would be interested in Susan. He was carrying an illegal weapon, which was enough to justify his death on the White House steps. The man was labeled an assassin and filed away. Susan was the only person who had access to the traitor's mind. She alone knew that corruption ran deeper. Evil had wormed its way into the very fabric of her country. How and why were the questions?

The energy was seeping out of her with each person Susan scanned. Most were people visiting their capital every day for the first or second time in their lifetime. Jittery, nerves frayed, she looked into mind after mind, every place they visited with York. Susan kept a ready smile for the child upon her face. They marveled at the image of Abraham Lincoln or told their children stories about the man. Others spoke of how relatives of many families stood on opposite sides. Their belief in what was right during the war between the North and the South tore families apart. Neither side was utterly wrong, and in the end, they became one country after years of adjusting from one to the other.

York heard some of these conversations and finally asked Susan and Tex about it. "The North won. Didn't that make them right?" he wanted to know.

Surprisingly, Tex jumped in with an answer. "Not entirely. The idea of freeing the enslaved people was indeed great. There were people in the North who wanted to keep their slaves. In the South, a lot of the slave owners had already freed their slaves. Or they treated them as if they were family. The idea that grated on people was being forced into doing something. The North mistreated the people in the South. They used the war as a means to take over the land. And to destroy the homes that had stood for generations. They harmed the women who lived in those homes. Soldiers who fought for both sides went home to the South only to find they had no home. Their lands no longer belonged to them. They had no rights. And just because the North won the war on the basis that it was freeing the enslaved people did not mean that they freed all their slaves. Whereas the enslaved people who had been so-called freed lived in poverty with no benefits. In the South, some people who had been enslaved refused to leave. They wanted to stay with the people who had always treated them kindly. Not all of the South treated slaves kindly, just as some of the slaves of the North had cruel owners. No side was truly wrong or right. They just went about things differently. A lot of it was because of greed. Men of the North wanted to get the rich lands of the South, which was a factor. Just as much as any other reason for fighting the war. Both sides suffered. Only one side was allowed to recover in peace."

York stared at the statue of Abraham Lincoln for a long moment and read the words. He turned to Tex, his face sober. "Do you think this President believed he was doing the right thing?"

Tex looked at the statue. "I'd like to think he did."

"Me too," York said. "But, I think the South believed they were doing the right thing too."

Susan kept her thoughts on the subject to herself. Being a black person, she knew that even here in the Capital of the nation, she was often looked down on in this day and age. Not that people said it out loud. She heard their thoughts, and they were not kind or understanding. When Susan lived in the United States's southern region, people accepted her. The people in the South saw her as a person, not a color. The positive people in the South far outnumbered those of the North. Around them is the statue of Abraham Lincoln. Some of those standing by them saw her standing with two white men and a white boy. They considered her a servant of the household. She was so thankful for her family, who always treated her as a person. Mentally, she amended that except for her Aunt Julian. Susan chuckled at that thought. Aunt Julian didn't think anyone was a person except herself.

Tex heard Susan's little laugh and wondered what had brightened her day, and could he make it happen again? One of his goals in life now was to bring her as much happiness as possible. She smiled more with York around; it was only often a fake smile. Like now, he'd see the strain beneath that smile as the burden of people's thoughts wore her down. He noted the slight tremble in her fingers. How long before they had viewed all that York wanted to see today and could return home? "Let's go to the bunker, and Simon or Roger can pick up something for dinner," he said, giving Roger one of those 'that is an order' looks. Roger nodded that he understood. Their day of sightseeing was over.

They both missed York's sharp look or that he turned to study Susan. He was no fool and understood that going to the bunker was for Susan's benefit. He looked up at the woman who was to be his mother. "When we get there, will you explain how to be a battery and let me see if I can do it?"

He hadn't fooled Susan. His thoughts of concern were projecting from his mind. That he'd feel relieved to be able to do this one thing for her was also like a glowing desire inside his mind. She nodded. "Of course." The relief he felt was so clear that she knew she was doing the right thing.

Simon volunteered to go pick up dinner. They had all looked stressed when they entered the bunker, so he took it upon himself to see they were all fed. Simon could feel that sense of dread hanging over Tex and Miss Susan. Knowing they had come across something Tex didn't feel he could solve had Simon on edge. This time, being with Miss Susan had been the most rewarding he had ever felt. She uncovered so many of the dark secrets in the underbelly of the government. Then they saw to it the evil traitor bastards were locked up. What had happened while they were out today? Something had that grim darkness hanging over them. At least the boy hadn't picked up on that darkness, Simon thought. He entered the bunker with their dinner and watched York as he stretched his arms out to describe some dinosaur skeleton he had seen.

Susan ate as if she were a starved waif of a child who had been given a crumb of bread and feared to have it taken from her. Tex watched her out of the corner of his eye. He did not want to appear to be staring at her. Many dark thoughts were crowding his mind about how he would keep her safe. Should there be a plot in the government of America to harm Susan? If they had time, they could prepare another hiding place for her. Somewhere that even the President wouldn't be able to find her or York. Time was unknown, as was who or what made up the enemy. He felt in need of a team he could trust. Trust, however, had flown out the window, along with his faith in the people. People who were supposed to be looking out for the country. And it's people. He listened to York and laughed when he felt he should. And Tex was glad that they could spare York the drama he felt weighing himself down.

Aware of the leaking thoughts from Tex and Simon, Susan stuffed her stomach full. She gulped down BBQ ribs, potato salad, and baked beans as fast as she could eat them. Simon did well, buying stick-to-your-ribs food for dinner. She smiled at the BBQ sauce smeared on York's eager face. Glancing at the three SS men, she noted they had sauce on their lips and mouths. Ribs were never food for people who minded using their fingers or couldn't stand a little sauce on the face. For the first time since reaching the safety of the bunker, Susan felt relaxed. Now, she could try to talk York through becoming a battery. First, they cleaned up after themselves.

Susan and York stood, picking up their plates like a well-oiled machine. The three SS agents were instantly upon their feet, taking pains to clean their messes up. Roger, the team's newest member, had already learned that this family included the SS in their home life. The interaction in cleaning up was a team effort and not placed upon one individual. He witnessed York tending to his clothes as if he knew this was his responsibility, not for Roger or Susan. It had all been hard for him to understand in the beginning. In his family, his mother did all the housework. And the rest of them were handed the things they needed or wanted. Never had he been expected or required to do manual labor at home. That life hadn't bode well for him as an adult, where people expected him to provide for himself and do his laundry. He had felt like a fool the first time he tried to do his laundry and ruined everything he owned. He found that he resented his bosses telling him to do things. He hid it well, but the anger was always beneath the surface. His journey into the SS had been through a chance to be in the right place at the time.

This assignment he fell into like so many things in his life. Then, Tex had found him wanting. He hadn't said anything to Roger, but the feeling was there. Inside himself, he began to see that flawed outlook he had held onto for so long. Something changed; now, he wanted to live up to this man he had come to admire. So he cleaned up his messes, learned how to do his laundry, and kept his eyes open, trying to see all the things he had missed.

"You guys all relax now," Susan said. "York and I need quiet as York wants to learn to be a battery." As she talked, Susan turned two chairs so they faced each other close enough a person could sit in each and readily touch the person in the other. She had York sit in one while she took the other. York and Susan each took a chair. The three Secret Service agents sat or stood where they could watch over the pair.

Immediately, Susan realized she would have to drain some of her energy to be sure she could feel York giving her his. She looked over at the SS agents, wondering which one should be her pretend victim. Simon and Tex both looked ready to do anything she asked of them. Roger was watching but also seemed a bit confused. "Roger, I think you need a boost of energy. Please come stand beside me for a moment," she told him. He did as he was told for once without being ordered to do so by Tex.

"I'm going to give you a little of my energy. You saw me do this for the woman stabbed. If you were injured, it would give your body a little more vitality to help keep you going. It wouldn't heal you, for I can't heal. But you would live a little longer. Ready?" she asked.

Roger gulped and nodded his head. He felt her hand touch his arm and stood fast, refusing to let his nervous body pull away. He didn't expect to feel anything, as in his mind, this was all phony bull crap. A warmth began to creep up his arm, spreading through his chest and giving him a feeling of well-being and peace. He wanted that warmth to hold him in its deep embrace. Then, her hand was gone from his arm. There was a lifting of his spirit he hadn't had before, ever. His eyes looked down at his arm in wonder, as he thought surely, his whole arm must glow with this feeling he had inside him. But it was just an arm. Looking over at Miss Susan, he could see how exhausted she looked. After dinner, she was almost jolly. He looked up at Tex and saw the worry in his mentor's eyes, the grim set of his mouth. And he saw the clenched fist at Tex's side. Carefully, he stepped back away from Susan, giving Tex a nod to let him know he understood.

"York, what you need to do is, to me, simple. I've seen many people try, yet all have failed. Only my father, my sister, and my brother, besides myself, have succeeded so far. What I do is think of sending all my strength, all my energy, to my mother. I do it because I love her and know she needs that energy to heal someone who will die if not for her. You can think of it in whatever way you imagine seeing your life essence going from you into me, okay?" Susan instructed York.

Nearly bouncing in his chair with eagerness, York nodded, then solemnly placed his hands upon Susan.

Tex had stepped up by Roger while Roger watched in fascination with Susan's instructions. "You need to stand by York. If he starts to get too pale, tell him to stop; if he doesn't, pull him away. This task is vital. York could die if he gives her too much," Tex whispered in his ear.

Roger had been riding the high he still felt from Susan's warm touch. Tex's words had him zooming to York's side. He ignored everything around him. Someone could have shoved a gun in his back, and he wouldn't even have blinked. He could feel it. That sense, he had seen in Tex and Simon when they were watching over Susan. This time, the job was his to do, and nothing or anybody else mattered, just York. He saw it when York began to send his essence into Miss Susan. The boy paled in front of his eyes. "Stop, York. Stop now," he said.

At that exact moment, Miss Susan pulled away from York. "Honey, you must stop now," she said.

York slumped forward, but Roger caught him. Blinking, York looked up at Roger and said, "Thank you."

Roger smiled at York. The boy was so formal in thanking him. "You are welcome, but next time I say stop, you better stop, or it will be no ice cream for you," he teased, pleased when York laughed.

"I did it!" York said, raising his hand like a

champion boxer being declared the winner in a
boxing match. He was too weak to give a victory yell.

Tex had chaffed when he had been kept
away from Susan during Ritter's healing. He had
seen enough to realize that this battery bit was just
as serious as being a healer was for her mother. It
meant Susan could die in the process. And now, the
same thing could happen to York. Knowing that
Roger didn't have a clue, in the same manner they
left him in the dark about caring for Susan, didn't
sit well with Tex. He would do his best to forewarn
Roger of the dangers.

First, they filled York and Susan with ice
cream and then popcorn. Tex knew that soon, the
pair would need to go to sleep. He waited until York
was asleep and Susan was in bed before taking Simon
and Roger aside. He wanted to be sure both agents
knew how to take over for him with Susan and York
if he died. "Sit," he told them. "I was sent on this
assignment without being given all the necessary
information, just like you. I've had to learn the hard
way, as you have, Simon, and you are, Roger. This
mind thing Miss Susan does is scary. You are told to
count to keep her from reading your thoughts. What
they didn't tell us was that the thoughts hurt her." He
saw Roger look surprised. "Imagine that you have an
earbud in both ears. Two people start talking to you
at once, then three, five, then one hundred. They are
all there, forcing their deepest, darkest thoughts into
your head. Some think lustfully, and some are angry
for petty, senseless reasons. And all of them shouting
at you. You hear men thinking of murdering or

raping, or molesting little children. Women are consumed with thoughts of killing their boyfriends or best friends. Children who think the only way to stop the abuse is to kill themselves. Then the ones who are crazy in love, desperate to win someone over, or brokenhearted and in deep dark shit in their minds because of being betrayed. Miss Susan is attacked with every bit of this, unable to block it out except in a place like this." Tex waved his hand sweepingly to indicate the bunker.

"She can't go out to dinner without being mentally attacked by everyone within the area. So, we count to spare her our thoughts, not to hide them." Tex paused to let that sink in before getting to what he thought Roger needed to know. "Now, to the reason I'm talking to you. York has just become one of the batteries that support Susan's mother on difficult heals. You stayed with York while Simon and I went to save SS agent Ritter. You didn't see what can happen to our subjects when they are batteries. Even you, Simon, didn't see those last minutes. Miss Susan was too weak to go on. They ordered me to take her out of there. She was unconscious with her heart barely beating." He looked meaningfully at Roger. "You have to guard York against himself when he is a battery. You saw how far gone York was on his first attempt to give his energy. He didn't have the sense to stop. It is up to us to stop them. We must try to be gentle and talk them down, but if that doesn't work, then force them to stop. I'm telling you this because this is now part of our job. The food they need to be made to eat before giving. They need to stop and rest and drink those brown drinks while eating those bars. All this is left up to us to do for them. You both need to know this and be prepared. Bring some of the bars and drinks with you.

"There is some evil coming. I can feel it. Miss Susan got a whiff of it from the guy we killed today. It felt big to her. Big and dangerous. If in the future I am incapacitated," Tex paused to give both men a commanding look. "I depend on the two of you to step in and take over. We are all that stands between her, York, and this thing so evil, so foul that one whiff made her shiver. She hears all the dirt and horror inside us all. And THIS made her shiver. Now I'm going to bed, and you should too, Roger. Simon, be alert," said Tex, stood going off to shower before bed.

Simon stood. Now he knew why Tex had looked so grim all evening. At some point, Tex thought he would have to give up his life to save Miss Susan. Now Simon felt grim. He stepped outside the bunker, triple-checking the locks before beginning his night patrol. Simon was going to update his will and increase his life insurance. Off and on, he flipped through anything in his life he needed to take care of before he died. It was something Simon did regularly since, like every other agent, he knew he was a meat shield; at least for part of each day, he had a subject to protect. Protection wasn't all the SS did, but it was a part of their life that required great sacrifice.

Roger was reevaluating his life. He had never made a will or thought of getting his affairs in order. But then, Roger had never faced his mortality either. Nor had he known about people who could do amazing things. Give the energy that made them live by touch and thought to someone else. He considered what that meant as to his duties and the tremendous commitment he was making. It was so giant that it dwarfed him, making him feel lacking. His job had become difficult and far more important to him. He remembered how he had resented having to count in his head. What a thoughtless idiot he had been. How could he not have reasoned that even thoughts hurt when you couldn't block them?

In the morning hours, three SS agents and their subjects of protection ate a morning meal. The bags, packed and ready to go, sat near the bunker door where they were. They looked like any family unit on holiday and were preparing to return home. Their faces were tired like the holiday had worn them out. And the air of impatience to be home in their beds once more hung over them. The three men, however, wore dark suits and carried weapons. There was a touch of danger in their eyes, which were always watching the world around them. To one of the men, that look was something new. He had matured overnight.

Roger watched York eating with a critical eye. Today, he saw the simple act of his subject being fed in a different light. Yesterday, he was annoyed with the kid when York needed to stop often and eat one of the protein bars York had carried in his backpack. Today, he knew the boy must be full of good proteins and vitamin-enriched foods. "Eat another egg and drink your milk, York. Now that you are a battery, you must always keep your body fueled," he told the boy. He was gratified when York listened to him. For once, Roger didn't check to see if Tex approved of him. York was his to protect. Today, he understood what that meant. In the back of his mind, he worried about who would look after York if something happened to him. He needed a night man, someone he could trust to watch over York.

Once airborne, Roger broached the subject of a second-night man—someone to be there with Simon should he have to chase a suspect. "It makes sense to me that we have that extra protection since we never know what will happen," Roger told Tex as Simon slept in the back of the plane.

Tex nodded. "Is there someone you trust, or would you like me to pick someone to be your partner?" Tex asked.

"I've seen some poor Representatives. Maybe you should pick someone. You picked me. I hated it when you selected me, but now I'm glad you did. You do it," Roger told him.

Nodding, Tex went to the back of the plane and made a few calls. Shortly, he returned. "He'll be waiting when we land. His name is George Jones. I would trust him to have my back anytime. Okay?"

"That is good enough for me. If you trust Jones, then I know I can trust him with York if something happens," Roger said in a whisper to not worry York. Nodding, Tex understood that Roger was also looking at possible future outcomes and moving forward.

As they taxied to a stop, Roger spied a long-legged man leaning against a post by the ramp they would be walking up to escape the crowded airport lobby. The man was lean, whereas Roger looked like a football player. And he wore a cowboy hat. At first glance, the man looked like a goof-off, not someone Roger thought of as an SS agent.

When Susan and York stepped through the plane's exit, the man took his hat off. He had coal-black hair with just a hint of gray at the temples. He stood up straight, ready to greet them.

"Howdy," George said in greeting as the group of people he was committing to approach. "Tex, you old dog, you haven't changed one little bit. Thanks for giving me a call. I was bored near to tears," he joked as if he had seen Tex every day.

"Let me introduce the others to you, George," Tex said, a tiny grin on his face. "Miss Susan and York are ours to protect. Everyone, this is George Jones, a retired Texas Ranger. He will be teamed up with Roger here. Simon is my partner. You and Roger have York as your main concern, but all of us, in reality, have both York and Miss Susan," Tex said in a commanding voice.

"George," Simon said, shaking George's hand. "You and I are available on nights and whenever they need us."

"You bet. I brought my night vision," George responded, clearly having already been told how things stood.

Roger wasn't impressed. He had expected another SS agent. That Tex had gone far afield didn't sit right with him. But he shook George's hand and kept his objections to himself. He knew he could trust Tex if he had learned nothing more. Therefore, he'd allow George to prove himself before mouthing off. After all, he knew he hadn't been on top of his game when he first joined the team.

Susan turned as if to look behind them. Tex and George both drew their weapons. Roger and Simon stepped to where they were shielding Susan and York. "Where?" Tex asked. Susan pointed up to a plane circling away from the end of the runway and leaving the area. For a moment, it looked as if Tex was considering shooting down the plane. It was a commercial airline, which meant many innocent people were on board. "Simon, check the passenger list. Roger and George protect Susan and York. I'm going to check the car for explosives," Tex ordered. Simon and Tex waited until the four had Susan and York in a building out of sniper sight before going on their missions.

It was the first time Roger had seen George in action. He was as hard-nosed and alert as Tex, and Roger understood why he was selected to join their team. The thought of explosives had Roger on extra alert. They would have to check the cars every time before using them now and for trackers.

Walking back to where his subjects were waiting, Simon's eyes searched for anyone out of place or suspicious. He had the feeling someone had declared war upon them. He had experience with fighting a war. It was seldom settled without blood spilled on both sides. He saw Tex returning ahead, increasing his stride to walk close enough to talk to him. "I also managed to talk them out of security footage. Anything on the car?" he asked.

"A tracker. I sent it off on a semi's load. It looks like it may be on its way to Alaska. We can't take any chances now that they know where she lives," Tex said, his eyes never pausing in their search for hidden enemies.

Susan insisted that George come early that evening so she could introduce him to the rest of the family. The three SS didn't even smile to indicate they knew what she meant by the rest of the family. George squinted with one eye at Tex, sensing that something was up, some test or joke on him. He smiled and said, "Yes, Ma'am," like Texans do to a woman they respect. Then he checked the second car they used for bombs and trackers.

That evening, while the last of dinner was baking in the oven, Susan, York, three SS agents, and a former Texas Ranger set off into the woods upon the mountain's side. Usually, the first to appear would be the doe Susan had befriended, but as fate would have it, a mighty screech rang out as the eagle dove through the trees straight for Susan. George didn't hesitate. He stepped in front of Susan and offered his arm to the eagle. "Aren't you a handsome fellow?" George said. Roger's mouth dropped open. He had never seen the eagle land on anyone other than Susan. The eagle fluffed out as if he understood what George had said. George looked over at Susan. "I have a couple of hawks back on the ranch who visit with me occasionally. Last night, I saw this fellow flying and thought he was grand. Is that pretty doe over there a friend too?"

"Yes, and Sly is peeking out of the bushes. He isn't fond of large groups of people, he says. This man is George. He will protect you." Susan said as

Chatterbox came down a nearby tree, scowling at Susan for bringing so many people into his woods. Susan offered each of her friends a treat before returning to the house. She was satisfied that George would not be hunting any of her woodland friends.

On the walk back, Tex told the others George had a way with animals. People in Texas were always after him to train their difficult horses.

"Yep, they can be a real pain in the… neck. I had to shoot one numb skull to get him to give up on horses. He had some idea that you spur them half to death to break them. I think he still walks with a limp. But to tell the truth, I meant to shoot him in the buttocks. His bad luck, he turned to run at that moment. At least it spared the noble horse his bad treatment." George said.

Susan made tacos and an enchilada casserole for dinner to honor George's joining them for his first meal. As the boys made their tacos, Susan served up plates of the hot enchilada casserole with some refried beans. George's eyes lit up, and he pulled a small bottle out of some hidden pocket, shaking hot sauce liberally on his food. Nobody saw when and how he dosed Simon's food with that Texas hot sauce. But they heard about it during Simon's first bite for dinner/breakfast.

"WHAT THE HELL!" Simon shouted, then he saw George's shoulders shaking in silent laughter. He narrowed his eyes at the bottle of hot sauce. Reaching out, Simon snatched it up. "Some dumb ass didn't use enough hot sauce for my taste," he mumbled, dumping nearly half the bottle on his plate. Then he sat back and ate with gusto.

George eyed his near-empty bottle of hot sauce. His eyes had an evil twinkle in them that worried Tex. He had experienced George's sense of humor and worried Simon wasn't up to the Texas-size jokes his friend could pull. "George, take it easy. I don't want to send you packing," he warned. Sobering, George nodded that he understood. "I should have warned all of you that George has a huge joking side. He once put super glue on my Stetson. I had to shave my head. We are not going to have a joke-pulling war going on here. Miss Susan is our main concern. Got it!" Tex said, giving George and Simon a pointed look. They nodded.

When Susan brought out dishes of steaming hot blackberry cobbler topped with ice cream, George took one bite and looked up at Susan with what appeared to be total sincerity. "Miss Susan, will you marry me?" He saw Tex stiffen out of the corner of his eye.

"You forgot to count while saying that, George. I won't let you use me for one of your jokes. Now tell everyone you are sorry," Susan said in that authoritative voice that came so naturally to her.

Lesson learned, George thought to Susan. "I'm sorry, guys. Miss Susan is too smart for me. So if any remarks slip, please attribute them to my hopeless joking side," he said.

York spoke up for the first time. "At least she didn't tell you you have the night off. If she ever says that, you might as well pack your bags," York said with a knowing look. Around the table, all three SS agents nodded in agreement.

As soon as they had consumed the last bite,

everyone stood and collected their dirty dishes.
George followed their example. He was impressed.
Their subject didn't fall into the known types
of people who needed looking after. Everyone,
including herself, was expected to clean up after
themselves. She cooked the meal and served them
but wouldn't clean up their messes. He began to
understand what the boy York had meant about
being given the night off. It would have meant he
was no longer a part of the team but an outcast.

It was during this group clean-up that the
phone rang. The SS agents stopped and stared at
the phone as if it was a viper. Tex was the one who
answered. "Speak," he barked, then listened intently.
Then he looked over at Susan, worry etched his face
in troubled lines. Hanging up, Tex began barking
orders, "Simon, all our go-bags. Miss Susan, we need
to talk. George, we need a fueled private jet when
we reach the airport. York, you get your and Susan's
go-bags. Roger, ready a box of each of the energy
supplies. York, don't forget Goldie's bag and vest."

Satisfied that everyone was off doing their
tasks. Tex went over to Susan. "It is your sister. We
need to hurry," he said, knowing that nothing but the
truth was needed. He filled his mind with numbers
to try and spare Susan the worry.

Chapter Eight

FAMILY

York was nervous as they rushed into the hospital. Susan explained that her sister was very ill and that York needed to fill his body with all the food he could before they reached her hospital room to be a battery. He ate everything she gave him on their trip over on the jet. He gulped down several energy bars and drinks on the car ride to the hospital.

Roger kept unwrapping bars and handing them to York as if he feared the boy would blow away on a stiff wind. He gave George a brief rundown on how to care for York when he did the battery thing. The tall man had nodded as if it all made sense to him. This only made Roger wonder if he was the only one who found this part of the job strange.

Tex was determined not to be shuffled to the hallway and kept from Susan this time. His previous experience in the hospital with Susan acting as a battery had soured him on the whole idea. He knew the score now and wouldn't let them treat him like a green rookie.

They did not have trouble finding Middy as men in blue uniforms and poker-faced Detectives lined the hallways. That sea of blue parted before Susan and her team. Bobby Jay was pacing just behind the curtained-off area where Middy was fighting the battle for her life. One look at Bobby and Tex went into super protection mode. "Simon, make certain everyone out here counts. Knock them out if they give you any crap. Roger, your main job is to be there for York. He will need more frequent breaks than Susan. George," Tex marked a line across the hallway with his foot. "Nobody passes this line unless I okay it."

Next, Tex went over to Bobby Jay for an update on what was happening. "It is grim, Tex. I'm worried about my boy. He is a full-time healer this time. This thing is too big even for Mrs. Whiting to heal. Mrs. Whiting and Eric had to work with one battery each until now. And I think Miss Susan's pep talk pulled them out of that dark tunnel of despair everyone felt. This thing has me scared. It shouldn't have been allowed to exist…" Bobby's head swung to look past Tex as a woman tried to get past George. "She has been a thorn in our sides trying to get in here. I don't knock out women, but she is trying my patience."

Tex noted the woman in a doctor's coat arguing with George. She didn't stand a chance. George was a brick wall when it came to trespassers. Tex turned back to face the curtain. It hung between himself and where Susan and York were giving their all to save Middy. He could see through a slight opening the healers working and his subjects with their hands upon the healers. They all looked worn already. And was that Ritter acting like a battery? "Ritter?" he asked.

Bobby nodded. "He loves his subject enough that he is capable of being a battery. I know it nearly floored me, too. He has it bad," Bobby said.

"They haven't reassigned him? I'd have thought at the first hint he cared for his subject they would reassign Ritter," Tex asked, knowing that he had feelings for Susan that he didn't want to admit even to himself for fear they would make him leave her.

"He'd have shot anyone who tried. Once his mind is made up, you step aside, or he runs over you. And from what I've heard, Middy has been hard on anyone sent to watch over her. Ritter is just stubborn enough to stick it out. I doubt the old man has any say now that Ritter loves her," Bobby told him.

Tex felt a hot breath upon his shoulder and realized Roger was worried about seeing an IV hooked up to York. Bobby saved him from having to say anything to Roger. "Get used to it. I've become an expert at hooking one up to Eric. I'll see to it you are both sent a supply of Andy Bags," he told Roger.

Roger bit his lip as he heard them send York to rest and eat. At least they were making him take breaks, he thought. That didn't stop the urge to run in there and throw York over his shoulder. He glanced at Tex and saw the worry in his eyes. Shit, if he was that worried, it had to be extremely dangerous. Roger stepped forward before realizing Tex was holding onto him to keep him in place.

"Susan's sister is dying. She has that thing we never heard mentioned when we heard it. She needs them all, and I hope they succeed without all of them going down in the effort. We have to be strong for them and think positive thoughts. I know those thoughts will help them," Tex told him. "Just as thoughts can hurt, they can also give hope." Roger gave a weak nod.

Simon came, bringing coffee and sandwiches for everyone. He didn't need to ask how things were going. A hundred uniformed officers were keeping vigil, and the grim faces thanked him for the coffee and sandwiches, telling him all Simon needed to know. He went to talk to George for a little while just to be doing something.

"That little gal in trouble?" George asked Simon.

"The whole family is. We could lose a lot of them tonight. Miss Susan's mother and brother died before healing. From what I understand, the batteries are drained. York is so young and small. His body can't hold much of the life force to give up. If Miss Susan goes, we need to take Tex's gun. The last time we were here, he wouldn't leave the hospital, so I'm not going to try to get him to rest this time. Let's keep them pumped full of coffee and food when we can get them to eat," Simon said, scrubbing a hand over his face. "Another thing, if Susan's sister dies, we may have a riot. That bunch sitting vigil shifts changes but hasn't shrunk in size."

By morning, everyone inside that healing room looked ready to drop. The entire healing team had to take frequent breaks, with the two healers alternating in short spats. George and Simon were holding Roger and Tex back as the two SS agents leaned farther and farther into the room, ready to run in and rescue their people. Tex loosened his gun once, and Simon immediately slipped it out of the holster. Simon hoped never to see the day when something happened to Susan. He didn't want to have to shoot his Friend.

Two hours passed in utter agony for everyone. Fred was on the verge of telling Felith to stop when she called everyone to her. "Come quickly. I have it isolated in one small spot. We need to all work at once to finish it off. Eric joins me. Everyone else supports us."

Fred looked more worried than he had all night. He knew this was it. They either got rid of this horrible thing, or Felith and Eric would pass out, and that would mean the end of Middy. Fred held his hand up to stop them all. "Hold a moment. Tex," he called out. Immediately, Tex stepped through the curtains. "Get that snooty doctor and two crash carts. She may need to revive several of us after this last attempt."

The hovering doctor was immediately shoved through the curtains, followed by two crash carts. The doctor swore upon seeing the people in the room who looked like death warmed over, but Tex shut her up. "You are to observe, and should anyone drop dead, save them." He held his hand up to stop her protest before she could voice it. "You will not interfere in any other way. Stand here." Looking daggers at Tex, the doctor did as she was told to, standing there watching what she thought of as a freak show.

Felith and Eric attacked the last bit of horror, drawing relentlessly on their two batteries. Felith could feel the darkness starting to creep up on her and pushed all the harder to kill the last bit. She couldn't, wouldn't let her daughter die. Eric was just as determined, fighting his darkness as his strength began to wither away. It was a suicide attempt given by both healers at the same time. The veil of darkness took them over, and they fell into the waiting arms of two SS men. York was already out cold. Susan was swaying and went down with a thump. Ritter and Fred just slipped to the floor. It had been an all-out effort by them all. Their last thoughts were for Middy to live.

Doctor Pierce's eyes widened, but she didn't hesitate to wade in and check pulses. The two who had been touching her patient's hearts had stopped. The rest were out cold, although the boy barely had a pulse. She needed help, but one look at the SS men standing over her told her nobody else would be allowed in.

Bobby Jay appeared out of the blue. He ripped Eric's shirt off and lubed the paddles of the defibrillator machine. Not waiting for approval, Bobby Jay shocked Eric as if Bobby had done this many times before. He started the defibrillator to charge again, even as he felt for a pulse on Eric's neck. Ignoring everything around him, Bobby Jay concentrated only on Eric. Saving Eric was his to-do. His part of this partnership was keeping Eric alive. "Come on, Eric. Bruce will kill me if I return without you. Then, they will come to shoot Bruce or send him to the gas chamber. You don't want that, do you?" That seemed to work, and Eric took a deep breath before rolling to his side and falling into a deep sleep. "Blankets and six cots," Bobby Jay called out to the men in black waiting outside the curtains. They were men used to there being such emergencies. Not only were blankets brought, but warm blankets.

Fred had crawled over to his wife. He shoved the doctor's hand away when she tried to check Felith's pulse. His voice croaked heavily with fatigue and said, "Your touch will drain her even more. My touch won't. I'll tell you once we get a pulse." He brushed Felith's hair off her face and began to talk to her. "You promised you wouldn't die for good. The kids are all here. You can't disappoint them. Come on, Honey, fight for the kids and me." He kept on in that same tone of voice, encouraging, pleading, at times even threatening.

Doctor Pierce shocked the patient once again, only warning Fred at the last moment. She was relieved when he nodded and said, "Pulse."

Susan and York were both attended by Tex and Roger. Tex looked particularly grim as he treated Susan. He would pause only long enough to direct Roger in treating York. Soon, everyone was in a cot with warm blankets covering them and hooked up to fresh IVs. Doctor Pierce was slightly impressed with the professional way this team of Secret Service men took care of their charges. She couldn't help but wonder if they had to do this often. Unfortunately, she was removed from the curtain area when the current charge breathed. She didn't even have a chance to ask one question or examine her actual patient.

Tex and Roger shared a look, and both sat down on the floor, leaning back against the cots where their subjects now slept. "You should have kicked my ass when I first joined the team," Roger said in a near whisper.

Tex nodded. "I thought about it a time or two."

Roger chuckled and reached over to tuck the blanket more securely around York. In a spattering of days, he felt like he had lived a lifetime. He settled back. The long vigil had begun.

In the hallway beyond the curtain, Simon gave George a thumbs up. "We live to worry another day," he told George.

"I thought Tex was pulling my leg when he said this was a serious as-death assignment. Now I see he wasn't joking around," George said in a whisper as if he thought he'd wake up those in that room sleeping the sleep of total exhaustion.

"You must have known him during a different time. I've never seen Tex when he wasn't dead serious. Well, I think he gets a bit of a kick out of shooting at the General," Simon said smiling, "That blowhard may yet learn to call ahead when he wants something from Miss Susan.

When they arrived at her home, Middy and the family briefly felt at ease with her fellow officers. Eric was the first to leave as he had to return to his practice. All it took was a call about a sick child to send her mother and father flying off to the rescue. Susan decided to entertain Middy and her friends. To demonstrate the dancing routine that Goldie, York, and herself had learned. She was pleased by the thoughts that ran through her sister's mind. Some of the shadows inside Middy seemed to be lifting.

There was a knock on the door, and the world was entirely of shadows once more. One of the officers opened the door, and General Richards walked in. Tex drew his gun out so fast it was like a Western showdown. General Richards threw up his hands. The rest of the armed officers in the room joined Tex.

"Oh, damn! Do we have to go through this again? You know who I am. How do you even know I am here for Miss Susan? I could be here to talk with Middleton." General Richards protested.

Tex turned to Ritter. "Did this man make an appointment in advance to see Mids?"

"He did not," Ritter said, drawing his gun.

"But I'm The General; the President personally assigned me as a go-between to the Whitings," said General Richards when faced by both Ritter and Tex.

"All contact with my subject must be approved in advance. This rule is a well-known fact. I will not allow Miss Whiting to be in danger," Tex said. "The standing order is an appointment first and approval."

General Richards' shoulders slumped in defeat. "I will be back after you receive approval," he said. With that, he beat a hasty retreat.

As soon as General Richards left, Middy fell over laughing. She looked at Tex and said, "You are my hero."

Susan laughed, "It does make my day every time Tex sends him packing. The time he had his car shot was a real highlight of my day."

Over in the corner of the room, Simon gave Roger and George a broad smile as if to say our boy is back.

"General Richards stopped trying to order me around about the second time he visited the farm," Middy said.

"That is because you scare him. He isn't foolish enough to tempt having your wrath pointed at him," Susan gasped out between laughs. The entire room turned to look at Middy just as Tex's phone rang.

"Yes, Mr. President. He may come for an appointment. No, Sir, I will not allow anyone to approach Miss Susan without an appointment. Tell him tough shit." Mouths gaped open at Tex's words to the highest person in the whole country. Tex hung up. It was clear he was irritated. "Next time, I'll just shoot the twerp."

There was a soft tap at the door. The closest officer to the door answered the knock. It was the General. "I have an appointment with Miss Susan Whiting," The General said, turning to Susan. "Miss Whiting, you are needed in a rather urgent matter. We will leave immediately."

"They didn't tell you, General Richards. Who thinks you are a security risk?" Susan asked. There was no doubt she knew the answer. She only wanted him to voice it.

"Miss Susan, you know we can't discuss this

here. Come with me, and the proper person will brief you," The General almost begged.

"General Richards, don't you think I may have plans already? Has that thought entered any of your minds?" Susan asked.

"But, Miss Susan, your country needs you most urgently. What can take precedence over that?" He declared.

"Finding my sister's stalker, a man who has killed numerous people to cause her pain. I can find this monster, and I will before I leave," Susan promised. Then she read the horror of her staying to face this man threatening her sister in Middy's mind and gave in. Susan would go off and play spy for her country. But she wouldn't forget the disregard for her desire to help Middy.

This mission would be the first mission where George was part of the team. He was to watch over York after dark while Roger got a good night's sleep. Susan and York felt depleted from helping to heal Middy. So, the first order of business for them all was to make sure their subjects ate hearty meals. They ordered a huge meal to be waiting on the jet for everyone to enjoy. George managed to sprinkle some of his hot sauce onto the plate served to General Richards, seasoning the steak. He felt this was one joke Tex wouldn't mind him pulling off.

They sat down with plates placed in front of them. General Richards began to question George. "You weren't part of Miss Whiting's team the last time she came to D C. Are you familiar with the area around the Capital? Will you find your way around our Nation's Capital?" he questioned.

"Well, sir," George began, thickening his Texas accent. "I do believe I am capable of following a trail there. My specialty, you see, is finding people. I can track where a flea has traveled on a coon dog's tail. And I understand that the number of people chewing on our country's rear is astronomical. I shall be right at home there."

At that moment, the General took a bite of his rib-eye steak. His face turned bright red as he struggled not to make a fool of himself. Richards downed his glass of milk, which was served with the meal. He drank it down without taking a breath. Eyes watering, he said, "Quite so, I imagine then."

Simon had to look away to keep from laughing.

Oblivious to the trick played upon the General, York wolfed down his food and asked for seconds. Susan kept her head down so as not to comment. George had forgotten to count again. It seemed he enjoyed pranks too much to keep in mind; she could hear his every thought. Tex couldn't keep the slight smile from creeping on his face for all of a second. Roger hid behind his napkin for a long moment. George had just won his partner over.

Susan and York fell asleep as soon as they finished their meals. Their systems were used to the limit when neither of them cleaned up their mess. Tex and Roger cleaned up, and then they fell asleep. All four protectors had stayed up for the entire ordeal of Middy's healing. The experience had cemented their relationships as few things could.

Still in the dark about the mission when she exited the plane, Susan was slightly irritated. She disliked being among people. To be around so many minds, with no reason given, just wasn't right. She had always known why she was being asked to endure this bickering place and had been confident she could do her job as quickly as possible. If she attended a dinner, they would provide her with the clothing needed for that dinner. Should she need to examine people's thoughts in a meeting, someone arranged it for her. She hadn't had a chance to recover from the healing. The countless minds in and around the hospital still haunted her. Her body was weak from the all-out push at the end to save Middy's life. The General did not know what the assignment in Washington entailed.

A cold wind began to blow as they crossed to where a car should be waiting for Susan and her team. No car and no escort were sighted. Tex looked back to where the jet was undergoing cleaning and refueling to prepare for the next scheduled flight. His gut was telling him this was a setup. George stepped up next to Tex. "I've spotted at least two unlikely people working on the field. This stinks of polecats." Tex nodded.

The General spoke up for the first time since they had exited the jet. "Gentlemen, I don't like this. We need to secure Miss Whiting at once." Simon was already on his phone, hunting for transportation. He looked over at Tex, shaking his head. "The lines all say try again later."

Susan's hand came up, and everyone alerted, surrounding her and York, making a meat shield around them. Even the General placed himself between her and possible danger. Susan closed her eyes as she was receiving such a jumble of confusion that it was hard to sort out what was happening. Several torturous minutes passed, and Susan was growing weaker by the moment. At last, she spoke, "There is confusion among the people at the airport. They can't get a taxi or car service. Several people are weeping, scared. The news channels are all broadcasting some disaster. I am having trouble sorting out what." She sagged against Tex as her legs became too weak to hold her up. "They are shouting in their minds. Some, screaming in their hysterical fear mentally," she whispered.

Three unwrapped protein bars from York, Simon, and Roger appeared before Susan. She ate them like she was on autopilot, a haunted, faraway look in her eyes. She started speaking again, more in a half-whisper than anything, "Car bombs. Car bombs are on each of the main entrances to DC. The Capital is in lockdown. A few people are starting to think again, worrying about how their families are and knowing that there may not be a way to reach them."

"That does it! We are getting you out of here. By air, if possible. If not, Simon, start plotting a ground route. We are going home one way or the other," Tex told them in a level voice. "George, go see about securing a rental. If none are available, buy one. Here, use this card. General, you see about a flight out of here. To anywhere so long as it is away from the danger. Whoever succeeds, return immediately. No calls, period. Move it!"

As soon as the General and George left, Tex turned to Simon and Roger. "We are in mission mode. Our task is to see Susan and York to safety. Simon, you have our route out yet?"

"The problem is leaving here. The area is locked down. There are car checks for miles. Traffic backed up, and people were passing out, just sitting and waiting to move. I have several routes mapped out if we can worm our way free. That is the hang-up to getting out," Simon growled.

While they talked, they moved Susan and York to an outbuilding near the runway gates. It felt like hours they waited. Yet, it was probably only thirty minutes that they stayed. First, the General and then George showed up. The air traffic was grounded, as well as the ground traffic. This attack was upon the Capital of the United States. So, everything was being kept from chance. Tex didn't feel they were safe in DC. Susan had become a target. They needed to be where they controlled things.

"Everyone, turn off your phone and take out the battery. Except for you, George. They may not know you are with us. We'll use your phone to keep on top of things. Give it to Simon," Tex ordered.

George didn't look happy about surrendering his phone. He nodded, adding, "Don't look up any of your known contacts. Use One-eyed Pete as a contact if we need anyone." Simon nodded. It wasn't his first hide and escape.

"Since travel will not happen, we walk out of here. First, George and Roger, you purchase water and whatever else we can carry to eat and drink along the way. Simon and I will look through the go-bags and dump anything possible to make room. Get us something hot like pizza or chicken to fill our guts before we start. Everyone needs to utilize the bathrooms. Except for Susan, I'm sorry, but this shed is where you'll have to relieve yourself. You too, York." Tex said, looking none too happy in ordering her to do something she might throw a fit over.

Susan nodded. "Also, guys, buy some outlandish tourist clothing for you, York, and me. Get me some big sloppy hat to hide my face. And some sunscreen. We will be exposed to the sun and wind, maybe some windbreakers with pockets. You will need them to conceal your weapons."

"What about me? I can carry a backpack. And I can shoot," the General said. They ironed out what to buy and set the plan into action. They decided that the General couldn't go into the airport again either. George was the least known of the team. He would be depended upon to do most of the public activity. Operation Home was underway.

Impressed, George and Roger headed out to gather supplies.

Decked out in the disguises bought in the airport shops, they were an unlikely-looking bunch of guards with a secret weapon and a human battery. The General looked like a grandfather, even sporting a cane to swing about as if pointing out sights to see. George was the most normal of them at home, wearing his usual clothing of jeans and a cowboy hat. They planned to walk until they could rent a car or buy one. It was slow as they needed to appear as tourists stopping to stare at known tourist attractions. Susan mentally told Goldie to stay beside the General to draw less attention. Susan was the odd man out, black and more complicated to disguise.

They were walking past a sidewalk apartment sale in one of the residential sections when the General came up with an idea. "See that baby carriage? Let's buy it and have Miss Susan push it along. We can put some harder-to-carry items in it and cover them with a baby blanket. Then, put the hood up with a light scarf to block the sun from the sleeping baby. They have some old clothes which might be part of a Nanny outfit. What do you think?" he asked.

"Sounds good. Susan won't stick out so clearly. Few people notice a Nanny. Go get it all," Tex told them.

Soon, they looked like a family who had lost their mother and wife with a nanny for the baby. The grandfatherly figure of the General added to the illusion. Susan even held an umbrella over herself and the baby carriage to make it seem she was serious about protecting the little one from the sun's rays. Whenever they paused to look at some statue or monument, Susan would squat down and pretend to check on the baby, even faking changing a diaper or giving a bottle.

George suddenly stopped walking and looked around. Everyone was alert while trying to appear casual. "I've been here before. If I'm right, I'll have our transportation soon. Go and eat at that Coffee Shop. Order me something that will stick to the ribs. I'll be back in a jiff," George said. He took off at a brisk pace.

True to his word, George was back within a

half-hour. His meal had arrived about five minutes before he showed up. Flipping some keys in the air, he had a smile on his face. "We can store our bags in our new home. I got us a house on wheels. It is a tad used but a sweet baby," he told them, smiling and sitting down to devour his meal.

"A camper? You bought a used camper?" Tex asked, then shook his head with a grin on his face. "One of the best disguises in a tourist area. You always had a bit of down-home flair, George. It is perfect, no hotel trail."

"Exactly! I tracked a nature boy here once and encountered this great contact in the area. He refits campers for guys like us. They are fast and efficient, too," George said between bites of food. "We have a few blocks to walk to where it is parked. If they don't haul it away before we get there."

"Then we move out now. The Nanny thinks Junior needs to be in a real home. Shall we?" the General said, just like any concerned grandfather might. Or someone who was trying to take over the mission.

"Not yet," Susan said. "First, I will do a mind sweep of the area to see if anyone unpleasant lurks nearby. "Then we go buy three cans of formula for the baby at the drugstore across the way. Simon and George will walk close to a block ahead of us to reduce our numbers and take Goldie. Roger and York will follow them, and we will bring up the rear," Susan said, laying out the plan and retaking charge.

Tex kept his smile inside. Susan one, General zero, he thought. "33,896, 33,897…." He was impressed by how she reasoned that they would draw less attention in small groups. It was something he should have thought. Only, in his mind, he considered them a whole unit to protect. And his protective instinct wanted everyone with him so he could keep them safe. He watched as Susan closed her eyes and began to search through all the minds within her reach. The pallor of her skin grayed as time passed. "Enough," he whispered to her, "stop now while you can still walk."

"Ahead appears clear. Behind us are two watchers scanning the crowds. We start moving out as planned now," Susan said.

The first group, consisting of Simon and George, headed off, followed by Roger and York. The Nanny group bought the formula for the pretend baby. By the time they all reached the camper, Simon and George had checked that it was safe and readied it so they could leave as soon as everyone was inside. It was a bit crowded, and Roger expected Susan to complain. He was wrong.

Susan looked over the inside of the camper. At the rear end, it held one full-size bed. A small table with seating was between the bed and the driving compartment. George demonstrated how the seating area opened up to two sleeping areas. There were seven of them traveling. The foldouts were rather cramped things that would sorely test the men to sleep on them. Immediately, she sorted the sleeping arrangements in her mind as her mother always set up the family chores. "York and I will each take a fold-out to sleep. You may all decide between you who will sleep on the bed. I suggest at least three of you rest there and one other on the pullout. I'm assuming that one person will be driving at all times. The most rested will start us out, and you will switch out every four hours. This way, nobody will be tired, in case we should have to fight. The driving schedule I leave to you. I will remain up until we have cleared the more populated areas. I suggest you set your schedule and let some of you rest. We are a family and must look out for each other."

Chapter Nine

FATIGUE AND RELIEF

Tex wanted to take the first shift as the driver. Only he is likely to be identified by any checkpoints set up they have to navigate. George was selected. Each time they came upon a checkpoint, everyone else would hide. They were approaching one such checkpoint when Susan spoke up. "George, there is a watcher here. He is with the organization that used the bombs. I get the impression that he is Muslim. You need to speak really country when talking to him, George."

George adjusted his Stetson and assumed a cowboy's howdy grin. "Why, howdy, young fellow. Y'all sure are making a fuss today. They didn't stop me even once driving in, but this old hound doggy is starting to believe you want him to stay and whoop it up here." George grinned and managed to spit some chew into a cup he had placed on the dash.

Susan felt the disgust the man stopping him felt as he looked over the camper. "What are you doing in the area?" he asked.

"Well, doggone it, that is a private business. I'm on my way to Virginia to see my gal. And I don't think my love life is up for gossipy doggies. If you get what I mean," George drawled. "She'd bust my balls if I talked about her to someone like you."

"Get moving, you disgusting infidel," the guy almost shouted at him. George drove on with a smile, knowing he had handled the guy just right.

"Well done," Susan said behind him. "Now count, please."

"1,2,3,4,5,6,7...." George counted, realizing his thoughts had not been nice about the checkpoint man.

Tex took over driving once they were in the mountains and on the best back road route home. He tried to study every area that looked as if it could hide away Susan for a new base to keep her. They had to prioritize looking for a new hideout. He wondered if she would put up a fuss about relocating and leaving her mountain friends. Those animals meant something to her, something special.

Waking, Susan wondered where they were. She had practically passed out once they were in the clear. Using her power for a prolonged period had drained her already depleted body. York had come to her twice and given her some of his energy. He had paid for it and slept as if dead himself before she had succumbed. She looked out a window and noticed the sun dipped behind a mountain ahead. They were entering a small town, more of a trucker stop. "Food," Susan said as if to the air.

"On it," Roger said from the driver's seat.

"We've made good time. If we eat here, we can refuel our bodies and camper. Look at all the truckers parked. You know they know where they serve the best food. We should make it home by tomorrow night. Maybe."

Susan sent her mind out to the people at the truck stop. "Not here. We need to drive on. Danger lurks within."

Roger nodded, checked the fuel gauge, and drove past what looked like good food. His stomach growled in protest. There was a downside to being dedicated to the job. Meals and sleep often needed to be improvised. He thought about pulling one of the protein bars he kept on him for York out and eating it. But what if York needed it? It would have amounted to dipping your hand in the cash drawer in another type of business. And he was not a thief.

When Roger saw a sign stating the next stop was five miles ahead, he wanted to cheer. Food and a chance to walk around sounded sweet. That is when he noticed the engine was overheating. There was a scenic spot where a person could pull over and look at the mountains just beyond the mileage sign. Roger eased into it and parked. Tex and Simon appeared at his side, guns drawn. They had been wound up so long that any stop had them ready to fight. "We are overheating. At best, we need to let the engine cool down. At worst, we need to do some repairs," he told them.

It was the year's colder months, and the temperature dropped fast once the night fell. George and Roger worked on checking out the problem with the radiator overheating. Simon and Tex kept vigil over their subjects. George mumbled. "Ah-ha!" He sent Roger in to bring water for the radiator only moments later. "That is an old hose," George said once they were back on the road. "We'll need to check them all once we are safe. Fortunately, the crack was near a connection, and the hose had a bit of play in it. I could stretch it to reach after cutting off the bad section. Sorry, boss. I should have taken the time to check them all out before bringing it to you guys."

"I think the need for the flight was dire enough to excuse taking time out to examine hoses," Tex said, crawling back into his sleep space. He was instantly asleep.

Nodding, George was soon snoring away. He was a ranger, and you grabbed sleep every chance you had. Their slumber was short as it was only a few miles before they parked outside another stop set up for truckers.

They entered the truck stop in small groups of twos and threes. York, George, and the General were in one, looking like a three-generation family, Tex with Roger like a pair of college seniors on break touring the mountains for thrills. Finally, Simon looks haggard, with Susan helping him walk as if she were his nurse. That they were all positioned to see the entire room went unnoticed by tired truck drivers taking a break or eating before catching a few hours' sleep. Susan could not help but think that this might be her form of life shortly, traveling about, trying to stay out of the notice of inquiring eyes and protecting York.

Tex had thought they would be home before now. Still, he didn't make a fuss when George insisted they stop and get new hoses and belts for the camper. They found a camping spot and stretched their legs while George and Simon ensured the van wouldn't overheat or break a belt. The SS agent understood that George felt responsible for the earlier instance and wanted to correct his mistake. They walked through the trees out of earshot of the other campers. Tex brought up the subject of cash with Roger and General Richards. "We each need to withdraw our money from the banks where it is. If we have to go on the run, we won't be using Credit Cards or writing checks. From now on, no cell phones, nothing electronic with a locating device attached. General, you may be able to go home, but be prepared to run." He gave each of the men his gaze of intense no crap.

"Gentlemen, no guns, and look down at the ground. Someone not human has sensed me and has come to visit. I met him once upon my mountain. York, clear your mind of threat; look at the ground also," Susan instructed everyone.

They could barely hear a soft rumble. As much as Tex wanted to look up, he didn't. He had to trust Susan, just like she had to trust him. He relaxed as he did for the doe and fox at home. As, in front of him, Susan knelt, opening her arms. The rumble quieted, and a shadow crossed the patch of sunlight where Susan knelt. Cougar! Tex inched his head up just enough to see more of Susan. She had her arms around a cougar, rubbing its head against her. A twig snapped behind him, and the cougar bounded off.

"Sorry," the General whispered when Tex glared at him.

Susan wiped tears from her eyes as she stood up. "I thought he was dead. I'm so happy he is still alive.

"He is beautiful," Tex whispered.

"Yes, he is. I only hope he lives a full life. Wildlife is so threatened by man these days." Susan turned around to return to the camper.

"What is his name?" York asked.

"He doesn't have one yet. He never stays for long when other people are around. He is like a trace of a breeze, touching only when in the area. Let's think upon it for a while, okay?" Susan said. York nodded, already thinking about what to name the elusive cougar.

They were almost back to the camper when Susan raised her hand. She stood very still with her eyes closed as if concentrating. As did her companions, the General knew to keep quiet when Susan was in this listening mode—minutes passed, with Susan still in that nearly frozen pose before she began to speak. "I can't move from this spot, or I'll lose her. Roger, you return to the camper and bring flashlights, a blanket, food, and water. Go now in case I have to move," Susan said. "Everyone be quiet. I have to be able to hear her mind. She is injured, and at a distance, she is crawling along. One leg is badly hurt. A teenager, I think, who was out on a nature hike. She is worried about a friend, a boy. Stand still. I have to move a little. She is fading."

Walking in a small circle, Susan sought to gauge the direction she needed to move in to find the injured hiker. She stopped and stood still for a moment, then moved a little to the left, then back to the right. She stayed to the right, taking several steps forward. "This way. Set a marker here. We will need a litter, more blankets, and some ties. The first aid kit. I'm going to call for some help, so stay quiet."

She hadn't done it for many years, not since she had been home on the farm, but this girl needed help and needed it now. "My friends, I need to locate this mind. Please help me find her. Help her if she lets you. If not, please keep watch over her. She has a friend who I can't hear. If possible, locate him for me," the broadcast sent; Susan seemed to wilt for a moment but then stood up, straightening her back. Tex was there handing her a protein bar to chew. Around them, the dark forest came alive. Leaves rustle with the rushing off of different animals. Overhead, the night birds took flight. Every creature and avian in the area responded to her call. They would let her know when they found the girl. In the meantime, she would follow the only lead she had, the girl's thoughts.

When Roger returned, he brought more supplies, including Simon and George, than Susan had first requested. They followed Susan as she tracked a mind whose thoughts were growing weaker and confused. The girl was clearly on the verge of passing out. "I'm going to lose her when she faints. She is so near to unconscious now that I'm receiving something like static," Susan told the others.

She stopped walking and closed her eyes, concentrating. "V is for Vince…. That was her last thought. Spread out, we will keep walking in this direction for now. Maybe we won't pass her up."

The team moved slowly forward. Step by step, they looked for any hint of a girl's body. Like a ghost drifting towards them in the still of the night, a white owl came gliding on silent wings to land on a branch near Susan. "Thank you," Susan said out loud. "She is just to the right of us. Beyond her is a team of forest rangers searching for her. They are too far to the left to see her. One of us needs to pretend to find her."

Tex took over immediately, "George, take the backpack. You are out for a hike and stumble upon her. Call out for help. Do you think they will hear him?" he asked Susan.

"Yes, call loudly. We will fall back towards where the camper is and wait for you. Let the rangers take over and join us," Susan directed. Turning, she moved away from the girl's direction.

Back at the camper, they sorted out the bits of food they had left between them, setting some aside for George. After eating, some lay down and slept while the others kept watch. With the camper repaired, they needed George to return to them before moving on. Roger's stomach rumbled, reminding them all that it was only a few miles up the road to a place to eat a hot meal. Susan sat quietly with York leaning against her as she sent "Thank you" out to all the creatures and avian beings who had helped to find the girl. She also had good news. They found Vince.

"Why are you doggies waiting around? I have a powerful appetite. Whose turn is it to drive?" George bellowed at them all as he climbed up into the camper. "Let's get our sorry butts home."

Roger burped. His stomach was happy once more. He let the others figure out the driving schedule and went fast to sleep in the camper. Looking down at Roger's sleeping form, George shook his head. The kid was like a Great Dane puppy, hungry and unaware of anything beyond his needs. He lay down on the far side of the bed, setting his mental alarm clock to go off in four hours. He'd learned long ago to sleep in short spats on the job. It was true that George wasn't tracking down a dangerous criminal as he used to, but in a way, this job was the most important one he ever had. He was in it for the long haul, so rest he would, then drive until relieved.

Every mile that passed, Tex became tenser. What if the creeps had raided her home? They'd need to park somewhere safe and scout things out before exposing Susan and York to danger. The phone and communication silence was only common sense. No phone line was completely secure. And what the heck were they going to do about the General? If they kept General Richards, he'd be shooting the prick. Then, there was an explanation of why General Richards was still at Susan's place. That brought up the fact that her home was now compromised. His mind was filled with all the possibilities that could now befall his subject. Every one of them stank. He drove at the best speed to get them home, which seemed like home to him. In the short time he had been Susan's security, he felt more at home than in any place he had been other than his own home. He didn't try to pick apart a reason for that feeling. He just accepted it.

The sun was long awake when Simon took a turn in the driver's seat. They were nearing home. The air around him seemed to be changing to the crisper, cleaner air of home. He hated the idea of giving up the spot. Miss Susan would be upset. Hell, he would be upset. They had clean, fresh air and delicious meals, and the company was not bad either. Sure, it could be boring patrolling around and around at night. But he'd take boring here over any other place he was assigned.

It started to rain with the wind gusting, making the camper sway from side to side slightly. Everyone was up and alert, aware it was time to decide the next move. York had been very quiet, feeling he had nothing to offer these men trying to get him home. Now, he sat wide awake and anxious to be home and see the animals in the woods. He bounced a little in his seat excitedly when he saw the big rock, which meant they were very close to the road up the mountain. The camper pulled over and went behind the big rock. York looked around at the others. He knew that look on their faces. They were going to tell him to sit tight or hide.

Susan raised her hand, putting a stop to the weapons check the guys were in the middle of performing. George posed with his hand on the camper's door, about to exit. It was clear he and Tex were going up the mountain on foot. "I can feel nobody between here and halfway up the mountain. I need to move closer. You will take me with you. York, you will stay here with Simon and Roger. You too, General. Hand me several protein bars and two drinks, and leave at least one drink for York and the rest of the bars. Roger, you will be in charge of keeping York's sugar up. Let's go," she told them.

"No," Tex said in a flat, this is not going to happen voice. "You need to be safe." He looked at her with something in his eyes she hadn't seen before. It looked like fear.

Susan tried to see his thoughts. Usually, she wouldn't think to invade one of her SS agent's minds. That look, though, upset her. He was having none of it, practically screaming his numbers out as he waited for her to respond to his blunt No. She nodded and sat back down. She watched his shoulders relax a little. It went against her very nature to stay out of the action. But, she now saw that Tex could defend himself better if he did not have to worry about her safety. She, however, would track their every move as best she could without access to their minds.

Once Tex and George exited the camper, Susan went to York. "Eat a protein bar now, and keep another on hand. I may need a battery," she said softly for his ears only before going to sit on the floor by Goldie.

"I know you have a plan, so clue me in," George whispered as he and Tex went up the mountain, dodging boulders and thick underbrush patches.

"We take the sniper's route. I'm thinking to check on them and get high enough to kill anyone who isn't supposed to be at the house," Tex said.

George nodded. "Just like old times."

George went over several feet so they didn't

present a group target if they were seen. The two men began making their way from tree to tree, going around about wide of the area where the house sat. Tex didn't have his ears on; they were silent, with no communication except through hand signals. The SS agent led his companion on a weaving path, sticking to the thicker vegetation. Tex would stop and use the scope of his weapon to scan the area ahead before continuing. Stop. Scan, then go. There were none of the forest sounds going on around them. It was like the animals and birds knew they were creeping through the forest and had all hid away.

At last, they made it to a carefully concealed path leading to where the snipers kept vigil over Susan's house. Slowly, Tex led the way to where he knew his snipers should be camouflaged. He scanned the area, looking for any sign of bodies, but nothing. Returning to the edge of the concealing brush they had been hopscotching to, Tex heard a harsh voice speaking low and dangerous to him. "If you are a damn fool, then take another step. If not, tell me what you are doing up here in a restricted area."

Tex drew a relieved breath as he knew that voice from talking to the man who owned it over his earbud. "It is good to hear a friendly voice. I was beginning to think we'd find your bodies up here. Has there been any activity down below while we've been gone?" he asked.

"No, sir. The phone has rung a time or two today. I take it things didn't go well in DC?" the voice asked.

"It went sour the moment we landed. We've

made our escape, so all is good. I'm glad you guys are all right. We are going down to check the place to be safe before bringing Miss Whiting the rest of the way home. We'll be in a camper, so don't shoot us when we return. Good hunting," Tex said. He and George took a more direct route down to the house.

Nothing had been disturbed at or around the house. George was left on guard while Tex hot-footed it back to get his gal and bring her safely home.

It was with a sense of relief that Susan walked into her home. Susan unpacked and repacked her go-bag. She then gathered the dirty clothing from each of the guys and York. The General didn't have a go-bag, so they had Simon take him into town to buy some clothing. In the meantime, everyone took a shower and put on fresh clothes. Glad to feel refreshed after the long, nerve-wracking journey home. Susan cooked a hearty meal and set the table when everyone finished their chores.

The house phone rang as they ate a steaming chicken and dumplings meal. Everyone turned and stared at the phone like a rattlesnake vibrating its tail. Tex got up to head off any thoughts Susan might have about answering herself. "Talk to me," he said flatly, then listened momentarily. With a strange look, he offered the phone to Susan.

"What? When?" Susan asked the person calling. "We'll be there as soon as we make arrangements." Susan hung up the phone and sat back down at the table. She ate a few bites before becoming aware that everyone was watching her.

She had forgotten that they couldn't read minds. Smiling, Susan explained what was going on. "We are going to my sister's place. She and Ritter are getting married."

Everyone started talking at once. Some were planning the trip. The rest grinned like fools at the idea one of theirs had got the girl. George looked a little confused. "Who is this Ritter guy? We need to vet him?" he asked with a frown of concern on his face.

Tex laughed, actually laughed, and that seemed to be more startling than the news that Middy was marrying Ritter. "He'll get a kick out of you wanting to vet him. From what I understand, Ritter is the best the Secret Service has in the way of agents. I think he was the one they wanted to take care of Miss Susan. Only, well, her sister is hard to guard. So the boss sent him there instead. It seems he has lasted longer than any other agent on her detail."

The General spoke up for the first time, "I heard a rumor that he refused to recall after that near-death thing. Pretty much just said 'NO' and hung up."

"He is a battery," York said with admiration. "Only special people can become batteries. He helped us heal Middy."

Everyone except George became solemn after that reminder. He didn't know what had happened. Tex stood up from the table. "We need to pack energy supplies just in case. Bring your vests, too, or have they captured the shooter?" He glanced at Susan for an answer.

"Middy got him. The fool kidnapped Middy from her bedroom. He didn't know what he had lashed onto. She managed to hold him even though she was battered and tied up like she was in the middle of one of her storms. I understand the storm brought the building down on her, but she held him. She didn't have a battery or any boosts. So she ran out of energy and came close to dying again. But, she held the creep," Susan told them.

Nodding, Tex continued, "Vest and tuxes. General Richards, you need to return to D C. before they decide you have been abducted or try to use that as an excuse to get to Miss Susan."

"Do we have to go now? Can't we spend the night here? I want to see Chatterbox and the others. Please?" York asked.

Smiling at York, Susan answered before Tex could, "We will spend a couple of days here, then go. I think we all need some downtime. Besides, I think we owe our mountain protectors some downtime." She looked up at her men, noting how wary they had suddenly appeared. "Nothing bad. Today and tonight, you are free to do what you want. Tomorrow morning, the day crew will split the day snipers' shift between them and the night crew, and the same will happen for our night snipers. We can't have all the fun," she said, almost daring anyone to disagree. "Now, Tex, your earbud thing so I can tell them the plan." Susan held out her hand.

They all stepped in the open so the snipers could see them, and Susan explained that they would have tomorrow off. A whoop of joy echoed all the way down the mountain. Tex looked over at Susan

with a tiny smile and nodded at her. He told himself
he should have thought of relieving the guys up top.
And he was glad Susan had thought of it. He felt
she must have heard their thoughts and figured they
needed a break. Soon, Susan and the rest would be
leaving again while the snipers would be stuck up on
the mountain watching over an empty house. They
had to be bored half to death.

The team broke up with the night crew, who
went to sleep and readied whatever they needed for
the wedding. Tex and Roger shadowed their subjects
through the woods as the pair sought out their
woodland friends.

Grabbing his stomach in laughter, Tex watched
the usually well-behaved dog, Goldie. She tucked
her tail and took off running in mad circles around
the doe when she saw her. The two of them bounced
through the forest, leaping over logs and doing their
happy dance of meeting up after being apart. The
doe came back panting to rub her head on Susan,
then offered to let Tex and Roger pet her. It was clear
the doe was happy to see everyone. Sly, the fox, was
a bit more reserved, but there was a moment when
the fox looked as if he was accepting of everyone.
Chatterbox took his time showing up and scowled
at everyone as if to say he would not tolerate them
being gone from his life for such a length of time
again. Eagle Eye didn't show up, and Susan worried
about him.

Some didn't end their downtime soon enough,
as they were itching for action after running from
D.C. to protect their subject. Running didn't feel
right. Now, they had to go and play nice and be silent

guardians at a wedding.

The wedding was simple but so beautiful that tears crept into the corners of Susan's eyes. Thoughts around her were those of joy and wonder. Her big sister was now a married woman. She smiled when Middy's fellow officers stopped her from leaving to give her a toast just from them. They knew her well enough to know she wouldn't stick around for the reception.

The look of surprise on Eric's face when the garter landed on his shoulder was so worth knowing Middy had cheated and directed it there with her wind. Her sister was quite the joker of the family. But, Susan supposed she would have had to have a good sense of humor to put up with all she had endured while in training. Police officers tended to gang up on people they didn't think belonged to the force. And there had been enough of that negative feeling over Middy joining that tough bunch of officers.

Susan was startled when the bridal bouquet came flying in her direction. "Oh, no, you didn't," Susan told Middy. A hand reached out and snatched the bouquet out of the air. Tex handed it to Susan with a goofy look on his face, his mind so filled with numbers that he nearly drowned out the thoughts around Susan. She had been horrified when the bouquet headed towards her. Here, he had just made sure she received it. She felt like hitting him over the head with it, but she smiled and laughed with everyone else.

Susan already knew she wasn't marriage

material. Her life consisted of finding people who lied and did the most terrible things to one another. She'd never be able to trust a man enough to marry him. Look at the guys she trusted her life to; they were all counting as if their lives depended upon it, and it may well be so, for each of them held some deep, dark secret that they didn't want anyone else to know. Most of them she knew already. She would see these terrible secrets no matter how hard she tried to block them out of her mind. She didn't want to see Tex's secrets. For just a little while, she wished to think he had led a life of honor. She knew it was a stupid wish, but couldn't she just like one person without being blindsided by their sins?

George was the first of the guys to tease Tex about catching the bouquet. "So, does this mean you are the next woman to get married?" he asked, straight-faced. Susan could hear all the jokes he was full of to say to Tex. She knew the pair went back to times before the SS for Tex. And that they were close friends.

"What? No, I just kept Miss Susan from being smacked in the face by the flowers. It doesn't work on men," Tex said, going along with his friend's teasing.

"Nope, it is the same. The person who catches the bouquet thrown by a new bride is doomed to be the next person to marry. It is usually to the person who caught the garter. You'd make a cute couple, the skinny guy and you, the tough man," George said, on a roll now.

"Hmm…" Tex looked at Eric. "I think you are a bit batty today. You just pointed out Miss Susan's brother."

The ranger's face turned a sickly shade of red as he darted a look at Eric and then back at Susan. How could he have forgotten the family dynamics? They were all adopted. "No offense intended, Ma'am. I was only teasing old iron breeches here," he said, trying to cover his blooper.

"Iron breeches? I think there is a story behind that name," Susan said with a chuckle. Now, Tex was turning red in the face. Tex frowned and looked down at the floor, and Susan was instantly sorry she had joined in the teasing. "Of course," continued Susan, trying to ease the tension in Tex, "they all think similar things about me. I know it is because I seldom will except the men they pick out to escort me to all those boring dinners and dances." She gave an exaggerated sigh. "Men just hate to be rejected, even when they think they'll get lucky when they take me out."

She gave a little shiver as some of the perverted thoughts she had heard over the years came up and hit her. Just thinking about them made her skin crawl. She gathered herself, lifting her chin a fraction. "My brother, Eric, I can trust," she said, smiling over to where Eric was being teased. She looked back at Tex, "And you."

She had blindsided him, Tex thought. Here, he felt so embarrassed that George was revealing his non-love life. Then, she said she trusted him after telling them she couldn't trust men to escort her in public. That placed a tremendous burden upon his shoulders. He'd have to live up to that trust now. He knew he'd fail because he did think about her as a woman. Sometimes, he even felt possessive, as if he had the right of a claim on her, which he didn't. He couldn't trust anyone else to protect her, not the way he would and did. That was the danger. He had been stupid enough to let himself care. Now, well, he was caught and helpless in his living hell. And she goes off and says she trusts him.

Filled to the brim with food and all the cobbler he could eat, York lay on the floor, petting Goldie. Sherlock came over with his long, wet tongue and licked York's face. He laughed. "You'll get my tux slobbery," York protested, then hugged the dog's neck. "You are sort of my doggy uncle," he told the dog. "So, I will be back to see you sometime." Sherlock licked him again and laid down for a tummy rub. This party was a dream come true, filled with peach cobbler and dogs all around you. York thought about the animals on their mountain and knew they had a special bond with his Mom. There, he dared to think of her as his mother. Now, if only they had someone to be the father, he'd have a real family.

Chapter Ten

WHEN A DEER COMES KNOCKING

Once home again, they settled back into the daily routine. It was a relief to Susan's frayed nerves. She relaxed, only worrying a little about the mental and physical health of the men around her. The General was back at the Capital. He blamed the bombing for not completing his mission. Or bringing Susan to D.C. York was excelling at his lessons over the Internet, and the team was back to two on days and two at night, meeting up at mealtime in Susan's house. Upon the mountain, the snipers were often relieved to visit their homes. Susan also started sending hot meals to the snipers. They were all leading the good life once more. All seemed right in the world.

Fourteen days passed before the outside world again intruded upon their little haven. Over the weekend, Susan had a BBQ and games day for everyone. The event began around noon. When Susan had the night crews of snipers and SS agents come to eat and horse around at whatever they wanted to do, tag football, volleyball, or even card games. Filled with good food and relaxation, they went on duty a little early to give the day crews a chance to eat and play whatever games they wanted. York and Susan played hosts, grilling and fetching platters of ribs, chicken, potato salad, baked beans, and cornbread. It was a fantastic day for all, leaving the men with full bellies and contented smiles.

Monday, armed guards came for Tex. He was summoned to Washington to answer charges of going rogue and endangering his subject. Anger blasted Susan from all sides. Men forgot to count, their thoughts outraged at the idea of Tex being taken off in handcuffs. Everyone on the team was ready to go with Tex and speak on his behalf. Only Tex told them all to stand down. His counting broke only once, which was a clear message to Susan. "I won't let them keep me from watching over you. Don't worry."

They cuffed him! He spent his whole life serving his country in one form or another. Mature looking at age fifteen, he had managed to join the Marines. More than excelling in marksmanship, he served his country well. However, he became disillusioned and returned to Texas looking for another helping method. The Texas Rangers seemed a good fit. They teamed him with a down-to-earth George, a practical joker when off duty, and a hard taskmaster when on duty. Their tracking and apprehending record was untouchable. Tex took every job seriously. A girl finally brought him to his knees and caused him to leave Texas. She seemed perfect for him but was only out for the thrill of saying she dated a Texas Ranger. After that, he refused to date again and resigned rather than pull George down with his irritable temper.

Washington contacted him, offering him an opening in the Secret Service. He had thought this was his calling to be the knight who watched over these people of power. Then they sent him to Susan, and his life took on a new meaning. This job was his it. He knew it after the first trip to D C. She needed him.

All these thoughts ran through his mind while he sat, cuffed, waiting outside an office. Hopefully, he will be told what he did to merit this summons. And why were there guards standing over him as if he was a security risk? He stood when the door to the office opened. His mind was taking in everything around him, like, who was this man? He'd never seen him before and didn't believe he had any authority over the SS. He decided to see how things would play out before attacking.

"Come in and take a seat," the man at the door ordered. Tex walked past the man at the door without paying attention to the guards. He neglected to give the man room, making the man step back to let Tex enter the office. It wasn't something he would usually do, but he was a tad on the pissed-off side. And his manners were balancing between kill and let live. So far, the no-killing was winning. Barely. This guy had yet to introduce himself.

"You know why you are here. Have you

anything to say regarding the charges?" the man asked, as if Tex had been read his rights and told what they charged him with having done.

"I have not been told any charges. I've been wondering why I'm here instead of protecting my subject. Please, enlighten me," Tex said, keeping his tone civil.

"The sarcasm won't help your case. You were told of the charges upon your arrest. You have endangered your subject and have become a rogue agent. In other words, you are now considered a traitor to your country."

Tex watched as those words came out of this stranger's mouth. It was unreal, like some evil joke. This guy couldn't be serious. "Layout the supposed reasons for these so-called charges for me one by one," he said, his voice now chillingly soft.

"Really? You want to hash this all out?"

"Yes," he answered, flatly holding his ground.

The man laughed loudly. "Alright, then. On Miss Whiting's first assignment, after you took over protecting her. Did you or did you not refuse to let her go?"

"No, I told the man who had just said he knew the assignment would hurt her that he wasn't taking her anywhere if she was in danger. Miss Whiting explained the circumstances, and I was then willing to proceed. My job is to keep her from harm. Therefore, being told she would be hurt, I reacted as any agent should," Tex responded.

"On numerous occasions, you threaten General Richards even to the point of having him fired upon. Do you deny this?" the prick asked.

"Of course not. General Richards knows that nobody sees Miss Whiting without first making an appointment. On each occasion you mention, he showed up unannounced without an appointment. I only prevented him from seeing Miss Whiting because he did not follow protocol. Being sloppy and letting anyone turn up whenever they want can get a subject killed. Even you could be a threat. My job is to protect my subject, period. It is not to wipe some General's boots when he is too lazy to call ahead and make an appointment," Tex said.

"And shooting the tires out on the messenger's car?" countered the prick.

"Most certainly. The man was an unknown, with, as far as I could tell, some made-up excuse for getting to Miss Whiting. He didn't have an appointment. He had nothing that even resembled authorization to access Miss Whiting. And to top it all off, he said, Miss Whiting needed to escort some strange man whom I had not vetted. If that isn't suspicious enough, he claimed to represent the General. Miss Whiting herself told him no. We were kind enough to direct him to a station where he could have his tires repaired," Tex said as if saying even a moron could figure that one out.

It continued like that for hours, with Tex repeatedly stating the reasons for his actions. He had reached the point where he was ready to give this prick a flat-nose job when he was released.

On the mountain, Susan prepared dinner for everyone. She believed Tex would be back in time to eat. Roger paced back and forth outside the house, clearly agitated over Tex being hauled away. It had looked like an arrest. It felt like one. Susan watched Roger as he tried to look everywhere at once. He was defeating himself by being so tense.

York stopped chopping vegetables for the salad to watch Roger. York had been quiet for most of the day. He didn't ask about it or why they came and took Tex. He was afraid to ask. It felt as if his family had been ripped apart—the father he hadn't had they took from him. York realized at that moment that he did think of Tex as the father of this family. Unofficially, he now had a father and a mother. What did that make Simon, Roger, and George? Uncles? They were like uncles or cousins. York knew it was foolish to daydream that Tex would become his adoptive father, but somehow, that belief was in his head.

George and Simon showed up just as Susan took the BBQ ribs out of the oven. George rushed to take the platter from Susan. He looked older than he had that morning. Lines creased his forehead, and his eyes held a deep worry. He was thinking of going after Tex. He knew many places a wanted man could hide and live in peace. That boy would never have done the things they were accusing him of doing. As he placed the ribs on the table, he had automatically set it down where Tex would have sat had he been there. Hot baked sweet potatoes were on the table already, Tex's favorite treat besides berry cobbler. That, he spied cooling on a rack. The little gal had also been thinking of Tex. George knew his boy had feelings for the lady. That could be a problem. The boy didn't do relationships.

They ate in silence, each lost in their thoughts and the worry about their missing companion. Simon took the prepared plates up to the snipers as their shift was about to change, and each set would have a chance to eat as they swapped out. "Any word?" was the first question asked as he stepped up to the hidden spots where the sniper nests were. Simon shook his head. "Damn shame, he is a good one. We've had more fun since he arrived than in all the previous years," one of the guys said. Their job was lying up there for hours, watching the people below going on walks or playing games.

"I saw a look in George's eyes that says he won't wait beyond tonight for them to release him. He is almost as scary as Tex," Simon said. I want to join him in the venture, but Tex would kill me if I left Miss Susan."

"I believe he would at that. I've seen him through my scope, watching Miss Whiting. She could do worse…. Forget I said that. It isn't any of my business."

It was getting dark as Simon made his way back down to the house. He felt that restless feeling he got when things were about to go sour. Taking out his weapon, Simon checked it to be sure it was ready. "Come home, boss, we need you," he thought to the silent darkness around him.

George had his gun pointed at Simon's head when the SS agent exited the woods to join him. "Sorry," he said, "I've got a tumbleweed feeling in my guts tonight."

"Me too," Simon said, checking his weapon once more. "Let's keep alert."

Susan and York said goodnight and entered the bunker to find their beds. Susan couldn't sleep because she was worrying about Tex. She decided to watch the monitors in case Tex showed up to talk to the guys. Despite her heavy heart, around midnight, she dozed off, resting her head on her arms, listening to the occasional bits of conversation that passed between Simon and George.

Two popping sounds woke Susan. She sat up straight and stared at the monitors. It was so dark she could barely make out Simon taking a stance in front of the bunker while George took off for the path up to the sniper's nest.

The shots had sounded from up top and didn't seem aimed at them. But Simon and George reacted in tandem as if they had rehearsed their moves many times. Simon stood fast, guarding Susan and York while George ran to check on the snipers.

George ran silently up the mountain, not daring to take the path. He reached the first nest and felt for a pulse, already knowing the man was dead. They hadn't seen it coming. Nobody had. The preps had crept up behind the snipers and took them both out before they could turn around. When he heard shooting from below, he grabbed the nearest long gun and turned around to scramble down the mountain as fast as he could.

The bullet hit Simon in the shoulder, knocking him against the bunker. His head bashed against the bunker, and his world went dark. He didn't even know he had managed to fire his gun off as he fell.

Inside the bunker, Susan saw Simon go down.

He was right there against the bunker. All she had to do was open the door and pull him inside. She knew it was against the rules. Simon would be the first to tell her she was doing wrong. But all she could think of was that Simon needed her, and she wasn't going to let him die.

Knowing her hands would be busy dragging Simon, Susan set the door to lock automatically when closed. Cracking the door open, she grabbed Simon under his arms. He was heavy. To get him moving, Susan had to jerk relentlessly on him. It made her cringe inside at the possible damage she might be doing to him.

A dark shadow rushed out of the night, slamming into her and knocking her hold off Simon. She bumped into the door, sending it to slam shut. Susan fought. She clawed at the man who was dragging her away from the house. Susan tried to kick his legs out from under him. She heard chattering nearby and, at the same time, saw George appear out of the trees with his gun drawn and aimed at the man who had her. The man pulled her up in front of him, aiming for George.

The creep was using Miss Susan as a shield. George weighed the wisdom of firing anyway. It was in the dark of night, with the person he was here to protect likely to be hit, too. He hesitated just a fraction too long. A shot rang out, as well as a scream, and George's leg folded under him.

Susan heard Chatterbox behind the man kidnapping her. "RUN!" she sent to the raccoon. She tried to free her arms to knock the gun hand of the kidnapper. Susan needed to dislodge the gun before he could shoot George.

She told him to run, but Chatterbox tried to save the woman. He dashed up and bit the evil man in the leg, ripping a chunk of flesh from the muscle where he had clamped his teeth. At the same time, the gun went off, startling Chatterbox enough that he jerked back. Scowling loudly, he went for the lousy man again. This time, when the gun went off, Chatterbox ended up still on the ground.

Susan was horrified at seeing Chatterbox lying so lifeless. She pulled her thoughts together and sent out a silent command to all in the area. "Run! Hide!" That moment was her last conscious thought as she was struck on the head and thrown over the kidnapper's shoulder.

Rolling onto his belly, George aimed the long gun with the night scope on it at the receding figure of the enemy carrying his subject off. To avoid even the slightest chance of hitting Susan, George aimed for the leg opposite where Miss Susan dangled over the man's shoulder. He heard a grunt of pain, but the kidnapper didn't stop. The kidnapper was limping, giving George some hope of catching him. He made his way to Simon and quickly packed the wound. George staunched the bleeding as much as he could while in a rush.

Snatching the long gun up, he used it as a walking stick until he was able to brace himself on the trees to search out traces of where the kidnapper went. Not too far into the woods, he found where the man had stopped and packed his leg wound. After that, the guy began to show some skill, making trailing him require George's tracker expertise. George found a medium-sized branch, which he stuck under his arm to lean upon instead of the gun. He thought he made better time and should be gaining on a man carrying extra weight and wounded.

At a small trickling stream, the trail stopped. George got down on his knees and examined the tracks. Not as deep as before. He spun around and backtracked. The fellow had put Susan down long enough to lay a false trail. Then he returned to pick her up and take off in a different direction. George smirked a wily one.

The wound in George's leg would not stop bleeding. He had stopped long enough to adjust the makeshift wrap over the seeping wound twice. He was losing more blood than was good for him. He wouldn't give up, though; nothing had ever stopped him from eventually getting his man. And this time, the stakes were too high to let a little blood loss stop him.

A noise sounded up ahead through the trees. It sounded like the trunk of a car slamming shut. George began to run as fast as he could, ignoring the tree limbs smacking him and the brush attempting to trip him. A car started up, and the headlights came on. George brought the long gun up and aimed. Anywhere but the trunk, he told himself. George aimed for the driver's side window, not hesitating this time, letting loose two rapid shots. Bringing the scope sighting down, he fired at the tires as the car sped away.

George watched until the car was out of

sight, memorizing as much detail as possible before heading toward the house.

Tex had been in bed for an hour and had just managed to sink into a decent sleep when some fool came banging on the door of the little house he and Simon shared. Automatically, his hand slipped under his pillow and pulled out his backup gun as he staggered up, bleary-eyed and annoyed. The noise was a persistent hard whack, whack, whack. Tex yanked the door open. A deer's hind leg came within an inch of hitting him. "What the hell!" he exclaimed.

A deer and a fox were on the porch. The deer butted him in the chest and turned to leap off the porch. At the same time, the fox yipped at him and grabbed the air in front of Tex. As if to clamp down on him but not willing to put his mouth on Tex.

Susan! That thought had Tex shoving his feet into boots and grabbing his cell phone. Damn the run-silence order he had given. He slipped the phone into the pocket of the tee-shirt he wore to sleep in and took off after the deer in his boots, and shorts, carrying his gun. His gal needed him. It was the only reason a deer would come knocking at his door. He detoured to the car, but the doe placed herself in front of it, making a clear statement. He needed to be on foot.

"Okay, lead on," he said gently to her. She immediately entered the woods with the fox shadowing him to make sure he went after her. They were taking him away from the house. His whole being screamed at him to go to the house. Only, for some reason, he trusted these woodland creatures to take him where he needed to be. They loved Susan. Tex was sure of that. They were just as concerned as he was about her safety.

The doe paused briefly, waiting for him to catch up. He saw the disturbance of the forest floor before seeing the footprints. Two men, one very heavy, one lighter, passed this way—one of the sets of footprints returned. There were traces of blood. One or both were wounded. Tex's grip on his gun tightened. The doe, Dewy, and Sly, the fox, had started moving again, following the returning pair of footprints. They didn't appear scared; they just had an urgent air. He trotted after them, and the doe sped up, outdistancing him.

The doe stopped and laid down next to a mound of leaves. Tex approached with his heart in his throat, thinking that this was Susan hurt, maybe dying. The person under the leaves gave a manly moan, and a man rolled out from under the leaves, hiding him. George.

George woke beneath a blanket of leaves. He groaned, realizing he must have fainted from blood loss. Pushing up, he tried to get back on his feet and fell flat on his face. Someone put a hand on him, making him frantically reach for his pistol. A strong hand stayed him.

"You shoot me, and we'll both be useless out here in the forest. Let me get you up, partner," Tex soothed. Doubts filled Tex's mind. If George was out here, where would Susan be? Suppressing his raging need to leave George and run to the house instead,

Tex helped George to sit up.

"Simon, he is down at the house. I chased after Miss Susan. Shot the creep carrying her off in the leg. I was afraid to do a body or headshot for fear of hitting her. I tracked him to a road and heard him put her in the trunk before I got there. Shot at him through the passenger-side window, then at the tires. Damn it! He got away." George gave his report in short sentences, not trying to elaborate. There was no need. He tried again to pull himself to his feet using Tex's arm. Once up, he swayed and would have gone down if Tex hadn't supported him. "Snipers dead," he added as if he knew Tex was wondering why they hadn't helped George and Simon.

"York?" Tex asked, fearing what George would say.

"Locked in the bunker. Whoever it was killed up top first, and Simon stayed to guard the bunker. I went up the mountain and found both of our guys dead. I grabbed a long gun to shoot the bastards. I heard the shot that took out Simon and rushed down to protect Miss Susan and York. He was using her as a shield. She must have left the bunker to help Simon. Before I got a clear shot, he popped me in the leg. The damn leg folded on me. He snatched her up. She was fighting like a demon till he hit her. I rolled over, then leg-shot him. He didn't even pause. I never saw but the one guy. There had to have been more." George stopped talking and nearly pulled Tex to the ground as he slumped, passing out again.

Slinging George's long form over his shoulder, Tex quick-walk towards where the trampled trail of desperate men led to the house. The doe streaked ahead of him. Like a faithful dog, Sly stayed with Tex, running beside him. Tex barely noticed Sly, even though he appreciated the fox staying with him. He had to get George to a hospital and see if Simon was still alive. And call Roger. He stopped long enough to work the cell phone out of his shirt pocket. There was no sense in running silent now that the creep had Susan.

"Hug ma," Roger mumbled when he answered the phone.

"Get your ass to the house, but first call for the medics to come double-quick. Simon and George or both down," Tex growled and hung up.

He began to double-time it, hoping he wasn't doing more damage to George as the man bounced against his back. The chill of sweat was on his skin when Tex broke free of the forest. He stumbled to a stop, seeing the doe lying close to a small, still form. Fortunately, Roger arrived in a cloud of dust, jumping out of the car with his gun drawn at that moment. Tex handed him George and ran over to check on Simon.

Simon was pale but breathing. He didn't appear any worse off than George was at the moment. There was a third casualty, and to that small still form, Tex next went. Kneeling by the coon. Who had a bit of the flesh clutched in his teeth. He thought Chatterbox was dead until he saw the raccoon's chest give a shuttering breath. The doe, Dewy, had been keeping him warm while Sly licked the coon as if trying to wake him up. They knew Tex realized. They had witnessed the whole thing. And from the look of things, Chatterbox had tried to be a hero.

"Roger, I need an evidence bag of some sort. Go into the kitchen and bring some baggies," Tex called. There was a bloody bullet groove across Chatterbox's head. Tex had the veterinarian they took Goldie to on speed dial. He punched that number, barely waiting for the doctor to mumble "Hello" before demanding he come out to the house right away.

"We've some trouble here. It means life or death for your patient. Get here as fast as you can," he ordered. In the distance, he heard the first rescue vehicle approaching them.

The bunker door was shut and locked. Tex debated the wisdom of having York unlock the door. He didn't want York to see all this bloodshed. On the other hand, Chatterbox needed a boost of the life-giving force. York loved that noisy raccoon and needed to know what was happening. Tex looked up into the security camera and gave the open signal, hoping, yet dreading, that York would be up and see him.

Roger ran up to Tex and handed him the baggies he had found and a serving tong. Tex had him hold a plastic baggie under Chatterbox's mouth as he used the tong to push the bits of flesh clutched in Chatterbox's teeth into the bag. There was also a bit of cloth, probably from the pant leg of whoever Chatterbox had attacked. This was placed in a separate bag.

A child-sized body slammed into Tex's back as York threw his arms around Tex's neck. Tex held the child to him and stood up, feeling doubts about using him on Chatterbox. York spoke. It wasn't the voice of an innocent child, but more a person used to disasters being part of their life. "What can I do to help?"

Tex knelt back down next to Chatterbox. Setting York on his feet, he nodded down at the coon. "He needs a little boost to keep going until the Vet arrives. Don't do too much. George and Simon are both down. But Chatterbox seems to need you first, okay?"

York gave a solemn nod and knelt, putting his hands on the coon. He shoved his life energy into that tiny body as sirens screamed up the road to the house. Dewy and Sly suddenly took off for the forest.

It is not easy knowing that people you work with and have your back have died. Especially when you feel you should have been there and done something, anything, to have prevented those deaths. Two of theirs had died. Yet two had lived, and a third life hung in the balance.

The people who had come to help had to walk up the mountain to carry down the bodies of the two dead snipers. Tex made sure they treated the bodies with respect. They loaded George and Simon in the ambulance. And they sent it screaming to the emergency trauma unit in the nearest city.

Chatterbox was on the kitchen table with a grumpy doctor working on him. He had suggested putting the animal down. Tex got in his face, and the man quickly changed his mind. The vet was shaking his head as he shaved the wound on the raccoon's head. He tried again to explain how keeping the animal alive was terrible. "There is bound to be swelling in the brain, which alone might kill him. About all I can do here is clean the wound and shoot him full of antibiotics. The trouble is that he is a wild animal. He is going to experience a shock upon waking if he does wake. Wild creatures often die just from the shock of being caged."

"He won't be in a cage. Chatterbox, this hero you call an animal, saved my men's lives. In doing so, he became like one of my team. He WILL be treated with respect and given what he needs to recover," Tex explained. He was holding his temper in check as he dealt with the doctor. He had men at the hospital he needed to retrieve and a young boy who had lost the nearest thing he had to a mother to comfort.

He tried not to factor in his feelings. Doing so might cause him to make a mistake. The biggest problem now was figuring out who he could trust. Someone had his girl, and he couldn't afford to make a wrong move here. As he watched the doctor, Tex called the State Trooper they had worked with on the child kidnapping ring a while back. A groggy voice answered the call, "Low?"

"I need a favor, Jess. We've had some trouble here. Miss Susan is gone, taken. You must alert the Troopers in our state. Contact only those you trust for this mission. I need the roads watched for the car a witness described taking her away. There should be evidence of gunfire in the car. Also, if you could arrange to watch the airport and bus stations, I'd appreciate it." Tex was curt and to the point; so much needed to be done. He only hoped he hadn't misjudged this guy.

"The Tracker Lady? I'm up. I'm on it. What else do you need? I can send some men, maybe. I'll come. Just tell me where," Jess said. He owed them big time. And would do anything to help rescue the Lady Tracker.

Knowing Jess would care for the trooper's end of things, Tex called in a few more favors. The grumpy doctor left, leaving a list of things they could try to feed the coon. Tex felt he wouldn't have to look too hard for food to give Chatterbox.

Next, Tex checked on Roger and York. He loaded them into the bunker and told them to keep an eye on Chatterbox. It was time to go and see what Simon and George could tell him about the person or persons who had taken Susan. And he had to visit the families of their two dead companions. They were good men and didn't deserve to die like that. He slapped his forehead. He had to inform the day crew about the loss and get them here to watch over York—his list of things to do kept growing while he only wanted to take off after Susan.

York pulled him up short. "I want to go see them, too. They are my friends." He stood there staring at Tex with the same look Susan had given when she had decided.

"Somebody needs to be here for Chatterbox, York. He is closer to you than either of us," Tex reasoned.

York looked torn as he considered Tex's words. "I… okay. I know you are right. Tell them I wanted to come."

"I will, but I have a feeling my biggest problem

will be keeping them in the hospital. Maybe you can see if there is any soup you can heat up in case they force their way out of the hospital," Tex told him, only half kidding about them wanting to leave. Both Simon and George were pretty hardheaded. "Roger, you have him," he said, letting the man know he trusted him with York. Roger nodded. He was tight-lipped and looking serious as all hell. Now Tex needed to get his clothes so they wouldn't throw him out of the hospital.

Tex was a block from the hospital when he spied two suspicious-looking men. They were hobbling down the sidewalk, hospital gowns flapping in the wind. Pulling the car up to the curb, Tex shook his head at the men. "Leave you alone, and you make a jailbreak. Come on, get in. York is worried about you two jailbirds."

Simon helped George to the car and piled in after him. George grunted, glaring at Tex. "You should have been here an hour ago. You know they pumped me full of who knows what person's blood? If I come down with some exotic disease, I'm giving it to you," George complained.

"Did you at least swipe some antibiotics?" Tex asked.

"Yeah," Simon growled. "The Lone Ranger here would sneak off and leave without them." Simon threw a glance at George only to find him sound asleep. "He did come to spring me first, though."

"Whew," Tex said. "For a moment, I thought you guys would have to share Chatterbox's pills. Of course, you might have craved crayfish later if you did." Tex looked over at Simon. The man slumped against the door and started to snore.

Chapter Eleven

SUSAN

The constant sound of tires on pavement hummed in her ears, barely penetrating her mind as Susan fought from the darkness holding her trapped. Slowly, Susan realized she was in the trunk of a car. She was supposed to do something if she found herself trapped in the trunk of a car, but what? It was like a part of her brain was missing, some vital part. SHE WAS ALONE!

Not one thought from another mind was in her head. Not even an animal. Alone. But that was not right. Somebody had to be driving the car. Was their mind blank? No, they were never blank. Some residual thought was there even in death. Susan had always thought being free of other minds would feel like freedom. The opposite was happening. She was terrified.

I need to get out of this car, she thought. What am I supposed to do if I am in the trunk of a car? Why was she unable to think? What was wrong with her? Think. Think. A memory of her Mother speaking came like a whisper to her. "Bad men may stick you in the trunk, but you are not helpless. Find the trunk release and use it."

She tried to move her hands, realizing they were bound behind her. Still, that did not mean she was helpless. It took a bit of maneuvering to turn her back to the side where her bound hands could feel around for something that would indicate you should pull it to release the trunk lock. It was more difficult shifting her body inch by inch along to search. She located what she thought was the latch. She was trying to get her fingers around it when the car skidded to a stop. Susan slid away from the chance at freedom.

"Get out of the road, you stupid cow!" an angry voice shouted. Susan heard and felt a car door open as someone exited the car. Now. If she could open the trunk and roll out of the car, she might be able to get free. She started inching back to where she thought she had felt the latch. Footsteps. They approached the back of the car. Susan held her breath.

There was a thumping pop as the trunk opened. Light flooded the car trunk, temporarily blinding Susan. A hand slapped her on the head, banging her head on the floorboard. "This is all your fault. You did this." A fist punched her, and the trunk slammed down again. Susan lay stunned at the sudden attack on her. She could not feel his mind or anyone, anywhere. What was wrong with her? Was this how most people felt all the time?   All alone. "Tex!" her mind screamed, but there was no answer to her silent call. Blessed darkness surrounded her mind once more as she passed out again.

Tex turned onto the road that traveled up the side of the mountain to Susan's house. George and Simon were both still asleep, and Tex wondered if he would have to carry them into the house when something tickled him inside his head. It was a weird feeling, almost an itch, but more a tingle. He felt rather than heard his name in a desperate whisper. Susan!

Tex slammed on the car's brakes, jarring George and Simon awake. Both men automatically reached for a weapon that was not on them. "What the hell?" George grumbled. Simon looked wildly around for whatever threat was near them.

"Quiet," Tex abolished. He knew there was a range limit on Susan's mind-reading thing. He wasn't sure how far she could reach, but he would not chance moving out of range. "Susan?" he tried to think back to her. Nothing. Maybe he had moved too far already. Throwing the car into reverse, he backed up to where he thought he had first felt that tickle. "Susan?" he tried again. Dread filled him. What if that had been her death scream? No, he wouldn't accept that. She was alive, and he was going to find her. He backed the car up farther and tried again, then pulled forward. Back and forth, back and forth, with nothing but that dreaded silence.

Simon was watching Tex closely. At first, he thought his friend had lost his mind. "You alright?" he asked.

"Yes. I think Miss Susan tried to communicate

with me," the frustration in Tex's voice was firm. "We know her range for picking up thoughts is limited. Could she have been moving away and have gone past her range?"

"She spoke to you?" George said. His tone was one of Are you crazy?

Simon punched George, "Just shut up if you can't help. You saw her tell those animals to search for that hiker. She can hear our thoughts. Who knows what else she can do? I believe she would try to reach Tex or one of us. Logically, she is closer to York, but she would still think he was in the bunker."

Starting back up the road towards the house, Tex mumbled angrily, "Of course, I know she talks to York. He'd have a better chance of hearing her." George wisely kept his mouth shut as the driver became reckless. Tex was in a hurry.

Even though Tex wanted to run in and question York, he carefully helped George and Simon get out of the car and into the house.

Roger had been on the roof of the house. He dropped down to assist the wounded inside. There was a hardness to his face that hadn't been there before. He didn't grumble as he had so often been prone to do. Roger took George's weight on himself, leaving Tex to help Simon.

York was on Tex like a magnet as soon as Simon was in a chair at the table. For a moment, York stood clutching Tex, then stepped back and got that all-business look that Susan was so good at presenting people. "There is some hot soup ready. Maybe we should all have a bowl with a glass of milk. Frito chips were all I could find to go with the soup. We must be out of bread," he said, sounding all mature. He acted like the host, bringing each man a bowl of soup and milk.

The table was silent while the men ate. Tex could barely choke down his soup but was determined not to disappoint York—each person consumed by their thoughts and the sense of urgency that hung thick in the air. Goldie was the only one who didn't eat. She lay in the doorway with her muzzle pointing towards the distant horizon.

Fed, their tummies full, the team of wounded and frustrated protectors armed themselves for combat. Where they were going was still up in the air. Usually, Tex would call on all the branches of law enforcement. With traitors in the mix, he tended not to trust anyone he didn't personally know. The trouble was that he couldn't think. His emotions were trying to paralyze him. Every fiber of his body screamed at him to kill the person who had taken his Susan. Only honor and common sense held him in check. He knew they needed a plan, and they needed help. There were just so few he trusted with something this important to him. Then there was York. He couldn't dump the boy on someone and leave him in the dark. York was as much a part of this as he was in every way. He loved Susan. And there it was, the whole thing he had tried so hard not to admit to himself, the reason his mind wouldn't function as it should, the love of forbidden fruit.

One of the objects of Tex's anguish stood in front of him. York looked at him with questioning eyes. "What is it, York?" Tex asked.

"Do you think Goldie could find her, sir? She listens to me like she does my mom. She has a good nose, sir," York said, his voice trembling.

"The kidnapper carried her out of here and then put her in the trunk of his car. I don't think her scent would be on the ground for Goldie to find, son. But it is a good idea. And we can use all the good ideas we can gather," Tex told him, placing his hand on York's shoulder to comfort him.

"It is worth a try. I had an old Bluetick hound that tracked a Jeep through a swamp. Let's do it now while the scent is hot," George said, struggling to his feet. "We know where the trail starts and stops at the road. If she can make it as far as the road, we give her a shot at car tracking…."

A crash and some angry growling interrupted George. Chatterbox was awake and feeling grumpy. It was York who reacted by jumping to his feet. He ran to where they had left Chatterbox resting on warm blankets. He closed his eyes and concentrated on the raccoon as he spoke and thought the exact words. "The bad man hurt you. Please relax. You may leave anytime you want. We only wanted to help you when you were unaware of the danger around you. You did well saving Simon and George. We all love you and do not wish you harm."

Chatterbox stopped growling and cocked his head as if listening to York. As if to cover being embarrassed at having misread the situation. The coon turned his back to York and sniffed the air. He could smell food. With all the grace of a lumbering raccoon, he approached the kitchen table and looked up at it.

"He is hungry," York said with a little laugh, relieved that he had been able to soothe the troubled animal friend. He couldn't do the things Susan could, but at least he was developing his mind a little bit.

"We should all eat again. Especially you, York, if we will be tracking. We are going to need all the energy we can store. Plus, let's fill a backpack with those weird drinks and bars," Simon reasoned.

"Yes, and some of the IV bags and catheters. Let's think ahead; we've done this before. Sure, we have wounded, but load you guys in a car and hand you a gun. I'd take you any day," Tex said, feeling more positive now. They had a plan of sorts.

Each of them had a task to do. Simon and George packed one of the cars. Tex made sure the snipers were informed of their loss and had backup. Tex took York and Goldie to where the trail started. They had an item of Susan's clothing in a bag for Goldie to sniff. Roger came with them as he was York's security. They would meet up with Simon and George where the trail ended at the road where the kidnapper had parked his car.

It was a solemn bunch that walked to where the kidnapper carried Susan into the woods. Even Goldie, who was usually a dog full of happy wags, walked purposefully. York looked to Tex for directions when Tex stopped walking. "Tell her to find Susan, son," Tex said softly before stepping back to give Goldie plenty of room to work her nose on the ground. Behind them, there came an angry chattering. Chatterbox had decided to accompany them. Tex shook his head, believing the raccoon would enter the woods once they reached the road.

"Find Susan," York told Goldie, holding down the bag with Susan's used apron in it. Goldie didn't hesitate. She was off in a determined effort to find and protect her person. Nose bobbing up and down, Goldie searched the surroundings for a hint of Susan. She caught her scent mixed in with that of someone evil. Goldie growled. Something she seldom would ever do unless there were intruders. Her nose could smell Susan, Tex, George, and the evil person. But, it was the evil who had her person. With hardly a pause, she took off running after that foul smell, now and then finding a hint of her person.

"Blood," Roger stated flatly. He stooped to look at the ground.

York paled.

"It is either George or the kidnapper's blood, son," Tex told him, then gave Roger a look that said do that again, and I'll clock you one. Roger nodded. He understood. He had to protect York even from his runaway mouth.

It was a while before Goldie reached the road. This spot was where the kidnapper had put Susan in the trunk of a car. There were signs of George having shot out a window or two and evidence that the car was running on the tire's rims on one side where the tracks speed away. Goldie frantically searched for the trail she had been following. The three humans kept a distance to let her work. They did not want to foul up any scent she could find.

Before long, Chatterbox reappeared and joined Goldie on the road. Although, Goldie seemed more able to follow a human scent. Chatterbox was familiar with the car scents of the road. It wasn't long before the raccoon was standing in one spot, appearing to curse at Goldie. Goldie went over and stuck her nose in the spot Chatterbox was smelling. It was almost as if they were having a sniffing conversation about that spot. Goldie suddenly began to sniff along the pavement in the direction of the car that Susan had gone in. Still fussing to himself, Chatterbox went back into the woods. The three humans traveled behind Goldie. Now and then, Tex glanced behind them. He hoped to see if there was a sign of the others in the car.

Everything was so quiet inside Susan's mind. She had always heard every thought around her, and having them silenced was creepy. Now she understood how other people felt waking up in total darkness. She never was afraid of the dark. She was surrounded by minds constantly. She always knew she wasn't alone, ever. Her head bounced against someone's back. She realized someone was carrying her again.

Knowing she couldn't panic the way she had in the car. Susan pretended to be unconscious. She was on her own now and had to try to use her brain in other ways instead of depending on grabbing the information she needed from someone's mind. If able. She did not like herself for thinking that. Her mother would face the problem no matter what. She always did whatever she needed to survive and protect her children. What her mother and siblings would do in this situation was the question she should be asking herself.

The man carried her into a building. And through it to a room where he dumped her on a mattress or something similar on the floor. Susan kept her body limp, letting it puddle in an awkward position upon being placed on whatever was on the floor. She almost stiffened when one of her legs was grasped and pulled in one direction slightly. Cold metal clamped around her ankle. The man chained her like an animal.

Time dragged on, and the man didn't leave as Susan hoped. Before long, the stress of worrying all day over Tex and the shock of seeing everyone shot right in front of her caught up with Susan, and she slept.

"Susan, tell me where you are if you hear me." That message kept running through Tex's mind as they slowly walked behind Goldie. Goldie hadn't let up, although her tongue was hanging out of her mouth, and her pace had slowed. As the sun rose higher in the sky, the pavement heated up. Traffic began to pick up. Both caused Tex and York to be concerned for Goldie.

George said, "We must stop and have Goldie drink some water. Do we have a towel or something to wet down and drape over her body? We can rig something for her feet with a bit of leather and some odds and ends.

Tex nodded. "York, can you make her stop and rest and drink a little water? I have an old tee shirt in the back, and we can get it to cool her body off some." Tex paused, thinking. "While York, Roger, and I treat Goldie, you two get whatever you need to put on her feet. We will trail behind her. You can catch up when you are finished."

Simon was reluctant to leave. They still had one subject to protect. Out here, York was exposed to any potential attack. The determined look in York's eyes cut off any protest he may have voiced. The kid was out to save his current mother. How could Simon deny him that chance to help? Reluctantly, he nodded. He found himself counting to hide his doubtful thoughts. It had become a part of him now. His phone vibrated. "Hello," Simon said, his voice reserved.

"Simon, this is State Trooper Kurt. I'm at the house, and it is empty except for a very angry raccoon. Where do you need me?"

"That will be Chatterbox. He saved George and my lives, so don't hurt him. Tex and York are following Goldie along the highway. George and I will get some supplies to make boots for Goldie. That pavement is hot. Let me text you directions to catch up to Tex and York. I'll feel better knowing you are there to give them refuge in case of gunfire," Simon told him. They hung up, and Simon sent directions on where to find the others.

George gave Simon a questioning look. "You trust this guy?" he asked.

"Yep, he is the guy who called about the kidnapped children. It was a child slave ring. Miss Susan located the children, and we got part of the group or killed them. York was one of the children. Only he didn't have a family or a home. She is in the process of adopting him," Simon told him, his voice trailing off as he thought back to that time.

"I can see why. The boy has common sense, not something you find in today's youth. I should have thought about setting the dog on her trail. I think they put some dumb person's blood in me. That's why I hate getting blood from people I don't know," George mumbled.

"You know that is just stupid. The Labs test the blood given in hospitals for almost everything today. You might have the blood of a genius or a priest inside you now. Or it could be from someone like our Miss Susan," Simon said.

"You think so? What if I start doing weird things?" George said in a thoughtful voice.

"You already do weird things. I'd feel honored to have Miss Susan's blood," was Simon's comeback. George shut up as they pulled up to a store.

Traffic was backing up behind where Goldie stood, refusing to move off the road. Tex stood directing traffic around York and Goldie. Several drivers gave them the finger, and one asked if he could help them.

York stood shielding Goldie from the sun's rays as much as he could. Now and then, he would pour some water on the tee shirt covering Goldie and give her a little water. Gradually, Goldie cooled down. When she put her nose down and started down the road again, York pulled the tee shirt off her back to allow the air to flow around her.

Behind them, a siren blasted and whipped around the remaining traffic to stop behind the man and boy following Goldie. Jess stepped out of his patrol car. It had taken longer than he thought to drive up here. "You guys keep going. I'll handle the traffic behind you," he said.

Tex barely nodded, his focus on Roger and York ahead of him. He was just relieved to have someone to handle the traffic problem.

The traffic was at a complete stop. Roger climbed on top of the car to see the problem. But the traffic was at a standstill stretched so far ahead that all he could see were distant flashing police and ambulance lights. Goldie sat impatiently, wanting to move on. All the pavement ahead of them was bumper-to-bumper cars. The trail was growing colder by the moment. Tex paced like a caged lion, his expression so grim that even George didn't want to approach him.

Finally, Tex stopped pacing. His eyes swept over the men with him. "Pull the car off the road. George, Simon, you stay in the car. Roger, grab a backpack. George, pack one with water and the tee shirt to cool Goldie down. Roger, pack plenty of power bars and an IV set up in your backpack. York, you will carry the small pack with drinks and bars just for you and Goldie's bowl. Jess, as soon as this mess clears up, you escort the car to us. We will hoof it till we get past this mess," he ordered.

As the others became active, packing their backpacks, Goldie stood. For the first time in a long while, her tail wagged. It was as if she knew they were finally going to move on. She walked after York at first, raising each foot high until she became accustomed to the boots George had made for her again. When they moved off to the side of the road, she looked at York questioningly. Her look said this wasn't right. They needed to follow the scent. Goldie sat on the pavement and watched the others preparing to walk off. The message was clear to them all. She wanted to continue following after Susan.

"Come on, Goldie," York called. "We are going to find Mom."

Goldie's eyebrows twitched as she looked back and forth between Tex and York. Tex patted his leg, and Goldie stood. She still appeared uncertain. When Tex and York both began to walk off, she reluctantly followed.

It seemed to take forever to reach the front of the long line of cars waiting to be allowed to continue on their way. During the entire walk, Goldie worked her nose overtime to find a trace of the scent she had been following.

Susan could hear the guy pacing back and forth, mumbling to himself now and then. Her muscles were stiffening up from trying to lie relaxed and still. She had almost ruined her pretense of sleep when she woke. Before she could jerk her body up and look around, she had heard the pacing and remembered where she was and what had happened. Thirst was like a burning fire inside her, making her mouth feel dry and gunky. The need for water didn't compare to the pain in her side. She could only take shallow breaths. She must have flinched because the pacing stopped.

Heavy footsteps came over to where Susan was on the mattress. Rough hands grabbed her and shoved her into a chair. Her arms were pulled behind the chair's back and tied. It was all she could do to keep a groan from escaping her as the movement caused her side to scream at her. Susan opened her eyes as a giant hand, almost gently, patted her cheek.

"How did you know?" the angry man demanded of Susan.

"Know what?" Susan managed to croak from her dry throat. He kicked the leg that was shackled hard. Susan felt the bones crack as they broke. It took all her willpower not to cry out as she stared up at the man.

"Don't act stupid, you know. How did you see me in the trees? I checked after it was clear, and you couldn't have seen me. Tell me, you…, you…," her tormentor raved as he kicked her again.

"I didn't…," Susan started to say, but the rage was on him, and he kicked her so hard her body broke free of the chair, and she fell, hitting her head, she blacked out.

A crew of clean-up personnel was sucking up what looked like a massive spill of something on the highway from a tanker. Whatever it was, the men wore hazard outfits to avoid contact with the substance. Green-faced officers had set up what looked like official tape sectioning off the area. In the distance, a helicopter sat well away from the road where medics were treating several people, giving them oxygen. Tex kept York and Roger well back as he approached to gather information on what was happening.

An officer wearing a mask waved him off and then came over to talk to him. "You can't come any closer. One hundred feet is as close as we can get to that stuff without dropping. Go back and wait in your car for now. The team is working quickly to clean up this mess."

Flashing his identification, Tex explained what he could. "We are tracking a kidnapper with the dog there. We must get to the other side as the path leads this way. Our mission is a matter of life or death. Tell me how to get to the other side."

The officer automatically tried to scratch his chin, but the mask was in the way. He ended up running his hand through his hair. "Go out two hundred feet or till you are past the helicopter. Then, continue that distance until you are at least one hundred feet past the spill. You will see the tape marking the distance."

"Thank you," Tex said and hurried back to the others.

Goldie objected until York calmed her down. Even then, she kept looking back at the road. When they turned and started paralleling the road, Goldie suddenly alerted. Her head swung to the right, and off she dragged York along.

It was a rutted track running off into the distance. Tex checked his weapon, as did Roger. He called the others to inform them they were going across the country. It wasn't long before a cloud of dust announced the others were with them. They all had a shared look, which boded ill for the person at the end of that rutted track.

A man was beating Susan when Tex crashed through the door of the run-down building they found. George reached out and tried to grab Tex before he could get to the man, but the enraged look on Tex's face made him hesitate a second too long.

Tex barely had enough reasoning to throw his gun over his shoulder at Simon when he saw the creep hitting his Susan. Every instinct inside him said, 'Kill the bastard!'. Only the fact that he knew York was watching held him in check. That didn't mean he couldn't do some damage. His fist slammed into the big man, never giving the creep a chance to touch Susan again, hitting the guy again and again. He did some damage of his own until Simon placed a hand on his shoulder. "Tex, he is down. We've got him now. I think you should talk to York. Okay?" Simon soothed.

Through clenched teeth, Tex managed to nod. The red haze lifted enough from his mind that he saw York eating and drinking to boost his energy. Going over, Tex blocked York's line of sight of the man he had just battered to a pulp. "See to your mom. I need to call your Grandmother to come to heal your mom," he told York. Turning to Roger, Tex continued. "Take care of York." Roger was already following York, opening a power bar as he walked.

Delusions crept into Susan's mind. Middy and Eric chased her, tickling her to make her laugh in the farm's yard. It switched to Tex telling her about tadpoles. They were all happy moments. Those are the little moments she held dear. She kept those memories hidden away deep inside. To be pulled out when the people around her were crushing her with their thoughts. She cracked her eyes open just a little, knowing in this figment of her imagination, she would see Tex sitting beside her bed in the D.C. bunker.

There he was, just like she remembered. She smiled a swollen lip smile at him. "I wish you were real. I'm so alone here. Nobody is here but the sniper. Even his mind isn't here in my head. I'm empty. All alone. Please don't fade away. Stay, so I don't feel alone for a moment." She whispered with her croaky, dried-out throat.

"Oh, my love, you are never alone. I'm here to stay, sweetheart. One day, you will find the man you love. You are going to break my heart. I won't be able to leave you. Not then, not ever. I'll watch him courting you and want to kill him. But I won't, because you love him. You'll look outside the window of the happy home you make with the man who wins your heart and will see me out there patrolling, keeping you safe. Rest now, I have you," Tex dared to let his thoughts express themselves. She had said she couldn't hear them. They had her back at the house, waiting for her mother to eat. And heal all the damage that the sniper, she had sensed hiding in the trees during the children's rescue, did to her body. He had beat her, breaking her legs and ribs. There was no telling what damage he did to her head. She couldn't hear him.

Susan tried to open her eyes wider to see if she was awake and in the real world instead of the insane thoughts in her mind. Tex hadn't thought she could hear him when he told her about the tadpoles, and now, when he…, she felt her mother's touch and slept once more.

When Susan next woke, reality surrounded her. All the minds she had lost were back in force. Those minds were confused and worried as they thought about what it would mean if she could no longer read minds. The SS were afraid they were going to reassign them, leaving her unguarded against the world. It was touching that they felt so protective of her and York. Tex... Tex was counting like crazy. She could feel his determination not to let her see his thoughts. A worry would creep out now and then, and she would hear it. He feared there would be a recall, but unlike the others, he had already decided not to go if the worst happened. York's thoughts, by comparison, were all joy and happiness that she was alive and well. He seemed unaware of the problem the SS were facing.

"York," Susan's scratchy voice called.

"Do you need some water?" he asked, hovering over her, his bubbly joy at seeing her awake coming through.

"Yes, but first, go tell the guys I can hear them so they will quit worrying," Susan said. She listened to York rush off to tell the SS she was okay. The relief that swept through her mind when York told them nearly made her weep. This team of SS was more like family than any of the others who had watched over her. Those other SS would have been happy to have been recalled. She could feel Simon's mind! A tear tracked down her cheek from her joy at learning he was alive. The fear that she had failed him when he needed her. It had haunted her all the while she was being held by...; she didn't want to think of that.

Tex followed York back to Susan. He had to

see for himself that she was awake. Carefully, he counted, concentrating on the numbers to not give her the slightest hint of all the thoughts jumbled inside his mind. Old man Whiting had yet to call him after Tex had sent word that they had rescued Susan and the terrorist was in prison. He hadn't mentioned the fact that the monster was a bit the worse for wear. Or that it had been him who had exacted the punishment on the creep. The filth had dared to hurt Susan. Even now, Tex's blood boiled in anger, and he wanted to lay hands on the monster who had harmed his woman. No, he could never let Susan hear those thoughts inside him. He kept those thoughts hidden in the darkness of his soul.

When he saw Susan, his world turned to the right side again. Tex let his eyes roam over her face to be sure all signs of the bruising, the damage to her body, were gone. A weight lifted from his heart, but deep inside was that lingering feeling of guilt like it was somehow his fault that the terrorist kidnapped Susan. And then, subject to all the terror and harm put on her. He was afraid to get too close to Susan. If he did, he might grab her and hold on so tight he'd scare her. So he stood back and watched as she drank the water York had brought.

Something was different about Tex, Susan thought. He seemed to contain himself as if he didn't want to approach her. She couldn't blame him. She must have looked terrible when they found her. "You got him?" she asked.

Tex first nodded, then found his voice. "Yes, he is never going to see daylight again."

"Darkness will suit him," Susan whispered.

Those negative words are not like her, Tex thought. She always seemed optimistic, knowing what direction to take and what to say and do. He was the one with darkness in his soul, not her. How did he know that she was so pure? She saw all the dark thoughts that were inside the people around her. How was it she was able to stay positive? Then he knew why she was the person she presented to the world. Because to be otherwise was to be like them, the cheaters, the robbers, the haters, and those who just thought they were above everyone else. She included them all in her meals and danced for them. She showed them through her actions that she was a person like them. Not better, not worse.

Chapter Twelve

CHANGE

He is acting strangely, Susan thought. It was like Tex was keeping his distance, blocking his thoughts aggressively. Tex was warm with York, treating him as an equal and showing York moves to protect himself. The thing was, with herself, he held himself in check as if afraid to get too close. Was he afraid she would break? Or was this the beginning of him preparing to ask to be reassigned? Tex and Simon had lasted longer than most SS sent to watch over her. Susan laughed at herself, realizing she had let her guard down, and began to feel as if Tex was there to stay. It was stupid of her because she knew they feared she would see inside their minds. Sooner or later, they broke away to live a less stressful life.

Tex watched as Susan began to prepare the large breakfast she cooked for all of them. He told himself he was only inside watching to ensure she was fit. It was true; her mother had healed her broken bones as well as all the other damage a madman had caused to her lovely body. But... who was he kidding? He was there for one reason: he didn't trust letting her out of his sight. It could happen again. Someone could storm the place and try to snatch her away from them, from him. He didn't know if he was strong enough to maintain a calm agent air if it happened again.

A shadow passed the window. Tex's hand went to his gun before his mind registered that it was Simon. He was on one of his final patrols before coming in for breakfast. Or, in Simon's case, dinner. He had to get a grip on himself, calm down, and return to his right mind. Every instinct inside him screamed at him to throw Susan over his shoulder. And take her far away from this place where they stole her from him. Only reason and logic, the small amount he had left, held him in check.

George came inside, leaving Simon outside to wait his turn to go in and eat. They had an unspoken agreement that one of them would always remain outside. Roger would show up soon to relieve Simon and allow him to eat. Then, they would find their way to bed to sleep the day away if they could sleep. None of them could rest, truly rest. They had failed to keep Susan safe, which ate at them all. Everyone seemed to be walking on eggshells, wary that one misplaced step would break them apart.

George boxed playfully with York for a few minutes as he waited for dinner to be ready to serve up. His leg was healed, as was Simon's shoulder, thanks to Susan's mother touching each of them. For the first time in his life, George felt lost. He had

failed. Two men he barely had known were dead.
All because he failed to sense the danger. Simon
suffered an injury. And... George could scarcely
think of the and part. Each time he looked at Susan,
he saw her lying on that dirty mattress, chained up
like an animal. Her body was broken, and her face
was nearly unrecognizable.

He repeatedly played that night like a movie
in his mind when he was supposed to be sleeping.
The monster who had taken Susan struck her broken
body. And Tex disarms himself as if he knew he'd
shoot the guy if he had the gun in his hand. George
had to fight the urge to join Tex in beating the guy.
He knew, as well as Simon did, that Tex had to vent,
or he would kill the guy. They were also painfully
aware of York in the room. Somehow, they had been
able to control themselves, be agents and a ranger,
knowing they had failed to keep the woman on that
disgusting mattress safe.

Simon walked in just as Susan was about
to call them all to come to eat. He silently helped
her carry the food to the table. Now and then,
he glanced to where George and York were
straightening the furniture they had moved around
to make the pretend boxing ring. Each took turns
showing York different ways to protect himself and
Susan. It was an unspoken pact they had made since
following York and Goldie to where Susan was held
and tortured. When his turn came, he had been
thinking of what he wanted to teach the boy. There
were so many methods and so much to learn. All the
observing that the boy needed to understand. Susan
was already teaching York how to vanish from sight.

It was unusual for a subject to be aware of the need to hide oneself. Simon had been impressed once he learned what Susan was doing with York.

He was worried about Tex. The man wasn't himself. Little things had changed in the way he talked to them and the way he interacted with Susan. The abduction was eating at all of them, but with Tex, something had happened. What that was, Simon didn't know, which worried him.

When the table was ready, the men and York took their seats. Susan took her seat. She missed the easy chatter and joking that usually graced the place. They were too solemn, these men of hers. "I'm thinking of walking in the woods today," she said, starting them all to talk. "I believe Dewy is expecting, and I want to see if there is a difference from the last time we visited her."

York bounced in his seat with excitement. "A baby? Who is the daddy? Do you think it could be that big, silver-looking stag? What should we name the baby? Is it a boy or a girl deer?"

"York, take a breath. Miss Susan can't answer all those questions just yet," George said. He looked to Tex for help in defusing the boy.

It was Susan, though, who spoke up. "It could be the big stag. That is if she is expecting. We won't know whether it is a boy or girl until Dewy presents the little tyke. But, York, we have to be extra quiet when she does come to us with the little one if she is expecting. Moms are very protective of their little ones."

"I can be quiet," York said, making it like he was zipping his mouth. That brought a soft chuckle from the guys, and they sat up a little straighter, thinking of the joy a baby deer would bring to York.

After breakfast, Simon and George took food up to the snipers. Also, they did a visual check on the guys. Physically checking the snipers had become part of the difference in their routines. Their patrols ranged around the snipers once or twice a night and daily. They had lost two of theirs and were not about to let it happen again. They gave the all-clear to their daytime partners before heading to bed.

Tex was tense about going into the forest with Susan and York. He remembered the blood that had been spotted on the vegetation from a kidnapper and their own George. George would have died without the deer and fox coming to get him. Besides the energy bars and brown power drinks, Tex carried treats for the animals who helped protect Susan, secreted about his body. He would never forget what he owed to them.

He stood outside, waiting for the others to prepare for the forest walk. In the distance, Tex saw a plume of dust, indicating a car was on the way up to the house. "Alert," he said softly.

"Got it," a voice said in his ear.

"Roger, take them to the bunker, now," Tex ordered, keeping that dust plume in his sight while speaking. He loosened his weapon and checked that he had clips on him as he waited.

The car approached the house and parked as if the person inside intended to stay. Tex pulled his weapon out and took an aggressive stance. "You are not authorized to be in this area. Turn your car around and leave," Tex said loud enough to be heard by the occupants.

A man opened the car door and stepped out. He was tall and well-built, with a darker coloration than Susan. He could be her brother from the look of him. "I'm Jarvis Adams, your relief if you are Robin Shadow," the man said. "You have been recalled."

"Your information is faulty. And nobody here has been recalled. Our team will not be ever recalled," Tex replied. He heard the bunker door open behind him. Damn, she was coming out. Had she learned nothing from…? He could not let his mind go there, not now when this stranger threatened to send him away.

Susan held her hand in her listen-to-me signal once she saw Tex. But it was to the stranger she spoke. "You will stand there until I talk to my grandfather. Do not move. Tex, I have this. You do your thing," Susan said.

Do his thing? Ah, keep his gun on the stranger, maybe shoot the mirror on his car out. He could do that. He smiled to himself. Yes, he could do that.

"Grandfather, there is a man here saying he is relieving Tex. You know I have not sanctioned this? What is the reasoning behind this? No, you will see to it this man stands down now," Susan said into her phone.

Tex felt relief at hearing her words. She did not want him to leave. So, this was not her idea? For one moment, he had thought she wanted to get rid of him.

"You are pulling the 'I am the President' card out on me?" Susan's voice held a tone of disbelief as she listened to her grandfather try to explain away the order for Tex to leave her. Pressure? Someone was pressuring him into this, or so he claimed. She looked over at Tex with his unwavering gun pointed at this intruder. "So, you are saying that if he does not return to Washington, they will fire him from the Secret Service?" There was a pause as Susan listened to her grandfather going on and on.

Susan faced Tex and spoke to him, ignoring the man standing still by his car. "Do you wish to be relieved of this duty, Tex?" she asked him.

"No," he immediately spat out with force, wondering what was happening.

"His answer is no. I'll ask him," Susan said into the phone. "They are threatening to fire you. I know you love your work. So, my question is, do you still want to stay here knowing you will no longer be a Secret Service agent?"

"Yes, they need not bother firing me, and as of this moment, I quit. I will remain here," Tex replied.

"Then, as of this same moment, you are now my private security. Where I go, you go without exception. Do you hear that, Grandfather? I expect you to issue credentials for him immediately so he may go everywhere with me. You will have no say in his inclusion, or you can remove my number from your phone. Got it?" Susan said, never raising her voice, but her tone said everything.

Susan listened for a moment as her grandfather sputtered and finally conceded defeat. Her grandfather explained to Susan what Tex needed to do at her end before hanging up to prepare a pass for Tex.

"Tex, turn your identification and issued revolver over to this man. I am hiring you as personal protection," Susan told Tex before turning on the stranger. "You will accept the items Tex gives you with politeness. If you ever sneer or make any comment about today, you will find your way back to D.C. Take up standing out here for now. I have to explain to my son why you are here and keep your fellow SS from killing you. Tex, please tell up top to stand down."

"Up top?" Jarvis asked.

Susan didn't answer. She turned away and entered the bunker, leaving Tex to explain. "They didn't tell you anything, did they?" Tex said. "Up top are the snipers. They could have taken you out at any time. Be thankful Miss Whiting came out to keep you alive. Here is a hint. When she holds her hand up, stay alert and wait to see what she says. I doubt they told you that much. You may have come here thinking you will be in charge. You can stuff that in your sock. She is in charge. Now start counting in your head, and never stop." Tex told the intruder as he handed him his issued gun and identification. Without pausing, he pulled out another weapon and placed it in his holster.

Gone were the plans to visit the mountain's forest friends. Susan was angry. They had gone too far by springing this new guy on her and trying to take away someone she had come to trust. If not for Tex and the others, Susan would be dead right now.

As far as Tex was concerned, he was still the head of her security. This Jarvis fellow had better watch his step.

"I'm ready," York said as Susan mentally vented her anger inside her mind.

"We are not going today," Susan stated flatly. "Or at least not this morning." Feeling York's disappointment, Susan thought to compromise. "Perhaps you and Roger can go. I have a few things to sort out here. Tell our friends I will see them soon.

"You are not losing, Tex. He stays no matter what. We do not play at caring about people. Tex is one of us; if he ever decides to leave, that will be his choice. But he says he wants to stay even though he has lost his job as an agent." She looked over at Roger before continuing. "Roger, Tex is still in charge. Are you okay with that?"

"Damn right, ma'am," Roger replied.

"Now go with York to explain this Jarvis guy to our forest friends. They deserve a warning," Susan said, dismissing Roger and York.

Walking outside, Roger and York approached Tex. "I'm taking York for that planned walk, sir," he said to Tex, adding the sir to ensure this intruder knew Tex was still in charge of this operation.

"Hold it right there," Jarvis barked, a scowl on his face. "Just who are you two, and what plan are you having going on?"

Roger walked off as if he hadn't heard the intruder speak. Let him take it up with Tex, he thought, not hiding the thought from Miss Susan. He glanced over at York walking beside him and smiled at the boy.

York, his eyes opened wide and looking a little scared, managed to smile back. They had tried to take Tex away, was all York could think. They tried to steal Tex from them.

Jarvis turned on Tex, his mind full of questions. "Are you going to tell me who they are and what is going on?" he asked Tex, trying to keep his temper in check.

"You just met Miss Whiting's son and his SS security. We had all planned on a walk in the forest, but it seems you have put Miss Whiting off of doing a feel-good walk. Play nice, and maybe the night men won't shoot you on sight," Tex told Jarvis.

"Is that a threat?" Jarvis said, his posture one of I'll arrest you if it is.

"No, that is a fact. We have just dealt with the last threat to Miss Whiting, and everyone feels a lack of friendly to strangers threatening to upset her or York," Tex explained before talking to the guys up top. "Be aware, Roger and York are walking in the woods. Miss Whiting is still in residence. Suggest each monitored."

"What?" Jarvis snarled, beginning to think he had entered some altered world.

Tex shook his head at the guy as if finding him lacking. "Up top needs to be informed of activity in the woods. It wouldn't do for them to mistake York or Roger for an intruder and shoot them."

"Surrender your earwig," Jarvis demanded.

"Nope, these are mine and not SS property. Play nice, and I'll let you have one of your own. I take Miss Whiting's security very seriously. Do you want to play on our team or not?" Tex laid it out for Jarvis to decide which side he wanted to support. Theirs or D.C.'s.

"Alright! For now, I will go along with what you are doing. I warn you. I WILL win Miss Whiting over to doing things my way. Now give me a damn earwig," He grumbled at Tex.

Tex listened to York talking to Roger while handing over one of his earwigs. They had spotted Dewy. He smiled as he heard how excited York was about the possible baby.

Jarvis stuck his earwig in, expecting silence. Instead, someone was carrying on a conversation that took him a moment to understand.

"Does she look bigger? Are we going to have a baby?" York asked Roger.

"I can't tell. The tummy still looks normal to me. I'm not sure I could spot signs of being pregnant. We'll have to sneak Miss Susan away and ask her," Roger said.

Listening to this conversation, Jarvis worried he had an expecting woman on his hands. They had been tight-lipped when giving him this assignment. Was that the reason for all the weird looks he had received before leaving? Did he have a hormonal woman to watch over?

"Tex, I don't see Chatterbox," York said, worried that the hero of the kidnapping was hurt worse than he let on.

"Take it easy, son. If he doesn't show, I'll have George go with me later to find him. He may sense an intruder and be lurking nearby. In case he has to come to the rescue again. Talk to Dewy and Sly. Let them know what is going on. I'm unsure if Susan wants to introduce this new guy to them. Any sign of Eagle Eye?" Tex asked.

It was Roger who responded. "Not out here. He only shows himself to Miss Susan, though. I did see him circle overhead at the house. So he is keeping an eye on things."

"Okay, I suggest you practice some hiding, York. We know the value of becoming invisible now. Okay?" Tex responded.

Roger chuckles, "Now, how am I supposed to keep an eye on him if he keeps disappearing like that?"

"You are looking for the enemy, right?" Tex responded.

"Understood," Roger said sheepishly.

A wormhole, Jarvis thought. I've fallen through a wormhole into an alternate reality. No wonder everyone was giving me the stink eye in D.C.

It was dark when George and Simon started their walk to the house to have the nightly meal with the others and relieve Tex and Roger of guard duty. Tex left them both a text on their phones to inform them about Jarvis Adams, so the men knew Jarvis was the tall black man standing outside the house.

George pulled a Tex as they exited the cover of the trees. Weapon out, he crept up behind Jarvis and poked him in the ribs with the gun. "You are not authorized to be in this area. All visitors must call and make an appointment. Leave now or consider yourself under arrest."

Surprised, Jarvis reacted automatically. He

tried to knock the gun out of the hand of the man threatening him. Only the man pinned his arms behind him and disarmed him before he had completed his move. At about that moment, what the man had said penetrated his mind enough to make sense. "I'm SS agent Jarvis Adams," he said through clenched teeth.

"We'll see about that," George said. "Simon, check this guy's identification. He claims to be one of you." George was enjoying himself. He'd shown a Texas Ranger could outsmart a Secret Service agent just by taking Jarvis without breaking a sweat.

Patting the intruder down, Simon smiled to himself. The man hadn't even drawn his gun when attacked. It was pitiful, just pitiful. He was reluctant to pull out Adams's credentials and end their fun. "You can let him go now. It seems he is an agent," Simon said, as if disappointed. Turning to Adams, he frowned. "You didn't alert when George attacked you. Not saying anything to the others puts Miss Whiting in danger. You'd best step up your game if you expect to stay here. STAY ALERT!"

Tossing Adams' identification to him, Simon stomped off towards the house door, calling over his shoulder to George, "We'd best eat and then take over for this bozo."

Eat? These two were going to share a meal with the subject? That wasn't right. You don't get up close and personal with the person you were protecting. No wonder they were recalling Robin Shadow. He had become involved with the subject. Maybe she was carrying his baby inside her, from how the boy and his security talked. Jarvis listened in on the chatter between the people at the dinner table without feeling guilty.

"I think we have razed the new guy enough. Like it or not, he is taking over for me. So you will need to work with him," Tex explained as they all sat at the dinner table.

"That is a bunch of crap, and you know it. This whole thing is just another attempt to get to Miss Susan. The other try at getting rid of you didn't work, so they changed tactics. How do we know this isn't just another attempt to kidnap Miss Susan again? And I thought they wouldn't give us another SS man," Simon said.

There was silence for a long moment before Tex spoke again. "I'm no longer SS. It was to be fired or quit. I quit," he finally said.

"No! I won't accept that shit. You can't leave us now when we know they are after Miss Susan. Miss Susan, tell him he can't quit," Simon said with growls of agreement in the background.

"You know that the man outside is listening to all of you talking? I think you do know Tex is not a quitter. He is staying as head of my security. So, nothing has changed all that much, except that he can't call for SS assistance any longer.

"Now, that has been settled. Roger and Tex, please take our up-top friends their meals. Simon and George, you finish eating and relieve the new guy. We all have to accept change and make the best of it. I believe you will all work together as you have in the past. After you have taken the meal up top, come back and have your dessert," Susan told them.

He was still fuming over everyone eating with

Susan when Tex and Roger came out of the house with a basket of food each. Tex nodded to Jarvis as they passed by him. That is okay, gloat, Jarvis thought. I will have a good meal in the house you used to occupy. He smiled to himself as he watched the pair of men trudge up the mountain to where the snipers were nested.

Tex and Roger's steps began to slow as they neared the spot where two of theirs had recently died. Then Tex straightened his shoulders and put on a good face for the four guys waiting for the hot meal Susan had prepared for them.

"The new guy sounds pretty arrogant," Alex Smith said as Tex and Roger laid out the meal for the guys.

It wouldn't make for a good team if they all were against the new guy, Tex thought. "Miss Susan says nothing has changed. It would be best if we try to fit him into our group somewhere. She will tell us if he is a spy for the people out to kill her."

"Okay, we won't shoot him on accident. But, if he gets highhanded with our bunch, I can't say he'll be covered when the shooting starts down there. After all, our main concern is Miss Susan," Alex said. "Tell her thanks for the great meal."

When Tex and Roger reached the house for their dessert, the night crew left to relieve Jarvis. Tex handed Roger a key. "Pack up my belongings and bring them down in my car, please," he told him, and Roger nodded and headed off. Next, Tex turned to Jarvis. "Miss Whiting expects you to join her now that you have been relieved. I will be in shortly."

"Do you have a place to move your

belongings? I'll need the area you used to occupy," Jarvis asked.

"Of course, Roger is bringing all my things as soon as he has them packed up. You will be sharing a house with Simon. Roger and George have the other house we use," Tex replied as if this was a given fact and not some power play by Jarvis.

Jarvis glanced over to where George was getting ready to start a patrol around the sniper's area. "This George is not on the roster. Why is he here? And who is he?" he asked.

About to take off on his first patrol, George did a turnaround and was next to Jarvis, making the other man's eyes widen. "I'll answer that. I'm a Texas Ranger hired to strengthen Miss Whiting and York's security since your fine SS officials didn't see fit to listen when the team required help. Now, I have a patrol to do," he said, spinning around and disappearing into the trees. They could hear him muttering to himself, "Frigging arrogant snot. He walks in here as if he owns the place, not knowing what is happening."

"A Texas Ranger? He is outside his territory. He can't operate here as a Ranger," Jarvis protested.

"True in the sense of being a Ranger. George is retired from active duty. He is doing a favor for me. I assigned him to the house with Roger as they worked opposite each other: Roger's days on York and George's nights on York. He will bunk with me if that irks your sense of what is proper. After all, the bunkhouses are for the SS. Our personal security team can share a bunk," Tex said, heading Jarvis off from throwing George out of the houses.

By then, they had walked into the dining area of the house. Susan set out Jarvis' dinner on the table and the heaping dessert plates for Tex and Simon. Although Tex did an excellent job hiding his thoughts, Jarvis was broadcasting his thoughts like crazy. Susan went around the table, sitting down at her spot beside York. She knew Tex was trying to be fair to Jarvis. Inside, he was upset about this whole business. Meanwhile, Jarvis was crashing around like some wild beast trying to assert dominance over them all. She would not allow that to happen.

"Did you say you and George have nowhere to sleep?" Susan asked, her voice not showing the slight anger she felt.

"We'll be fine. I can set the camper George bought up near the house for us if needed," Tex said, trying to reassure Susan and downplay the whole thing.

"That won't do at all. You and George will sleep here. There is a bedroom here in the house that we do not use. York and I sleep in the bunker. So that is settled. You can move your belongings into the room since you switch off sleeping hours. Now, Jarvis, eat your dinner and go to the houses where you can settle in. Tex, move the two of you into the spare room here after you enjoy your dessert," Susan told them. She briefly saw a crinkle of relief flash around Tex's eyes and smiled. He didn't know she had heard his thoughts just before she woke up.

"Miss Whiting, you shouldn't be put out like that by your security. We will make room in the houses for the two of them," Jarvis said, protesting the arrangement.

"I'm not being put out at all. I'll feel better with Tex and George in residence. If not for them and the others, I would be dead right now. There will be no more discussion about this," she pronounced, holding her hand to indicate she had finished the conversation.

"Do you feed them like this every night?" Jarvis asked.

"And morning. These are my protectors and deserve a decent meal. York and I also put on a show for everyone occasionally. Although we haven't lately had the time to make up a new show," pausing, Susan turned to Tex. "Tomorrow, we need to go shopping for new clothes for York. He is growing so fast. And at the same time, I want to get some plants for your room. Nothing like a few plants producing fresh air to make a person sleep well."

"Are we going to eat out?" Tex asked.

Watching this exchange between the two, Jarvis felt they behaved more like a couple than a subject and her security.

"Mom, I want to get Chatterbox and the others each a treat. Will that be okay?" York asked Susan.

"Of course, it is fine with me. What do you think, Tex? Will we be taking too much of a chance?" Susan asked.

Brow furrowed, Tex sat in thought for a moment before answering. "I think it might be best to make up a list of what you would like to give each of our friends and let George pick it all up while we shop for your clothes. It will cut our time out in half and allow us to all meet up at a place to eat out before coming home."

Jarvis had to say something before he burst, "I thought George was on nights? Won't his going out in the day hinder his awareness that night?" It just made sense to him.

"Not if we set the meetup time to just before his shift. Besides, George will know just what to get our friends. That way, Simon can come too, so we can all eat together," Susan said, closing the subject. "I'll prepare top side's meals ahead and make sure Simon takes them up before he comes."

"This sort of thing gets subjects killed," Jarvis said. He was here to stop this reckless endangerment of the subject and make her accessible to those in power. "You are all acting like this is a family outing instead of a shopping trip. There should be a structure and a plan for where your subjects will be shopping and how quickly you can get them there and back. Exposure can get your subject killed. I'm vetoing this whole shopping venture."

Susan held up a finger to signal one moment. She held her hand out to Tex. "Hand me your phone." She thought to Tex. He pulled his phone out and gave it to her. Susan knew her grandfather was on speed dial and which number it was. Tex had let that slip into his mind once. She pressed the number and waited for her grandfather to pick up the phone. Usually, she wouldn't pull out the grandfather card on anyone, but this bully had to stop. "Hi, I have an overbearing SS agent here trying to stop me from shopping for clothing for my son. Yes, I would appreciate you having a word with him." She handed the phone to Jarvis.

He put the phone to his ear, unsure who was on the other end of the call. "Hello?" Jarvis said.

"Tex, what in the Hell is going on there? What do you mean stopping Susan from shopping for my grandson?" the President barked into Jarvis' ear.

"Sir, this is Jarvis Adams. I've ruled the outing as too dangerous. They plan on meeting up at some restaurant and eating out after shopping. This will tire out the night shift and put the subject in additional danger, exposing her more to the public," Jarvis said.

"She is not a subject. The woman you are speaking about is my granddaughter. And why do you think you are calling the shots on anything? You listen to Susan and do what she tells you." There was a loud click on the President's end of the call. He slammed the phone down.

"Your plans stand," Jarvis stated, his voice tightly controlled.

Chapter Thirteen

DUTY CALLS

The outing was going as smoothly as Tex had thought. They were on the way to meet up and eat when his phone rang. Roger was driving. Tex answered the call, listening to the person on the other end of the phone without commenting. "Just why is she needed?" he finally asked.

Jarvis sat up a little straighter. This call was about his subject. Should he not be the one talking? "I'll take that," he said, reaching over the seat for the phone.

Ignoring Jarvis, Tex spoke one last time and hung up. He turned to Jarvis and said, "After our meal, we will go to the airport. Simon will go with George to pick up our go-bags. I assume you have one ready. If not, don't feel bad. Most of us didn't realize how much traveling would be involved here. You can go prepare your bag with Simon and George if needed." Tex raised a questioning eyebrow at Jarvis.

If Jarvis realized Tex was trying to be

reasonable, he wouldn't have shown it. His expression was sour. He glanced over at Susan and forced out a smile for her. "No, I haven't unpacked everything yet. They will grab my duffel bag. Although, I would appreciate having my razor placed back inside it," he said. She had to believe he was playing nicely there, even though he should be in charge of this whole thing. First, it seems, he must win her over to his side.

For once, Susan was looking forward to the mission. Not that she wanted to be among all those plotting, stressed-out minds. A break from the new guy's plotting was what she needed at the moment. However, someone was stopping her with his thoughts. She raised her hand.

Roger pulled the car over to the curb, stopping when he saw Susan's hand go up. "Where?" Tex asked as he looked around. "SS or security mode," he told himself now.

Scoffing, Jarvis then snorted out something like, "No restaurant here, doughhead."

Doing her slow turn thing, Susan rotated in one direction and then the other. "There, the photoshop. A man, armed, holding them up," Susan said.

What crazy shit was this? Jarvis thought they were all insane. Tex took over once more. Loosening his gun, he opened his car door. "Roger, take Miss Whiting, York, and the SS guy to safety. I'll call it in and remain here. The story is I saw it happening through the window. You were never here. If you need to, go on meet up with George and Simon. Now go," Tex said, stepping back and shutting the door.

The car lurched forward before Jarvis could even voice his opinion of the craziness of the whole thing. "Miss Susan, York, you both get down low. Jarvis, contact George and Simon to update them," Roger ordered, sounding so much like Tex it could have been him barking orders.

"Update them on what? Reporting nothing is crazy," Jarvis grumbled.

"I'll do it, sir," York told Roger. York seldom had a reason to call. Pulling out his phone, he speed-dialed George. "Tex is making sure that they arrest a crook that Mom spotted. Roger has Mom and me secured away from the action." York called up to Roger from his spot on the floor in the back seat, "Anything else?"

"Yeah, tell them to swing by and pick Tex up. I'm taking you on to our meet-up spot," Roger said. He felt like a proud father at how York stepped up and gave the message. The boy delivered the report in the same to-the-point sentences they all used. He let York finish talking to George before speaking again. "You did great, York. Okay, you can both sit up again and relax. Miss Susan, any news on Tex?"

"The police arrived, and he could slip away without being noticed. Nobody was hurt," she told him. "Jarvis, when we reach the meet-up spot, we will go in and get the table for us all. George and the others should be along shortly. Count."

That last word was said as an order, causing Jarvis to bite his tongue to keep from making a comeback remark. Count? That is the same thing Tex had told him to do. Why the hell did he need to count? They had arrived at the meeting spot before he could pull up reasons for counting. He stepped out of the car, sweeping the area with his eyes. Nothing suspicious. He opened the door for Susan and helped her out of the car, holding her hand just a little longer than was needed. He thought he knew how to win women over, smiling to himself. She didn't stand a chance.

"Walk between us, York," Susan thought to York. York walked up to her and squeezed between Jarvis and her, putting his arm around her waist. Roger was back behind them, sweeping the area for any sign of danger to his subjects. He was unaware of the tension that was building up in Susan.

The kid was getting in the way of him making his moves on the subject. Jarvis had planned on placing his hand on the small of her back to walk her to the table. But the kid kept his arm clutched around the black beauty. Guarding this subject was the worst assignment he had ever drawn, Jarvis grumbled to himself. His subject smiled slightly. Maybe he was winning her over after all.

Tex's eyes immediately sought out Susan the moment they entered the restaurant. He found it hard to be separated from her, fearing he would lose her again. And thinking Jarvis would make a move on her. Both possibilities made him nearly crazy and worried. It was as if he was a person split into two parts. He knew he could never be the man in her life and had to let her find someone to love her. At the same time, he couldn't accept another man having her love. So he took whatever small moments came to him. He gloried in her sticking up for his decisions, yet tried to always think of what was the honorable thing to do. His life sucked big time now, but he wouldn't give it up. Committed to the impossible, Tex walked swiftly to the tables pushed together to accommodate their group and nodded to Jarvis and Roger. That nod said I'm back and in control, boys.

Once they were all seated, everyone looked to Tex to explain what was going on. He alone had the details of the assignment that called Susan to D.C.

Tex waited for their meal before telling everyone about the assignment. "President Whiting is worried about one of the people who has been with him for many years. He did not send the General to get you this time. He does not want it known that he is concerned about this particular person's behavior. So we are going on a visit with your grandfather so you can do your thing. We will go from there," Tex told Susan.

"Does it involve parties or dinners?" Susan asked.

Looking worried, Tex answered, "Frankly, I do not know. We are being kept in the dark this time. I got the impression that the person your grandfather is worried about is a friend. Something is not right. My gut is saying this is rotten." Tex looked around the table at the others. "Keep alert. We may have a fast trip to D.C., so you do not have to take this assignment. Give me the word, and I'll see that this assignment is void." He wanted her to tell him to call and cancel, but as he watched Susan, he saw her chin raise just a fraction and knew she had committed already.

"If something is wrong, we have to find out what is wrong so the country is kept safe," Susan told them as she looked into the distance.

"What about York?" Roger asked, "Is this too dangerous for him?"

York spoke up at that. "I go with my mother. I'm her battery," he stated as if there was no doubt he should go.

"Leave the kid here. He would be underfoot," Jarvis said, inserting himself into a command position. Or so he thought.

"My son stays with me. I will not leave him behind where he could be vulnerable. We have seen how easy it was for a monster to kidnap me. I will not take a chance on being separated from York. We lost two of our men during that time. I do not want to have more deaths weighing on my soul," Susan said, and that killed any debate about York coming.

Deaths? Jarvis suddenly felt out of the loop on what had happened here. There hadn't been two SS reported killed, not that he knew of anyway. He'd do a record check while they traveled. Jarvis felt Susan looking at him. Looking over at her, he asked, "What?"

"I am not certain you should go with us. How do we know we can trust you?" Susan said bluntly.

Shock raced through him. How could she question his trustworthiness? Before Jarvis could express himself, Susan spoke up again.

"Every step of the way, you have questioned and tried to counter-command each move my team has made. How can I trust you if you are unwilling to accept Tex as the team leader? Your only thoughts have been about taking over and doing things your way. In truth, you don't even know what is going on. Yet, you expect everyone to listen to you. I can't, won't listen to a man I can't trust with my life and that of my son and my men," Susan told Jarvis.

Sitting back as if struck, Jarvis thought of what she had just said. He could see how she might feel that way. He had thought he should take control of the team and her. But they were the ones who blocked his every action and word. How was that his fault? Then her words sank into his mind because he didn't know what was happening. He just wanted to take charge. The president seemed to want Tex to stay with her. The others had pressured him into making the changeover, recalling Tex. Oh shit, he thought, some creeps have used me.

"Exactly," Susan said as if he had said that out loud. "What are you going to do about it?"

"Follow Tex. Be the low man instead of the leader. And protect you," Jarvis finally said, his face still not looking as if he had accepted things.

"And count," Susan said.

His brow furrowed at this condition of his serving her. He wanted to ask why but was afraid to make waves. Jarvis nodded and started mentally counting. He saw a look of relief appear on Susan's face. Did his counting do that? "You mentioned deaths? Who died? There isn't a report on it."

Tex looked at Susan and waited for her nod before he began talking. "Recently, we had an intruder kidnap Miss Susan. The guy came in at night and knew about the snipers. He first went up and took out the snipers. Then, while George rushed up to check on the gunfire up top, the guy came down and shot Simon. Miss Susan exited the bunker, something against all our rules on keeping her safe. Only she did it to try and pull Simon inside and keep him safe. The creep grabbed her and used her as a shield against George. The guy raised his gun to shoot George, but Susan's protector, Chatterbox, nailed the guy in the leg, and his hand auto-swung down, wounding George in the leg. Then the creep shot Chatterbox. George hit the guy in the leg and limped after the man as the slime carried Susan off.

"George nearly died from blood loss but is a tough old bird. Anyway, we all tracked the traitor down, and he isn't going to harm anyone again. But we lost our two topside guys. That is hard to even think about."

"We?" Jarvis asked, thinking two would have been in the hospital.

Susan spoke up, "All of them came except for Chatterbox. York directed Goldie to follow the track. I understand Simon and George drove the car, and Tex led to the fore. They all found me, although I was pretty out of it, having been beaten to a pulp, I knew they were there."

"This was recent?" Jarvis's voice held tones of disbelief.

"Yes." They all said.

"Okay," Jarvis said in a small voice. His eyes searched over them all. He could see no indication of the trauma they had mentioned.

"Count," Susan said.

He had forgotten to count, but how did she know? Jarvis started counting and concentrating so as not to stop again.

The team stood, exiting the restaurant. They piled into the cars. They had an assignment duty to which they had to take their subject.

This trip was Jarvis's first time with them on an assignment. He felt like all their eyes were on him, judging him. Jarvis was feeling the pressure to be at his finest. He held doors for Susan and fetched anyone who wanted something. To their credit, they didn't haze him or make him do anything. They didn't seem to expect anything from him, which made matters worse. It made him feel lacking as if he wasn't good enough. Never before had Jarvis thought he wasn't up to a task. So, he watched his tongue and didn't say anything sarcastic. Jarvis brought out the gentlemanly manners his Mamma had pounded into his head. He watched everything the others did and listened to their conversations. The problem was that he didn't understand half of what they said. It was as if they were talking in some form of shorthand.

"The bunker is all set, Miss Susan," Tex told Susan. "I've set up the Secret Service guys in a house nearby. Are you certain you can sleep with George and me in the bunker?"

"Yes, think of tadpoles," she said with a smile.

Tex nodded. He could do that. It warmed his heart that she remembered his tadpole story. He'd set aside all the thoughts of barbed wire and anthills to give her tadpoles.

"We never did see if Dewy was having a baby," York suddenly said.

"I think it is too soon to tell," George grumbled from the back of their plane. He knew he should sleep, but he had seen the doe on one of his patrols, and it was hard to see any hint she was expecting a baby.

It went that way for a while, with them talking about things he didn't know until they all fell silent and tried to rest.

As the descent to the airport began, Susan's team went on alert. The last experience here had not been good. The difference this time was they had been called directly by the President, not some go-between minion. That didn't mean letting down their guard, though. Everyone but Jarvis checked their weapon as the wheels touched down. "Check your weapon. Be certain it is loose and ready to fire," Tex told him, looking at him until he did as he ordered.

"George, you do a quick visual. Check if the car is in place this time. We know they had planned some attack last time. Let's stay on top of things," Tex told them all as he had Susan and York both crouch down and wait for the all-clear to proceed.

"The Limousine is in place, and two men are waiting. Do either of you recognize them?" George asked, stepping back so Tex and Simon could have a look-see.

"One of them, I know. The other is a stranger to me," Simon said. "Go, no go?"

"Go. Form a shield around Miss Whiting and York. Weapons out," Tex finally said.

Susan thought of meat shields. They considered themselves as nothing more than meat shields. They are so much more. Look at Roger, who is still a boy at heart but has grown up with us. He is so intense, yet I can see the child in him. Simon, the sturdy, feels like he has to be there for Tex and us all. George, the practical Joker, jokes to relieve the tension and give the others a bit of laughter. He is committed to Tex, his job, and us all. Then there is Tex. He considers himself only a meat shield. He can't see his worth, so they all look up to him. They are here because of him because they respect him and even love him as a brother. He thinks nobody loves him. So he will let himself die to protect the rest and do his job.

Her thoughts had become so morbid that Susan felt she had to let them all know she would not accept their deaths. "You are not to risk death protecting me. Besides, there are no threats here. So relax. You are not Meat Shields. You are my friends and family," she said in an ordering voice, wanting to look over at Tex but not single him out.

Tex didn't seem to have heard her as he firmly planted himself between her and the two black-suited men in the limo waiting for her. The others took their cue from Tex, staying firmly beside her. York reached out and took Susan's hand. "It is okay, Mom. They don't want to lose you again," York silently told her.

"Identify yourselves," Tex told the two men by the limo.

"Clark, I'll be driving you while Miss Whiting visits in the Capital. This man is Sanders. He came along as my trainee," Clark said, producing his identification and showing it to Tex. "I didn't expect so many of you. Do I need to order a second car, sir?"

Tex glanced at Susan and noticed the slight shake of her head. "No, we can manage. Jarvis, you ride up front with the drivers. The rest of us will share with Miss Whiting." It sounded like Jarvis was going to object, but the man quickly cut off whatever he was going to say. Tex still didn't completely trust him.

They crammed themselves into the limo, the SS sitting so some faced forward and some to the back. George and Tex are on either side of Susan and York. The tension in the men was high. Each remembered the time before when they had to get Susan and York out of D.C. as fast as they could. They didn't talk with men they didn't know in front of the car. Trust. The trust of even fellow agents had gone out the window.

"Where to, Ma'am?" Clark asked.

"The bunker first. I think we could all use a little freshening up. Then, if my grandfather isn't busy, I'd like to visit with him," Susan said. It did not go unnoticed that she hadn't just told the driver they would go next to see the President. The detour to the bunker was new. Usually, she would have gotten to business immediately to lessen the time spent in the Capital.

Susan seldom heard her grandfather wasn't available for a visit, perhaps never. The voice on the other end of the phone call she had placed said in a no-nonsense tone, "The President will be in meetings all day. I'm sorry, Miss Whiting, but you must try again tomorrow."

"Are you saying I need to make an appointment to visit with my grandfather?" Susan asked.

"Yes… No, no… well, I cannot comment on that. With all these meetings, right now is a critical time for the President. So much so that a casual visit, I guess, needs to be scheduled," came the hesitating reply.

"Okay then, let's do that. Where is there a ten-minute break when I can visit with my grandfather?" Susan asked.

"You're not upset?"

"No, I understand. You are doing your job. Grandfather is doing his job. Now, why would I be upset over that?" Susan said. She could feel the woman's relief at the other end of the phone. She had feared that Susan would complain to the President about her not being allowed access to him. "Now, do you have time for me to speak with my grandfather?"

"He has a full schedule for tomorrow. However, I know it won't take him twenty minutes to speak with Senator Garbo. Could you get here at 9:30 in the morning? I will hold off Representative Denver for a couple of minutes when he shows up while you chat with President Whiting," the woman told her.

"You are wonderful. Thank you so much. I'll be there, but don't you feel pressured to fit me in if things go sideways? Okay?" Susan replied. Putting down the phone, she wondered what they should do with their free time that day.

"York, where would you like to visit today? We have some free time." She called out.

Amazingly, York was out of ideas for places to see. It was Roger who finally spoke up,

"The newest Marvel movie is out. How big a problem would it be to go see it?" he asked, glancing to where Tex was standing guard in the bunker.

"A darkened theater will not make it easy to guard Miss Whiting and York," Tex said. He noticed York trying not to look disappointed and continued, "But I happen to know where we can have a private showing of the movie."

"Really?" York yelped out in joy.

A snorted laugh came from Roger, but he, too, looked at Tex with questions in his eyes.

"Yes, someone I once helped will give us a showing. That is if the room is available. Let me call him," Tex said, walking off a distance from the others to make his call. Returning to the others, Tex winked at York. "All set. If we leave now, we can have our private viewing and still have time for dinner and a drink. I can't reveal my source. You will not meet him, but he has made a crew and viewing available for us. Ready?"

York was up, walking to the bunker's door so fast it was as if he had flown. Roger wasn't far behind him. Both had a look of great anticipation on their faces.

Much later, they met up with the night crew for dinner. Jarvis didn't even grumble about it under his breath. He was becoming used to the whole group thing this subject and team had going on. It still chaffed Jarvis that Tex was the one in charge. When they sent him, it was his understanding that he was taking over for Tex. Tex was the team's leader, so didn't that mean he became the leader? He had been put in his place by his subject. Her threat to leave him behind, he did not believe for one moment, was an idle threat. So, he was biding his time watching for something he could report. And have Tex removed? He thought this whole dinner and drinks would be a check on the bye-bye-Tex list. After all, you didn't drink on duty. You were on duty all the time.

When they pulled up to the restaurant, George and Simon were already there, waiting just outside the door for them. The smell of frying fish and boiled crabs hit them as they entered the building. Sweeping the area with his eyes, Tex nodded to the others to proceed. He watched as York talked a constant flow of exciting words to Roger about the movie they had just seen. The boy was on cloud nine, and Tex was sorry his friend hadn't agreed to meet up with them to cap off the night for York. He could almost see York's enthusiasm at meeting the movie's star. The kid would be floating for days. A half-smile briefly graced Tex's face. Then, Jarvis held Susan's chair, and Tex's face returned to all business. He tapped down the jealousy he was feeling. Tex didn't have the right to have those feelings. Or so he told himself.

So far, guarding this subject had been a cakewalk. Jarvis didn't see why they felt she needed so many men watching over her. It was hard for him to keep up the humble act. She was just another rich subject more full of herself than most. She had browbeaten the rest of the team. It was up to him to figure out a way to handle her. He smiled at her as he held her chair for her. Brownie points, Jarvis thought. He had to make stupid brownie points.

"The only thing you need to do is your job," Susan told Jarvis in a low whisper. "Count, please."

"45600, 45601," Tex counted like mad when Susan whispered to Jarvis. He was losing her. No, she was living her life. Tex wasn't part of it. The waiter came, and Tex made a circle with his finger to include the whole table. "Some of your famous iced tea for the table, then we will order," he said. "This place serves the nearest to down-home iced tea I've ever found. Only my Mamma made it better."

"Tea? I thought we were having drinks," Jarvis said.

"None of us drink. And you are on duty," Simon corrected Jarvis, taking the burden of the correction on himself to spare Tex.

"Of course," Jarvis said with a frown, so much for counting drinking on the job against Tex.

"I drink," York piped up, saying, "I like tea." He looked at Susan and added, "And milk."

"Milk's good," Roger said.

"Hum… I'm beginning to suspect what happened to the last of my cereal milk," George grumbled, and everyone except Jarvis laughed.

Shortly before 9:30, Susan and the day team showed up for the appointment to speak to the President. Susan felt a whirlwind of thoughts from the people in and around the area where she sat waiting. These people were worried about her grandfather. The problem was they did not know exactly why they were worrying. He seemed off, not himself. Whatever was bothering her grandfather was noticed by the others. What she found most disturbing was that Susan could not hear her grandfather's thoughts. Her grandfather was counting!

"Something is wrong, Tex," Susan mentally told the non-SS agent. "Grandfather is counting. He never counts when I am near him. He trusts me with his secrets." She saw out of the corner of her eye Tex ever so slight straightening of his body. His head nodded as if confirming something in his mind.

This assignment was more than they believed it to be. If the President himself was trying to hide information from Susan, Tex thought. He looked over at Roger, who was standing stiff and proper behind where York was sitting. Should they remove York from the area? A glance at Jarvis confirmed the agent was unaware of Susan's tension. He needed to drill both men in hand signals once they were in a safe zone. For now, he would depend on Susan to alert Roger. "Please tell Roger to be alert. And do you think we should remove York to safety?" he sent silently to Susan.

"Not at this moment. I will alert York, and he can tell Roger. I think it would freak Roger out to hear my voice in his head," Susan responded. She thought to York: "Whisper to Roger to be alert. I think we need to be careful here." She didn't look directly at York as she watched him motion for Roger to bend down. York whispered in his ear.

The child is getting restless, thought Jarvis, as he saw York whispering to Roger. The very reason he had not wanted to bring a child with them. They had no attention span. They took up time and got in the way. He probably wanted to use the restroom. It was a mistake for Tex to have included the child in this whole scatterbrained trip. Jarvis wanted to make sure everything was clear while meeting the President. Jarvis stood up straighter. He figured this could be his chance to secure a place guarding the President.

The door to the meeting room opened. The President had finished with his current appointment. A man with a grim expression walked out of the meeting room. The secretary motioned for Susan to go in and see her grandfather. Rising, she and the others stepped forward. "Jarvis, stand out here and watch. Roger and I will shadow Miss Whiting and York unless the President wants to talk to her privately," Tex told Jarvis. Jarvis opened his mouth, then shut up. Once the others had entered the other room, Jarvis stood against the door. He was not trying to hear what was going on inside the other room, not really.

"Grandfather," Susan said, hugging the elderly white man with her dark arms. "We came for a little visit before taking a trip to show York the countryside. Will you be able to take a few minutes to visit with us? Would it be possible to have dinner with us tonight? If not, we can wait another night or two if you have an opening." All the while she talked, Susan was hugged tightly by her grandfather. The action was unlike the man. Susan felt as if he was holding on for dear life.

Finally, Stanley Whiting let go of his adopted granddaughter. He walked over and shook York's hand. Then shook hands with Roger and, last of all, with Tex. He held Tex's hand a little longer than was needed and squeezed it before letting go. "I am sorry, dear. You have come at the most inconvenient time. I have meetings in this room for the duration of your stay. I can have the chief bring us up something if you are hungry. But maybe I had better check my schedule before committing to anything. You know my life belongs to the country. I'm so sorry, Susan dear," Stanley Whiting said. He kept counting like mad, trying to block off his internal thoughts.

"It is okay, Grandfather. We can have a visit once we have finished our little vacation trip. I will let Mom and Dad know you are looking good," Susan told him, noticing the hint of panic in his eyes when she mentioned her parents. She kissed him on the cheek and gave him a huge hug that he did not seem to want to escape from, but eventually, he let go of her, and then he hugged York.

Susan left the meeting room, smiling and looking as cheery as possible. She thanked the woman who had allowed her to see her grandfather, collected Jarvis, and left the building.

She waited until they were back in the bunker, and Tex had swept the bunker for hidden bugs before she spoke. "He is in trouble. I think he is, more or less, held against his will. More than anything, I believe he wanted me to get to safety. Also, he did not want my parents involved." Susan paused to look at Tex. "He was counting the entire time, so I could not get anything from him. Tex, Grandfather never counts when I visit him. I think he wanted to warn me to stay away. And that was the only way he could tell me."

"What about the others nearby? Were they counting?" Tex asked.

"No, but they all worry that something is wrong with him. Most of them thought it was a health issue. Or to do with his age," Susan told him.

"But you do not think so," Tex said. He paced for a moment, deep in thought. I am open to any thoughts the rest of you have," he finally said, looking at each team member.

Given the opening, Jarvis said, "I think you are all being a little paranoid here, seeing things that are not there. The President is likely under great pressure to run the country. I doubt he is in trouble just because he does not have time for a social tea."

The others all looked at him as if he had lost his mind. Oddly enough, it was Roger who spoke up. "Between what you said, the people around him are thinking. And his treatment of you, given he was the one who asked you to come, has to be an internal threat. We need to be as covert as possible here."

"I agree," Simon said. "Operation Darkness is what we are in now. What do you think, Tex?"

"Operation Darkness it is. All phones are off, and nobody talks to anyone outside the immediate team about this. We behave as if this is a vacation for everyone. It will be up to you, Miss Susan, to dig deep and find the source of the problem," Tex said, looking at each team member. "Phones out, turn them off, and take the batteries out." Tex turned off his phone as he gave the order.

Chapter Fouteen

THE FEW

Loony bin. These people are all crazy, Jarvis thought. They had concocted this insane theory of some fictional danger to the country from a conversation that anyone could see was innocent. The man was busy, simple as that. Jarvis saw his subject looking at him, studying him like a bug. Why? He was not trying to order her around. Instead, he was letting her go her crazy way. Yet, she seemed to judge him as if he lacked good sense.

Susan thought it may have been a mistake to have allowed Jarvis to come with them. His mind just was not on the job. He pretended he was going along with what they were doing, but Jarvis was only biding his time until he could do things his way. Unfortunately, what he wanted had nothing to do with the reality of her life. The attempts to further his career could become a problem if they had to go in and rescue her grandfather from whatever was threatening him. Could she even trust the man to keep her secret? That may be the problem. He did not know what was going on, what she did.

"Tex, I think you and I need to sit down with Jarvis and explain everything to him tonight," Susan thought to Tex. She could feel some resistance in Tex. Then he nodded as if he had come to the same conclusion.

Later, once George and Simon were awake, the joint meal was over. Susan motioned Jarvis over to her. She noticed how he brightened as if he believed this was an opportunity to get her to his side. When Tex joined them, Jarvis frowned.

"What I will tell you stays here between the team members. Any breach of the trust we are placing in you will result in your imprisonment or death. Do you understand and swear to remain forever silent about what we will reveal?" Tex asked Jarvis.

The SS agent sat with his face a study of confusion. Finally, he spoke, "And if I don't agree?"

"Then you will not participate in any missions Miss Susan is assigned. When we leave in mission mode, you will be left behind. You will become a glorified doorman. This decision is the most serious decision you will make in your lifetime. Consider carefully if you are willing to commit completely to being one of the Secret Service agents guarding Miss Susan. If not, then walk away now and do not look back. If you commit, then you are to carry to your death the information we will give you. You will need to sign several documents. Do you need time to think things over?" Tex asked.

Jarvis realized Tex was serious about leaving him out of missions. The fact that Tex gave him an out convinced him that more was happening here. More than they told him when he received this assignment. He knew his mission was to eliminate Tex and send him packing. He was to take charge of the team. They had yet to tell him the reason for removing Tex other than he was not doing his job. He finally answered with a sense of dread, "I agree; just tell me what is going on."

"We, this team, and three other teams are the Few, the only people privy to this information. Many of the SS have had assignments like ours. They never knew the true reason behind being the security of this family. It might be hard for you to accept the truth of what is going on here. But accept it you must if you are to remain on this team. First, however, you must sign some documents," Tex told him, lifting a briefcase onto the coffee table before him. Tex set the contents in front of Jarvis, taking out a folder. "Signing your full name to these documents will constitute swearing to all the stipulations. This commitment is for life. It does not mean the life of the job but your life, even unto death. And beyond. Do you understand?"

Arching an eyebrow, Jarvis looked as if he wanted to object somehow. "And beyond," he said under his breath as if mocking Tex.

Tex's mouth became a hard, straight line. "Yes, and beyond. Should you, in some misguided manner, decide to talk about, write about, transmit, record, or divulge in any manner this information placed in your trust to another. Or other individuals, during your life or upon your death bed, those individuals will be imprisoned in your stead. Do not take this lightly. If you are not going to commit completely to this Vow, leave now," Tex stated, pausing to allow Jarvis time to get up and leave. "You can go back and report that your mission was a success. You have managed to get me out of the SS. If not off the team."

"You knew that was my main task?" Jarvis asked, his brows scowling.

Keeping his eyes locked on Jarvis, Tex answered, "Yes, of course. This attempt is not the first time whoever is behind all this has tried to get rid of me. That fake arrest they pulled to keep me away using the so-called investigation into my competence in guarding Miss Susan. That was a bunch of bull crap too. And look at what resulted. I was not there to protect Miss Susan. Two of us died, and George and Simon were wounded.

"They kidnapped Miss Susan and hurt her. I'll never forgive them. They caused her harm! When I find out who is responsible, the rest of you had best be somewhere else." Realizing his voice had become deadly, Tex reined himself back. Now was not the time to let anger rule him. Susan touched his arm to offer comfort and reassure him everything was okay.

Again, that bit about a kidnapping was not on the records. If for no other reason than to find out what happened. Jarvis picked a pen from the table and began signing his name and writing his initials in all the places indicated in the documents before him.

"Raise your right hand and swear you

understand the restrictions now binding you. Do you swear to remain true to this oath and all it entails, so help you, God?" Tex asked.

"I swear, so help me, God," Jarvis swore.

Having sworn his solemn oath, Jarvis cleared his throat. "Now, will you please tell me about this so-called kidnapping again? There is no record of anything like that happening," he asked. "And none of you appear to be recovering from injuries."

Tex motioned George and Simon over. As they seated, he said, "Let's tell him the whole story. My part started with two goons showing up. They handcuffed me and hauled me off to D.C. It was late into my sleep cycle before I arrived at my house. Well, your house now. George and Simon need to speak of what happened while I was traveling home."

A dark, haunted look was on Simon's face when he took up the tale. "We were all worried about Tex that day. Miss Susan made all of Tex's favorite dishes for dinner when we expected him home. When he didn't show up, I knew some deep shit was going on. George and I had decided to fetch him home if he wasn't back the next day. We ate, then took food up top. We saw that Miss Susan and York were locked in the bunker for the night. My gut alarm was blaring damn loud by the time I figured our subjects were asleep. There was a pop, pop up-top. George went up to check it out. I remained to watch over Miss Susan and York. The prep stepped out of the woods and popped me in the shoulder as I fired at him. George needs to tell the rest.

George scrubbed a hand over his face, trying

to wipe the vision in his mind of the two snipers up top sprawled dead when he reached them. "We both knew our roles once we heard the shots up top. I sprinted up the mountain in silent mode. There was nothing I could do for our men there, so I grabbed a long gun and scrambled back down, having heard the shot that took Simon down. The truth is, I was hoping Simon had killed the bastard. Instead, Simon was down. The creep had hold of Miss Susan and was trying to drag her off."

George looked over at Susan with admiration in his eyes. "You were fighting him like a wild cat. I was so proud of you, Honey," he told her before continuing. "The filth pulled her in front of him. so I paused a second too long considering my shot, not wanting to hit Miss Susan. He popped me one. He wanted a kill shot, but Miss Susan was fighting him. And then Chatterbox attacked him. The creep leg shot me, and my dumb ass leg folded on me. He knocked Miss Susan out, threw her over his shoulder, and headed for the woods after shooting poor Chatterbox. I'd rolled to sight him with the long gun aimed at his leg to avoid hitting Miss Susan. I got him, but he kept going.

"I field-packed Simon's shoulder and began tracking after Miss Susan using the long gun as a crutch. There was blood along the way, so I knew I had hit him and tracked him to a road where he had a car stashed. I heard him close the trunk of the car as I approached. I shot several rounds in his side of the car and the tires. I headed back to check on Simon and get a car to follow him, but I had lost too much blood to stay conscious. The bastard had Miss

Susan, and there was no chance we would stop until we got him and brought our gal home."

"He got away?" the question just slipped out of Jarvis. He had become wrapped up in the telling of the story.

Looking down at the floor, his face woebegone with guilt, George nodded. He sat up straighter. "For that moment. We don't quit, not ever. Tex, you tell your part. I was out at that point."

"I had gone to bed, knowing I needed a few hours of sleep to protect Miss Susan. Dewy nearly knocked down the door, waking me up. The moment I opened the door, I knew Susan was in trouble. There was no other reason Dewy and Sly would come knocking on my door. I slipped into my boots and grabbed the cell phone, gun, and keys. Dewy indicated that taking the car wouldn't work for what she wanted. So she showed the way with Sly urging me on. Soon, it was apparent that two individuals had tromped through the forest. One of them returned. One or both were bleeding out. My instinct was to rush to the house and bunker to see if Susan was secure. Dewy took me to a pile of leaves, under which George was bleeding to death. George came to enough to give a report. He told me Simon was down at the house. Someone kidnapped Miss Susan, but York was safe. George had lost too much blood to make it to the house. We don't leave anyone behind. With George in my arms and Dewy and Sly escorting, I managed to carry George home.

"Then I checked on Simon. I realized there was another victim, Chatterbox. I called a specialist for him, started treating him for shock, and collected the evidence he had managed to acquire when he bit the kidnapper. After the Doc treated Chatterbox, I went to pick up the rest of the team. I figured they would try to escape by the time I arrived. I was a few minutes too late. And the two of them were trying to walk home in their hospital gown. We regrouped, fed our wounded, and formed a plan to track the creep who took our gal down," Tex said, pausing; he looked over at Susan. "I heard you call out to me. But I couldn't get the connection again. If I had just been able to get close enough to hear from you again, maybe he wouldn't have been able to hurt you so badly. I'm so sorry…" Tex stopped and looked away, guilt choking him as he tried to control his anger at letting her down.

"Stop. Not one more moment will you continue feeling guilty over something you were not responsible for doing. I couldn't contact you. Or York. After he struck me on the head, I was mute and deaf. I was alone. Do you understand? I was alone," Susan told him, her voice sharp and demanding. "Mother said there was a bleed in my mind that caused it. It was not your fault."

Susan turned towards Jarvis, pinning him with a commanding look. "The truth is I'm a spy for the United States. For the President. Whenever he needs me, the General carts me off to D.C. My family is talented. We each serve a purpose. Mother heals, Middy enforces, Eric sees, and I hear every thought anyone has within a certain distance. For example, you were thinking, what a bunch of lunatics. You think that fairly often. You also tend to look down on all of us. And feel you can use me, if you can win me over, to get yourself promoted. You forget to count and shout your thoughts out almost constantly. You have a very unorganized mind. And I am still not convinced you will not be more of a liability to us than help. Perhaps, if you think of things from our side of the equation, it will help you. You were forced on us by someone determined to either cut me off from helping our country or out to use me against this country. And you don't even know who is using you. That part is sad. It is what has kept me from sending you packing. I can not trust you until your view of things has changed. Thus, we are giving you this one chance."

A cold chill swept over Jarvis. He had thought that they were all lunatics. She had him pegged and put in a peg hole. Had he been that transparent? He sat up a little straighter, wondering what he should do now. "So, you read minds?" he said, knowing how stupid that sounded.

"No, minds sort of bombard my mind. It is like walking into a room where a hundred radios are playing. Each set is on a different channel and turned up all the way. Thus, I live on my mountain, away from all the noise. And all the bickering thoughts, the blame everyone else thoughts, the rage, the greed, the hate, the lust, and the paranoia," Susan answered. "But all those voices were silent for what seemed like an eternity when I was hurt. You never know what something means to you until you have lost it.

"These men, the few who know the truth, are made of the stuff that real heroes have. They don't seek recognition for it, nor do they seek to gain anything. They are here because they believe in this country and want to keep her safe. So, I will continue to do my thing. When someone is trying to trick the President, I will let him know. If someone is out to assassinate the President, I'll let him know. Tell me, what will you do?"

Jarvis rubbed his forehead, squirming slightly, wondering what she was asking. There was only one answer he could give. "Guard you." Yet she was still looking at him as if he was lacking. What was he supposed to say? They kept saying she was kidnapped and hurt. She looked fit, with no bruising, no scars, nothing to indicate she'd had so much as a pimple. "When did all this shooting happen? There is no report on it, and there is nothing to say that this happened. You could be putting me on."

"Fair enough, trust for trust," Tex said. "It has been two and a half weeks."

"Don't give me that shit!" Jarvis blew up. He jabbed his finger at George and Simon, "You claim they were leg and shoulder shot. And her…" Jarvis indicated Susan with his head, "badly beaten. Yet here they are, hale and hardy."

Susan put a hand on Tex's arm to stop him from saying or doing anything. She turned a face of stone towards Jarvis. "One of your greatest faults is you don't listen. Did I not tell you my mother is a healer?"

"So she is a doctor that doesn't explain the three of you looking like you never had a sick day," Jarvis argued.

"Yes, it does. Mrs. Whiting heals. Do you understand? Heals. Completely," Susan told him.

"A general practitioner. It takes the body weeks to heal and recover. Unless she is some miracle worker, the three of you should still be recovering. George should be limping, Simon. Over there, he is having therapy for his shoulder, and you too," he said with disgust in his voice.

"From a doctor having treated us, yes. My mother heals. Even though she has her degree and license to practice, she instead heals," Susan explained. The thoughts coming from Jarvis were like a scream inside her head. He was cursing and calling them all lunatics. Susan raised her hand.

That was all it took to bring Tex to his feet. "What do you need?" he asked, his hand moving to his gun as he swept the area inside the bunker and checked the security monitor.

Closing her eyes, Susan pointed at Jarvis. "I need him out of here. He is screaming curse words in my mind. Very loud. So much anger."

Before Susan stopped speaking, Tex had Jarvis' arm twisted behind his back and disarmed him. Tex counted like crazy and tried to think of anything besides killing this bastard. Simon was beside him, a concerned look on his face. He didn't try to stop Tex and even card-swiped the security door for Tex and stepped outside with him. As soon as the bunker was secure again, Simon spoke. "I don't think she would approve of you killing him. What are you going to do?"

"Talk to him," Tex grunted. He took a breath as if bringing himself back under control. "At the SS house. He will not be allowed back in the bunker. Susan will decide if she wants to allow him to go on missions. He is going to learn to count before I finish with him. Don't expect me back for a couple of hours. And take possession of his gun… and mine, for now."

Simon nodded, securing both weapons. "I'll keep her safe," he promised. He reached up and smacked Jarvis on the back of the head. "That is for being so stupid as to hurt Miss Susan. Wash your mind out."

Thrust into a chair in the house set up for himself and the other two SS, Jarvis felt creepy crawlers running up his spine. He had never had cause to fear for his life, but that fear was running wild inside him now. This man had a reputation. He hadn't believed it up until the moment he was disarmed and roughly taken to this house. Tex shot at Generals, for God's sake! And he killed without so much as breaking a sweat. Rubbing his shoulder, Jarvis dared not take his eyes off Tex. For the first time, he noticed the steel in Tex's eyes and the way he held his lips so tightly shut as if afraid that if he opened his mouth, he'd kill him.

It took a long moment before Tex trusted himself enough to speak to the creep before him. The fact that he had hurt Susan right after she had explained how thoughts affected her made him want to knock the guy out and then put him in a room with a million recorded voices blaring at him. "Tell me what you said to Miss Susan," he asked once he was in control.

Jarvis cleared his throat. "You were there. You

heard everything I said."

"What were you saying in your mind? Have you already forgotten she can hear every thought you think?" Tex asked. He gripped the back of the chair in front of him so tightly that his knuckles turned white.

"What?" Jarvis yelped out.

Taking a deep breath, Tex let it out slowly, trying to calm his inner demon—the one who wanted to kill this bit of scum in front of him. "You are dense. I'm going to have to treat you as if you are a child or else beat you to death. What did you think hurt Miss Susan so much she needed you out of the bunker?"

Oh, hell, Jarvis thought, maybe she is one of those freaky mediums. Grinding his teeth, he decided to tell a vanilla version of what he had been thinking. "I thought that you were all crazy and needed to be in a mental hospital. And I was cursing the assignment that sent me to watch over a lunatic."

"I think it was more than that. Miss Susan doesn't get upset easily. The last time she couldn't be in a building with a person was when a man was so filled with grief and guilt that it was affecting her. I've seen her come out of a formal dinner and tell how a man is planning on killing his brother to take over a country. I've seen her wade into a building filled with terrified children who had been kidnapped and abused. With nothing but support for those children. She faced all the pain in a hospital, first to save Ritter and then to save her sister. You were cursing at her, weren't you?" Tex stated, his voice soft yet deadly.

Jarvis gulped, then looked down at the floor and nodded his head. "The whole thing is just not possible. The two who you say were shot can't have recovered so quickly. The subject would still show some signs of her beating, a scar, or something. Any sane man would agree with me that you have to all be insane."

Tex sighed, "You haven't listened. Nothing has gotten through to your tightly closed off mind. Her. Mother. Is. A. Healer," he said slowly. It was clear Jarvis had trouble thinking beyond his preconceived thoughts. He didn't need to be on this team if he couldn't open his mind and learn to accept people different from his idea of what they were. "The first person I saw her heal was SS agent Ritter. He was crushed. All his bones, in his arms and legs, were shattered. That he was alive at all was a miracle. Miss Susan's sister called her mother. And they called us because Susan is one of her mother's support people. The doctors said Ritter would never use his legs or arms should he survive. Mrs. Whiting healed him completely in hours, except for some surface bruising. Within three days, he left the hospital and resumed his duty.

"I contacted the President when we had recovered Miss Susan. She had fractures of her legs and one arm. Her face was beaten so badly that I barely recognized her. I called to have her mother sent to heal her. Within one day, she had healed Miss Susan, Simon, and George. Now, you can believe whatever you want to believe. You can remain closed-minded and miss out on seeing wondrous things happen. I am warning you right now: if you ever think bad thoughts that Miss Susan can hear again, I will do some beating of my own. As long as you are allowed to be with Miss Susan, you will count softly in your mind. It is up to you to adjust your attitude and decide if you are here to promote yourself or do your job and protect Miss Susan. Your job, no matter what you think of your subject or the rest of us, is to keep Miss Susan safe. Now…" Tex slammed his fist into Jarvis's face. "That is for hurting her. Remember, even thoughts hurt," Tex said in a low, deadly voice. He didn't look back as he walked out the door and shut it.

I want to make your body hurt, Jarvis thought. As he calmed down, he realized that type of thinking had gotten him in trouble with his subject. This whole assignment had been weird from the start. He thought he should try to conform to how this crazy outfit operated or seek reassignment. Standing, he started pacing, thinking about what was best for him. It occurred in some dimly lit part of his mind that thinking of his own needs was the cause of his problem. The other thing was, should he take at face value this crazy idea that the subject was a mind reader?

Walking over to his bag, he searched for his laptop. One thing he could do was look up information on all the crazy people here. Time passed, and his frustration grew by the minute. His subject didn't seem to have any official records. Neither did her family, except for briefly mentioning her parent's wedding and the information about her father being Stanley Whiting's son. He did find records of Simon and George having been admitted to the hospital for gunshot wounds recently. Then, those records, too, disappeared. They were hiding everything. Why cover it up? They shouldn't unless it was true. Now, he was going nuts. She had known he was cursing them. She knew he was planning on using her to advance himself. Crap, she could read his mind.

In the morning, Jarvis felt the vibration of the bunker elevator. And he heard the bunker door open. Through the window, Jarvis watched Susan and York escorted away to only who knew where. It sank into his brain that they planned on leaving him behind. What he had signed up for was to protect. It was true he felt he should be assigned to guard the President. He was her protector. Then act like it, he told himself. Standing, Jarvis loosened his weapon and exited the SS house.

Chapter Fifteen

SOMETHING WICKED

They didn't have any real plan, only to follow their instincts. Tex didn't like being without a plan. He placed his trust in Susan as they went out into the world of D.C. Susan had decided she wanted to visit the so-called watering holes of the D.C. officials. There were many spots where people had formed the habit of drinking their morning coffee or eating their meals. The SS knew of these watering holes, and so did Susan. It didn't sit right with Tex. She shouldn't expose herself to so many slime-filled minds. And, there was the fact that people would remember her. If those people compare notes, they might expose her as a spy later.

Watching Susan as she stepped up on the curb, Tex knew he might make her mad with what he was about to say. "You don't have to be in the building with these individuals. How about we visit places close to our goals?"

Stopping, Susan looked over at Tex. Tex held his breath, afraid he was alienating her. "You are correct. We will do as you suggest. York, I want you to eat at every establishment where we sit. I'm going to need you."

York watched the people around them with interest. He tried to think like Tex and Roger. These people were all suspect; they all had hidden agendas, and York tried to reason out what each person was thinking. A strange thought entered his mind as he watched people talking and smiling at one another. Their teeth all looked the same. He knew his teeth and those of his family, the people he now considered his family, were all different. Each of the people he called family had differently shaped teeth. These people all looked like their teeth were produced by a machine. There was no individuality, nothing that identified them as being separate people. Yes, their hair and their clothing were a little different. Yet their teeth were all the same. He'd have to ask Tex later why everyone here had fake teeth.

Minds beat at Susan, trying to drown out her thoughts. She resisted by sticking them into boxes inside her mind. Susan had many such boxes inside her mind. Sometimes, she wondered what would happen when one of the boxes was stuffed full. Would her head explode? And which one of the boxes would fill up first? Would it be greed, lust, envy, hate, hopelessness, betrayal, or love? Some part of her cheered love. If she must have any box of thoughts explode in her mind and kill her, let it be love. Only that box held less than all the others.

They entered a tiny antique shop, and Susan froze as if examining a small wooden jewelry box. Her hand rested upon the jewelry box for a long moment before she moved on to look at a display of ancient necklaces. In truth, Susan was trying to step a little closer to the source of the thought Susan heard when looking down at the jewelry box. There, she had it again. "He keeps saying his wife is shopping or visiting a friend. But she would have called by now. It just isn't like her to ignore her family."

The trickle of thought moved beyond Susan's range. It may not have been anything after all. Only, it felt like someone was in deep trouble.

Susan barely noticed when they left the antique shop and moved to a small tea shop. It wasn't until an elderly waitress approached that she returned to herself enough to look around. They ordered hot tea and some small sandwiches for everyone. As York and Roger ate, Susan sent her mind searching beyond the tea shop. Random thoughts beat at her mind. Some made her want to cringe, while others left her wishing for a long, hot shower to wash her brain. Another trickle of thought about the missing woman hit Susan. She sat up straighter, concentrating on that whispered worry. "He is covering for her. I know it. She didn't show up for the meeting with Angry Housewives. I know her heart wasn't in this meeting. But her husband needs the goodwill that will come from this group."

The feel of the woman this person was worrying over felt the same as that of the previous worrier. Susan was sure she was on the right track. They left the tea shop and strolled along the sidewalks. They worked their way towards the next likely spot for thoughts of people from the White House.

Susan was engrossed in searching thoughts around her. She hunted for the next hint of what was happening to the missing woman. Tex placed his hand on her back to steer her around obstacles. He was worried about Susan straining herself with such a prolonged search. He motioned to York to come and walk close to them. Goldie was already pressed tightly against Susan as if she sensed Susan needed her.

"I need to contact the Secret Service. But if I do, they will kill her. Marge, honey, I'm so sorry I didn't say I love you before leaving for work that day. Please stay alive. I'm trying, darling. What do I do? What the Hell do I do? If I betray my country, they will still kill Marge. There is no way out. I should kill myself."

Raising her hand, Susan stopped and slowly began to turn in a circle. She stopped and opened her eyes to see a gray-headed man standing before a mail dropbox. He had a large envelope in his hand and held it over the slot to drop it into the mailbox. "Tex, I need you to keep an eye on that man by the dropbox," Susan paused, considering the wisdom of the next move. "Goldie, go grab that envelope and bring it back here. Quickly now, he has almost decided to drop it in the box."

"Jarvis, be ready to catch the man at the mailbox if he runs," Susan's mind spoke to Jarvis, who had worked his way ahead of them while she stopped to give out orders.

Jarvis almost screeched like a little child when he heard Susan's voice inside his head. He crouched and looked around him frantically for a speaker. He saw the man at the mailbox, and his eyes felt glued to that man. A golden retriever sped by his hiding place and leaped up as the man at the mailbox let the envelope go. It was his subject's dog. He could tell by the strange vest she wore. The dog snatched the large envelope from under the man's hand and spun around, running off.

The white-haired man at the Dropbox took one look at the two SS agents with the woman and boy before he turned and ran. He thought, "They are on to me," and he sprinted as fast as his old legs would take him to the nearest building.

Jarvis was slow to react. He had to chase the fleeing suspect for several feet before tackling him. His takedown was awkward, but it worked. He glanced over his shoulder to where Miss Whiting and the men protecting her stood. Feeling slightly superior at having been the one to subdue the suspect, he gave them a thumbs up. He failed to notice Susan's hand raised, stopping anyone from interfering with his takedown.

Roger had placed himself squarely in front of York. He felt slightly insulted that he hadn't been allowed to capture the suspect. If Roger had learned one thing from this team, it was to trust Miss Susan. So he sucked up his irritation and made damn sure he was protecting his subject. Part of him wanted to snicker at the amateur manner in which Jarvis stopped the fragile man from running off. Jarvis would have a few bruises. Roger realized that the aged man wasn't someone he should tackle. Roger thought he might have broken some of the venerable guy's bones if he had, and he felt better about the whole thing.

"Sir, are you alright? Did this man hurt you?" Susan asked, kneeling beside the man Jarvis was cuffing. She felt the jolt of shock in Jarvis' mind at her words. But the man in cuffs immediately melted towards her in his thoughts.

"He just killed my wife. I think," Jacob Combs whispered, closing his eyes in grief.

"Someone took your wife?" Susan prompted, holding the man's head cradled in her arms. He nodded. "You were paying them with information." He nodded again. "I will do my best to find her for you," Susan promised. "For now, go with this man to a safe house he is staying in. Think about everything that they wanted from you and where your wife was the last time you knew she was safe."

His mouth twitching with angry words he didn't dare voice, Jarvis helped the man to his feet. She had told him to stop the man, for God's sake! And then she makes out as if he is the bad guy? What the hell?

"Sir, get some hot food into this poor man. Please, treat him well," Susan said. Jarvis understood that every word out of her mouth was an order. Somehow, he managed to keep his mouth shut as he took the cuffs off the suspect. However, Jarvis patted the man to ensure Combs wasn't carrying a weapon. He risked a glance over to where Tex and Roger stood guarding York. Tex gave him a thumbs up, which irritated him all the more. Was he making fun of him? Jarvis wondered.

As he hustled Combs away, the phone Jarvis carried pinged. It was a text from Susan. "Well played. Text any information he gives you. His wife's life depends on it." The message calmed some of the anger he was feeling. So, she had set up an opportunity for him to gather the suspect's information. It made sense.

A smile formed in Tex's mind. Tex let it show so Susan could see it as he watched her walk back towards him. "You knew he was following us, so you gave him a job to keep him occupied and out of our way. You are one smart lady, Miss Susan," he said.

"It is up to us to teach him how to be part of the team. It would help if he could remember to count. He is so angry," Susan rubbed her forehead before continuing. "Jacob Combs was sending off information to try and save his wife from terrorists. I think she is the woman I have heard so much concern and worry over. Now, we have to find and rescue her if possible," Susan told them.

Terrorist. The thought had Tex's eyes narrowing and his lips thinning. They were slipping in more often with the illegal aliens who came into the nation. It was a concern for everyone who sought to secure the country. They needed help if they were going to bring down a bunch of slimy terrorists. He couldn't think of anyone else he could trust.

"We need to move on to another area. I think

we have learned all that we can from this area. What about areas where they are holding the woman? Any suggestions?" Susan asked.

"Normally, I'd say warehouses, but this is D.C., and I think that whoever is behind this threat will have taken a kidnapped victim into one of the nearby states. Maryland or Virginia," George said. Simon and Tex nodded.

"I'd head into Virginia if I was them. The area is more open. You could go up into the mountains where they would never find you. Any other time, it might be smart to give the FBI a chance to run some of their trainees in a look-around for hiding spots. I'm finding it hard to trust anyone else at this point. We don't know what departments they have infiltrated," Tex said, looking at each of his men. He wanted to be sure they all understood the implication his words implied.

They did not go to any of the places they had discussed. Instead, they headed to the bunker to let Susan recharge her energy and make plans.

Susan sat at the table listening to the ideas thrown out on what their next step should be. All she could think about was the terrible fear and grief that Jacob Combs was feeling. Her mind filled with his certainty that his wife would die because he had failed to mail the envelope off.

"What do you want us to do?" Tex asked Susan, having noted the distant look in her eyes.

She was staring at that envelope of secrets, which was a betrayal of their country when Tex asked her opinion. They could destroy it and let

Combs go, taking the chance he would not repeat his treason. Only there was a slim chance they would find his wife before they killed her. Her forehead creased in deep worry as Susan thought about losing that one life. "We mail the envelope," she said. "Go through it and see if you can create a forged copy that might convince the enemy that it is the information they want. Make certain nothing you send is real."

"Then we stake out the post office and see who picks it up?" Roger asked as if it was a given. He nodded to himself.

"Yes," Susan said, her expression clearing somewhat. "Split the night and day surveillance between all of you. We will continue to play tourist, hopefully picking up some stray thoughts from the enemy. Wonderful idea, Roger." Roger blushed, trying his best to keep a straight, serious face and not show how pleased he was to have his suggestion put into play.

A day later, the first stakeout began at the postal address on the envelope. They divided the twenty-four-hour day into four 6 hour shifts. Everyone was on edge, fearing to leave Susan for their brief time of box-watching. Guilt sat unbidden upon their shoulders for Susan being kidnapped. Fear of a repeat ate at their guts. That is all but Jarvis. He still did not believe the kidnapping had happened. That lack of faith in Susan caused the rest of the team to hold back any trust they wanted to place in him.

Deciding where to place himself in the schedule for his turn in the stakeout was a pain for

Tex. He did not want to leave Susan even for a few hours. There was a nagging fear that something would happen again. It was like a sore tooth making itself known. No matter where he placed himself, it felt wrong to be away from Susan. The Secret Service was not a bunch of bodyguards. They did investigations of all sorts. Only, something had changed in Tex. His focus had switched. Since his early teens, Tex had served as an investigator or protector in one form or another. He did his duty to his home and country. Never for a second did he hesitate to do the hard or the near-impossible assignment. His record was spotless. Yet here he was, feeling things that went against how he lived his life. It was black and white for him. He knew what he should be doing. Only it did not feel right.

Tex relieved Simon at the box drop stakeout at six in the evening. Simon would go to the bunker to catch a few hours of sleep before waking to resume guarding Susan. George would relieve Tex on box watch duty. Roger would take over for George on box-watching, leaving Tex to watch over Susan. Jarvis was grudgingly allowed to be the extra eyes for guarding Susan and York during the day.

As Tex scanned the area for likely suspects, the schedule kept running through his thoughts. Everything hinged on someone collecting the envelope inside that blasted box. No matter how he rearranged the schedule, this time frame was the best he could come up with for taking his turn. He had been with Susan and York all day except Simon; the night crew was fresh from rest. However, Simon would be resting inside the bunker. And Roger was still able to function at peak conditions. Susan had consented to let Jarvis into the bunker for a few hours while Simon slept and Roger tried to relax. It could have been better. Nothing would ever require him to be away from Susan.

The shadow creeping slowly along a windowpane caught Tex's attention. The movement was too hesitant. His body and mind switched into stalk mode. Tex faded into the shadows, watching intently for any hint that this was the person belonging to the box they were watching.

The figure inside the building finally walked more normally, approaching the area where their box was situated. Tex realized it was a teenager, barely even that. The slight form hesitated before poking a key into the box lock and turning it. The only thing inside the box was the incriminating envelope. Quickly, the boy snatched the envelope and stuffed it inside his hooded jacket. One frightened look around, and the boy took off, trying to appear nonchalant. In about ten or so years, the kid might be able to pull that look off. For now, he was failing miserably.

Pulling out his phone, Tex connected to the other team members. The app appeared simple and like a group chat program—but it was not.

George felt the vibration in his pocket. His phone appeared in his hand as if by magic. He saw Simon pop up off the cot where he was sleeping. At that moment, Roger turned grim-faced towards Simon. It was the moment they had all been dreading. They had one question to decide. Who stayed to guard Susan, and who would join Tex? Each of their phones now displayed a map showing that Tex was tracking the person with the envelope. Roger and George both looked at Simon.

Simon's eyes looked worried as he turned to Miss Susan. "Miss Whiting, you need to remain here in the bunker until we return," Simon said, raising his hand to halt her protest. George…"

Before Simon could continue, George gave a sharp, "No, I'm going after my boy."

Sighing, Simon continued, "Go next door and drag Jarvis and friend over here. Be gentle…, to the old guy…, but get Jarvis' ass over here." He turned towards Roger. "You need to gear up. I can't leave Miss Susan's side, so it will be up to you and George to help Tex. Put on an extra vest. Take extra clips, a knife, a med kit, bars, and drinks." Simon tried to think of anything he hadn't covered while watching Roger load himself up. "A flashlight," he finally added.

Roger had grown up since joining the team, and it was time they showed their trust in him. He was grateful to be the one sent to aid Tex, yet, at the same time, he worried about leaving York and Miss Susan to the likes of Jarvis. Motioning York over, he leaned close to whisper to the boy. "You are going to have to be extra alert. Always keep bars and drinks on you, and be sure you and your mother stay in the bunker. Listen to Simon. If Jarvis gets out of line, you have my permission to put some hurt on him. We understand each other?"

York nodded, then pulled an IV bag from one

of the boxes near Roger. "Take this too… just in case something bad happens. Please," he told Roger.

Never in a million years would Roger have thought that a child could fill him with so much emotion as York did then. He couldn't talk about all the feelings trying to drown him, so he nodded while keeping his expression as blank as possible and accepted the Andy Bag from York. His pockets were all filled with equipment. Nothing was left to do but shove the Andy Bag under his vest. It lodged there like a lump on his heart as big as the one in his throat. Holding his hand out, he waited for York to offer his own, then gave him a handshake of approval.

The bunker door gave that hiss it had when it was open—this time, it seemed to be hissing in displeasure at the individual shoved into the bunker. Jarvis staggered as George pushed him inside. His face was red with anger when he first entered. There was a visible struggle to correct that expression when his eyes noticed Susan. Straightening up, he pretended he hadn't just stumbled inside from a shove in the back. Behind Jarvis, George was laughing with the man whose wife they would try to rescue as if nothing was going wrong.

George cut his eyes to where York and Roger stood. He gave Roger a nod of approval and motioned to the door with his head. "Now, stay in here and keep Miss Susan company and whack Jarvis on the head if Jarvis gets out of line with our lady there. I'm counting on you," he told the elderly man he'd been laughing with a moment ago. George was in tracking mode now. His whole being was leaping onto that flashing red dot on his phone. Still, he took a moment to get the old guy relaxed, trying to keep him from worrying about his wife.

"Don't worry, young fellow, I've got his number now. I haven't survived in D.C. by letting bullies boss me around. You go and get my lady. I'll watch over yours for you," Jacob Combs assured George, giving Jarvis a stern look.

George patted Jacob on the back, grabbed extra ammo for his weapon, gave Simon a thumbs-up, and left. He knew it was up to Roger and him to back up Tex and save Jacob's wife. He was determined not to lose the woman or Tex.

Once the door of the bunker snickered shut, Jacob turned to Simon. His face had sobered so that Simon knew he had only been putting up a good show in front of George and Roger. "Tell me the truth," he said, looking at Susan. "What are the chances they will find my wife?"

Simon answered Jacob. "I have personally witnessed George's tracking ability. However, I was out when he tracked a kidnapper, while wounded himself, through a forest. I was there for the rest of it. If I or someone I loved were missing, I'd want him on the track," Simon said.

Jacob said one more word that made him slump as if he would faint: "Alive?"

"He is a Texas Ranger, sir. Let that thought keep you going so you'll be there for when your wife needs you," Simon said, even though he wasn't convinced Jacob's wife wasn't already dead. No matter the outcome, Jacob would have his wife returned to him, of which he was sure. But would he lose someone in the effort? Life, unfortunately, held no promises, just possibilities.

"They found me," York said quietly as if talking to himself. "Nobody believed they could, but they did. I'd be dead if they hadn't," his voice strengthened as he recalled the snatches of conversation he had heard back when his name was Useless. "The bad guys were planning on shooting the kids who were weak or sickly. We all heard them saying that as they loaded us on that last truck. I was already weak. The move took the last out of me. When I was blacking out, I remember thinking that I wouldn't be waking up again," he paused, looking over at Susan, then Simon, and back to Susan. "I know you saved me. You stayed with me to be certain I was okay, and let me pick my name." He looked back to Simon. "And you bought me some of the best ice creams I've ever had." He gave a little laugh when Simon blushed. At last, York looked over at Jacob. "Don't give up hope. You were found by the best. And now they are going to find your wife."

Jacob nodded, too choked with emotion to speak.

Stealth was something in which Tex excelled, not because of the native American blood that was part of his heritage. It all came down to his time with his friend George. When he had been in the Texas Rangers, the older man had taken him under his wing. Tex had learned to fade into the forest, whether woodland or concrete structures. He followed the youth carrying their bait as the kid went from eating ice cream to tacos and ended up at a video arcade. Sooner or later, the boy would hand the envelope to someone to lead them to the kidnapped woman. The day's word was patience; Tex knew how to draw on it.

It was at the video arcade that George and Roger caught up to Tex. Tex had been thinking about the wisdom of stealing a car as he watched the youth hailing a cab when Roger pulled their rental up beside him. The window rolled down, and George drawled, "Need a lift, cowboy?"

Tex chuckled, responding to the teasing, "Only by Redheads, Blondes." It was an old joke between them from when Tex would turn down any attempt by a girl to pick him up after being heartbroken by a gal. It had felt like he'd never find that one person to gladden his heart. Now, he prepared to watch her from a distance for the rest of his life. He couldn't even let himself think about what he felt around her. How often did a man find that one person who made his heart sing and laughter roll through his soul? He was determined to hang onto her, even though he didn't feel worthy of telling her how he felt.

Shaking himself mentally, Tex indicated the taxi slipping into traffic. "He has our package. I think he is just a runner. We have to follow the package to see where it leads us."

"The taxi driver?" Roger asked.

"No, the kid passenger. Watch closely to see if he passes it off to the cab driver, George. Roger has a point. It could be him," Tex said.

"On it," George grumbled.

When the taxi pulled onto the main highway heading out of the D.C. area, Tex knew the cab driver wasn't involved. It was a feeling, but experience taught him to trust his gut. "Anything new from the old guy?" Tex asked to be sure he wasn't missing some obvious clue.

"I don't think he would tell Jarvis anything. Miss Susan should talk to him," George said, and he saw Tex try to keep from smiling. The boy was too close to Miss Susan. George didn't know if he'd survive another letdown from a woman.

The taxi had pulled off the main highway to a gas station, letting the youth out. The boy stood there for a moment as if uncertain as to what he should do next. His shoulders were tense, indicating the meet-up wasn't going exactly how he had pictured it. Just as the teenager was about to go into the gas station, a car pulled off a side road into the station. The youth ran over to the car, opened the back passenger side door, and climbed into the darkened interior.

Roger allowed the car to pick up speed and get back up on the highway before pulling out onto the road and following. He could feel his body readying for whatever might come up next. The kidnapping of Miss Susan caught him unaware. And, in truth, had shaken his confidence in himself. With Tex being yanked away from the job, Roger had felt like he should have suspected there would be a try for Miss Susan. Only he was worried about what was going on with Tex and let the man down by not taking extra precautions for her and York's safety. Since then, Roger tried to keep his focus on the job. Gone was the naive man he had been, and a man on a mission was in his place. He now knew that all that stood between disaster and his charges was this team of men and himself.

The night was upon them before the car they were following pulled off the highway to a side road. They encountered a group of buildings spread over several acres of ground about four miles later. They appeared to be large warehouses or some industrial offices. Why they were isolated and hidden here in nowhereland wasn't clear. George had a road map out to pinpoint the area. He rubbed his eyes and shook his head. "Amarillo," he mumbled.

"Amarillo?" Roger asked, confused.

"Too many ins and outs," Tex clarified. "We once had a case that looked like it was going sideways on us. We tracked this drug runner to a neighborhood in Amarillo. The trouble was that there were many ways in and out of the area. It looked as if George and I would miss our chance to catch this guy."

"He got away?" Roger said, his voice carrying a note of disbelief.

Tex laughed, "No, George told me about the snake and the sparrow. To keep sparrows from nesting in places like the eaves of his home, his father would place these rubber snakes in those areas. The sparrows had learned to avoid snakes and didn't try to build their nest in the rubber snake areas. There were six exits from the area we needed to cover. And only two of us. No matter where we each set up to watch for this guy, he still had four exits we couldn't see. We parked our car at one of the exits with the light on top flashing. At another, George hung a vest with Texas Rangers displayed on it. Now, we only had two exits we couldn't completely cover. We narrowed down the odds, and we got our man."

The three men studied the map George had spread out. It wasn't the number of exits they had to cover this time. It was the number of buildings they needed to search. And hoped they would find the elderly victim and the men who held her captive. The question beating Tex up inside was how to go about the search. Together from building to building, or did they split up to cover a larger area? No matter how they searched, the time factor would hang over their heads like an Executioner's Axe.

Chapter Sixteen

PECK AND HUNT

No jokes were tossed around by George or Roger as Tex, his face grim, handed out the earwigs. However, Roger silently wondered where his boss kept this endless supply of toys in his suit. He watched as some message passed between Tex and Texas Ranger George, and some unspoken agreement was reached. Roger wondered if he and a partner would have that same rapport one day. The one where a look or nod would communicate some knowledge these two men shared. Then he caught it. A slight tilt of Tex's head sent George fading off to the right. "With me," Tex whispered to Roger. Roger knew that George would solo the buildings to the right while he and Tex went right. Maybe he was learning their partner code after all.

His gut tied in knots, Tex focused on the interior of the first building they entered. Everything inside him said the building was empty. They had to check it out to be sure. Odd bits of machinery were scattered here and there in this warehouse. It looked like storage for machines built for some function Tex could not phantom. Things with long arms ending in clawed grasping tools. Others looked built for suction. Large and small machines, each built for some specialized use. He signaled Roger to go right while he went left, gratified when Roger seemed to understand. The boyish man was coming along well in his training. They just needed to keep him alive until it finished.

George was clearing his buildings quickly. There was a feeling in his gut that had George twitchy. More importantly, there was the feeling George should have stayed with Tex. He knew Tex would sacrifice himself to save his team. There wasn't a Ranger who had ever worked with Tex that wouldn't put their own life in harm's way to spare Tex. They owed him a life. This constant twitching tended to hit George on assignments where Tex would play shield. George couldn't let him do that. For once, Tex might have a real chance at a love life. That is if George could keep him alive long enough.

They were heading to the third building on their side. Tex had seen George slinking up one building ahead of them, and he hoped his old partner was careful in his searches. Something about the building they were approaching sent off alarm bells inside him. He raised his hand, causing Roger to freeze and wait for Tex to creep over to him. As soon as Tex was in whisper range, Tex sent Roger off. "Go to one building up on the other side and bring

George here," he said, pointing at where they stood. Roger nodded, leaving immediately. Tex almost sagged with relief. He was free.

His real name was Robin Shadow. People only called him Tex because he had earned the nickname Texas when he'd been a Texas Ranger. The name had followed him when he entered the Secret Service. He hadn't bothered to correct anyone. Over the years, he started thinking of himself as Texas. That didn't stop him from being a shadow, for, in truth, he was a shadow. A shadow of a man, living only until he died protecting the people who lived in the real world, like Susan, Roger, and George. Taking a deep breath, a man called Texas went into the terrorist den, entering the shadows.

George knew the moment Someone started following him. He did not indicate he was aware the person was behind him. George slipped off to the side, doubling back. Creeping up behind the man stalking him, he placed his knife's sharp point a quarter of an inch into the skin on the man's back while keeping his gun aimed at the stalker's head.

Roger froze for only a beat of a second before taking evasive action. It meant he suffered a small cut on his back, but the killing blow would not sever his spine. He was lifting his weapon to fire when his brain registered that the man who had struck him was George. "What the hell? I'm on your side, Cowboy." The fact that George only nodded didn't satisfy him, but he'd take it. "Tex sent me to fetch you. He seems to think we have found the building. He is waiting for us," he told George, still irritated that the Ranger had bested him.

Spinning on his heel, George started running, not caring if he made noise in this empty building. His boy was in danger. "He isn't waiting. Tex is going in alone. Damn him! He needs his ass beat with a bullwhip. I'm not going to let him die," George swore. Beside him, Roger realized he had made an error as a partner, making him sprint ahead of George.

When they reached the door to exit the building, George held up his hand. Roger's mouth twitched. "Hold on. Let me go out first. Take two breaths and then follow," George told Roger.

"No," Roger snarled, his voice filled with anger. "I made one mistake already. We go together, or I knock you out and drag your body outside. Got it?"

"Welcome aboard, Rog," George said, impressed with how fast this one-time boy agent had grown up. They slipped out of the empty building. Both immediately saw that Tex was not waiting for them. "He would have gone in before you even reached my building. That is his M.O. He wants to shield us, offering himself as a target. Let's go save our leader's sorry ass."

The two eased silently into the building, letting the darkness inside swallow them whole. At the first intersection, a hand sticking out caused Roger's heart to almost stop. They were too late. He had caused Tex's death. Anger spread through his body like a wildfire burning in his veins. Exploding inside his skull into a hot rage, it took him over. George pulled him back to sanity with two words.

"Not him," George whispered. How George could tell from the shape of that lifeless hand, Roger didn't know. He did, however, trust George. "Knife, he used a knife on this guy," George said. Do you have one on you?"

With a grimace, Roger yanked out the knife Tex had forced upon him one day when they had been sparing. He heard Tex's words in his mind as he showed the weapon to George. "Always have this on you. Silent kills are your friend."

That hand seemed to mock Roger as he crept up on the intersection and peeked around it. He tried not to look down, not because he was afraid of seeing a dead body. No, it was because he feared George would be wrong, and the body was Tex, after all. Then, he looked down. Almost he sighed, but the team had taught him to control those giveaway signs of emotion. It wasn't Tex's body. George pushed past Roger, and he had no choice but to follow or let down another partner. He wasn't going to allow that last part to happen. Fear and regret already had him by the throat at the thought of losing Tex. Tex had been his mentor on this protection assignment. Roger now knew what it meant to be an SS agent. The rest of the world didn't count. Only the subject counted. So, yes, fear had him by the throat. It was a fear he had to ignore, conquer, and save Tex. Droplets of blood here and there disappeared down the hallway. Determination followed that trail of blood.

Night had claimed the Capital. Others went off for a few hours of sleep or did deals in secret meetings. One woman, a youth, an aged man, and two Secret Service agents kept a silent vigil.

Worried about Tex and his mother, York suggested they create a dinner to serve when Tex, George, and Roger returned. The bunker held the barest of kitchen arrangements. A hot plate and a microwave. Plus, an electric teapot. Simon took over the microwave, claiming he had learned much from cooking his meals. Somehow, he managed to cook hot fudge brownies, while Susan managed BBQ sauce and ribs with just the hot plate. The beans and cornbread were a challenge. Somehow, they managed. York took over making a potato salad.

Making the meal had been a good idea to keep all but Jarvis busy. It did not stop Susan from worrying. Again and again, she reached out, trying to sense Tex, but not only was the bunker damping her ability, but the distance was also not her friend. The horror of when she had been kidnapped and had been without her powers kept eating at her. She felt helpless. Once all the frantic activity was over. All the various dishes they had been able to make in the kitchen cooked and waited for their three companions to return. Susan knew she had to step out of the bunker. The not knowing was fraying her nerves.

It was late. The prepared dinner had grown cold and looked sad as it waited for Tex and the others to return to feast on it. York had finally fallen asleep sitting up. Simon covered him up, placing pillows to make the boy comfortable without moving him. He had noticed Susan's restlessness, and that had him trying to think of how he could relieve her worry. Unfortunately, he felt just as out of sorts as she looked. It was rare that Susan displayed any emotion.

When Susan approached him, Simon steeled himself to refuse her request. At the same time, he wanted to agree with her and put a plan into action. Anything was better than not knowing.

"Simon, I want to step just outside the bunker." Susan held her hand up to stop the protest she sensed battling in his mind. "Just outside so I can mentally reach Tex and the others. If they prove to be beyond my range, we step back inside. Does that fit within the allowed options?"

"Yes," Simon said, perhaps a little too quickly. He battled with himself over letting her go outside. Tex would have his hide. He'd skin him and tack his skin on a tree for the creatures to chew. If the slightest chance existed for Susan to connect with the team and let him know what was happening, he'd take it. Simon would guard her with his life, but he had a partner out there in danger. "Rules first. We leave the elevator doors open. You step back in and hit express down at the first hint of danger. You do not wait for me. Also, you stay behind me. Do not expose yourself to anyone out there. Swear you will do as instructed," Simon said, showing his most serious face.

"Yes, I swear to follow your instructions," Susan replied, relieved Simon would allow the outing. Everything inside her screamed for her to check on Tex and the team.

Jarvis stood as Simon and Susan went to leave. "I don't like this. It is the middle of the night, and any bit of crud could be out there," he said as if holding his own life in his hands.

With a nod, Simon motioned Jarvis over. "That is why you are going to stand just inside the elevator. You will pull Miss Whiting back into the elevator and slam the express down button at the least hint of trouble. Should the unspeakable happen and both Miss Susan and I go down, you will pull her body inside and go straight down. Your sole purpose will be to protect her and York. You will not allow anyone to enter the bunker except authorized medical personnel or Tex. Understand?" Simon was in Jarvis' face while he spoke, driving in the seriousness of his words. He waited for Jarvis to swallow and give a weak nod before doing a weapons check. He glared at Jarvis until the man checked his weapon.

It was a tense few moments as the elevator traveled up to ground level. Simon kept the doors closed, giving Susan a sign to remain inside until he checked things out. He allowed the doors to open wide enough that he could squeeze out of them. Carefully, Simon looked around until he felt it was safe to let Susan exit the elevator. Opening the door, Simon motioned for her to step out.

Droplets dark in color spaced at irregular intervals. George squatted at one and studied it for a moment. He kept his mind from leaping to all the dark thoughts that begged his attention. His boy was alive. That was all that counted. They had been in worse spots. His stomach lurched. There it was again, that foreboding, like a knife twisting into his gut. Damn you, Tex, do not die on me, George silently cursed.

Slightly behind George, Roger felt a chill on the back of his neck. He had heard guys talk about how they seemed to have a sixth sense of danger. Was this going to be his indicator? If so, he had best listen. It was time for his instincts to turn on. For the first time, he felt he had become a real agent.

As the pair glanced around another corner, they found another body. The dead man was dressed in robes with his head wrap still on his head. His throat had been slit. "He is taking them out one by one," Roger mumbled.

George nodded. He was worried. The first guy must have been rounding the corner as Tex approached it. That one got a piece of Tex. George knew from this kill that Tex was using full stealth mode to creep up on them. No, he was hurt and didn't trust himself to take down someone charging at him. The blood was fresher here, indicating they were closing in on where Tex was ahead of them.

Stepping over the dead man, George checked that he had a couple of clips. He offered Roger one of the ammo clips. Roger shook his head and pulled two loaded clips from his suit pocket. George motioned to Roger how to set the clips so that when he reached for one, he would not have to turn it around to insert it into his weapon. The agent nodded and followed the example, realizing they would soon not have time for even the second it took to look at a clip. He said a silent prayer that they found Tex before reaching that point.

The droplets grew larger for a few feet. A

door off the hallway had a bloody print on the handle. George took a deep breath and eased the door open. Empty. It was an office of some sort. The required desk and computer were against one wall. The only other pieces of furniture were three chairs. Something about the desk drew George's attention. The blood trail led to the desk but not away. The answer was on the desk. A stapler had traces of blood upon it. Tex had pulled his skin together and stapled it in place. The wound had to be worse than George had feared. His jaw clenched as he turned away from the desk. Good for Tex, maybe, bad for them as there was no trail to follow now. Tex had to have exited the office, as there was only one door in or out. George stuck the stabler in one of his pockets. You never knew what might save a life. He already had a fondness for this stabler because it had helped Tex.

George remembered the boy/man Tex had been. He had been nothing like Roger. Tex had always had a seriousness about him. Tex stayed focused on a job until he finished it. His single-minded determination had impressed George. Recruits were often teamed with George to train. He turned them into Texas Rangers. Tex was a different story. The boy was so focused on the job that George began to worry he never had any fun. So the jokes started between them as George sought to loosen Tex up. Their partnership became a legend among the Rangers. They always succeeded in bringing in their man or woman. Then that rat-fink woman came along, pretending to love Tex and leaving him crushed. That determination Tex had took over. He never trusted a woman enough to date her again. He loved one now. George knew it even if Tex would not admit it to himself. George just had to keep him alive tonight…, and maybe whip his butt for not letting his heart accept what was in front of him.

All we can do now is keep going forward, Roger thought. He watched George closely, trying to pick up on what George sought to find. The blood trail was gone and had been their guide until now. He thought about Tex stapling his skin and shivered. He guessed he could do it to himself if it meant living. Only, he was squeamish over getting vaccinated; to stick metal in himself was just creepy.

All thoughts of staples and needles went out of his mind when George held up his hand. That hand twisted behind George's back and motioned Roger to back up. He edged slowly backward, expecting George to follow him. When George didn't move, his temper flared, and he walked silently to where George was peering around the corner. He looked around that corner.

Roger sucked in a breath. At first, he thought he saw a dead body until one of the hands reached back and produced a wicked-looking knife. Why was Tex on the floor? There had to be a logical reason. He looked back to the corner behind him, trying to find logic to what he had just seen. It occurred to him that he had looked at a person's height, which made sense to him. Where did you look when you expected someone to come around that corner? You did not look down at the floor. He would, from now on, look at both places. Even now,

Tex was teaching him how to survive.

Tex slid back and started the painful process of getting to his feet. He cursed his carelessness at approaching a corner too quickly. It had been a Greenhorn's mistake. He'd had to fight with the guy who was hurrying towards him. It had taken a fraction too long to take the man down. Long enough to be stabbed himself. It was so stupid of him. He wanted to whack himself upside the head. Right now, he had to figure out how to take out whoever was behind him. Feeling the staples pull as he finally managed to get to his knees. He whirled, prepared to throw his knife and kill whoever was behind him. George gave him a wide-eyed look, causing Tex to abort the throw. George pretended to wipe sweat from his brow and grinned like a fool at Tex.

Tex held up three fingers, bending them down slowly one by one. On three, he and his team stepped around the corner into the room beyond. Three knives streaked through the air, taking down all but one of the men inside the room. Roger moved fast for a big kid of a man. He was on the fourth man and had him choked so the man couldn't alert anyone else in the building before the third dead man hit the floor. When dead weight pulled on his arms, Roger was still amazed that things had gone so well. His stomach had been in knots when he'd been the one Tex assigned to do the takedown on the fourth man. Tex had told him not to overthink anything but to react. Throw, run, and choke were all he had to concentrate on doing. And, damn, it worked.

Watching the look of pride spreading over Roger's face almost made getting stabbed worth it. Almost. Tex was still mad at himself for getting too comfortable checking out the building. "Good work," he told Roger. "Now bind and gag him. We will question him later." He held out some zip ties to Roger. "From here on, things may get a tad messy. The entire building will be on alert once we fire a shot. Roger, you hang back," seeing the rebellion that entered Roger's face, Tex added, "with me. George will take point. Agreed?"

Roger nodded, keeping the same tight-lipped expression that indicated he wasn't pleased yet would obey.

"First," Tex said. "Let's get our signals straight. If you see George hold up his hand with his fist clutched like this," Tex demonstrated with his hand. "It means stop, enemy ahead. If he then starts raising his fingers, he is indicating how many. And this means scatter and hide." Again, Tex indicated the hand signal by waggling his hand, with his fingers spread, in a shooing motion, then pressing his palm down towards the floor. "The rest is pretty standard."

Roger swallowed and nodded again as he realized why George was on point. He knew how to communicate with Tex. The muscles around his mouth relaxed slightly so Roger didn't look so stubborn. He saw Tex nod to him. They were still a team and were not babysitting him. He'd worried that, in some manner, he had messed up the takedown.

George stepped close to Roger and saw the

young man tense up again. Leaning in close, George whispered in Roger's ear, "You see him stagger; get him out of here. Knock him out and carry him out if you have to. The boy is running on adrenaline and is bound to crash." He waited until Roger nodded before slipping away from Tex. George disappeared around the corner long enough to see the area ahead. Suddenly, he was shooing Tex and Roger back to a different door. George held up his hands once they were secure in a side room. He flashed all ten fingers twice.

Twenty. There were twenty enemies in the room ahead of them. With a solemn nod, Tex pulled a notepad and pencil out of his endless pockets. George took the pad and pencil from Tex. He quickly drew the room he had spied out. Blobs, which were the furnishings, appeared here and there, and stick men represented the men inside the room.

Taking the pad back, Tex made a circle around the outside of the room with a question mark. George rubbed his forehead and shrugged.

Watching Tex and George interact, Roger could tell they had encountered a roadblock. He was about to volunteer to look for a different route through the building when Tex looked around the room where they hid. He glanced up at the ceiling, then wrote two words on the notepad. "Fort Bend?" George nodded.

Writing on the pad again, he showed Roger the words. "Air vent." Roger glanced around the room and then up at the ceiling. Seeing the grill over a vent up there, he nodded. Roger felt a little doubt that his body could fit into the vent. But he was willing to try. Thinking of pulling himself up into that vent, Roger thought of Tex and his wound. Would he have the strength to pull himself up there? Looking at George, Roger tilted his head toward Tex with a questioning expression.

George twitched his mouth and spoke up, "I'll go first. Roger, you boost Tex up to me and then follow him." Before Tex could respond, George removed the grill cover and pulled himself into the above space.

His brow down in a deep frown, Tex nodded. He wouldn't be doing the team any favors by aggravating his wound. There was no room for egos in teamwork. "Pull a chair over here, and I'll stand on it. That way, you won't have to lift me from the floor," Tex told Roger while holstering his weapon. He also double-checked that his gun wouldn't bump against the sides or bottom of the vent. "Don't forget to place the chair back where it was." Tex stepped up on the chair. Roger grabbed his legs in his large hands, and, for a moment, Tex wobbled, trying to balance as Roger lifted him to George.

Reaching his long arms down, George scooped Tex's underarms in his hands, gently lifting his friend as he scooted backward. It was a slow process, but finally, Tex was far enough in the vent to wiggle away from it to allow Roger to climb up.

It was tight. Roger wondered how he could reach back and replace the vent cover. He felt wedged in as it was.

"Now, wiggle back over the top of the vent cover and replace it," Tex whispered to him.

I need to lose some weight, Roger thought,

as he did the impossible and moved his body in the tight vent backward over the vent cover. Carefully, he replaced the cover over the space they had entered the vent through. If Roger had dropped it now, all this wiggling would have been for nothing. Mentally, he sighed once the cover was snug back where it belonged.

When the first split in the venting system came, George signaled for Tex and Roger to wait as he explored the side vents. Tex relaxed as much as he could, trying to regain some of his strength. The muscles over his belly were becoming tight. Tex knew that indicated bleeding internally. He only wanted to get his men through this with the hostage alive. After that, death could take him. Except, who would look after Susan and York? That one problem nagged at his subconscious.

The tightness of the vent was getting to Roger. He never feared tight places. Angry at himself for sweating at the thought of the vent closing in on him. The space is the same, he told himself over and over. It wasn't closing in and squeezing the breath out of him. That was his imagination taking over. It wasn't rational, but the air seemed to be turning stale to the point he felt light-headed. He couldn't breathe!

Returning, George pulled himself past Tex and backed into the forwarding vent. Turning himself around so he could head in the direction from which he came, pointing forward and motioning for Tex to follow, George squirmed forward.

As Roger was about to crawl over Tex to try and get out of the vent, Tex moved forward, turning into the left side vent. Roger took a breath and another before following Tex. He had almost lost it back there. A bloody trail followed where Tex crawled ahead of him. That sight was enough to pull Roger back to his senses. Tex was counting on him. His boss was able to keep going, even though he was wounded. Surely he could stand being in a damn vent. Mentally, he kicked himself in the backside, squirming forward as fast as his wounded leader. He didn't even realize that the vent no longer felt as if it was crushing him.

Ahead of Tex, George stopped moving forward. He tilted his head, trying to see the entire room beneath the vent cover. In the center of the room, a gray-haired woman was slumped forward in a straight-backed chair. Only the bindings around her body held her in the chair. Odors of urine and other bodily waste wafted into the vent. Anger flared inside George for how they treated the woman below him. Scrunching his body to one side, George looked as far as he could to the left of the bound woman. He could barely make out the wall of the room on that side of her.

Flipping so that his hands were free, George signaled Tex. The goal is here. Forward, left zero. Right, back unknown. While he waited for Tex to form a plan, he drew his knife and placed it between his teeth. George loosened the vent cover, preparing for fast entry.

Scribbling his orders down on a tablet, Tex steadied his breathing. He passed the tablet to

George first and let him read it. George's head shook
in a negative motion. Tex swiped the tablet back and
added a note. "I need you two to be able to carry
the subject, and possibly myself, out," he jabbed his
finger at the tablet, emphasizing his message. George
glared but nodded. Satisfied, Tex sent the tablet back
to Roger.

Action, finally, Roger thought, grabbing the
tablet a bit too eagerly. He had to read it twice before
the words made sense. According to this, George
was dropping Tex into the room, armed with two
knives. George and Roger were to follow. That last
part had Roger's brow furrowing in a frown. Did
Tex expect to be out of action? No way! Reaching
forward, he grabbed Tex's leg to get his attention.
Then he pointed at himself and made a motion like
walking over Tex. Tex shook his head, pointed at
the tablet, and back at his wound. Closing his eyes,
Roger nodded. For a moment, he felt the sting of
a tear in his eyes. The boss was right; Roger had
to accept that bitter truth. He pulled his knife and
readied himself, staring forward. There was no trace
of the kid he once had been upon his face; that part
of him had grown up accepting the fate that might be
in store for his boss, his friend.

His team's reaction to the plan made Tex
worried about them. He had prepared to die as he
had already felt so weak from the blood pooling in
his belly. He thought the best option for the team
was for him to go first. And draw any fire from
those in the room to himself. That would allow
George and Roger to take the enemy down and save
the woman. He hadn't considered the fact he'd be

putting a scar on Roger's young soul. "I'll try to live," he silently promised Roger and George.

Angry at Tex but understanding his reasoning, George removed the vent cover. He motioned Tex to come forward. Tex hadn't much room to turn his body and ready himself for dropping into the room. He needed to be facing the right direction. So he could deal with anyone in the room out of sight.

George brought out a small mirror and angled it. So they could both see the blind area in the room. Two men lounged in office chairs close to the far wall. Two. George knew Tex could take out two people when he was healthy. The trouble was that George was about to drop Tex into the room, and his partner was wounded. He pressed his spare knife into Tex's off-hand. They hadn't practiced off-hand throwing for a while now. Still, he knew his boy was good with both hands. Nodding, he was ready to lower Tex; George flashed a look at Roger. Roger nodded readily to spring into action.

Chapter Seventeen

SOUL'S LINK

Simon knew Tex might kill him for allowing Susan to exit the bunker. Hopefully, Tex would remember that Susan was a force of nature when she wanted something. Even though he knew Tex was in love with their subject, Simon told himself. It grated on him that he needed Jarvis to come outside with them. If the stuck-up jerk endangered Miss Susan, Simon was prepared to shoot him.

Susan searched for Tex and the team, sending her mind out farther than ever. It was more than likely that they were beyond her reach. However, she counted on the fact that she had recently received a boost in her mind power. Every time she had to scan whole crowds, her power would increase. The constant searching felt like it had broken through a wall inside her. Or, at least, it felt like that had happened. It could be wishful thinking as she was desperate to know the team was safe.

Thousand upon thousands of thoughts bombarded Susan's mind. This time, she ignored them all, focusing only on one man's mind, Tex. Then she was with him. She felt his efforts to ignore the discomfort in his belly. "He is wounded," she whispered to Simon.

Clamping his mouth closed, Simon fought the need to question Miss Susan. He didn't want to distract or make her focus on Tex harder. Simon kept his eyes sweeping the area around them. His job was to keep her safe, and he had to keep his personal feelings in check to do the one thing Tex had charged him with: caring for Miss Susan.

"I don't like the plan," Susan mumbled, wanting to speak to Tex and tell him he couldn't risk himself as he planned.

Tensing, Simon wondered what was going on with the team. His mind battled with him over going to Tex or watching Miss Susan. He knew it was impossible to get to Tex and the team in time to help, but that thought kept him on point while watching their subject.

Miles away, George dropped Tex into the room where the woman was held captive.

Tex threw both knives as he dropped to the floor. Both of them hit their target. The only problem was the off-hand throw didn't kill the intended target. Tex dropped and rolled away from the subject, who was tied in a chair to draw fire to himself. George and Roger both dropped down behind him.

The wounded enemy was fast. He had a knife out and threw it, hitting Tex high in the back. The pain surprised Tex, but it didn't last long. All feeling just ceased. He heard the flight of two knives and their soft thuds hitting the enemy. Tex smiled. They had succeeded to this point. Now, all they had to do was escape.

Susan felt the knife enter Tex's back. She felt the nerves sever. Then, blackness claimed her with its dark curtain.

Simon lunged for Miss Susan when her legs folded, saving her a nasty fall. Picking up her tiny body, he turned towards the elevator. "Send it up, you damn fool," he growled at Jarvis, causing Jarvis to spring into action.

Clutching Susan to his chest, Simon carried her inside the bunker. He wasn't surprised that York was there waiting for them. The boy had the bunk ready for Simon to place Susan upon it.

Once Susan was settled in bed, York placed his hands on her arm. He tried to send his energy into her body, but her body rejected him. With a gasp, Susan woke up and took control of the room.

"Simon, call my mother, then hand me the phone. Jarvis, order us a large meal filled with protein. Make it enough for five people. No, make it enough for ten people. York, you clear two cots and warm some blankets.   Simon, once you hand me the phone, fill a table with bars and drinks. Tex and Jacob's wife will need all the help we can give them. I must go back outside once I've connected with my mother." Susan paused to ensure everyone was doing their assignment.

Simon handed Susan his phone. For once, he wanted to shake Miss Susan and ask her to tell him what had happened to the team. Instead, Simon waited and shamelessly listened to what Miss Susan told her mother.

"Tex and the woman they are rescuing are injured. I can only tell you some of Tex's problems for certain. He has been wounded in his belly and possibly his leg with a knife. The reason I need you is that his spinal cord was severed. The woman, I'm not certain of her condition. From the small flash I got, she had been beaten and was unconscious. Come straight to the address Simon is going to read out to you. I'm going to start eating bars and having drinks," Susan told her mother.

Reaching his hand out, Simon took the phone from Miss Susan and gave her mother the address where they were staying. While he was on the phone with Mrs. Whiting, Jacob, having heard his wife was injured, approached Miss Susan. Simon put his body between Susan and Jacob. "From here on out, you are not to touch Miss Susan or York. They are preparing, readying themselves to help your wife. Either settle down somewhere, or I will return you to the house. Understand?" he told Jacob.

Looking stunned, Jacob seemed to tremble for a moment before gathering himself. "She is alive, right?" he asked Simon.

"Yes, we know she is bruised, but not to the extent of what she needs medically yet. Have faith. The best damn doctor in the world is coming to treat her and our wounded team member. You should rest. So you can be there for your wife. Think of her, okay?" Simon soothed.

Miles away from where Susan and the others prepared to treat the woman and Tex, George knelt beside Tex. Tex opened his eyes and looked up into George's face before speaking. "I am paralyzed. You may have to leave me here in the vent while you take the woman to safety. I will be okay. Just pull me back to that spot where the vent splits up and stuff me in a side vent, okay?" he said.

The expression on George's face said it all. There was no way he was leaving Tex behind. "Do you remember that serial killer we found in Austin? Did you leave me behind then?" he asked, knowing Tex had not.

"It is not the same. I am going to be a deadweight. I can not help you get me out. You, at least, could shoot. I can not feel anything, George. Nothing at all." Tex's voice seemed to drift off as the meaning of what he was saying hit George. Until then, he had been only thinking of how hard it would be to stuff his limp body into the vent to be left behind. It dawned on him that he would never be with Susan and York again. His life would be one of a hospital bed and maybe later a respirator.

Roger had been freeing the woman and had her laid out, looking her over for broken bones. He was listening to the conversation between Tex and George. They had not asked Roger what he thought; he was part of this team. "Let us take a vote. All those in favor of taking Tex out of here raise their hand," he said, raising his hand. George had his hand raised already. Tex lay there helpless. "Looks like two to one. You can go with us. Now shut up the whining," Roger finished, proud of himself for getting the last word in on the discussion.

Back at the bunker, they were set up and only waiting for Susan's mother and the team to arrive. It dawned on her that they did not know to bring Tex and Jacob's wife to the bunker. "I need to go back out and contact Roger or George to let them know to come here," she said.

Simon grimaced. "I think you need to remain in here and beef up. What if I go out and call them?" he asked.

"No, they were still inside that warehouse. It is too dangerous for them if someone hears a phone vibrate," Susan countered.

"I will do it," York said. "Let me try," he said, reasoning that an attempt did not cost them anything but his energy.

Realizing that York might be feeling left out, Susan nodded. "Simon and Jarvis, go out with you," she told him, and it was York's turn to nod.

Simon felt twisted in knots at the thought of York going outside. If anything happened to him, not only would Tex kill him, but Roger would help him. Taking a deep breath, he motioned York and Jarvis to the door. Simon knew when to give in to one of Susan's commands. He gave Jarvis a wave of his head towards the bunker entrance.

They are crazy, Jarvis thought. These people are stark raving mad. The air gushed out of his lungs as Simon slammed him against the final door. Simon got in his face. "You best bring your A-game outside, or I will shoot you in the kneecap. Understand?" Simon said. Jarvis nodded.

Turning to York, Simon told him, "Either George or Roger. Do not bother, Tex. Tell them your grandmother is on the way, and they will come directly to the bunker."

York nodded as he stuffed a bar in his mouth and washed it down with one of the brown drinks. Swallowing, he said, "Stand close to me in case I go down." Simon had already planned to be next to York. He would yank him back inside at the first sign of trouble.

Jarvis was not feeling the love. From the start, he had been the outsider, someone they picked on when they felt like it. Despite every attempt he made to fit in. They did not trust him. Nobody could give their A-game in this type of atmosphere. B, maybe, but not A. As these thoughts ran through his mind, he scanned the area around the bunker. That was his job, after all.

Back in the warehouse, George and Roger had two limp people. They had to move them through an air vent and to the car. Getting them up into the vent was the first task to figure out. Roger watched as George went over and stripped the ties holding the robes of the dead men. He then took off his belt and held his hand out to Roger. Fortunately, Roger had brightened up working with the team and was already pulling his belt off.

It was easy to figure out what George was doing. He was fashioning a harness of sorts out of the sashes and belts. He worked fast. Roger had never seen anything like the quick, deft way George whipped together a safety harness. When George finished, he motioned Roger over from where he had been tending to the woman. From one of the endless pockets, George and Tex seemed to have George pulled out a tablet. He passed the tablet to Roger after scribbling on it. It said, "You take the harness and go up. Drop the belt buckle end down to me. I'll lift the woman high and hook her up. Take her to where the vent divides, secure her in a side vent, then return."

Roger nodded. George cupped his hands to offer Roger a boost up. Roger reached up and pulled himself up into the vent chest first. He felt a tug on his pant leg. Looking down, he saw George twirl his fingers in a turn-around motion. Turn around? Oh, he needed to be facing the vent so he could pull the woman up and drag her down the vent. So much for thinking he was on top of things, he thought. Crawling across the vent, he raised his legs to where he had been about to enter the vent.

George held the woman up before him as if she were standing. Then he pulled the belt end of the harness down until he could unbuckle the belt. George slipped it under her arms and secured it in place. He hoped it was not so tight that it would hinder her breathing. It had to be snug enough not to slide over her arms and slip off. He gave Roger a thumbs-up and raised the limp woman as high as possible to ease the lifting.

Having watched every move George made, Roger pulled on the two sashes looped around the belt holding the victim. He thought she was heavier than she looked, realizing why George had him on this end of the lifting. He had been marveling at the effortless manner George used to harness the woman up. Feeling the dragging dead weight of her body, he wondered if he would have been able to lift her and hook her up the way George had.

It was a relief when Roger finally rested her chest before him. Now, he needed to figure out how to pull her behind him. Roger did not want to try pushing her in front of him for fear of hurting her, so he crawled backward and pulled the woman along with the harness.

Moving the unconscious woman was more difficult than Roger had thought it would be. She was a dead weight, wholly limp and unable to help him in any manner. No matter what method of pulling her along with him he tried, it seemed her body fought it. When he allowed her shoulders to rest on the vent, they caught each time she slid to where one section joined another. So, he would lift her shoulders at each vent joint. That made her slide over the area a little smoother but strained his shoulders from the constant lift action. Never was he so glad to reach the cross-section of a vent when he felt it with his feet.

Trying to make sure the woman was lying so she could breathe. Roger pushed her into the side vent. That was not as easy as it would have been with someone who could at least straighten their body. Once done, he removed the harness and scrambled back to where George and Tex were waiting as quietly as he could.

George had been busy while Roger was struggling to move dead weight. Thinking about how to immobilize Tex's neck and head had taken some thought. Moving him, in the condition he was in, could kill Tex. They were underpowered and unable to fight their way out of this den of evil. So, a stealthy and fast retreat was their best option. And that could be death for Tex.

There was nothing in the room but the chair, which had held Jacob's wife and the dead men. George knew he'd have to devise something out of what was on hand, a chair and what they wore. What was needed was a material that was somewhat rigid yet pliable enough to wrap around Tex's neck.

Removing Tex's shoes, George cut the leather away from the soles. It would be a difficult fit, but he thought he could shape this leather to curve around Tex's neck. Next, he cut the dead terrorists' robes into long strips, using the strips to pad the leather from the shoes and secure the sections together. It was crude and would not completely protect Tex's head from moving, but it was better than nothing.

"Sorry, old son," George whispered to Tex as he did his best not to cause more damage securing the makeshift brace. He felt the air shift when Roger lowered himself into the room. "This is going to be difficult for you," he wrote on his badly used notepad. "You have to pull Tex up without jarring him in any way. Then you leave here and return to where you left our victim. First, leave half of the harness for me. Attach the belt to our victim and use the other sash to attach her to you. It will be best to place her on her back and rest her head on you. Go up!"

Roger had a hundred questions, but he sucked them up and went back up into the vent. Don't bump Tex. Roger repeated those words to himself, dropping the harness back down so George could attach Tex to it. With great care, Roger pulled Tex up into the vent. He took his time, caring he never bumped Tex's head or shoulders. Once he had Tex facing lengthwise in the vent, Roger scrambled back to the woman they had rescued as quickly and quietly as possible.

There was no way George could move Tex through the vent without doing some harm to his injury. No matter how he considered moving with Tex, things didn't look hopeful. He ended up placing Tex's chest and head upon his chest and securing him there with the harness and his arms. George found moving while on his back was difficult. His legs had to do most of the work. Even then, he felt the strain on all his other body parts as he tensed his muscles, trying his best to keep Tex stable. But to keep Tex stable, he did, pushing forward until he passed the spot where Roger had left the woman. George was relieved Roger had managed to rig the harness on their victim. And that he was moving ahead of him. One less worry.

It was amazing how easily the woman moved once Roger figured out the whole harness. George was right about elevating the woman's shoulders so they didn't catch on every vent connection, making moving her along less stressful. He still wanted to get her out of that tight vent so he could breathe again. Upon reaching the room where they had accessed the vent, relief surged through Roger. Looking through the slits in the vent cover for that room, it seemed undisturbed. Roger had to decide whether to exit the vent and pony the woman in his care out. Or wait for George to make it to him with Tex. He couldn't visualize how George could safely lower Tex out of the vent alone. Roger knew the woman was their mission, and Tex would probably kick his butt for not getting her safely out. What sort of man would Roger be if he stepped up and left his teammates? So he warmed the woman with his body heat and waited and listened for some indication George was coming.

Any moment, George expected the alarm to be raised and men to come scrambling through the air vents after them. His whole body was tense in anticipation of the coming battle. They were lucky so far. The enemy had not found any of the bodies the team left behind. Truthfully, he had sent Roger ahead to save the woman and himself. George didn't expect to get out alive with Tex. So, when he saw that Roger was waiting for him, he wanted to string the boy up with barbed wire. The kid's chances of making it out had dropped dramatically.

The difficulty in training someone to think on the go is that you also have to boost their confidence. You could not do that if you strangled them, which George reminded himself as he reached Roger. Before, George could form a thought that did not include stringing Roger up. The boy passed him a note. "Felt we could lower Tex with less trauma together." George closed his eyes, admitting that Roger had a point. He nodded. And saw Roger relax in relief.

George took a moment to gather his thoughts and readjust his plans to lower Tex out of the vent. George scribbled out the instructions. "Lower our victim first. Then, you lower Tex directly on my shoulder, head, and chest to the front. You help bind him to me. So he does not bounce when I move. Take the victim and hightail it to the car. I will follow slowly with Tex."

As George laid the victim out on the desk, he had an idea. Motioning Roger to wait, George pulled out the top desk drawer. Located in the back of the drawer, he found the remains of a roll of duct tape. Perfect. With swift strokes, he then pried the bottom of the drawer free. Gently, he removed their victim from the top of the desk. He prepared his backboard using strips of tape to wrap around Tex. They had to move fast. It was a safer way to secure the head and shoulders from movement.

The Secret Service Agent and the retired Texas Ranger moved as fast as possible towards the door they had entered the building through. The door was in sight when an alarm blared inside the building. Their luck had ended. "Run!" they both said and ran, carrying their limp charges, trying not to do more damage to them.

"She's in the front. Open the back door for us," George instructed. Holding Tex tight, George dove into the car. Roger slammed the doors shut. With one arm, Roger kept their rescued victim in her seat as he peeled out of the area. There was a thud and then another as shots sprayed towards the fleeing van. "Are you alright back there?" Roger asked, his voice tight.

"Right as a Horny Toad," George grunted back. He was happy to be alive. Now, they might be in time to save Tex.

Susan and York were preparing to act as batteries for her mother at the bunker. They set up two cots close together to place Tex and Jacob's wife. A table had been laden with enough food for an Army. Hot water-filled bottles were ready to place around the injured. There was no need for bandages. Felith could heal anything as long as the dimmest spark of life was inside a person.

Jarvis thought preparing a banquet of food should be the last thing a reasonable person would do. He suffered his growing irritation in silence, having gleaned the fact the President's son was coming to visit. So much for this being a mission, Jarvis thought. He was not about to let the opportunity to impress Fredrick Whiting slip away. Twice, Jarvis stepped into the bathroom and went over his appearance. He buffed his shoes and ensured the edge of his embroidered handkerchief peeped just the right amount.

"Grandmother is here," York excitedly announced. Two Secret Service agents entered the bunker, guns drawn. Once satisfied that the bunker was a secure area, Felith and Fred Whiting entered. If the agents were intimidating, Fred Whiting was like a nuclear weapon. His cold gaze swept the room, zeroing in on Jarvis.

"You, I do not know," Fred said in that quiet, piercing way.

Beaming, Jarvis stepped forward, his hand extended towards Fred. "Jarvis Adams, sir, here to serve you," he said, thinking he had finally scored big time.

Ignoring the offered hand, Fred looked to

where Susan and Felith stood. The frown lines on Susan's forehead told him all he needed to know about Jarvis Adams. Fred hooked his thumb over his shoulder.

Suddenly, two burly men grabbed Jarvis by the arms and dragged him to the elevator. He let out a yelp when one of the men twisted his arm roughly behind his back.

After his initial excitement, York returned to sensing Roger and George. He tried to sense Tex repeatedly. And the fact that he could not feel him at all gnawing at his worry. Unable to calm the fear overtaking him, York reached out to Roger. "Did you all get out?" he inquired, desperately hoping they had.

A grunt escaped Roger when he heard York speaking in his head. Fighting to clear his own emotions, Roger tried to answer. "Yes, but I think we have some damage to the gas tank. The gauge is dropping fast."

Silence. Roger was kicking himself for scaring the boy when Miss Susan's voice sounded so clear that he looked at the limp woman beside him, thinking she had spoken. "Hide. Help is on the way."

Taking a deep breath, ignoring the pain in his side, Roger looked for a place to hide the black rental car. The only cover he could see was a clump of scrub trees inside what looked like a pasture. Finding a gate, Roger eased the car through and shut the gate. He drove slowly not to stir up the dust like intruders did when coming up Miss Susan's mountain. Now, all they could do was wait. Help was coming, but of what sort?

They didn't have long to wait before a silent ambulance bombed across the pasture to them with a black car escort. Two men in black wheeled a gurney out of the ambulance to the car. Roger insisted upon carrying Jacob's wife, leaving the gurney for Tex to be placed on. He thought he saw Jarvis attempting to exit the security car. Someone yanked Jarvis back inside the vehicle. A smile creased Roger's face for the first time in an eternity. He dared to ask the question the sight of Jarvis brought blurting out. "Was that agent Adams?"

A face filled with belligerence zeroed in on Roger. "No way are we leaving that user near our fine lady," the angry agent said. Then he smiled, "Although, if he touched her, her hubby would have killed him. Nope, he stays in the car."

Chapter Eighteen

SAFE

George insisted on riding with Tex, although he was content riding with the driver, leaving the attendants to care for their injured. That didn't keep him from watching the men tending Tex and the poor woman. "Looks like your team had a rough go," the black-suited driver said, trying to draw George into the conversation.

"A bit," George said, taking a deep breath as if bracing himself. "Classified," he whispered. Relaxing when the dark-suited driver nodded and kept his mouth shut. They had been operating with no official orders, completely off books, and as illegal as hell. He'd willingly do it again if his boy came out of this whole. As if he were afraid Tex would die if he couldn't see him, George kept his eyes glued to the rise and fall of Tex's shallow breaths. If he could only see Tex safely to Miss Susan's mother, Tex stood a chance of living. That was a lot of ifs. Sometimes, it was all you had to keep you going.

York was out of the bunker before anyone could stop him. He had to see Tex for himself. Deep inside, that nagging fear of losing the closest person to a father York ever had scared him. Then he froze. That sight of Tex strapped down, not moving, not even his eyes, those see-all eyes, open. It hit him hard, for that moment seemed to stop in time. Deep down, something happened to his insides. It was as if part of who he was grew up and took over the scared little boy he felt like he was. "Bring him in and place him on the second bed. Leave him strapped up for now." It was an effort for York to switch his attention to the bruised woman Roger had in his arms.

"I've got the victim," Roger said, his voice holding determination and command. This woman was his to-do, something he could do for Tex. Hold and complete the job. Then... he could fall apart, give in to that constant fear that Tex was going to die. Mentally, he kicked himself. No, that wasn't the end of the job. He still had a subject to protect. He couldn't let Tex down now, of all time.

Several men in dark suits positioned themselves around the area while a disgruntled, worried man sat in the black car where the others had arrived. His future didn't look as bright as he had thought.

Inside the bunker, Felith Whiting checked the wounded. Jacob immediately claimed a spot where he could hold his wife's hand. He didn't understand the people who had come. All they did was eat. His wife and that Secret Service man needed a hospital. Why were they wasting time eating? The older woman had touched his wife's head before walking over and doing the same to the man who looked nearer to death than alive. Jacob watched in frustration as the woman sat down in a chair and held her arm out. One of the men came over and inserted an IV in the woman's arm. Shouldn't they be doing that to the patient instead?

Simon walked up behind Jacob and spoke softly to him. "I must ask you to sit quietly while the doctor works on Agent Shadow. He is near death. Tell me now that we can trust you to behave, or must we remove you?" Simon asked.

Jacob was not about to leave his wife's side, so he said what he could, "I'll behave." The agent stood at his side to ensure he kept his word.

"He has a hot bleed from the knife wound in his side, but I need to heal the spinal cord first, or I'll lose him. Susan, York, if your guys tell you to stop, do so. Understand?" Felith said.

Roger stepped up to keep an eye on York. When George started to do the same for Miss Susan, Simon stopped him. Who signaled for him to take his place, watching Jacob. He gladly relinquished the spotter duty as he had no idea what he was doing. By the next time, he would as he watched everything that happened that night.

Nerve damage to such a vital section of the spinal cord was one thing doctors were sure they had little hope of success in treating. Felith knew she could heal that wound. She closed her eyes and began searching out the severed ends. They did not want to reach out to each other. She fought them silently, directing them to relax, and guided the sections towards each other. She induced growth where it had never existed, feeding it with her life force and that of the three human batteries giving their life force to her. Together, they could do the impossible.

Within minutes, York began to feel the strain on his young system. Still, he kept trying to give, to support the one person who was able to save Tex. Roger was watching York closely. When York began to sag, Roger stepped close to him.

"Don't touch him; talk him down and catch him if he falls. Then get him to eat and drink," Simon told Roger in a whisper to not disturb the others. "Warm blankets."

"Step back, York. Take a break. Eat and get warm so you can help some more," Roger urged. I sound like Tex, Roger thought. His forehead frowned as York stood a moment longer. He had to bring York out of whatever place in hell he had gone. Think, Roger told himself. The kid would do anything for Tex. Roger had to play to that. "York, you have to stop and beef up to help Tex. Stop now and come back strong," he reasoned with York. Relief rushed through him when York leaned back on him. Simon gave him a thumbs up. Roger realized his job wasn't over as he helped York to the table. Where two rugged giants brought and set out food. One went and came back with a warmed blanket in his hands. He gave Roger a nod of respect, which would have made Roger's day once. Now, Roger had more important things on his mind than his ego.

Roger ensured that York filled his tummy and ate at least one protein bar before the boy returned to help heal. By then, Susan was sitting, stuffing food into her mouth and almost swallowing it whole. Simon wrapped her in warm blankets, dreading letting her go back while hoping she recovered fast and could go back. The conflicting emotions had his stomach wanting to rebel, but Simon held strong, doing what he needed to do.

Before York or Susan had recovered enough to return as batteries, Fred was talking his wife down. Soon, she collapsed back into Fred's arms. He held her, motioning Simon to bring a blanket. "We'll do more once you eat and rest, dear," Fred assured Felith.

"They are fighting me. I almost have it all aligned. The sections are going to have to join each other. Set the kids up on IVs," Felith told Fred. She felt the zing of fear that hit her husband and leaned close to kiss him. "It will be alright. We are winning," she whispered. She knew he was remembering when they hadn't been winning. That time, they came close to losing their eldest daughter, Middy. They were all haunted by how close they had all come to death while fighting a lab-created nightmare. Since that time, they had all begun carrying portable defibrillators. You never knew when your healer's heart might stop.

Young ears hear everything, and York becomes worried about his grandmother. He was there the night she died while healing Middy. Like the rest of them, he had been scared. He looked over at Tex and knew it was worth him dying to heal the man he thought of as a father. Returning to the table, he sat down and ate a second meal. He drank two energy drinks and ate another protein bar. He'd try not to die cause dying scared him, but if he had to die to save Tex, he would. His face became a copy of his grandmother's face, not showing any of the terrible fear that rested in his heart.

"York, no! You get that thought right out of your head. Nobody is going to die here tonight. We are going to save Tex. And heal Jacob's wife. They don't have the thing your Aunt Middy had. We can do this," Susan swore to him, hoping to get his mind off anyone dying.

The frown line on Roger's forehead drooped down so far it looked like he was scowling. He kept his mouth clamped tight, fighting a wave of dizziness that threatened to take him down. He had to be strong for the boy in his care, for Tex. Grabbing one of the disgusting-looking brown drinks, he guzzled it, thinking he hadn't eaten since breakfast. There wasn't time for more; Susan's mom was back touching Tex, and the batteries were back in full force. York, with a determined look on his face, hid the fear Roger now knew he had.

Fred had Felith stop as he still had to insert the IV hookups into York and Susan. Simon took the setup from Fred and began to prep Susan's arm. George stepped forward and motioned for Fred to attend to Felith. He had used many catheters in the field on his boy Tex and other Texas Rangers. George was confident in not hurting York. He didn't know York was well-versed in IVs from when they healed Middy. "This arm is the easiest. Just go right about here, and you will find the vein," he told George. George believed him and had the kid set up, and brownish fluid dripped into him quickly. He was proud of how York stepped up and took on a man's load to save Tex. His boy had to marry that gal and be a father to this remarkable child.

Felith mended the delicate spinal cord back together. They would have to wait for Tex to wake up before knowing if she needed to make adjustments. She had stopped the bleeding earlier and knew he was now out of danger of dying. Before completing his healing, she needed to tend to that poor woman. Sitting back, she looked up at the worried faces of those around her. "He will live now. I may have to adjust some nerve tissue. And I'll complete his healing once I see our lady. She has waited long enough," Felith told them. The looks of relief were well worth every struggle she had with this stubborn spinal cord.

When he heard the good news and knew that Tex would live, Roger let go of his tight control on his body. He seemed to wilt, sliding into a puddle on the floor, out cold. York was instantly at Roger's side. When he touched Roger, he saw inside him. York saw where a bullet had penetrated his abdominal cavity. "Grandmother, he has been shot," he called out. "I can see it inside him," he said in wonder.

Turning from starting towards Jacob and his wife, Felith knelt beside Roger. "He certainly has been. And you see it?" she asked York.

"Yes, Ma'am," York said, his mind still full of wonder at what he saw.

"He is going to be okay, York. He isn't in danger. I doubt he even knew he had a wound. Let me heal the lady. We will work on him together. Eat again because healing takes a lot out of you," Felith told him. They had a budding healer in the family.

They had cruelly beaten Jacob's wife. She was, however, an easy heal for Felith. Small fractured bones, once such a challenge for Felith, now healed with little effort. Each time she died while healing, she received a boost to her skills. Soon, with Fred as her battery, she had the woman looking in the pink of health. She patted Jacob's hand. "She will wake up soon and feel wonderful. You must see to her mental health. She may have many nightmares and fears from this. Are you prepared to see her through all that mental trauma?" she asked Jacob.

"Unto death, we are one," he replied. "Thank you. I swear to keep it secret what you can do. I swear this unto death, my lady," he said with tears.

Felith hugged Jacob Combs before returning to the table, where her SS agents placed new hot food dishes. Fred had trained them well.

They all ate again, filling themselves with the food that would sustain them the longest. With new bags of fluid connected to the catheters in their arms, they were ready to heal Roger and finish up on Tex.

York was nervous. He had never thought of himself as anything other than a battery. Now, his grandmother was saying he could heal like her. Well, a little, but not really. How did she do it, the healing? Could he do that? What if he failed? Would his new mother be disappointed in him?

"York, come stand by me," Felith said. She had to figure out how to heal on her own. Now, she could pass that knowledge on to York. If it were not healing, which he was tuned to do, then his ability to see the wounds would help determine when Eric or herself needed to summon. Fortunately, her children never called her unless it was a dire emergency.

Trying not to let his hands shake and show how nervous he was, York stood by his grandmother. She motioned for him to sit in a chair while she checked the flow of the brownish fluid dripping into his veins.

"Good, now place a hand somewhere there is exposed skin on Roger. Let your mind flow through his body and see if there is any other ailment we need to investigate," Felith told York.

The moment he touched Roger, he saw the gunshot wound. Try as he might, he couldn't get his mind to see anything except the wound. His face scrunched up in concentration, and he thought his head would explode with the effort. Only that one point showed bright and clear to him. He had to concede defeat. Holding back signs of the fear he felt at having failed, of being useless, he looked up into his grandmother's face. "I can only see the wound. My mind won't look anywhere else. I'm sorry, Grandmother," he said with only the slightest quiver.

"You did excellent, York. What you did was stay focused on the most threatening wound. It will make you invaluable when we have many hurt people to care for in the future. You can zero in on the life-threatening wounds and let us know who to treat first, who can wait, and who to send to regular doctors. You are a treasure," Felith told him.

Automatically, York swung around to see if his mom and Tex had heard his grandmother's words. Susan had come to stand by him, and she beamed down at him. "You are a treasure, son," she hugged him. He looked to where Tex lay still and not moving. And it all hit him so hard his body went limp, and he fell to the floor off the chair.

Helping York up, George shoved a bar and a drink into his hands before checking that he hadn't dislodged the catheter in his arm. They were putting too much on a young boy like York. He was about to light into the healer woman when he realized she was healing Roger. And the others were being batteries again. Even York had his hand on the healer woman while chewing the protein bar he had shoved into his mouth. No way was George going to interrupt them now.

The bullet wound Roger had was easy to heal. He had been driving, walking, and supporting York for hours before he gave in to the wound. He blinked awake as the team over him left him to refuel before finishing the healing on Tex. George leaned over him and explained what was going on. "You were hit by some fire when we drove off. The healer woman fixed you. York diagnosed you. He can see wounds," George told him. "Rest, then get up and take over watching over him."

Slowly, Roger was able to see what George was saying. York could see inside people. "For real?" he asked, remembering George was a joker. George nodded. "For real," Roger whispered to himself. He didn't have time to lay there in wonder over what

York could do. The family was up and headed towards Tex. Sitting up slowly, he realized he felt better than he had in quite a while. The healer had healed him alright, all over. His focus was entirely on York as he walked up behind the boy, prepared to do whatever it took to keep him safe.

"Touch Tex like you did, Roger, and tell me what you see," Felith told York.
Reaching out, York touched Tex's cheek, and he was instantly zooming in on a knife wound in Tex's leg. It was the only bright spot he saw. "His leg. It is the only thing I'm seeing," he said.

"Wonderful. If left to me, I'd have fixed his belly first. I had dismissed the leg wound as non-life-threatening. But now that you have pointed it out. I can see how the blood flow is restricted more and more. If we don't do the leg first, he will lose it. You have saved his leg, York. I want you to touch him again after I fix the leg, okay?" Felith asked.

York nodded, placing his hand on her shoulder, sending his strength to her as a battery should. He didn't know how he felt about not being a healer. He was just happy to be a battery.

Once Felith had healed Tex's leg, York touched him again and could see the bleed in his belly that had almost bled him dry. He could see why his grandmother would think this was the first place to be healed. But his weird seeing thing had shown him the leg, which his grandmother had told him had saved Tex's leg. Grandmother fixed the rest of Tex, and then they began the long wait to see if his spinal cord was healing correctly.

It was nearing the noon hour in Washington D.C. when Tex woke up from the healing coma he had been in before they exited the air vent in the terrorist warehouse. He didn't move or try to sit up, just lay there. Susan heard her mother's worry that she hadn't repaired his spinal cord correctly. That fear was also in everyone in the bunker. Both Susan and York sat on either side of the bed.

Young York watched Tex's face for some sign that he was okay. When Tex did nothing but shift his eyes, York reached out and touched his forehead. That caused Tex to look at York. York's eyes were closed as he tried to get his new power to work. Nothing. Nothing at all appeared before him as needing immediate attention. He looked over at Susan and barely shook his head. To his surprise, Susan smiled at him.

"You've lounged in that bed long enough, Tex. You have to tell us what went on in that warehouse. I need to be able to report something to grandfather," she said, then paused as if considering something. "Are you hungry? You haven't eaten since yesterday; of course, you are hungry. See what our dear SS friends can provide us for lunch."

Once York was out of hearing range, Susan narrowed her eyes at Tex. "You are scaring York. He needs to know you are okay. Now suck it up and get out of bed."

Get out of bed? I would if I could, Tex thought, remembering the moment he lost speech and then blacked out. Not one muscle of his body would ever listen to him again. She had to let him go, let him die.

Susan stood up. Fury was etched on her face. Just as quickly as that sign of temper flashed, it was gone. "You are wrong. Mother has fixed you as she fixed me and Ritter. You remember Ritter, smashed to a pulp. Do you think you were in bad shape? Consider the hell he went through while being healed. Now, Smile for York is bringing us some lunch. And sit up."

Tex did smile at this tiny, bossy woman. She wielded so much power and was so down to earth. How could you not love someone like that? Love. He had forgotten to count, damn. "1,2,3,…" "I don't know if I can sit up," he said. An overpowering force moved up to his bed. Susan's father. "Sir?" Tex managed to get out. He remembered this man having a talk with him about not hurting Susan. Or had he dreamed that?

"I'll set you up. My wife wants to be certain she healed you correctly. Those researchers who want to experiment on her have her doubting her abilities. I'll set you up. Then you show her you are fully functional," he said or ordered Tex.

This man managed to intimidate Tex, which was not easy. He nodded, then marveled at the fact he could move his head. Slowly, he tried to flex his fingers, and they obeyed. Hope sparked inside him. He tried to keep that tiny spark from growing and hidden away. But hope is a strange thing. It doesn't take much to place a bit of it inside a person. A word, a look could place it deep inside you. And it could grow to such proportions that it spun a miracle, or it could wither and die with one careless, thoughtless word.

York arrived with a tray so laden with food that the boy could barely carry it. He walked slowly and carefully, keeping his eyes glued to several tall glasses of milk.

Fred pulled a table closer and took York's tray, placing it there. He gave Tex a pointed look. And began sorting plates around the table as men in black suits brought in more food, enough to feed everyone. Fred knew that this was something his wife organized. She was feeding everyone again. He so loved that woman.

Susan turned to the bunker door, now open so the SS, which had accompanied her mother, could come in and join the meal laid out. Tex tensed up. He knew that look on her face. She had heard some thought she was about to respond to it. Without thinking of the paralyzing he had previously endured, Tex stood up and felt for his gun. His weapon wasn't on him. "Simon, guard Susan. And someone, bring me a weapon," Tex barked in full guard mode.

The room erupted as every SS agent and person, except Susan, became battle-ready. Susan calmed the room down with one word: "No." She gave Tex a look of apology before continuing. "It is only Jarvis who is still out in the car. We should let him come in and use the bathroom, then eat. He has an inflated ego but is still one of you."

Eyes narrowing, Tex looked at Susan. "What did he do?"

It was Susan's father who answered him. "He carelessly stuck his hand out, expecting me to shake it. The danger of him touching my wife was too great. I had him removed," Fred said, not concerned about what anyone thought about him sending Jarvis out.

"Then I will talk with him before he is allowed to come in here. Excuse me a moment," Tex said, walking out still in his stocking feet and looking like he had been through a hurricane.

It wasn't hard to tell the car where Jarvis sat. Only one had two burly armed men standing guard over it. Tex nodded to the men walking straight up to them as if he was fully clothed and wore a sign saying he was in charge. "There is no sense in you two having to stand out here. I'm going to have a little talk with him," Tex indicated the dark shape in the car's back seat. "Perhaps I'll allow him inside. If not, then you two go eat and relax a moment, and I'll see to it he stays put."

The two men stepped back, a spark of amusement flashing on their faces, to let Tex into the car. One of the men unlocked the rear passenger-side door for Tex.

Without bending down to let Jarvis leave, Tex held up his hand, stopping the man from exiting the black car. "I understand that the Secret Service had you removed for being too touchy with the President's son. He feels you are a threat to his wife. Everyone knows they are not to touch her. You have pretty much blown any chances with the family. Should you remain quiet and stay where you are allowed to sit? You may enter the bunker and use the bathroom, then eat. Do I have your word that you will follow those rules?" Tex asked. Jarvis's face blazed red, but he nodded. "Be certain to wash your hands after the bathroom," Tex added before stepping back to allow Jarvis to exit the car.

The two SS agents stood beside him in case he didn't remember to behave himself.

Chapter Nineteen

PARENTS

Jarvis behaved and even apologized for coming on so strongly with Fred. He did not endear himself to anyone. The man had much to learn about the word team and how to function as a human being. Before Susan's parents left, they saw that the home office recalled Jarvis. He didn't have what it took to be part of the security for anyone in the family. A weight lifted from Susan and her team once Jarvis was gone.

Goldie was watchful of not only Susan and York now but also of Tex. She often sat or laid by him for a few moments each day before they boarded a jet home.

The jet home was quiet. They had managed a peaceful family dinner with Susan's grandfather. They filled him in on what had his loyal friend acting so weird. The President nodded but didn't elaborate on what his thoughts were. Mentally, he told Susan that he had feared having her investigate since he had worried that this involved a new threat to the United States of America. And he feared his office was bugged. All the SS agents exchanged looks of worry at this information later when Tex and the others silently learned what had been told to Susan. Several hand signals passed between the men, Tex and George.

Now, on the jet home, the men were quiet, each inside their heads worrying over the signs of times changing ahead.

In the car, as they drove home, York broke the silence. "I want to get back into training," he said. "You must be serious in teaching me what all of you know. I must be prepared to help if we have to fight Someone."

He was so grown up and serious about the subject. Every man on the team swore to himself that they would teach everything they knew. Susan's mountain came into sight, and the tension rolled off their shoulders. They were home.

A piercing scream in the sky sounded when they pulled up in front of the house and bunker. Eagle Eye came down in a steep dive, and Tex feared the mighty bird would crash into the ground. At the last moment, the eagle backwinged and landed lightly on Susan's shoulder. It was clear Eagle Eye was injured at some point, which would explain his long absence.

York used his budding ability to see wounds as he petted the fretful bird. He not only located the place where Eagle Eye had been shot but saw how the wound had healed. "Eagle Eye has healed, Mother. He may feel a bit stiff in the cold of winter. But he is okay."

"You were a brave boy fighting that intruder, Eagle Eye. I was worried for so long about you," Susan told the bird. I shall tell the others what you have seen over dinner. Thank you for being such a good friend," Susan said, her mind filled with the images that remained with the eagle. Now she knew why they had only had glimpses of him soaring in the sky occasionally. Satisfied, he had warned Susan, Eagle Eye took to the sky to continue his endless patrolling of the area.

Dinner would have been delayed without meat already thawed out. Susan and the others had been away for nearly a week while they searched for Jacob's missing wife. Susan found some canned tuna fish and prepared a casserole with it. She made a creamy sauce with finely chopped mushrooms. Then, she cooked some noodles to be nearly done. Draining the noodles, Susan combined them with chopped onions, tuna, grated cheese, and mushroom sauce. She baked the casserole until it was bubbly and delicious.

Roger and Simon eyed the casserole with critical eyes. Both men had become spoiled with the man-pleasing meals Susan had served in the past. But they sighed in pleasure once they dug into the creamy tuna casserole and tasted the hot greens and delicious cornbread. "Ma'am, you must give me that recipe so I can send it to my mother. She will love it. And I understand she is on a very restricted diet within the meal you served tonight," Simon told Susan.

Since Susan had not made a dessert, George

volunteered to make some ice cream while the others carried meals up top for their sniper friends. It was good to be home and to have their peaceful routine back, even though their minds still held dark shadows and worries over all that had transpired in D.C.

They consumed mounds of peach vanilla ice cream. The subject of Tex and George and the SS houses came up. "Are we to resume our previous schedule of two in the houses and two here?" Simon asked. He had missed having Tex around. With his attitude and cutting voice, Jarvis had become a thorn in his side.

The entire table became silent. All eyes went to where Tex sat. Only moments ago, he had felt so upbeat and satisfied with life. He sat with a deep furrow on his forehead and brooding eyes. We should, he thought to himself. We only moved up here because Jarvis was an ass. The thought of leaving Susan open to any threat without him standing between her and danger irked him no end. He had to try and calm down his protective instincts. Only now that he could move, he felt the full force of his often awkward emotions. How could he leave her? How could he stay? Count, damn you, don't let her feel the turmoil inside you. Count. "1, 2,4, now 3, now 4…." He couldn't even count with all his insides pulling apart. How could he decide? What was wrong with him? He'd never found a decision so hard to form before.

The raised hand stopped Tex before he left Susan's and returned to the SS house he had shared with Simon.

Everyone at the table turned their full attention to Susan. She was used to having Generals and Secret Service men stop and look at her when she spotted some danger. Only this time, it was personal. She didn't want Tex to go back to the house. But what she had seen in his mind when he forgot to count made her decide to send him back. "I think it only proper that you return to the house for now," Susan said, watching Tex tense up and feeling the profound hurt her words had brought him. "It is only proper that you come courting from there rather than living here. I trust you to figure out the rest."

Heads swiveled from her to him, obviously shocked at her forwardness. All but Tex, he had dropped his eyes to the melting ice cream when she said he should return to the house. It was a long moment before the rest sank through his hurting heart. Courting? He sat back as if poleaxed. No words could pass his tongue to come out of his mouth. After what seemed an age, Tex just nodded, pushing his bowl of ice cream aside. He stood and walked to the bedroom to pack his few belongings. Courting, he could do that. He heard York's voice behind him, "For real?"

Susan nodded, hoping she had not misread Tex's unguarded thoughts. She feared that should she leave him to decide to go beyond the SS agent and his subject. He would walk away out of some misguided idea of honor. Look how hard he had held himself in check when he thought Jarvis was a fitting husband, as if she would want an ego-ridden man who never thought of what others may feel. Susan liked what her mother and father had, that sincerely devoted caring that could survive any crisis that came their way. If she had to push Tex into stepping out of the shell of his previous heartache, then she would.

Tex came out of the bedroom with his duffel bag over his shoulder. "I'll be back shortly. Simon, I believe you are starting your duty early. George, pack your bag, and I'll take it with me," he ordered as if this was an everyday occurrence.

Soon, Tex had both bags in the car and drove off. He hadn't spoken to Susan or even looked at her. He was counting like mad so that Susan couldn't hear his thoughts. Now, she was nervous, wondering if she had pushed him away instead of nudging him towards her.

Resigned to living with whatever path Tex took, she went with York and George along the woodland path to visit their animal friends. Dewey had been waiting for them on the forest trail. Her tummy was showing definite signs of a baby on the way. York was so excited and showed his concern with gentle caresses. His eyes sparkled in anticipation of seeing a tiny version of Dewey in the Spring.

Chatterbox and Sly arrived at the same time. Chatterbox scowled at them for being away so long. But Shy seemed to be concerned about something. When Eagle Eye called out overhead, letting them know he was on patrol watching over them, Sly stared up at the eagle circling in the sky. Susan felt he was worried about their old friend in the sky.

Coming home should be a time of joyous

reunions, not this constant worry. Did everything and everyone around her have to suffer because of her? Looking at York so happy over the thought of a fawn in the Spring, Susan wondered if she was doing him any good as a parent. Too many of the people she cared about suffered harm. First Simon and George, then Roger and Tex. Who would be hurt next? York? That thought sat heavily on her mind for the rest of their walk.

Tex unpacked his duffel and then packed up Jarvis's clothing and items. Tex wouldn't let loose all the thoughts that had bombarded his mind when Susan mentioned courting. He had to think about things and do this right. She had said courting, and Tex wanted to be sure she felt fully and truly courted. He needed to fill her with romance. Good grief. Tex had no idea what people do nowadays on dates. What was he thinking? He couldn't take Miss Susan on a date with crowds! He had to avoid crowds. And normal. He didn't want just a normal courtship with flowers and candy. He wanted something she would remember when they were old and gray. Memories she would smile over.

York! Good grief, he was going to be a dad, too. York needed to be courted by the man soon to be his father. Or was he just crazy thinking Susan had been serious about them courting? I could be overthinking this whole courting idea, Tex thought. But she was the one opening the door to these crazy thoughts he was having. And he was going to take advantage of that opening. Was he prepared to be a husband and a parent? Damn right.

His soon-to-be son wanted to learn how to

fight. They had all given York lessons in defense, but Tex needed to prepare him for anything the world might throw at him. Tonight, Tex would give him the first lesson.

Of course, plans always turn out differently than you think they should. When Tex returned to the cottage, York was so worried about the fawn Dewey was carrying that he couldn't talk of anything else. He wanted to know if she would need a doctor to check her out. George reassured York that Dewey could have the fawn in the woods. And that people being there when the fawn was born would upset her.

So much for starting out being an example of a father, Tex thought. He smiled at all the right moments and agreed with George about how Dewey would feel about people being there when her baby was born. He offered some advice to York before calling it a night and leaving. "You must allow Dewey to decide when to present her baby to you. New mothers are protective of their babies. Never place yourself between an animal of the wild and their baby, son," Tex told him, wondering if he was overstepping by calling York son.

Her heart felt like it was cracking. Tex had returned last night as he promised. Only, he hadn't looked at her. York seemed to be his focus. Then he was gone without a word, not even a good night. She had been wrong. The push had gone the opposite way from what she had hoped. That would teach her to meddle with things to do with the heart. She must accept what she had brought about and let Tex go. You couldn't tell what another person held in their heart or wanted. It was clear she couldn't.

Susan began to cook the large breakfast she cooked each morning to sustain her menfolk. Her men, how arrogant that sounded to her. She had thought of them as hers for years. They were here to protect her, that was all. She was just a job they had to work. She was nothing else.

Simon's brow furrowed in a worried frown. Where was Tex? He was usually the first one there to relieve him and George so they could go in and eat. Had he taken the coward's way out and ran after Miss Susan's announcement about courting? I'll kick his butt, Simon thought, if he hurts Miss Susan. A cloud of dust caught Simon's attention. A vehicle was coming up the road to Miss Susan's house. "Alert," Simon called out, pulling out his weapon.

George, who had been making one of his last patrols for the night, scrambled down the mountain. He leaped upon the roof of the house. George lay prone on the cabin roof, securing the long gun he had oiled and wrapped up to have at the ready. That kidnapper had shown there were flaws in their security. George had been updating the security, bit by bit. Sighting down the barrel, George grunted. That was new. A delivery truck? For flowers?

Simon had Miss Susan and York secured in the bunker with orders to wait to open the door until one of them gave the all-clear. He had already sent an alert to Tex and Roger. They should be arriving at any moment.

Roger came running out of the woods, his weapon out and an expression on his face that Simon would not like to see in a dark alley. Simon looked for Tex but didn't see him. His stomach soured a bit. Tex, the dirty low-down coward, Simon was going to shoot his balls off.

The flower truck slowly crept up the mountain towards them. Seeing several weapons pointed at him, the driver slowed to a mere crawl. Then he stopped some distance away, trying to decide if he should turn the truck around.

It was a standoff. The driver dared not drive closer, and the men were not budging in their stances. The team felt sorely tested without Tex to guide them in this situation.

Behind him, Simon heard the vacuum suck of the bunker door opening. "Ma'am, you are to close that door and not open it again until you get the nod from me," he barked at her, aggravation eating him up inside. No Tex. Now, a stubborn subject.

"Stand down," Susan countered. "I could not hear the driver's thoughts while in the bunker. He is frightened. I will go back into the bunker, but you must go and do your thing by putting your gun away before questioning the driver," she commanded.

If he hadn't had to keep his eyes on the driver, he would have closed his eyes in a God save me from fools manner. Simon nodded instead. Simon wasn't sure who that fool was.

Once he heard the bunker door snick shut, Simon began to give orders, "Up top, hold steady on the intruder. Miss Susan thinks he is innocent. Roger and George hold ready. I'm going to approach the intruder."

Holstering his weapon, Simon walked to where the driver sat as if frozen in the flower truck.

"You have entered an area that is restricted. Please state your business," Simon said.

The teenager in the flower truck gulped once, then sat up a little straighter. "Sir, I have a flower delivery for Miss Susan Whiting. My boss said they had to be delivered by…, well, five minutes ago. Do you shoot people for being late here?" he asked.

Despite all the drama and anger he had been feeling, Simon chuckled. "No, but we require you to have an appointment in advance. That way, we don't have to draw down on you," he said.

The teenager looked down at his hands. "They did tell me to call ahead. I forgot," he confessed.

"Tell me, who sent these flowers? Was it a woman or a man? Describe how they looked. What sort of vehicle were they driving, and did you get a look at the license plate?" Simon questioned the teen as if he were a witness to a crime, which he might be.

"Whoa, man. I only deliver, and I don't take orders. You will have to ask the owner for that information. Usually, it is some guy who stepped out on his wife or someone's funeral, or it could be a new fling starting," the guy paused, "and on occasions, birthdays, and such."

"A card?" Simon asked. He needed information and would if he had to rip the flowers apart to find it.

"Yes!" exclaimed the teen, relieved he could finally produce something for this man with a gun. He reached back, got up, and searched his many deliveries before picking up a potted orchid. "Here, this is the plant, and a message is attached. See, right here."

Simon saw it. He also saw the writing and knew with a sinking feeling. He was going to be the butt of many a joke. The card read:

This orchid will tell me if
You have decided to accept this
invitation for a date today.
Place it upon the tree stump,
In front of the house, if yes.
In the window, if no.

Robin Shadow

His face was red. Simon tipped the delivery driver generously and accepted the orchid. "Stand down," he ordered the team. Under his breath, forgetting that the team and snipers could hear him, Simon mumbled several curses with Tex's name involved in them. He heard a soft chuckle and shut up. Holding the orchid before him for Miss Susan to see, Simon stood where the camera had his full view and gave the nod she was expecting.

Susan and York walked out of the bunker with Goldie prancing at their side, wagging her tail in delight. "Thank you, Simon," Susan said, softly adding, "You need to count. Please tell everyone breakfast will be soon."

He felt a great weight lift from his shoulders as his anger at Tex was released. The man was late because he had been ordering flowers and arranging a date. Okay, I won't kick your butt, he thought, but that does not mean I won't tease you a hell of a lot, you sneaky devil. Smiling, he turned toward the others and glanced up at George as he jumped down to be with them. "Miss Susan says breakfast will be ready soon," he said, thinking of all the mischief they could pull on Tex soon.

Susan had taken the orchid inside with her to show to York. The boy was happy beside himself, seeing this as the first step for Tex becoming his father. Susan carefully sprayed the orchid with water before taking it outside and placing it upon the tree stump indicated in Tex's note.

Returning to the kitchen, Susan had York help her prepare breakfast. Biscuits were mixed and baked, eggs and bacon were cooked, and a milk gravy was made. Then, the feast was placed on the table. Individual baskets were made up for the four snipers to dine on during their changeover from night to day crew.

George entered to take up the baskets of food for snipers up top. He frowned at the table setting. "No pancakes? Miss Susan, you wound my grumbling tummy. It was all set to eat your light-as-air pancakes this morning," he teased.

Susan swatted him with a dishtowel. "Oh, you poor baby. I'll make some for you. Now, scat. Up top are hungry men," she told him, grabbing a mixing bowl to make pancakes. On this day, she was allowed to be happy, to have a break from hundreds of people's thoughts beating on her happiness. Tonight, she was to have her first date.

Roger and Simon came in to eat while George stayed outside on watch—there was still no Tex. Roger had a huge appetite and devoured his food almost without chewing it. Simon had yet to hear from or see Tex. He was too filled with worry to enjoy the feast set before him.

Then there was York, who forked food into his mouth and chewed it as fast as he could, for so many questions were erupting in his mind. He felt it would blow up if he didn't get answers to them. Only as fast as a question popped up, another shot into his brain, leaving the previous questions unasked. And there was a deep-seated fear that he was having a dream where all his wishes were coming true. Dreams. They are not real. Please don't let me wake up if I'm dreaming, he silently begged.

"Alert," George's voice over the earbuds said. Roger and Simon pushed back their chairs, drew their weapons, and hustled York and Susan out to the bunker built into the mountain to keep her safe.

A cloud of dust hid the vehicle or vehicles coming up the mountain to Susan's place. Two SS agents and a Texas Ranger stood armed and ready, watching as that cloud of dust revealed a battered truck and a horse trailer bouncing along the dirt road.

The truck pulled up in front of Susan's place, dust swirling around and over it. The driver's door creaked and popped when it opened, and Tex stepped out. He ignored the men staring at him, turning away to look towards the tree stump. There it was, his orchid to Susan. "Please tell Miss Whiting her date has arrived. I understand that one of you must accompany us. I expect whoever comes to keep a respectful distance. You may sit in the bed of the truck," Tex said, watching the facial expressions of his teammates and friends closely for any sign of disapproval.

Stepping forward, George said, "That would be me if you are going by horseback. I assume you have a horse built for a tall, long-legged man."

"Yes, sir. I do," Tex said, trying not to laugh. He saw Roger looking back and forth between Tex and George as if they were speaking in a code he couldn't understand. "I also brought a Molly Bug for our young child," Tex said, knowing George would remember the pony Tex had trained. It had been for the daughter of their Captain in the Texas Rangers. He had named it Molly Bug.

"Simon, inform Miss Susan and York they need to wear jeans and boots for their date," George said. "And Roger, you must go with me since York is going. I suggest you go like the wind and change clothes too."

Roger started to argue that he had never ridden a horse, but he kept his mouth closed and took off running to change clothing. He thought he heard the guys up top laughing in his earbuds, but he was too worried about being on a horse to care or feel embarrassed.

Susan and York exited the bunker. When York heard he would be going on this date, he jumped in the air, giving a whoop that had Eagle Eye answering with a screech overhead before rushing inside to find some boots.

Doing his best not to laugh at York's wild excitement, Simon volunteered to clean up the breakfast dishes and lock up the house before he retired to catch some sleep. Someone had to keep a level head around here and rest up for duty tonight. He had underestimated Tex. He was grateful he was the only one who knew the doubts he had thought before Tex revealed his planned outing. Leave it to a Texan to go hog wild on a first date. Despite trying to keep a straight face, Simon smiled.

Chapter Twenty

NOW AND FOREVER

Tex watched York's jump of joy and felt pleased that he had included York on this first date. Hopefully, it was not the last date with Susan. He had racked his brain for some idea that would not subject Susan to other people's thoughts. The only solution was to stay clear of any town, city, or dwelling. Such spots are not easy to find on short notice. From listening to her talk with her brother Eric, he knew Susan liked riding horses. With that helpful information, he left his job guarding her in Simon and George's hands while he vetted the nearest ranches with horses he could rent or buy— five local or at least within a distance of traveling to pick up the stock and saddles. Two Tex immediately left upon seeing the horses they stocked—a third he held as a maybe. The fourth ranch had what he wanted.

The Molly Bug pony Tex was found at the fifth ranch, along with a fine mare for Susan. He had spent the morning saddling horses, loading, and gathering everything he needed for the outing date. He was nervous when he came with the truck and horse trailer to pick everyone up. Simon had given him such a glaring look that he felt like a teenager facing a date's father. He decided to play up to that side of things like a stranger coming to pick Susan up.

Driving up, he hadn't seen the orchid on the stump because of the dust thrown up. His heart had thumped in his chest so hard when he thought perhaps he had read the whole situation wrong. Surely, Susan wouldn't tease him about courting her. He had never seen her be cruel like that. One of the many things he admired about her was the even-handed way she treated people.

Once in the truck, George and Roger were situated in the truck bed. And York sat between Susan and Tex in the cab as Tex fired up the old but dependable beast. He swung wide to head back down that long, dusty road to the highway. York bounced in the seat even when they hadn't hit a bump. The boy was so excited to see him that you'd think it was Christmas morning. Susan sat quiet, and that worried Tex no end.

The green of soft rolling hills lay before them when Tex finally pulled off the highway. He turned to Susan and York. "York, you can help me set up the grill and unload the horses. We will set some coals in the grill to slow burn so they will be ready for cooking our lunch once we return from the ride."

It took a great deal of effort on Tex's part not to laugh as a grumpy George jumped down from the truck bed. Dust covered George so thick it was hard to tell what color his hair and clothing were. Roger looked like a hulking ghost covered in dust. Both men had bandannas covering their faces.

Having left the BBQ grill slowly burning coals for later, they unloaded the horses and pony and led them around to get the kinks out of their legs. York was trying to act all grown up about getting on his pony. The brown and white painted pony stood still while York climbed into the saddle. Once York was settled, the others mounted, with Roger nearly flinging himself clear over the saddle, trying to make sure he made it up there. He sat, his feet dangling until George told him to stick his feet in the stirrups.

The horses Tex had selected were excellent animals, their coats shiny despite the layer of dust on them. Roger and York were settling in nicely when George rode up in front and raised his hand haltingly. His far-seeing eyes had spotted movement ahead. He pulled a scope out of one of the pockets in his padded vest to get a better look.

Behind George, the others had tensed up. What had moments ago been a carefree outing now seemed filled with foreboding. Three grownups surrounded York, and Tex softly spoke to York. "If I say go, you should turn Molly Bug around and ride back to the road as fast as possible. Don't stop at the truck. Keep going, and if you hear shots back here, head off the road but travel alongside the road until you come to a building with someone in it. Call Simon from there. Understand?"

Nodding, York hunched forward, prepared

to dash off to get help. George called York to come up beside him and passed him the scope. "Look towards that rounded tree," he instructed.

Hands trembling, York did as told. The image in the scope was bouncing up and down and around the tree. Until it finally settled upon a small herd of deer grazing on the lush grass there. "We will have to ride up slowly to not scare them," George told him. "Let your mom have a look."

Once everyone had a look at the herd of deer, they went on. Tex led them onto a twisty path around one of the steeper hills. The sounds of water falling reached them long before they rounded a rock cliff and spotted the waterfall spilling into a clear pool below it. There, they stopped, allowing the horses to drink and washing some dust from the truck ride and the trail off. A tall stand of trees blocked any farther travel, and they realized this was the turnaround spot about which Tex had told them. Roger kept watching over York as he explored the waterfall and the pool. Roger even allowed York to check out a stream spilling down the hill to the green valley below. Here was where Tex had thought to propose to Susan. However, that did not look possible as George kept watch over them. It was time to head back. Tex had to decide to get down on a knee or to wait.

Frustration began to build inside Tex as York came running up to tell them of a fish he saw swimming in the stream. He did the fatherly thing and let York lead him to the spot where the fish was swimming in lazy circles. After Tex explained that they were watching a catfish, Tex looked over to George, catching his eye. With a hidden movement of his hand, he signaled his friend.

Alone? The boy wanted to be alone. What the hell for? It was their job to protect Susan and York; he wanted to be alone! Right about then, he saw Tex glance at Susan. Well, duh. Okay, but he thought you'd better kiss that gal while I distract the others.

Gathering Roger and York, George took them to the pool's far end, where the stream began. A smooth surface of clear water simmered in the sun until it stirred and trickled down the stream below. He showed Roger and York how to skim rocks across the water's surface. Soon, Roger and York tried to make the small stones skip across the pool's surface. George encouraged them and kept an eye on Tex and Susan.

Tex took Susan by the hand and walked to where a tree leaned over the water, giving them shade and privacy. Looking into Susan's eyes, he thought, I must be crazy. He hadn't even kissed her yet, and he would ask her to marry him. Being paralyzed had shaken him up and made him realize that you can't keep putting off doing what your heart desires. He had given up too many of the moments he wanted out of life. And she had brought up the word courting, right? Reaching into his pocket, he pulled out the ring he had pushed in early this morning and got down on one knee.

Across the pond, George muttered, "I'll be damn he is proposing already."

"What?" Roger asked, turning so he could

see Susan and Tex.

"What?" York gasped, spinning around and almost falling into the pond. He saw Tex down on one knee, holding a ring out to his mom. Wide-eyed, York looked up at George. "He truly is going to be my dad?" he asked in a voice so raw with feeling that the words seemed to tremble.

"Looks to me as if he is asking her right now. Let's hope she says yes," George said.

Tex gazed into Susan's eyes as he slipped the ring onto her finger. He stood, taking her into his arms and gathering her to him. Tex closed his eyes and kissed her. He lost himself in the feeling of kissing Susan. Tex didn't even hear the wild whoops from their audience. When the Kiss finally ended, Susan glanced over Tex's shoulder. "They need to count," she said, smiling as she said it.

On the ride back to the truck and the heating grill, York stayed with his two guards to allow Susan and Tex a little privacy. York kept asking Roger and George when they would get married. Was Tex his dad right off, or did he have to adopt Tex? And did he have to go to court and tell them he wanted to adopt Tex? It was all they could do to keep a serious face on as York kept trying to get information from them but was too impatient to let them answer.

Tex was silent for a bit as they rode up ahead of the others. Everything inside him wanted to charge full force ahead and see the preacher before they returned to the house. However, he needed to consider Susan's feelings about the wedding. "Any ideas on how we can pull the wedding off? I'm all for going now and finding us a preacher. But I'm certain your father would kill me if we did that. Save me, please," he said, half-joking, half-serious.

"No problem, we'll set my mother loose on it. She will be straightforward. By morning, she will have the wedding arranged. I imagine we'll have to get started on the paperwork right away. We can expect the whole family to attend," she said, watching Tex's face go from amazed to grim.

"All of them?" he asked, remembering that her Aunt Julian wasn't a favorite of anyone.

"Mother will handle them, don't worry. Considering that half the SS will be there, she might have us with immediate family in some out-in-the-country church. I'll hint at that. Sound good?" she asked.

"Sounds like a dream to me," he said, leaning in for a kiss and nearly unseating himself.

Never had hot dogs gone down a boy and his keepers so fast as they did that day. The horses were walked and unsaddled. Tex showed York how to rub down Molly Bug and treat her legs for traveling back to the ranch.

York became shy once they were in the truck heading home. Just before they reached the turn-off up the mountain, he found his voice. "I'm going to adopt you, so you'll be my legal dad, Tex. You can help me fill out the papers. And if we have to go to court, you need to wear your SS suit and gun so they don't argue with me. Okay?"

"We'll do it upright, son. Just leave it to me. I won't let you down," Tex assured York. He felt moved that York was considering making him legally his dad. He swore a silent oath never to let down

York or Susan. Dust billowed around the truck as they stopped in front of the house.

York leaped over Susan and out of the truck as soon as they had stopped. He ran full force to where Simon stood, raising his arms over his head and shouting, "Whoopee!"

Simon grinned. "I take it you enjoyed the ride today," he said.

"We are getting married. And I'm going to adopt Tex. He will be my real dad then. And I get to keep Molly Bug once we have a place to keep her. And Tex put the ring on mom's finger then kissed her for about an hour," York said so fast he forgot to breathe and had to bend over to gasp.

"Well, congratulations, York. You are about to become a son," Simon said, patting York on the back.

Placing her wedding in the hands of her mother had been the best idea anyone had. Already, her mother had booked the spot where her mother and father were wed. There were strict orders not to inform the national newsgroups. The townspeople all agreed to abide by the order. Felith had saved at least one member of every family in the area. The tiny church polished its bells and had them ready to announce that Susan and Tex were married.

The dress was the only sticky point of the hasty wedding preparations. In the family, some loudmouth had told Susan's grandmother about the wedding. Fred, the bride's father, threatened the woman to keep the news to herself. However, Virginia Whiting felt she had the right to choose the wedding dress. She had dressed Susan over the years for every occasion attended in D.C.

Susan balked, saying it was their wedding and that they would determine how they dressed alone. Tex and York selected formal Tuxes. Susan did not like or want the dress her grandmother picked out. Feeling frazzled and out of sorts over the dress, Susan agreed to meet with her grandmother at a famous bridal shop. Susan did not like any of the dresses she had seen in the photos her grandmother had sent her. She was not in the mood to argue with her grandmother yet again.

They sat as gowns paraded down the walkway. None of the wedding gowns looked or felt right to Susan. She was about to get up and leave when a pale blue butterfly flitted across the runway and towards the back of the store. Susan stood and followed after the butterfly, for she had learned to look at whatever the butterflies showed her.

Virginia followed after Susan, her voice showing her displeasure at Susan, ignoring the dresses offered. "You can not just up and walk out on him. He dresses Queens for their weddings, Susan."

Following the butterfly, Susan didn't even register the complaint. Back in the dimmest of areas, a lone woman sat at a sewing machine, working on a dress. The butterfly hovered over her. "May I see the dress?" Susan asked.

Startled, the woman jerked back from the machine. "W…what?"

"The dress you are working on—may I see it?" Susan asked again, her voice soft enough not to startle her.

"What? No, it is not any good. It was just some leftover material I was playing with, wanting to be a designer. The master makes all the best gowns," the woman managed to get out.

"And suppose this turns out to be the perfect dress for me? Would you want me to miss out on that perfection?" Susan said, smiling gently.

"No, Ma'am. I mean, this is just a bit of nothing, nothing fit for you," protested the woman.

"Oh, for goodness sake, let her see it, or we will never return to the special gowns," Virginia demanded.

"Yes, of course, my lady," the poor woman was humbled in front of Virginia, and Virginia was eating it up.

Tying off the spot she had been finishing up, the woman gently removed the gown from her workspace and held it up. It was perfect—simple yet elegant, with delicate butterfly lacework.

"I will take it," Susan said, her eyes sparkling. "Can you fit me now? And I'd like to take it with me when we leave if possible."

"But it is made from scraps. Surely you can not want a piecemeal dress," Virginia said in shock.

"I can, and I do. It is perfect," said Susan, ending the argument with her grandmother.

The day dawned with sunshine and nerves on edge. The men were all decked out in tuxes, with George insisting on wearing his cowboy hat. Tex told them it was not a wedding without a few Stetsons among them.

York kept touching his pocket, holding the

papers that would be signed, making Tex his dad. He was trying so hard to act like a grownup.

The only person who looked comfortable in his tux was Simon. He had attended many functions requiring a tux that was like a second skin to him. He chuckled at Roger, who kept running his finger around his neck as if very uncomfortable.

All the family came, Emily bringing tons of food and the other Aunts decked out in finery. Julian only made one remark about Susan's dress. It was Virginia who put her in her place. She stated that the dress was original and unique, and the pattern was never repeated.

People took their places. Black-suited men were in clear view and not in the mood for anyone to act up. They protected the best people in their world, and nobody would rain on this wedding.

The tiny bridge where Susan's mother had been married to her father still stood. It had been made safe and decorated for the occasion. Tex, York, and the rest of the team, with Eric, stood waiting for Susan and her father to walk to them. Tex fretted with worry that other agents were guarding his Susan. It didn't sit right with him, and Simon and George had to keep telling him to settle down. The piano struck a chord, and the music announcing the wedding march began. Tex came to attention, his eyes glued to where Susan was to appear.

The bride's maids followed two local children who spread rose petals in front of them. Silence reigned long before the music grew, and Susan and her father appeared on the path. As if they had been waiting in the trees, butterflies filled the air, descending on Susan and forming a multicolored train behind Susan. This display was what the people were here to see. Those who had been children or hadn't been born for Felith and Fred's wedding had seen the pictures, and now they witnessed the event in person.

With the last I do, a starburst of butterflies burst into the sky, ending the wedding. The church bells began to ring, sharing in the joy and peace of the day.

For a honeymoon, Fred and Felith emptied the farm of people and gave the house over to the newlyweds for the night. Morning came too soon, in Tex's opinion. Morning meant the family returned with York and enough black suits to paper a house.

York broke free from the crowd of relatives surrounding him and ran to the farmhouse. He made a mad dash to the bedroom, where they told York his mom and new dad would be sleeping. Then he did the one thing he had dreamed often of doing if he ever had a family. With a Tarzan yell, York launched himself into the air and landed smack dab between his parents. The bed bounced, and Tex was on York, pinning him down and tickling him. Susan let out a tiny squeak and jumped on Tex's back, and they had a free-for-all pillow fight. It was fortunate for Tex that Susan had clued him in on this fantasy York had. Between them, they made York's family dream come true.

They noticed a longboard tacked over the house's door while driving up the dusty road to the house. It said Welcome Home, written in double lines of bullet holes. On the bottom of the sign were signatures in marker from all of the snipers who, over the years, had rotated duty watching over Susan and the team. Susan had brought half the wedding cake for the crew up top. She smiled as she filled up baskets of good food and the cake for the silent watchers on the mountain. Susan insisted on taking the baskets up herself with help from Tex and York.

Tex had moved his few belongings into the house and bunker before they left for the wedding. The settling in went smoothly, with the only hiccup being where to charge his phone and instructing York never to play with his gun that he kept under his pillow when sleeping. Life was good.

York worked hard on his martial arts and all things to do with fighting with weapons. Susan didn't object to teaching a young boy survival skills, for she had been taught how to survive at a young age. Soon, York's Aunt Middy and Uncle Ritter gave him twin cousins. A few years later, they followed that up with the news of another baby on the way. That was the only thing missing from York's family life. He wished for a brother or sister.

One day, in the wee hours of the morning, when Susan was up mixing pancakes for breakfast. York was bugging her to try some canned peaches in the batter. She finally gave in, and York rushed to open the can for her. It was his idea. He was dicing the peaches up as Susan had instructed him to do when suddenly Susan ran for the bathroom. The sounds of Susan being sick could be heard from that room for a long time.

Panic set in as York set the peaches aside, now all diced up. "Dad!" he yelled as he ran for the front of the house. "Come quick. Mom is sick."

Tex had walked outside so the rest of the team could hear his conversation with Eric, Susan's brother, and Bobby Jay, Eric's main bodyguard. "Do we know how soon this will all happen?" Tex asked. Eric and Bobby Jay had called with the dire news that they were all in trouble and needed to prepare to move to a secure, hidden place.

"Dad, hurry, she sounds like she is dying in there," York interrupted the intense phone conversation.

"York," called Eric over the phone. "Calm down. Your mom is expecting a baby."

"A baby?" York and Tex both shouted. That was how they learned they were about to complete their family. There, with words of doom hanging over them all, they felt this incredible joy.

And Tex knew that now more than ever, he needed to make plans with the SS and his team to keep his family safe from a war of the worst sort.

The End

www.ingramcontent.com/pod-product-compliance
Lightning Source LLC
Chambersburg PA
CBHW071150020726
47502CB00002B/345